JULIA FRANCK

Back to Back

TRANSLATED FROM THE GERMAN BY
Anthea Bell

VINTAGE BOOKS
London

Published by Vintage 2014

2 4 6 8 10 9 7 5 3 1

First published with the title *Rücken an Rücken* in 2011
by S. Fischer Verlag GmbH, Frankfurt am Main

First published in Great Britain in 2013 by
Harvill Secker

Vintage
Random House, 20 Vauxhall Bridge Road,
London SW1V 2SA

www.vintage-books.co.uk

Addresses for companies within The Random House Group Limited can
be found at: www.randomhouse.co.uk/offices.htm

The Random House Group Limited Reg. No. 954009

A CIP catalogue record for this book
is available from the British Library

ISBN 9780099572251

This book has been selected to receive financial assistance from English
PEN's Writers in Translation programme supported by Bloomberg and
Arts Council England. English PEN exists to promote literature and its
understanding, uphold writers' freedoms around the world, campaign
against the persecution and imprisonment of writers for stating their
views, and promote the friendly co-operation of writers and free
exchange of ideas. www.englishpen.org

Supported using public funding by

**ARTS COUNCIL
ENGLAND**

The Random House Group Limited supports the Forest Stewardship
Council® (FSC®), the leading international forest-certification organisation.
Our books carrying the FSC label are printed on FSC®-certified paper.
FSC is the only forest-certification scheme supported by the leading
environmental organisations, including Greenpeace. Our paper
procurement policy can be found at www.randomhouse.co.uk/environment

Typeset in Janson by Palimpsest Book Production Limited,
Falkirk, Stirlingshire

Printed and bound by Clays Ltd, St Ives plc

The cards
Fall
Luck falls
From one
To another
On and over
A face falls
The eyes fall
Under the table
And over . . .
The players
Shout
And God
Is silent
Smiling to see that
Now
Clubs are trumps
Luck falls
Under the table
And over

And God
Is silent
And smiles

Tormented
At man falling
From living by the cards
To death by cards
Silent
Unyielding
And over

12 August 1961

Swaying

The boat lay hidden in the reeds; they had found it a few days earlier by the landing stage, rocking on the water, and the wind drove it into the marshy inlet, along with leaves, twigs and larger branches broken off in the storm and washed ashore. It was not tied up, it obviously didn't belong to anyone. One oar lay in the boat, the other was floating a little way off among the branches.

Thomas and Ella took the things they would need from the house and down the steps to the yard: a quilt, two small saucepans, potatoes, carrots and a chunk of bread. They also took a box of matches, some paper and an empty wine bottle, because Thomas thought they might want to write a message and send it by bottle post. Finally they carried the camping stove and a flashlight over the marshy ground; in October it got dark early, and in the morning there was hoar frost on the leaves and the blades of grass. They would be cold.

They had been on their own in the house for the last two weeks while Käthe was working in the quarry. Just before she left, Eduard had walked out after a row. Thomas and Ella had been looking after themselves; they had boiled potatoes and mixed salt, chives and water with curd cheese, they had been to school, they were ten and eleven and they could do all those things. When Käthe returned at the end of those two weeks, they hadn't meant to do more than tidy the place up a bit: they

1

had washed the dishes, and while Ella was still drying them Thomas had begun scrubbing the kitchen floor; they scoured the dark marks off the door, they polished the handle with ashes, washed the door frame with soap, whacked the doormat with the carpet beater and scrubbed it in the rain butt. Gentlemen, today you see me polishing up door handles, and soon I'll sing everyone a song, said Ella.

Laughing, Thomas always put his hands over his ears at that announcement; he didn't want to hurt Ella's feelings, but she rarely hit the right note and changed the tune just as the fancy took her. The chandelier would really shine if you polished it up. The smell of brass clung to your fingers. It was fun; they would get the house into such a state of perfection as it had never known before. Thomas dusted the books and the shelves with a dry duster, then wiped the shelves over with a damp cloth, he sorted the art books by period and size, works of literature by alphabetical order, and political writings by subject. In a rumbling voice and looking through their dead father's field glasses, he called across the expanse of the room: Miss Ella, with all this splendid literature available what will you borrow, a romantic love story or an adventure novel? Are you studying the tale of the Trojan War and all that fighting over Helen? I'll be happy to make out a borrowing slip for you. Ella took no notice; she was lying under the table with a knife and a sponge, cleaning its underside, something that obviously no one had done for decades. Remains of something clung tenaciously to it, traces of food, maybe, or wax. Ella had soaked the Italian damask tablecloth in the zinc tub in the garden. It needed a thorough wash; over a long time, crumbs and dark stains of sauces and wine had made themselves at home on it.

If Ella and Thomas hadn't wanted to get their house-cleaning done in two days, Thomas would have enjoyed playing the part of librarian; he was going to draw up a card index for the library and its future readers, he would design borrowing slips for all the books. When she hung the saffron-yellow tablecloth on the washing line, Ella's arms hurt from the hard work of wringing it out. Armed with a toothpick and a cotton-wool ball, she climbed on a stool to clean the picture frame of the Sicilian landscape. The cobalt-blue sky shone over the rocky countryside where only olive trees would grow. But the shiny stuff coating the frame stained the cotton-wool ball dark, and Ella was afraid she might get not just the dirt but some of the paint off as well. She even tidied the workbox, winding cotton back on reels and embroidery silks around pieces of cardboard, she sorted the buttons into three black boxes and put needles into their little envelopes in order of size. Probably no one but Ella had used that workbox since the housemaid was fired. She played alternately the part of her distinguished grandmother and the seamstress; with her mouth pursed, and in her grandmother's stilted voice, Ella commented on her own handiwork in French: *Alors, c'est si parfait!*

Perfetto, perfettamente, Thomas replied in passing, and his tone of voice, rustic and theatrical, imitated Käthe's criticism of her mother's upper-class French.

They tidied up all the rooms, square metre by square metre, cleaned and straightened up the whole house as it had never been tidied before. They had washed the curtains in the zinc tub under the elm tree, and hung them on the washing line in the garden to dry in the wind. They ironed them smooth – Käthe wouldn't believe her eyes. They were maidservant and man-servant, singing a duet of admiration for their employer in tones of goodwill. Just once, the tenor of their conversation about their mistress changed – only recently she had raised her hand in anger to the maidservant over a stolen jar of apple compote, striking the girl so hard that she was knocked almost unconscious. Manservant and maidservant weighed up their mistress's kindness against her violence, wiping down kitchen surfaces as they talked. They cleaned the oven with a piece of wire wool, making such generous use of scouring powder that they emptied the container; they tidied up the larder, and found a nest of nine tiny, naked mice in a basket full of old shoes. The soft pink of the little creatures' skin trembled in time with their rapidly beating hearts, they didn't squeak or squeal, maybe they were too young for that. Thomas picked up the basket, took a boot out and looked at the nest. Little naked mole-rats, he said, his voice soft and velvety. Ella was disgusted by the blind little creatures. She didn't want to look at them. Ella was in favour of drowning them in the water butt, Thomas was against it. If he took the baby mice down to the cellar their mother would never find them again, and they'd die miserably. So as an animal expert he decided to lure the mother mouse into a trap, and then he could take her down to the cellar alive as well. He put a piece of cheese into a deep stoneware jar and covered it with a board, leaving only a little crack open. That afternoon he found the mouse in the jar, heard her jumping up at the walls inside it and slipping down them again and again. Thomas took the mouse in the jar and the basket containing her litter over the veranda into the garden, and from there to the door of the coal cellar. Ella followed close on his heels; she knew he couldn't go into the cellar. He didn't dare go into the dark, he was afraid of it. He knew how to get Ella to bring coal up instead. If you fetch the coal, I'll do your maths homework. If you fetch the coal, you can have some smoked sprats. If you fetch the coal and take it to the hazel bush beside the cellar door, I'll carry it up the steps and into the house, and what's more I'll heat the stove all week and chop the firewood.

4

Please, Thomas said, handing her the jar and the basket, you only have to put them down on the floor and take the board off the jar, then they'll do fine on their own.

What do I get in return?

A story this evening.

It'll have to be a long one. And something else.

What?

Because that's not enough.

I'll carry your bag to school all week, I promise, and I'll do your maths for you, and your German homework as well.

Oh, all right. Basket in one hand, holding the jar well away from her with the other, her arms outstretched, Ella staggered down the steps into the cellar. At the bottom she fell full length. He heard the mouse squeaking, the jar was broken, only the basket with the litter of baby mice in it had landed intact next to Ella's head. She struggled to her feet, her trousers torn, her knees sore, her hands black and grazed.

Hesitantly, one foot at a time, Thomas went down the steps and tiptoed into the darkness. His fear of the dark and the fright he'd had didn't cancel each other out, but it must have been the cold making his teeth chatter. He stopped on the bottom step and held out his hand to her. Sorry, he said, putting an arm round her shoulders. Then he examined her knees, helped her up the steps and took her indoors, where he washed her injuries and put iodine on them.

Later, Ella and Thomas had beaten the carpets and swept the floors, then wiped them with a damp cloth. When they were dry, they had rubbed in beeswax, then brushed the floors and finally polished them shiny with a cloth. They had been cleaning the house for hours, and then they fell into bed well after midnight, exhausted. Next morning they got up early, while it was still dark outside, and set to work without stopping for

5

breakfast. They lit all the stoves in the house, including the bathroom stove; it was possible that Käthe might want a hot bath when she got home. They scoured the bathtub and wiped down the doors, they hung the freshly washed curtains at the windows they had cleaned. At midday they put more coal on the stoves; acting the part of stokers they took the ash bucket out with the rubbish and cleaned the outside of the dustbin, they raked up the leaves under the elm tree, pulled dead plants out of the flower beds and swept the steps from the veranda down to the garden. Ella went all round the house with a feather duster, getting cobwebs out of corners and dusting the paintings. Something in her chuckled when she came to the oil painting of the cherry blossom in the garden on the Wannsee. That picture, Käthe told admiring visitors when they looked at it, was a masterpiece. Their reverent nods always delighted Ella. A few years ago, when she was sick and had to stay in bed, and no one came to keep her company for weeks, she had tried to paint a picture of her family in oils on a wooden board. It had not been a success: she herself was huge, larger than her mother and hovering in the room, her brother looked like a gnome, the tiny twins were attached to their mother's breasts like rodents, and her breasts themselves, emerging from her blouse, were far from rosy – against the green fabric of the blouse they were a strident scarlet. It was true that Ella had only just started school at the time, but the picture had made great demands on her, and she knew she could never show it to her mother. Then, however, her glance fell on the cherry blossom beside the Wannsee, and she couldn't resist it; she had got out of bed and added tiny white dots to the grass on the banks of the lake with her brush. She had also added a hint of yellow, only a slight one, because white was never sheer white. And didn't they seem to be daisies if you looked at them closely? No one was to notice those little

6

white dots, so that over the following years Ella kept altering tiny details of the great master's picture. There was no time for that today. She just smiled as she flicked the feather duster over the cherry blossom beside the lake. Thomas and Ella dusted every piece of furniture in the house, they rubbed down the chairs with warm, soapy water and then oiled them, leaving a glow as golden as honey on the wood. Only Eduard's room remained as it was; they were strictly forbidden to go into it. In secret, Ella opened the door; the room smelled nasty, of stagnant flower water. But Ella couldn't see a vase of flowers anywhere. Eduard's absence was a provocation to Ella; she felt she simply had to go into his room, as if she were looking for something and wasn't sure what. She slipped in quietly, although there was no one within earshot, and she knew that Thomas was far off in the kitchen. The desk drawer was locked. How often had Ella tried to open that drawer already? With a hairslide, a safety pin, a stray key that she had found while sweeping under the carpet. Was she the person who had scratched the varnish round the lock?

They left everything exactly as it was in the studio, they didn't touch any of the wax models, although the older ones had layers of hairy dust sticking to them, and one of them had lost its arms through drying out and age. They didn't touch the plaster models either, all Ella did was stroke the rounded hips of the reclining figures. No one had told them not to touch, but it was an unwritten law that nothing must happen to these fragile models, and more particularly, children must not play close to them. The broken bits of sandstone in the bin under the gallery, the clay keeping moist, and the smaller scraps of marble on the window-sill, it was all left as it was. They didn't even pick up a broom to brush up crumbs, they didn't remove cobwebs here. Dusk was falling when Ella, her legs weary, went out into the garden to pick a bunch of mauve Michaelmas daisies. She also broke some bare twigs of bright red rose hips off a rose bush.

Thomas made lentil soup, although he'd never made it before and there were no cookery books in the house. He was breathing through his mouth as he did it, because it cost him an effort to fry the bacon. The smell of smoked meat frying made him want to retch; it wasn't that he liked pigs any better than, say, hares, but he disliked the idea of any animal being killed solely to be eaten. He suspected, however, that Käthe would think lentil soup inedible without any bacon in it. Ella made fun of the way he breathed through his mouth, saying he looked like a fish gasping for air. The bacon was sizzling over the flame; later, in the soup, it would turn transparent and flabby. Thomas cut up the potatoes and carrots small, and he had bought celeriac because he remembered Käthe's grunt of pleasure at the mere mention of the word. He added two cloves of garlic to the pan. Nor did he forget the bay leaf; he spiked an onion with a bay leaf and a clove and put it in the pot for flavour. Käthe would never in her life have had such good lentil soup. Ella sat on the flour chest, swinging her legs and folding the napkins she had ironed, she watched Thomas cooking, and now she too was breathing in through her mouth.

I can hear her! Ella jumped up. There was a high-pitched clattering in the distance. It came closer, and now it was echoing across the yard as the sound was cast back and forth between the house, the studio and the shed. Nothing else made a noise like Käthe's two-stroke motorbike; its sound was unmistakable. Ella and Thomas went into the dining room and looked down to the yard from the window to make sure. There she was: Käthe with her leather pilot's cap on her head. She was bending over the wooden crate on the carrier and unstrapping a large, rather shapeless bag. Then her dog arrived, jumping happily around her now that he had caught up. He spent most of the time on the way home in the crate on the carrier. Käthe would let him out near Rahnsdorf, in the woods on the Püttbergen, so that he could run the last few kilometres. Dogs and children loved the tall dunes into which the sand had formed on the south-eastern side of the glacial valley where Berlin stood. 1954, there were woods as far as the stream of the Fliess and the banks of the lake, the Müggelsee. Isolated houses, a part of the city like a village on the edge of Berlin, the tall pines of the Brandenburg Mark with their red trunks rising above the tops of oak, maple and beech trees. Käthe seldom went out of the city without her motorbike, but she would have liked a car for transporting her materials and tools. Small sculptures fitted into the trailer of the motorbike. And when she took models to be fired or cast, she had to telephone and claim friendship with neighbours who were really just acquaintances, so that she could borrow their car.

Thomas went back to the kitchen, tasted the soup and burned his tongue. How was he to tell whether or not there was too much salt in it? He liked salt. Thomas turned down the flame. You taste it, he asked Ella, but she was already running past him. From the front hall they heard a clatter, and then the barking of Käthe's dog. Thomas followed Ella into the smoking room.

With her pilot's cap on her head, Käthe was standing at the long table with a stack of post in front of her: letters, newspapers, flat packages. Hello there, Käthe sang out in her high voice; she had heard Thomas coming into the room, but her eyes were on a newspaper as she hastily leafed through it. When she came home from a visit of any length to the stone quarry, even when she came up to the house after hours in the studio, she could suddenly break into song in mid-sentence. Cheeks slightly flushed, she licked her lips as, with the dog's leash over her arm, she opened a small envelope. She skimmed the lines inside it, uttering a sound like a little whinny. An invitation from the

Artists' Association! Proudly, she propped it against the vase of flowers. She couldn't help sighing. She had been waiting a long time for that invitation. Impatiently she opened the next letter.

Ella sat down in one of the two deep armchairs at the table, watching Käthe in her pilot's cap looking through her post.

Thomas would have liked to hug Käthe; he was realising how much he had missed her. He liked her cheerful whinny, there was desire in it, a sense of rejoicing. When Käthe was out of earshot, Thomas and Ella would sometimes imitate her little whinny all of a sudden, on their way to school or going shopping. Thomas wondered whether to take her pilot's cap and the dog's leash from her, the way you take visitors' hats and umbrellas when they come into your house. At the wrong moment, she might find such a gesture intrusive, for the cap and leash were a part of Käthe herself, and you don't just take such things away and hang them up on a hook. He liked Käthe's smell of leather and dog. But Käthe avoided hugging, it was as if she froze in physical proximity to anyone, she would press her arms close to her sides, stiffen her back, shake herself. There must be something she disliked about a hug; Thomas thought that was possible. She often used to tell the children: Don't cling like that – when they were only close to her. There were never any hugs. Nor had Thomas ever seen her hug Eduard or any other man. Maybe, as Käthe saw it, hugging was simply civility, doing a favour, showing affection that she simply did not feel. So Thomas stayed where he was, hoping she might put out her hand or at least look at him.

Käthe slit open a large envelope with her silver letter opener, produced a magazine and a letter and began to read. Without looking up, she reached her hand out to one side, searching for something in the air. Maybe Thomas was meant to take her hand?

Come on, then, she said, come here. Her hand flapped as her eyes gazed at the letter. Thomas took a step towards her, wondering whether she meant him, whether he should take her hand, or shake it; he took another step her way – but the dog got there first. Agotto licked Käthe's fingers, nipping her outstretched hand, rubbing his ears against her to make her pat his head.

Are you hungry, Käthe? I cooked something. Thomas put his head on one side. She must be able to smell the lentils.

Käthe nodded, briefly looked up and then turned back to her post. She nodded again, as if she had forgotten why first time. Thoughtfully, she put the letter away and picked up the next envelope. Ella-ella-ella, you'd better ask the good Lord to make you a pair of legs. The table isn't laid yet.

Ella stayed where she was in the huge armchair, sinking into it like a doll draped in fabric. She had put on her best dress, the check one, and her lace collar. She hadn't often worn the dress since her grandmother brought it back from London two years ago, and now the sleeves were a little short, showing her wrists. Ella's hair was brushed smooth, she had even cleaned her shoes until they shone – and not just hers, but all the shoes she had found on the shoe rack in the bedroom. Ella rubbed her finger silently over the green velour covering the arm of the chair. She was reluctant to stand up. The carefully arranged flowers stood between herself and Käthe, who hadn't opened the last envelope yet and shook her head now and then as she read, or made a sound of approval or disapproval. Ella was hoping for a glance, for a remark, however tiny.

What is it? Now Käthe did raise her head and looked challengingly at Ella. Do hurry up.

Taking no notice of her dress, no notice of her hair. Ella elaborately got to her feet; her left leg had gone to sleep, so she limped as she followed Thomas to the kitchen. Once in the kitchen, Thomas and she had only to exchange glances; their eyes expressed their growing suspense, their impatient waiting, it could be any moment now. Käthe's eyes didn't necessarily have to fall on the flowers, or the best dress and the shining clean windowpanes, but surely the smell of the polished floor would tickle her nose, Käthe would notice the rearranged bookshelves. And then she would have the taste of the celeriac and bacon and lentils in her mouth. How surprised she would be! Ella carried a carafe of tap water and three glasses into the smoking room.

Oh, for goodness' sake open a window, Ella, it's unbearable in here. Are you two aiming to make this house into a sauna? What a waste of money. We don't go heating the garden in October, understand?

Käthe cast one brief, reproachful glance at Ella. She poured herself a glass of water and emptied it in a single draught. Käthe's cheeks were flushed, she passed the back of her hand over her forehead, now she was studying the sender's address on a letter with close attention. Indecisively, Ella shook her head. Maybe she'd overdone the heating.

Back in the kitchen, Ella rolled up the napkins, which were already folded in half, and put them in silver rings. She drew a heart on a piece of paper in red crayon, and then two smaller, intertwined hearts inside it. She wrapped the message in the green-and-white napkin that Käthe liked to use.

There was still some parsley in the garden. Thomas showed Ella the blue bowl. Ella cut several slices from the loaf of bread, as straight and as neatly as she could, put them in a basket and covered them with a cloth. They poured the soup into a festive tureen. Thomas carried the steaming tureen in, Ella brought the tray with the plates and spoons, the bread and the napkins.

Oh, this is too much! We're not mixing with every Tom, Dick and Harry!

Käthe was talking on the telephone as Ella pushed the door to the smoking room open with her elbow, holding the tray steady in her hands. They laid the table. Thomas ladled the soup into the plates. They waited. The phone conversation went on for quite a long time. Through the big double doors, they could see Käthe standing by the chest of drawers, gesticulating wildly; it was probably about some decision that her group had taken. While whoever was at the other end of the line tried explaining something to her, Käthe did a charcoal sketch on the back of a large envelope. No, Käthe did not agree – she waved her stick of charcoal in the air – I've said so already, not in any circumstances. An idea like that needs to make sense. After a while Käthe hung up and came to the table. Has Eduard shown up?

Thomas and Ella shook their heads. Eduard didn't tell the children when he was coming or going. He seldom said hello to them, and if he did it was like a greeting to strangers; then, just to be awkward, he expected those strangers to reply politely. If they were all in the house at the same time, he regarded the children as part of the fixtures and fittings, like furniture or household pets: sometimes he noticed them, sometimes he didn't. There were times when he admired Ella's shoes, there were times when he admired her dress. It was perfectly possible that he had in fact been here during the last two weeks, maybe in the morning, but they hadn't seen him.

Not once? Käthe sat down and unrolled her napkin. The heart message, unnoticed, sailed to the floor. She tucked the napkin into the neck of her sweater, like a bib, and dug her spoon into the plate. Can't you even heat the soup properly?

We did. Thomas was watching Käthe slurp, chew and swallow. It got cold once it was on the plate.

Käthe shovelled spoonful after spoonful into her mouth. And I suppose there's no salad? She looked from Ella to Thomas and back again to Ella. What's the matter, what are you waiting for, why don't you eat up?

Bon appétit, murmured Ella.

Enjoy, said Thomas. No, sorry, there isn't any salad.

But surely there are still dandelions in the garden? Haven't you been eating any salad at all while I was away?

Thomas shook his head.

Ella said: Yes, we ate dandelion leaves. And carrots.

Käthe cleared her throat, spooned the last of the soup up from her plate and helped herself to more from the tureen. Ah, wonderful, at least this is lukewarm.

Thomas and Ella ate in silence, exchanging surreptitious glances. Under the table, Ella touched Thomas's shin with her foot, Thomas kicked gently back. It couldn't be long now before Käthe noticed the clean tablecloth, the freshly ironed curtains in the next room; in spite of the lentils and celeriac she would smell the beeswax and her eyes would go to the shining floor, she would see the clean carpet. She could look out at the garden and see the veranda door, with the electric light reflected in its panes in the dark. There were no curtains over it, so Käthe couldn't help noticing the sparkling reflection in the glass.

What's that? With a sudden jerk of her chin, Käthe indicated the flowers standing next to the tureen. A spoonful of lentils disappeared into her mouth. What's the idea of that? Käthe looked from Ella to Thomas and back at Ella. Käthe was noticing things now, looking around her at last. Have you two given up talking? She brought her fist down lightly on the table.

Was that anger in her eyes? Was she joking, and would she laugh next moment? Thomas and Ella looked expectantly at Käthe. Ella couldn't help smiling now, a smile spreading all over her face. At last Käthe was seeing what magic her brownies had worked in the house.

You picked those in the garden? What's the matter, cat got your tongues? Käthe threw her spoon down in the empty soup plate with a clatter. Once again she struck the table, and the china clinked.

No more glances were exchanged. For an indefinite length of time, Ella just listened to the slight crackling in the stove, her smile had disappeared, fallen into the embers, there was a tingling inside her but she couldn't breathe. Her gaze was fixed spellbound on the tablecloth that she had taken off the line and ironed this morning. Whining, Agotto put his muzzle on the table.

How often have I told you the flowers in the garden aren't for picking? At least, you two aren't to pick any there! Agotto was whining miserably, whimpering.

It's autumn. Ella's voice failed her.

The flowers will wither now anyway. And if they don't wither they'll soon freeze overnight. It wasn't easy to defend Ella, but Thomas kept trying all the same. She was the elder child, she was first to bear the brunt of all the blame, he was younger, Käthe loved him, he was sure of that.

Don't be impertinent. If I say none of the flowers in the garden are to be picked, then kindly don't pick them behind my back! Understand? Käthe took a gulp of water from her glass. You two can't even be left on your own for two weeks!

Thomas and Ella hardly dared to lower or raise their heads. Their feet touched under the table.

Käthe drained her glass and opened the newspaper that she had put on the chair beside her before supper. You can wash the dishes, I'm going down to the studio. One of you can take the dog for a walk.

Silence for a minute, two minutes. Were those going to be

Käthe's last words? Ella banged her spoon down in her plate, splashing soup into the air. What about the twins, Käthe, when are you fetching them? Ella knew only too well that Käthe didn't like to be reminded of the twins. The twins were a nuisance. They couldn't look after themselves, at the age of three they couldn't be left alone while Thomas and Ella were at school. So in those weeks while she was away, Käthe usually took them to the Werder peninsula near Potsdam, where there was a reliable children's home.

The twins are coming back tomorrow, the Winters are bringing them. Käthe stayed hidden behind her newspaper as she said that; she had not reacted to the clatter of Ella's spoon, nor did the question about the twins impress her. Silently, Thomas rubbed his sleeve over his eyes.

Ella and Thomas looked at their half-full plates. They would have to eat it all up if they wanted to avert a row. There were only the little bits of bacon left on Thomas's plate; he had picked them out and put them on the rim. Without attracting Käthe's attention, he pushed them onto Ella's plate. Ella loved bacon, if she had her way she would eat nothing else, no lentils, no parsley, just bacon.

In silence, Ella and Thomas cleared the table. Ella washed the dishes, Thomas dried them. They couldn't think of anything to say to each other.

Doors opened and closed, and Käthe marched through the kitchen and straight down the steps to her studio.

The two of them took the dog out to the Fliess, where the woods began on the other side of the stream. There was mist among the trees. They didn't talk.

Before the children put out the light at bedtime, Käthe opened the door to their room and said: There are bottles all over the back stairs. Didn't I tell you to clear them away? Do it tomorrow.

The door was closed, Thomas switched off the light. The ticking pendulum of the grandfather clock in the corridor could be heard through the door, it began to strike the full hour. Thomas counted along under his breath, it struck ten times.

Let's run away, Ella whispered in the dark.

Where to?

Doesn't matter.

She'll search for us.

Good. I look forward to that. She'll realise we're missing, maybe she'll think we're dead.

When?

I'm sure that boat will still be in the reeds. Think of it – our tracks go down to the water and then they disappear.

If Agotto helps her to look for us he'll stand on the banks of the lake howling. Thomas was lying on his stomach, chin propped in his hands, frowning. Ella could see that it gave him no pleasure to think of Käthe's anxiety, he was already feeling sorry for her. His defencelessness annoyed her.

Serves her right.

When?

Tomorrow, we'll take our things there after school. We ought to have something to eat with us.

I don't want to freeze.

For a while they lay in silence on their separate beds in the dark room.

How long will we stay away? Thomas's voice was unsteady. He certainly didn't want to frighten Käthe. He didn't like the idea of her anxiety. He tied one corner of his handkerchief round his finger.

She'll be bound to miss us by supper time at the latest. We'll stay out on the water until midnight.

We may hear her calling from the bank when she comes looking for us.

Let's hope so. Maybe. Maybe she won't look down by the lake, maybe she'll go to see the neighbours first and ask if anyone's seen us.

They had taken off their shoes and socks on the bank. With their socks tucked into their shoes, their trouser legs turned up, they had waded through the icy water to the boat to stow the last of their things away in the bows and under the seat. The reeds cut into Thomas's calves; he gritted his teeth and took a few steps back to take the camping stove and the basket of provisions from Ella. Finally Ella carried their shoes, all muddy from the marshy ground, out to the boat. They had forgotten to bring a towel, so they dried their frozen feet as best they could with the quilt. Putting their socks back on took some time, the boat was rocking, and the socks stuck to their damp, cold feet. Their shoes felt clammy as well.

Ready? Thomas waited until Ella had her second shoe on before digging the oars into the black water. He could still feel the bottom. He pushed the boat out. The blade of the second oar was broken, half of it was missing and the wood was rotten. Thomas put both oars in the rowlocks and rowed steadily, while Ella sang. The dark blue of evening was sinking into the mist.

Where do we go?

Ella shook her head. She felt chilly. How was she to know what the distant bank would be like, or what now lay behind them? So she said: Just out on the lake.

Thomas rowed. *Softly, down in the water, crazy, I lost the dream . . .* Thomas had often revised the lines of his latest poem, added to them, crossed them out. *The little elvers' joy in water, on the stone, it is always theirs, never my own.* Ella thought up a tune to go with it and hummed in time to his words. As she hummed she stamped her feet on the bottom of the boat, hoping that would warm them up. The sky above the lake was pitch dark now, they couldn't make out a light or see the bank any more.

My tummy's grumbling. On all fours, Ella crawled over to search under the seat for the basket of food. The bread was wet and cold. Soft bread? She tore a piece off, tried it. Not so bad after all. She offered her brother some, but he didn't want any, he had to row to keep from freezing. She chewed the bread until it tasted sweet in her mouth. She washed two carrots in the lake by holding them in the water and rubbing the earth off with her fingers. Thomas didn't want a carrot, so Ella ate both. She went on stamping her feet, but it was no use, the night air above the lake was implacable. Ella lay down in the bottom of the boat, wrapped herself in the quilt and tried to forget the cold. The splash of the oars made her sleepy. She turned from side to side, she lay tucked up as tightly as possible, knees to her chin, arms wound round her legs. But the damp had permeated her clothes and the quilt, Ella's back was cold and her feet frozen. Could she still feel her toes? Käthe would be alarmed, panic-stricken, she'd come looking for them. The first thing she'd notice would be the missing quilt. Ella dreamed, and knew it was only a dream when she saw Käthe running over the marshy ground calling out loud: Thomas! Ella! The cold stifled her cries. The waves grew larger, lapped louder and louder against the boat, broke on the bank, the stones of the landing stage, the wooden boat. Was Ella asleep or awake? Suddenly she couldn't hear the splash of the oars, she woke with a start, raised her head, and couldn't make anything out in the dark.

Thomas?

She heard only the waves.

Thomas?

Ella felt sick. She groped around, the quilt, the timber of the boat. Thomas!

19

What is it? Thomas sounded hoarse, he must have dropped off to sleep.

Why don't you answer me?

I am answering you.

I . . . I . . . Ella's hand worked its way up to the side of the boat, she felt her stomach churning, there was no stopping it; in a kneeling position she leaned over the side, the sudden pain made her body rear, she vomited.

What are you doing?

Ella was throwing up. She wanted to say something, but she had to throw up and still keep hold of the edge of the rocking boat. Now she felt Thomas's hand on her back.

Can I help?

Ella shook her head, although Thomas wouldn't see it in the dark. Ella got her arm over the edge of the boat, held her hand in the icy water, rubbed her fingers against each other and cupped them. The water of the lake tasted good, soft and sweet, its icy cold numbed her throat and took away some of the sour flavour in it.

Thomas had put his arm round Ella's shoulders.

What's the time? She turned to him, everything was still swaying, she felt dizzy, but the retching had gone away. Cold sweat stood out on her forehead, on her back.

Wait a minute. Thomas crawled over the bottom of the boat, looking for something. Ella heard the faint hiss of a match. Too damp. Thomas wasn't giving up, he rubbed every match several times to expose its tiny head, a third match, a fourth, until at last there was a little flame. The candle burned faintly, and Thomas had to shield the flame with his hand to keep the wind from blowing it out at once. Three thirty. He held his wristwatch to his ear.

Ella's dizziness overcame her, she closed her eyes. She imagined her brain like a water level in her skull, bobbing up and down inside it. Her brain glowed blue, it gave off tiny bubbles that popped with a faint sound before they softly broke. She felt Thomas putting her woolly gloves on her hands. They were frozen, stiff and cold. It took him some time because Ella could hardly move her fingers. Then he moved away, and Ella heard banging, bumping sounds. He raised her leg, the quilt; the boat was rocking, obviously he was searching for something under the seats. She wanted to ask what, but she couldn't speak. Her tongue was heavy and sour in her mouth. When the noise had died down again she blinked at him. In the light of the candle that Thomas had put in a preserving jar, she saw that he had jammed the camping stove between his knees. He was trying to light it.

The gas canister's empty.

Or damp, thought Ella.

I don't think damp is bad for a gas canister, why would damp affect gas? It's empty.

Who cares, Ella wanted to say, but she couldn't get the words out. Maybe she'd have to throw up again, even though her stomach was empty now.

Thomas scratched the gas canister with his fingernail. He smelled it. Nothing but the smell of burnt keratin left on his nail by the match.

How much longer were they going to stay out here on the water? Ella's nose was running, the handkerchief that her fingers could feel in her trouser pocket was a wet clump of cloth. Ella summoned up all her strength, she tried to open her roughened lips, move her mouth, wiggle her tongue. Let's go back. I can't stay out here any longer.

Thomas nodded, he looked at his compass. You take this, will you? I'll row. He handed Ella the little container.

Where do you think we are?

Thomas looked around, there was no bank in sight; he put his head back, neither moon nor stars, nothing but darkness. No idea. He rowed faster. If we keep going north-north-east, we ought to reach our side of the lake.

The wind was rising; a gust blew out the candle. Ella didn't need a compass to know where north was. She closed her eyes. Now and then she said: Over to port a bit. The wind was driving them too far east. A duck quacked, another duck, the children heard the flapping of their wings.

She couldn't move her toes separately. With her legs drawn up, Ella was half sitting, half lying under the clammy quilt, her head resting on the side of the boat, one eye open, the other closed. Careful! A little buoy was visible in the water. Ella craned her neck, but she still couldn't see the bank. Take it slowly, the fish-traps must be somewhere near here.

Thomas firmly raised an oar out of the water and held it aloft, he was sure they had come to a net. Then he sat down again. Thomas rowed, there was never a calmer, better oarsman.

Soon after that, they saw the first poles sticking out of the water. The marks on them and the arrangement of the fish-traps looked familiar to Thomas. He said something that was meant to encourage Ella, but she couldn't quite understand what it was. Ella and the cold had become as one, so much so that she felt hardly anything now, neither the cold nor herself.

They were rowing north. Shadows appeared out of the darkness, swathes of mist drifted by, parting for a few moments to offer a clear view. The bank traced a vague outline, maybe trees, a fairly long landing stage; now they recognised the place as Rahnsdorf from the two weeping willows and the faint lights. In the distance, Ella saw a red light, then a green one showed, the little harbour must be over there. They bore west and rowed past the first houses and the harbour itself. They recognised the boathouses; in the summer they had often played in one of them; Michael who went to school with them kept his boat there. They had made a sail, in

Käthe's studio they had soaked a large sheet in warm, liquid wax, they had dried it and sewn it and practised sailing with it as long as it lasted. But at this early hour there wasn't a human soul in sight. Ella watched the white clouds of her own breath; if they were still there she couldn't have frozen to ice yet. They did not put in and tie up the boat until they reached the stone landing stage. It was nearly four thirty, no sign of dawn yet.

Thomas clambered out of the boat. He held it firmly, close enough to the stones for Ella to get out of the boat and over the parapet, rolling rather than climbing. She couldn't bend her fingers; in her woollen gloves her fingers looked like a doll's, stiff and lifeless. Ella crawled on her knees, on her stomach; using the strength in her elbows and supporting herself on both hands, she hauled herself up on the landing stage. She could hardly walk, her feet were two lumps of ice, numb, she couldn't even feel her knee joints. She came down on one elbow, her left hip struck stone, one shoe fell off. She caught herself with her stiff hand, tipped over, and found herself sitting on the stones.

Thomas hurried over to her. Are you all right? With difficulty, he got her gloves off, took her hands, rubbed them between his own, and together they rubbed Ella's knees; she raised her legs to cycle in the air. Thomas leaned down a little closer to Ella and massaged her calves. She groaned and gritted her teeth to keep from screaming. Her body dropped back with a thud; she could hardly feel one shoulder.

Ella! Thomas shook her. Ella! He was bending over her, breathing the warm vapours of his breath into her face, but by the time it reached her it had cooled off again. What's the matter? Ella, say something! Ella didn't move, she was lying still, as still as she could. Before long Thomas, her little brother, would be shedding tears of desperation. He rubbed and pummelled her

23

stomach, her chest, he bent down to her nostrils, about to try artificial respiration. His voice was full of fear. Ella.

Her limbs really did threaten to freeze. All of a sudden Ella was afraid that any moment now the act she was putting on for him might turn real. She ought to laugh, so that he'd know she had been joking. But her mouth wouldn't obey her. Ella loved to scare her brother. She must laugh, she must, and she did laugh, a gurgle emerging from deep down inside her.

Ella! His relief and happiness to find that she hadn't died was so great that Thomas couldn't feel cross with her. He gave her a hug.

Help me. Ella couldn't raise her voice, it was a croak. Please warm me up.

Thomas went on rubbing her as hard and as fast as he could. The effort warmed him up too. He told her, smiling: your lips are made of ice, they look as if they have hoar frost sticking to them.

Ella cautiously moved her cold lips against each other; the skin on them was cracked and rough, but that was all. When she looked over Thomas's shoulder, she saw the beams of two flashlights probing the gaps in the mist, sweeping on over the water as if searching it.

They're looking for us!

No. Thomas had looked over his shoulder only briefly and then went on rubbing. It's the first fishermen going out to the fish-traps.

Hold on to me, I want to get up. Ella supported herself on Thomas.

In the wood, they could hardly see their hands in front of their faces, there were cracking sounds underfoot, they had to take care not to stumble. Once they stopped when they heard a rustling, a grunting, and then the trampling of several hooves. Wild boar might attack, better not get too close to them. Only when they reached the nursery garden could they make out shadowy shapes, the clearing with the young fir trees, the rows of bushes, and over to one side the unadorned framework of the glasshouses. Going past them, they reached Käthe's garden by going through the orchard. Ducking down low under the branches, they took care not to lose their footing; the mouldering leaves and withered autumn grasses were slippery under their coating of frost. The house was dark. They climbed the steps to the veranda; luckily the door wasn't locked. A brief bark from Agotto – then he came to welcome the two housebreakers, wagging his tail, and lay down in his place under the bench again. All was still in the house, not a sound but the ticking of the white grandfather clock. Thomas and Ella slipped into the kitchen to make some tea. Ella found a note on the table, in Käthe's familiar handwriting: Don't forget the bottles on the back stairs!

They made the tea and poured it into a Thermos flask. The hot drink was to help them get through the early hours of the morning. They fetched their hot-water bottles from their bedroom. Making sure that all the doors were left just as they had found them, they removed all traces of their surreptitious presence. They even wrapped the soft, used tea leaves in newspaper, to be thrown away later on the wooded bank of the lake. There must be nothing to give them away. They left the house down the back stairs. It was still dark. In the yard, they quietly opened the door of the shed, where a gas canister lay on a shelf. They would be able to make some soup in the woods or on the boat, never mind just where – they would stay away all day. By afternoon at the latest Käthe was sure to notice that they were missing, and then she would wonder when she had last seen Ella and Thomas. They would be back at the boat again before dawn, before anyone saw them, and they would stay out until someone did notice that they were missing.

Climbing

It's strange, such silence on a Sunday. Do you remember what it was like? Thomas thought of all the noisy scolding, the bellowing, the shouting. The standard lamp broken and stamped on, broken china.

Ella nodded, and stretched out full length on the floor of the tree house. I'm glad he's gone at last.

Thomas put three nails between his lips, holding them there so that he could make a loop in the cord better. The silence was astonishing; only the elm leaves rustled in the late-summer wind. That morning Ella and Thomas had gone swimming in the lake. Ella's hair was still damp. She was lying on her back with her eyes closed, carefully brushing it away from her face; it fell on the wooden floor, a wreath round her head, and the wind lifted only a few strands into the air. Ella looked like a black sunflower.

Thomas made a second loop, took a nail out of his mouth and picked up the hammer. He hit the nail, but it dropped to the floor.

Ow! Ella sat up, covering her eyes with her hands and groaning: I've gone blind, Thomas, I can't see.

Thomas shook his head; he guessed that Ella was pretending, he knew her. Putting the hammer down, he tightened his lips round the remaining nails, with one hand he touched both of hers – whereupon she lowered them to her lap and laughed at him. You fell for it, you fell for it! She lay down on the wooden floor again and watched with amusement as Thomas searched for the nail he had lost.

Had it fallen right down into the grass? Thomas groped around on the wood, changed to a crouching position, looked under the soles of his bare feet; the nail was nowhere to be seen. Carefully, he took a second nail out of his mouth, held the loop in place and picked up the hammer. Why on earth had Käthe married that man? Perhaps she had wanted to neutralise the disgrace of having children born out of wedlock, get rid of the stigma of her unmarried status? She often spoke of racial defilement, once she had told him and Ella: Your existence was the proof of racial defilement. The term clung to her. An idea like that didn't just go away after the war. But then she could marry anyone she liked. And who was left? In the year after the end of the war Käthe had come down from her mountain to satisfy her curiosity, and went to the election for the local district association. Anyone who didn't want to give the impression of having been in favour of the war was tentatively on the lookout for communists. That was where she had first seen Eduard. Later, he had taken her to area headquarters in Freiburg and given her a ticket to travel to the assembly. She first went to a communist meeting after the war; it was some three years later that she and Eduard had got to know each other more intimately after an assembly. Käthe said it had been in Freiburg, just before Christmas when the temperatures were below freezing. It must all have happened very fast. The tiny twin babies who had to fight for survival were born near Berlin a year later. She expected her parents to help out; she herself had neither money nor anyone to look after Ella and Thomas. Although they called it getting engaged, Eduard and Käthe could only clasp hands and promise to meet again before she left, because he still had a wife and family. Did she feel attracted to those who suffered? Did she

27

consider Eduard's grief as deep as hers? Both attracted and repelled; the strange lustre of his mind lying fallow had probably intrigued her. A man who had once had to endure a mountain of corpses lying above his body? Swept up, stacked like rubbish. The guards had run for it, leaving the place as it was, the liberators were trying to tidy things up and bury the dead. He couldn't breathe or cry out. Wasn't it just by chance that someone had noticed him at the last minute? There's something moving! He remembered that cry, he had told Thomas about it, just once, after a noisy quarrel with Käthe. There's something moving, he repeated bitterly to himself, using those words as a way of saying where they came from, where he came from, who he was. Thomas had felt sorry for him. Nothing but his arm had been sticking out, and he tried to move it with all his might, squashed as he was by the weight of human bodies, the masses of them in which he was being turned over, the bony, fleshy stink of decomposition all around him. The vehicle sweeping them up stopped, the engine was throttled back just before it reached the edge of the pit. They had to separate the corpses, throwing bundles of bones individually into the mass grave, until he was freed, dazzled by the light, and two arms took hold of him and carried him away from the pit. He couldn't speak for months afterwards. A man who had fought in Spain and ended up in Dachau, that had impressed Käthe. He was an unusually poor sort of hero. There he sat for months on end, incapable of working, and perhaps he hoped that some day Käthe would find time for a kiss, hold his hand, look into his eyes. Thomas didn't know anyone who could be as persistently silent as Eduard, for hours on end, days on end, his silence always lasted until the next occasion for a quarrel. There was only one person to whom Eduard sometimes talked in whispers, and that was Ella, if she had not walked past his silent form but steered a course his way and sat down beside him. Then she would smile and dance attendance on him until he patted his knee, and she was quick to comply with the request for her to climb on his lap: Ride-a-cock horse! But after a year or so Ella didn't like his lap so much, she stopped sitting on it of her own free will, no longer leaned back at her ease purring like a cat. She avoided him, got out of the way of his arms reaching out to her.

The last quarrel between Käthe and Eduard had been early this year, 1957, and it had taken place in the room next to Ella and Thomas's, so that they heard every word: Käthe shouting that she wanted to go to the theatre, he had never once gone with her, he took no interest in anything and blamed her for throwing money out of the window with her visits to the theatre. Throwing money out of the window? Could there be a finer, better, more important window on the world than the theatre? Whose money was it anyway? Who worked for it? In her indignation Käthe set about exploiting his latest symptom of paralysis in the arms; before his eyes she took a chisel and forced the drawer of his desk open. He had to watch, with his arms hanging limp and useless. She found a mountain of money in his desk, over two thousand marks, a whole bundle of banknotes. Käthe had expected almost anything, letters and pictures, documents and souvenirs of dubious merit, she had even thought there might be some money, twenty marks, fifty, perhaps a hundred. But not this. Ella and Thomas stole out into the corridor and watched the scene, unnoticed, through the open door. A painful scene. Its painfulness seemed to egg Käthe on to act like a monster. She threw the notes at Eduard, they wouldn't stick to him, his limp arms couldn't catch them, they sailed to the floor. Beside herself with fury, she shouted at him that he lay there idly like an invalid, had left her to provide for a family of six by herself all these years, didn't bother about anything, drove away their household helps, left her to do all the work on her own – she had to watch every mark! He shouted at her not to treat him like a small child. She had broken open his desk, he shouted, that was a criminal act, she was a criminal, he had to live under the same roof as such a person, he had rights as well. Käthe could give as good as she got when it came to shouting, but now she yapped, short and sharp: he was the criminal. All these years she'd toiled on her own, while behind her back he was hoarding money like a madman! What kind of money was it, anyway, where did it come from, what was it for? That was nothing to do with her, he retorted, he had a right to that money, he'd worked for it. Oh, worked for it, had he? Käthe snapped back. When and where, might she ask, had he been working recently? Did he think she didn't know what he got up to, lounging about and doing his friends a favour now and then?

Here he interrupted her; he'd fought and suffered, he said, she didn't understand the first thing about that, he hissed, she'd better shut up or she'd get to know him better, and not just him either. Not just him? It wasn't for her to put on airs, she knew nothing about doing friends a service. To which she asked if he thought she was stupid? Doing friends a service? Maybe it had never occurred to him that she too did friends a service, but for free, entirely unlike him. He was not a true communist, he was a greedy scoundrel and an old miser, keeping what was theirs from her and the children. He wailed that he was an injured man, maybe she remembered who it was she'd married, and he added further furious recriminations. Käthe said she had married him for the sake of the twins, hoping at least to give them a father – but he was the kind of father to cheat his own children, he was a crook, a miserable villain, keeping money from them, hoarding it in his desk on the quiet for years. He ought to be ashamed of himself, said Käthe, he could go to hell, get out of there, never mind where to, she just wanted him out.

She put her peach-stone necklace round her neck, picked up one of the banknotes and let the door latch behind her. The play she was going to see began in an hour's time.

And he disappeared. A few weeks later, his room was empty.

Thomas tied the cord round a small branch and knotted it firmly. He took the other end of the cord and wove it into the hanging roof. Ella had said she wanted a little bench, and this afternoon he was going to build one into the tree house for her, he knew where already, he would use the big fork in the branches for it. But the roof wasn't windproof yet.

Ella's voice was unusually flat, it sounded almost casual: I hate Eduard.

Oh yes? Then why were you always sitting on his lap?

Wasn't.

Yes you were, all the time. Thomas was trying to tie the leafy roof of their tree house firmly in place with the cord. He had woven twigs together to stabilise it. Ella sat up, crossing her legs.

It was from longing. I was thinking about our father. And wondering what he was like. I was sitting on his lap, not Eduard's.

Really and truly? Thomas shook his head; he didn't like to think about it. Anyone else would have seen you sitting on Eduard's lap.

Ella pushed Thomas with both arms, making him bump into the tree trunk. Don't be stupid – she was furious – you know perfectly well what he did.

Thomas lowered his eyes. He did know. It was just that Ella hadn't told him. He could still see old Eduard sitting in his big armchair, plucking at Ella's arm as she was walking past to get her to sit on his lap. Ella's giggling, his giggling. Thomas saw

Eduard's hands on Ella's hips, on Ella's legs, he remembered Eduard, grinning mysteriously, whispering something in her ear. Only later did Ella tell him what it was. Thomas hadn't liked the way the pair of them sat together, he hadn't liked the look on Ella's face as she sat on Eduard's lap. Come and play, he had asked Ella at such moments to get her off that lap. Once Eduard had told Thomas: You're Käthe's darling, Ella is mine.

He's a poor bastard. Thomas laid an arm on Ella's shoulder. Let's forget him.

Poor bastard? Poor? So what are we, then? You're just saying that because you didn't come to my rescue!

Rescue? For a moment Thomas didn't know what she meant.

Didn't protect me. Ella sniffed. Her eyes were reddened and running with tears.

Thomas put the hammer down and took Ella in his arms. Her crying was infectious, he felt her tears on his cheeks, her heavy breathing against his chest; if she cried it would start him crying as well. And wasn't she right? Shouldn't he have protected her, couldn't he have kept Eduard from whispering those things in her ear, from touching her and looking at her as if she were the buoy to which he could cling and so save himself?

You mustn't tell anyone. Ever. Ella rubbed her face against Thomas's throat. Understand? she whispered.

Thomas nodded. She had often made him promise that before. But what he did to you –

Quick as a flash, Ella put a finger over Thomas's mouth, her eyes were flashing. You know perfectly well what he did, stop asking questions.

Thomas wanted to go on asking questions, he wanted to know more, because what he did know was by no means all. But he sensed Ella's anxiety and obeyed her without reservations. Her tears made his throat tighten.

Come on, let's enjoy being nice and quiet here. Ella leaned against him.

He nodded. We'll sit back to back and you can tell me about our father.

Thomas knew that Ella loved telling stories about their father, stories that she sometimes invented because she didn't have enough memories. She had been just two when he died, Thomas was only one year old.

They sat back to back in the tree house. Ella closed her eyes. I see him coming out of the fir trees, climbing up the mountain in his black suit, with a hat on his head, it's a top hat, his dark hair is falling over his forehead, he has a rucksack on his back and his easel over his shoulder. He's handsome, only I can't see his legs, they're blurred. I can see his face, his eyebrows, he didn't have a beard then. He had to shave it off for the war.

Did he have a gun?

Severely, Ella leaned back and whistled dismissively. You and your gun. No, our father didn't have a gun. He did sometimes carry his easel over his shoulder. After all, he was a painter.

What did he paint?

He liked painting rocks and olive trees best. Funny, he never painted the sea. I think he didn't like Caspar David Friedrich. When he and Käthe were living on Sicily he must have kept turning away from the sea.

What's he supposed to have painted in the war? Battles?

No, he was too nice for that. Our father was a sensitive man. A fine gentleman with fine brushes. She took a strand of her hair and tickled Thomas's face with it until he turned away. He painted the soldiers. For their mothers. He painted pictures for the soldiers that they could send home. If they had sweethearts they sometimes needed two pictures, one for their mother and one for their sweetheart.

Did he paint murder and death?

Ella turned round and pinched Thomas's arm. What makes you think of that?

If he painted soldiers at the front they were all either murderers or dead. Thomas had to laugh with the shock of it when it suddenly occurred to him that this version of their father could have seen his models as heroes.

Ready to kill, perhaps. But I think he painted the death out of their faces. Ella assumed a blissful expression. I saw a few of his last drawings in Käthe's studio, and none of them looked like a murderer or a hero. It's quite an art to do that in the middle of the war, don't you think?

I don't know. Maybe he was a coward. The idea was painful, but it could hardly be avoided.

Our father? A coward? Now Ella punched him with her fist. It hurt, and Thomas raised his arm.

It was enough to satisfy him to see Ella duck away. It would have been brave of their father to paint the soldiers as murderers. It would also have been brave to stay with Käthe in defiance of his call-up papers, to go against everyone's expectations. What was he supposed to do at the front? What did he want to do there?

Get killed, maybe? Ella whispered thoughtfully. Have you seen those drawings? Perhaps he was doing them on a production line. Photographs and chemicals to develop them are expensive and sensitive, his charcoal could show everything, his pencil too, soldier after soldier. If it hadn't been for the uniform they'd have been nice brothers and nice sons and nice husbands.

What do you mean, nice husbands? Thomas would have liked to understand what Ella really did mean. Perhaps he could be a nice man some day, the kind of man his father was, perhaps. But Thomas didn't even know if that was a good thing.

34

You know what I mean. Men who didn't want the war.

You're crazy, Ella. Everyone wanted the war.

Not our father, he was made to go. He hid away in Italy with his beard for too long. They went looking for him, his parents wanted him to give himself up and go to fight.

So then he joined up . . . How important to their father had his parents' opinion been, the opinion of the mindless society to which he had returned from his romantic Italian refuge? It was idiotic, thought Thomas, but he didn't say anything. He knew that Ella would defend their father, would find reasons for what he did. She loved their dead father, and he was easy to love. Odd that you could go on leave from the front, isn't it? Someone stands there shooting, or painting people, and then he looks at his watch and says: time to knock off work, I'm going on leave for three weeks.

That was before you were born. I was sitting outside the house in the meadow, catching beetles.

Now Thomas leaned harder against Ella; that was part of their ritual, a gesture of humility in case of doubt. You were only one then, Ella, how could you know about that? It was only a game when Thomas asked her that, he liked this story and had already heard it hundreds of times. It was always the same story, so it must be true, even if Ella had been only a year old when he was born.

I caught the beetles and ate them. Honestly. There was a tickly feeling in my mouth when he appeared among the firs. I called out to him.

How?

Pa-pa! Ella relished the sound of the two syllables, Papa, Papa! She repeated it at length, longingly, just as she must have called to him at the time. Her voice was a little girl's voice, there were tears of joy in her eyes, of happiness at seeing him again. Thomas looked over his shoulder; Ella had turned her own head that way, and he could see her, little Ella who had known all this, just as she was. What a wonderful father it must have been who came striding up the mountain. Thomas saw Ella's love, he wanted to believe in it and suddenly find himself sharing it.

Did you know who he was at once?

Of course. Ella's eyes were sparkling with emotion, she was carried away by her story, by what she called memory; after all, no one else came up that mountain for months on end. The only person we were waiting for was Father. Thomas picked a small leaf off the elm tree and dried Ella's tears.

Back to back, Ella ordered, and they turned their backs to each other again. It was up to Thomas to ask a question now.

What did Käthe eat, did she just eat beetles too?

On Sundays she went down to the farmyard. No one must see her. They were all at church. There was bread, a can of milk, some vegetables, and sometimes a few potatoes left ready for her on the table outside the house. Ella sniffed: mmm, it was good bread, the farmer's wife had baked it herself from stoneground rye and there were little linseeds in it, it smelled delicious. I always got the first bit of crust. To stop me crying.

Didn't Father sometimes send the farmer money?

Of course, the farmer didn't like strangers and people hiding from the authorities. He didn't mind whether she was Jewish or a communist, she had no papers and no marriage certificate. He didn't ask to see her papers, but he got money. When she came to fetch the milk and the bread, Käthe sometimes left pictures on the table for him, pictures of our hut and the fir trees – that was all she had to give. After the war she found a potter's wheel that no one was using any more down in the village, and dragged it up to the hut. She knew how to make pottery, she sold the dishes and jugs in the market.

Do you remember the spiced biscuits? The first time she took us to school, and afterwards she sent us to the marketplace and the woman in the blue-and-white apron gave us a spiced biscuit each?

Ella nodded. One for the little girlie, one for the little boy, they said in chorus; it was their shared memory. How often, over the last few years, they had reminded each other of the woman in the huge, blue-and-white apron? To them, she was the quintessence of rustic kindness.

I remember about the hare – Ella's eyes sparkled – I remember how one day she brought a hare . . .

Thomas put both hands over his ears, ready to shut out all sound entirely if the story turned out as badly as Ella's chirping voice suggested.

. . . put the skin out to dry in the sun . . . cooked with thyme . . . with bacon . . . pepper. The roast smelled so delicious I waited by the stove to be the first to get a bit. Well, she told me as she took the roast out of the oven, because you're so greedy we'll put it out on the balcony in front of the door, and wait until tomorrow, tomorrow is Sunday, we'll have a Sunday roast! Ella turned indignantly. She was asking for Thomas's sympathy.

Yes? His hands flapped, there was a scared look in his eyes.

What's the matter, don't you want to hear the story?

Yes, yes, I do, begged Thomas, but he was afraid.

Well, next morning I went outside the moment I woke up. And there was the hare, all eaten except for its bones, and the dried roast meat that still had a shine where it stuck to the paws.

Thomas screamed.

Don't be silly. Ella nudged his back. Guess what, I was crying when I went upstairs to where Käthe and Eduard were comfortably lying in bed under the roof, and she told me, laughing, that it had been the fox!

The fox?

Yes, the fox. So then every evening I thought of the fox coming up our steps after dark, or jumping up from the meadow outside and polishing off our roast with his sharp teeth.

You really believed her? Thomas raised his eyebrows; he had to laugh.

Ella nodded, rapt in her thoughts. Or if not the roast, polishing me off, she whispered quietly. Only now did she seem to be thinking it over. Why ask?

Well, surely the fox didn't sit at the table, gnaw the roast neatly off the bones and leave the bones lying there! Thomas was in a fit of giggles as if someone were tickling him.

Don't laugh in that stupid way. Who else would it have been?

Who do you think?

Ella bit her lip. Not the fox? she wondered in a quiet voice. That was mean of them. They just ate it up on the sly, all by themselves. While we were in bed asleep.

We?

The fox was later, after you'd been born. So there. Her voice was brusque; perhaps her feelings were hurt by his doubts.

Come on, Ella, tell me more. Thomas was afraid he had annoyed Ella, and she wouldn't want to go on with her story. Remember when Father arrived. Käthe had a big belly and I was going to be born.

Yes, but you weren't there yet. I was sitting in the meadow by myself, catching beetles and putting them into my mouth. I called to him. I couldn't stand up yet, maybe I couldn't even walk.

There was snow still lying in the mountains in February when I was born.

It had already melted outside the house, so there.

And the moment the snow melted the meadow was right underneath it? .

38

If you don't believe me I'm not going on with the story.

Thomas listened hard, but Ella persisted in her silence. He leaned against her back, wanting to hear more. Go on.

No, I don't feel like it any more.

Go on, please. And I won't interrupt. Please.

Hard as Thomas might beg and plead, she stayed silent.

He thought of the other stories she usually told, of how she had nearly choked on the beetle scrabbling inside her mouth; it must have got into her windpipe. But then Papa had arrived, turned her upside down and shaken her. Ella knew just what their father smelled like. Sometimes she caught the smell of him in her nostrils, all of a sudden, unexpectedly, it could happen in the tram, the school playground, the kitchen. She knew he was there. Their father had asked Käthe to stop hitting little Ella with her wet nappy. She was only a child, he said, not a cat. She had only just started to walk. She'll learn to sit on her potty, he said, like any other child. Ella didn't remember the wet nappy. But she knew about it from a letter that she had taken out of Käthe's chest of drawers in secret and shown to Thomas.

Who says he's dead? Fallen at the front, maybe, but he isn't dead.

There was something that scared Thomas in Ella's voice; she shifted the intonation of words in a way that took the sense out of them. At the end of such sentences he tried to think backwards in his memory. She believed her story now, every detail of it. He didn't know whether she was just pretending to him that she could change the world with nothing but her own ideas and assertions, or whether she believed it herself.

Gypsy children, they called us, do you remember? Stinking gypsy children and bastards. Ella laughed.

Thomas turned to her. She had let her hair fall over her face so that he couldn't see her eyes. Ella-eyes, sparkling green gypsy

39

eyes. It was a good thing the other children at school hadn't sniffed out the Jewishness in them. A Christian name for the son, a birth announcement by a priest – the invention of a difficult birth, fever while Käthe was lying in, had helped. At school they had been the only children whose fathers were not farmers or war heroes. Whether dead or alive. And who had no capable farmer's wife or housewife for a mother. The only children who bore their mother's surname and had no father at all. Later, the priest had wanted to baptise the small children, but Käthe failed to keep appointment after appointment. She always had a new excuse. That probably told the priest that he was being used; two birth certificates within twelve months. Rumours began spreading. The other children's fathers were beginning to come back that summer. Other fathers were dead or crippled somewhere abroad, or in prison.

I'd love to be a gypsy child, a real gypsy child, sighed Ella. Perhaps that's what we are, too? One day a gypsy woman came by, begging – and as soon as she had gone Käthe heard babies crying. And then she found us in the meadow outside the house.

Do you think the twins like it in that children's home?

Abandoned. In her hunger and her hour of need our gypsy mother simply abandoned us outside Käthe's house.

Thomas moved away from Ella's back, leaning on the trunk of the elm, and looked at her. We could just go and visit them?

Who? Ella did look up now, in curiosity.

The twins.

Why are you always going on about the twins? Käthe has to work. She'll be busy at the quarry again by the end of the month. Ella raised her eyebrows and pursed her lips. Nobody here needs the twins. Eduard's gone. We can't help them.

You imagine being a gypsy child. Abandoned. It's a fact that the little twins have been in the home for weeks. Baffled, Thomas shook his head. If in doubt, you're sorrier for yourself than anyone else.

Ella thrust out her lips, offended, and looked at the house. The corners of her mouth twitched, and she wrinkled up her nose, which made Thomas want to laugh. However, she took a deep breath as if to dive underwater and stay there for a long time. Ella's face distorted painfully, her eyes rolled so that Thomas could hardly see their irises, she groaned from the depths of her throat with an almost animal sound.

What is it, Ella? Thomas put one hand on her shoulder. What's the matter with you?

Oh! Ella shook her head frantically and abruptly hunched her shoulders forward; she writhed, her head struck the cracked planks of the tree-house floor, and hissing, wrenching sounds poured out of her mouth.

Come on, tell me what's wrong. Can you hear me, Ella?

Now he saw her tears; she was sobbing, she had red marks on her face, she was weeping uncontrollably.

Aaarrr! He knew that growl of hers; it was the growl of a dangerous beast of prey. But was she playing a game, and if so, what game was it?

I can't bear it! I think I'm dying, Thomas, hold me tight. Gasping, she clung to his arm with all her might, she was sinking her teeth into his forearm. Ella could turn into an animal from one moment to the next, become another being. When Ella let go of him, she didn't even notice the blood on his skin from the bite-mark, she dug her nails into his arms, let go and tore her own hair, hammered the floor in front of her with her fists. This is hell, it's hell!

Thomas knelt down in front of her and tried to hold her head, her fists, but she struck his hands away and punched his collarbone.

Let go of me, Ella shouted at him. He saw a soft tuft of hair in her hand; she had obviously pulled it out of her head – or his. He felt a burning sensation on his scalp.

He was talking to her as if she were a horse now: calm down, lie still, lie still. But Ella took no notice; she drummed her fists, she groaned, she screamed. Then all of a sudden she stopped; Ella looked around her, glassy-eyed, quiet now, she sniffed and shook herself. Thomas waited.

All right now?

She bowed her head; softly, almost reproachfully she said: Nothing's all right. What's pain good for anyway? It's all so pointless!

Thomas had his own doubts, but he sensed that Ella wasn't expecting an answer to her question.

And it'll be every month from now on, she went on yet more quietly, I can't bear it, I'll go mad, I really will.

That crazed pain of hers – how odd that it came over her so abruptly just when he asked about the twins. Ella loved her imaginary worlds; she soon felt that any sudden distraction from herself was boring, perhaps an injury, a danger.

I'll make you a hot-water bottle, said Thomas, kneeling in front of her, hands in his lap, and as she did not reply he added: If you like.

Giving

Darkness, colourful shadows cooled and moved away in Ella's dream; what remained was empty, cold darkness. A ray of light, thin as a hair, fell through the keyhole, luminous dust poured through the gap under the doorway, there were footsteps, the sound of knocking at a distant door. Without making a sound, Ella sat up in bed, felt with her hands for the edge of the sheet, the edge of the cloth, the fortress where she was still sitting, if uncertainly. It could be the lodger, a man to be avoided. She bent forward, felt her way along the floor, soft wood, lowered herself to it on her knees and lay face down. Her ribs felt sharp, one hip met the floor, her breasts were too young, her mount of Venus too low, she pushed herself and her bones and her hair under the bed, making her way along on the palms of her hands, she pressed her knees down and pushed herself well back to the edge of the night, where she could feel the skirting board against her hip bones. The skirting board was pleasantly cool, it gave her firm support, she was safe here, or almost. She heard a note in her ears, was it a gong, a bell? Ella couldn't place it; her skin longed to be cool, but the bowl she had fetched in the night was too far off, the soothing water was out of reach. A soft patter of feet, someone coming along the corridor without shoes on, it couldn't be the twins, they weren't here; the pattering sound grew louder, its movement like a wave, its sound a regular, apparently innocent rustling. Dwarves maybe,

43

little kobolds who wanted to bathe in her lakes, in the pools in her basins, a scratching sound, that could be the dog. Ella could deal with sounds, the knocking grew louder, that wouldn't be the lodger who, after all, had a key, although no door apart from his was ever locked, and he always came into rooms without knocking.

Abracadabra! The yodelling note of the female voice was reminiscent of a jackdaw. A kind of grating gurgle, she knew that voice, yes, it reminded her of Käthe. Maybe it was the effervescence of a woman's voice, a cheerful warbling, as if to wake nightingales from their winter inactivity. Why would she be calling to Ella, what did she want from her in here?

Light shone in, fell on the entire room. Ella could see two feet in Mongolian shoes, the kind that Käthe wore.

Good morning, Ella! The feet came over to the bed. Ella heard the covers being pulled back. Ella?

Happy birthday! That was Thomas, whose bare feet Ella now recognised in the doorway.

Where is she? Have you seen her? Is she up already? The covers slipped halfway off the bed and hid the view. Ella? In surprise, Käthe went round the room, stopped at Ella's desk, paper rustled.

But Ella didn't want to show the two of them where she was hiding. She saw the feet go out of the room; they would go on looking for her in the bathroom and the smoking room. Ella crawled out from under the bed and knocked the dust off her nightdress, stardust from her hiding place in the ground. Wouldn't it be much better to sleep under the bed in future? She'd feel as safe as in a cave. Why did modern people sleep on beds, unprotected, visible from afar?

Where were you? The figure of Thomas reappeared in her doorway. We were going to wake you up, but you weren't here.

I was in the loo, lied Ella, and saw from Thomas's look that he didn't believe her. Maybe he had just come from there himself, and let her little lie pass only out of kindness because there were much more important things today. He put his arm round her shoulder, pulled her close and whispered in her ear: I hope all your wishes come true, dear little big wild sister. His cold nose brushed her cheek. I have a little present for you, it's in the shed at Michael's place.

Ella nodded.

Is anything wrong?

No. She had to say something, think up an idea quickly so that he didn't notice anything. I don't have quite enough money yet, but a promise is a promise. This evening in the Johannishof?

You look so scared. Thomas was watching her.

Ella pulled her nightdress over her head and dropped it carelessly on the floor, so that Thomas would pick it up and put it over the chair. Scared? She was going to need at least ten marks. Ella had only thirty pfennigs. She put on her trousers and sweater.

I have one mark twenty, you're welcome to that. I told you you don't have to invite me – anyway, it's your birthday. A person doesn't get to be sixteen every day, we were still the same age yesterday, now you're a year older than me again. And Thomas, laughing, nudged her in the ribs.

We're the Löwenthals, I reserved the table for us last week. They're sure to think: oh, what an attractive couple, how young they are. Just married? Ella disguised her voice and rolled her eyes; she enjoyed going out with Thomas as a married couple. Michael had told them about the Johannishof, his parents had celebrated their bronze wedding there with their relations from the West. Ten waiters serving one table, the food was carried over to the customer under a domed cover, the waiters wore snow-white gloves, it was a really classy place. Young people didn't

45

go there, it was only the upper classes who ate in the Johannishof. Like the Löwenthals.

Thomas took Ella's hand and led her out of the room and along the corridor to the smoking room. There was a smell of Earl Grey tea in there, and the room was full of the music of stringed instruments.

So there's my birthday girl, where have you been hiding? Cheerfully, reproachfully Käthe lit the big candle. This child was born sixteen sweet years ago, she sang.

Ella clapped her hands like a small child.

But as soon as Käthe had finished singing her little ditty, she said sternly: I have something really special for you this year. She turned to the green curtain behind her back that, together with the big sliding door, divided her bedroom from the smoking room. Picking up the poker, she waved it like a magic wand. Hocus pocus fidibus, three black cats! Now she opened the drawn curtain with the wand. Abracadabra!

Ella couldn't see at once what Käthe was conjuring up. She pulled the tea trolley through the doorway. There was a pale mound on the tea trolley, a white hill, a shining, glittering mountain.

Who stole the chocolate out of the pantry at festival time, who stole the nuts and raisins if it wasn't my magpie of a daughter?

Ella looked at Käthe, shocked.

Maybe you think I don't notice anything? But I don't like being robbed, particularly not by my own child. The crystallised ginger and candied grapefruit slices, who stole those out of my Czech bowl in the glass-fronted cupboard? Who nibbles the bacon before it gets to the table? Whose fault is it that I've stopped buying such things?

Ella shook her head. It wasn't me, she said in a hoarse,

helplessly indignant voice, knowing that she was a very good liar so long as she believed what she was saying herself. She didn't know about any theft, anything, she knew nothing at all about it, and she wasn't a magpie.

Your brother then, was it? There was anger in Käthe's voice; the simplest way, she thought, to convict Ella of lying was to cast suspicion on her brother. Ella wasn't going to let Thomas be wrongly accused, she would want to confess.

But Ella shook her head again, looking incredulously at Käthe: Do you really think . . . would you believe it of . . .? Thomas? How could Käthe drag him into it? Neither Käthe nor Ella took their eyes off each other even for a moment to look aside at Thomas, who didn't defend himself. He knew as well as the two of them what game they were playing, and he didn't want to be caught between them.

It was you. Käthe clapped her hands; she wanted to finish this conversation. She had no doubt at all that Ella had been stealing her provisions. That was why she was getting something really special this year. This is your birthday present!

What? Ella stared at the tea trolley.

Sugar. Käthe didn't reach out a hand to her, did not make any loving gesture, did not wish her a happy birthday. She turned on the very low heel of her Mongolian shoe and walked out of the smoking room.

Sugar? Ella went over to the tea trolley and incredulously touched the white mountain of fine crystals. The sugar rustled beneath her fingertips.

I expect she thinks she's giving you a treat.

Is that meant to be a comfort? Did Thomas really think that Käthe wanted to give Ella a treat with all this sugar? A real treat? Why not crystallised fruit, then, why not crisp bacon rind, why not onion pie?

47

My birthday present is sugar? Plain sugar?

The door opened and Käthe came in with a tray. Breakfast for everyone, she filled three cups with tea, put small boards at her place and Thomas's, held the loaf of bread to her breast and cut several slices. Whenever she cut bread like that, moving the blade of the bread knife towards her body, the bread in front of her full breasts, Ella thought that in the posh nursery of Käthe's childhood no one had shown her how to cut bread on the table.

Ella sat down at her own place. She had neither a little board nor a knife in front of her. She reached for the bread, but Käthe smartly slapped her hand, making it tingle.

You eat your sugar, she said sternly, triumphantly; there was no doubting that firm voice. Only when you've finished it all up do you get something proper to eat again.

Incredulously, Ella looked from Käthe to the tea trolley and back at Käthe again.

I'm sure you'll manage it easily, little magpie. And then perhaps you'll be cured, and see for yourself how stupid stealing is.

You want me to eat that whole mountain of sugar?

What do you mean, that whole mountain? It's a little hill weighing ten pounds, no more, no less. Ought I to have bought sixteen, one for each of your years of life? Ninety, a hundred, one for each pound of your weight? Käthe cut her bread twice, quartered a clove of garlic and put a quarter of the clove on each piece of bread. The salt was in clumps in the salt cellar; Käthe salted her food generously. The first quarter piece of bread and garlic was already disappearing into her mouth, she chewed noisily, munching, smacking her lips. In between meals I shall lock the sugar up here in my cupboard so that you don't go throwing it away on the sly. That would be a shame. There'll be nothing else for you until you've finished it, only sugar.

Ella rubbed her eyes with her fists; if she went on rubbing

like that for some time not only would her eyes be red, she would make tears flow, pitiful, heart-rending tears that would soften any heart. The warm tears ran down her cheeks, her eyelids fluttered, her nostrils widened and quivered.

Don't make such a fuss, there are millions of people in the world going hungry. You're too well off here, you're ungrateful, sly, disrespectful. I'm teaching you respect, that's all. Käthe cut another slice of bread, broke it in two and gave half to the dog. The arm of the record player made a dragging sound; the disc had come to an end and the needle was scratching over the vinyl. Käthe put the other half of the slice of bread on her board, buttered it and took a mouthful.

Ella's eyelid twitched; sheer rage took hold of her.

And by the way, there are also postage stamps missing from my desk. Here Käthe opened a thick quarto magazine, *Meaning and Form*, its title spontaneously arousing Ella's desire to mock.

To keep herself from snorting with laughter, Ella sucked in her cheeks and bit her lip. Next moment she widened her eyes and puffed out her cheeks. You think I stole them? Her indignation could not have been greater. She felt no shame – although she had in fact been to blame. She had taken postage stamps from Käthe's desk, and not for the first time. She nodded vigorously, so vigorously that Thomas gently kicked her under the table. Oh yes, of course, I steal everything! Ella was incandescent, shooting sparks. But I left the letters there – the letters you were writing because you wanted to marry a dead man.

You did what? *Meaning and Form* sank to Käthe's lap. What letters?

To the Ministry. Ella picked up the dessert spoon on the table in front of her, went over to the tea trolley, pushed the spoon into the sugar and carried it to her mouth as if there could be nothing more delicious in the world. Curiously, she observed Käthe's wandering eyes. It was beginning to dawn on her what letters Ella meant.

My desk is nothing to do with you. You have no business with it, none at all!

Retrospective acknowledgement of my marriage to the father of my children. Ella was obviously quoting; her tone was sarcastic. You were positively begging: You must understand! The man who –

Keep your hands off my things or I'll throw you out!

– who had certainly wanted to marry you, only unfortunately he couldn't, oh dear! Ella rolled her eyes.

What do you know about it? Käthe slammed *Meaning and Form* shut. Enough was enough; she banged the journal down on the table.

There was no stopping Ella now, in her delight at scoring off Käthe with something that would hurt at least as much as that comment on a magpie daughter and the mountain of sugar. But now that he's fallen at the front, and you have to make your way alone with two small children, oh, how glad you'd be of a widow's pension!

You don't know anything about it! Käthe's voice rose, if only to drown out Ella's, to keep from hearing what Ella was saying. She went on, undeterred, as if Ella were not speaking the painful truth. Both fell silent for a moment, breathless, red in the face. At this point Thomas picked up his board and left the smoking room in silence, while Käthe shouted at Ella: You can take your school bag and go and live somewhere else, it's as simple as that!

Oh, and where am I supposed to go?

Just get out.

You really wanted to marry a dead man? Have a common-law relationship made official after the event? Because you felt sure that but for the laws he'd have married you? What makes you so certain of that? Ella laughed; she had never before seen Käthe so sober, so nonplussed, in a state of amazement that she would have liked to interpret as shame, but couldn't, because Käthe wasn't denying anything, her face hid nothing, it merely showed sheer horror as she looked at the girl.

Käthe opened her mouth, took a deep breath, and said nothing.

I won! Gossamer-thin, malicious jubilation streamed through Ella. True, Thomas had not come back, so there had been no witness to her exposure of Käthe, but an important question had been asked, the curtain had been drawn back. As for the postage stamps and the raisins, and your stupid camping stove which capsized with us that time we were out in the boat, so it's lying somewhere at the bottom of the Müggelsee today – I ask myself what you mean by communism. Aren't your goods ours as well? And our neighbours' goods? Why do you give a mountain of sugar to me and not the Republic?

Because you're a thief.

Let me share it; I'll share the ten pounds of sugar with everyone who comes to see us, we'll let the tea trolley stand there in the corner, and you can tell your friends the story of your criminal child, and I'll tell them my story about communism, and we'll invite them to help themselves – go ahead, take as much as you want.

I'll be in the studio. With these words Käthe stood up and marched to the door.

Why didn't you come looking for us when we were out in the boat? Ella called after her. You didn't even notice we were missing! Not for three days, not for three nights, and all the time we were out on the stupid Müggelsee until our boat capsized. The water was icy. We were lucky it happened so close to the bank; who knows how long we could have swum in the lake?

What were you thinking of?

You didn't miss us one whole evening, one whole day, you didn't miss us for a moment! Not until we came home dripping wet and shivering, and then you were beside yourself. We had to tell you we'd been gone for three days, out on the Müggelsee at a temperature of zero. And you wouldn't believe us. People don't exist for you unless they're in front of your eyes. You don't bother about anyone but the poor –

You two taught yourselves a good lesson. A sense of responsibility for yourself begins –

You're cruel, you and your sense of responsibility. You want to be a heroine for everyone in society, people can't be poor enough to please you, you're sorry for the poor – but with your children you suddenly go on about taking responsibility for themselves! Every man for himself, and where will your society be then?

Don't shout like that, Ella, it reminds me of your father.

As if there were still poor people today. There are only good people, heroes every one of them.

Käthe coolly scrutinised her from head to toe. Take a look in the mirror, my girl, you're sixteen today, it's about time you stopped wailing and complaining so much. Clear the table. She pushed the door handle down and turned back once more. It's eight thirty, school has begun, so why are you still hanging around here?

Just as you like. I'll be off.

Ella didn't have to explain anything else, because Käthe had already gone out of the room, closing the door behind her.

Ella did not clear the table. She stuck the handle of the spoon into the top of the sugar mountain. The spoon tipped over sideways. Ella switched off the light; it was fully day now. Thomas wasn't around any longer. He must have gone to school, he hated arriving late, while she was late all the time. She hadn't been to school much at all recently. Two boys were in love with her; she made eyes at them both and didn't love either of them. She enjoyed the soulful looks of a handsome lad known to everyone as Johnny, who had all the girls hanging on his every word, what with the circles under his eyes and his slight squint, but few sounds ever passed his lips. Everyone at school knew about him. They had once danced rock'n'roll together, Ella in the petticoat she had made for herself and nothing on underneath it, he with the circles under his eyes and his longing glances. At the end of the night Ella had turned away, drunk with his unspoken love and already rather tired of it. She had given the last dance to short-legged Siegfried, who had then triumphantly taken her home on his moped. Inflamed by the jealousy with which he had watched Ella and Johnny all evening, Siegfried kissed her stormily before she had made it to the steps up to the front door. Legs, Ella, legs! His thick hair smelled of grease and the night's cigarette smoke. Ella had only just opened the door when he came in with her, she hung her jacket up on its hook, and he kissed her arms and the hollows of her armpits. She laughed, and he kissed her open mouth; she retreated, and he followed her until they had both landed in her room and on her bed. Door closed, Siegfried on his knees, he had kept his leather jacket on, the peaked cap was still on his head, slightly askew and crumpled; it was meant to make everyone think of Marlon Brando. The rough, see-through chiffon of her petticoat was scratching Ella's throat, a brief pain, a slight burning sensation, and Siegfried was rocking up and down in defiant delight. Ella didn't move, she didn't think of Marlon Brando, she was watching her toes in the air. The petticoat was tickling her nose now, and she didn't want to sneeze.

Johnny and Siegfried were not the only boys to have fallen for Ella, but they had fallen so heavily that within a few months Ella could hardly walk into the school without finding herself faced with making a firm decision. A decision that she didn't want to make, and still less *could* she make it. Ella listened for sounds in the house, for anything that might tell her Käthe was coming upstairs to her studio, for a key turning in the lock and the lodger coming in, although he hadn't been here since early January. But nothing stirred, she heard only the pendulum of the grandfather clock and, in the distance, the dog barking, perhaps because the postman had come into the yard. Käthe's shoulder bag was hanging over the armchair; it was made of green leather and printed in a way that made it look like the skin of a reptile. She found the large purse embroidered with a black-and-white pattern. She opened the catch, took out a ten-mark note and six large silver coins, and put it back inside the reptile.

Ella waited at the tram stop until she couldn't feel her toes for the cold. She let six trams come and go before she boarded one, and she stayed in it until it reached the terminus. On the way back she got out at Friedrichshagen. For twenty pfennigs she sat in the cinema, where there were only children and pensioners at this time of day. All winter the same film had been showing, *The Tale of Poor Hassan*, who was blamed for his naivety as a believer; of course the rich and powerful had blamed him for his poverty and thought up God only to enslave people like him. God as a calculating instrument of the exploiters. When the film ended it was nearly two. Ella bought herself a roll and dripping and munched it as she waited under the suburban railway bridge for Thomas. He would change trains here when he came out of school.

What have you got me as a present? she asked breathlessly when she had spotted him in the crowd streaming out of the station doorway, had run after him and put both her hands over his eyes from behind.

Thomas ducked to shake free of them, and turned to face her. The headmaster wants Käthe to come and talk to him. You can't stay on at the school if you don't attend.

So?

No final exam, no university studies. Thomas was looking earnestly at Ella.

Will I need them?

Here, I'm to give you this from Johnny. Thomas opened his briefcase and took out a small picture frame containing some pressed flowers behind glass. Ella squinted at the picture they made, oh no, please not!

Thomas took a letter out of his jacket pocket. And this is from Siegfried.

Ella turned away. I don't feel well.

And happy birthday from Michael too, he'd be pleased if we go to the garden at the weekend. We were going to tell you together, but you didn't come to school.

A surprise?

We've been raising a plant for you. It really grows only in South America. We made a biotope under glass for it. You'll see.

Is it in flower?

Let it be a surprise. And Roland says happy birthday, he asked if you're having a party.

We're having a party on our own, just you and me. I've got the money, we're going to the Johannishof.

I'm supposed to give this to you. The letter shook in Thomas's hand; he had been holding it out to her for some time. Siegfried wants you to read it when you're alone.

So what? I don't want to read it at all. She looked down the street, and a fleeting smile appeared on her face, as if she recognised someone in the distance. The tram from Adlershof squealed as it came along the curving rails.

Here, take it. Thomas tried putting the letter under Ella's arm, which she was pressing close to her body, hand in her coat pocket, because it was cold. But at that Ella raised her arm, took a step back, and the letter fell to the ground.

You threw it away. Ella laughed.

Thomas shook his head. You're so childish. You could at least take it.

But suppose I don't want to read it? I don't want it. Ella crossed her arms and, as if by accident, trod on the letter. The ash-grey slush under her feet sucked at it.

Then why do you go dancing around in front of him? With your hair like Brigitte Bardot's, hopping around on the dance floor in a petticoat?

Is that forbidden? Ella rolled her eyes and squinted with one of them, not sure whether to suggest to her brother that she had a guilty conscience when in fact she didn't. His fit of morality annoyed her.

Do you enjoy tormenting them? They all seem to be crazy about you, and you are too, crazy about yourself and no one else. Was that contempt in his eyes or lack of understanding?

This is my birthday. Ella was pouting, but Thomas turned away from her.

Here's to you, darling. Thomas held out the glass of sparkling wine to her.

Cheers! Thank you, my dear. Here's to us, Achim. Ella giggled. Shall I call you Achim?

I'd rather be Hans-Joachim. Thomas cleared his throat.

As soon as they had finished their sparkling wine, the wine waiter came along and changed them for cut glasses for red wine. Would you care for a Hungarian wine? It's a little young, but I think you will like its mellow aroma.

Bring it on. Thomas adopted a jovial tone. The wine waiter let him taste the wine and then filled both their glasses.

Two waiters carried in plates under silver covers, put them down in front of Ella and Thomas and said together, in solemn tones: The festive menu for Herr and Frau Löwenthal. First *solyanka* Moscow-style. The covers were raised to reveal surprisingly small porcelain bowls of a brown soup that smelled delicious to Ella.

Do you have a plain vegetable soup for my husband? He's a Buddhist and doesn't like eating dead pig.

The waiter hesitated only briefly, then bowed his head and came back a few minutes later with another cover. *Solyanka* Moscow-style without meat. He raised the silver dome and took three steps back, head slightly bent, expectantly waiting to see if there would be any further request before turning away and going back to the kitchen.

Amazing, they've rehearsed it all, whispered Thomas, every step, every glance. Reaching for it and shaking it just once, Thomas unfolded the fabric napkin and stuffed one corner in the neck of his sweater, as he had often seen Käthe do, and he had once seen her father the professor do the same.

You look like a baby. Ella giggled. Infected by the general formality, she put her hand over her mouth as she did so.

So? That's what you do. We start with the spoon on the outside. They both picked up their spoons at the same time and, while Ella tried to drink her soup as quietly as possible, Thomas cautiously stirred the thick broth. They've taken as many of the bits of meat out as they could, he said, nodding appreciatively and letting the soup fall back into the bowl in a glazed steam. He preferred not to drink it.

How could they get all those tiny scraps of meat out of the soup? But it tastes really good, do try it. Ella sighed with enjoyment. Their glasses were refilled; as soon as they had taken a sip the wine waiter came along to top them up. A waltz was playing in the next room; through the large, open double door they could see the other guests dancing there. They were getting on in years. A graceful elderly lady with hair dyed deep black was wearing a mustard-yellow dress cinched in at the waist, its wide skirt seemed to have thousands of little pleats. She had pinned her hair up on top of her head and she danced almost perfectly, as if the music had been written for her. Perhaps she was a professional dancer?

So who's the fairest of us all? Ella had finished her soup, was leaning back in her chair, arms folded and was watching the dancer's light steps with envy and admiration.

What a question, darling. Thomas took a slim blue folder out of his case. It had a dark ribbon round it. For you, but I don't want you to open it.

The bowls were taken away.

'Dream Sleep', it's called, said Thomas, leaning over the table so that guests sitting near wouldn't notice. *On my left a stone cries out in the dark / slowly my being ends . . .*

Ella sat opposite him, wide-eyed. She wanted him to think she was listening, he knows those wide eyes, the show of astonishment before there was anything to be astonished by. He wasn't going to let that annoy him now, and without finishing the verse he went on, further down in the poem: *Hands reach out, grasp the void, / faces take distance by storm, / circle a consuming light / that burns a dazzling white.* Ella was playing with her fork, her expression didn't show whether she was even listening, so Thomas skipped the next verse as well in order to get to the end of his poem, which now seemed far too long, as quickly as possible: *Gone is the image that brought delight, / the yearning song has died away, / and through the dark and russet night / cold silence blows this way*. He also left the next verse out and went straight to the last one, which he wanted to read, even if Ella was yawning now and covering her mouth with her hand . . . *The wind moves, moves its eyes / And my Self changes, as I see, / the world is silent, all sound dies, / a world cold and dead with no comfort for me . . .*

Ella was beaming, her happy gaze went to the two waiters carrying in new plates with silver covers over them.

Chicken breast in aspic with leeks and mustard seeds.

Putting his forefinger to his lips, Thomas asked her to keep quiet and not show him up again over the meat. Ella loved aspic, he wasn't going to send his back, she simply ate half of his serving. She put out her fork right across the table to his plate as if it were the most natural thing in the world.

Oh, wonderful, how good that tastes! Poor Thomas, you're not going to get much to eat today. Ella bowed her head in pretended regret. She was enjoying the meal, she didn't want to suffer pangs of conscience. Doesn't that smell good? Go on, do try it. I mean, the chicken's died for us already. You can't just send parts of its body back, then it would have died for nothing.

Leave me alone. Thomas was red in the face. He was embarrassed by the attention she was drawing to them.

Chickie chickie chickie . . . Ella's fork reached over the table to Thomas's plate again as if there were a little chicken there to be enticed out.

Tongue with mustard sauce and green pepper served with boiled potatoes in butter and parsley for the lady, bean casserole for the gentleman.

Ella looked triumphantly at her brother. Serves you right! She nodded eagerly to the waiter and took the fork from his hand even before he could put it down beside her plate, as a substitute for the big fork that she had used by mistake for the chicken breast in aspic, and she dug its prongs into the ox tongue. A poem! Ella was quoting Käthe, who described any delicious meal as a poem. Ella chewed, closing her eyes. I can see our Baltic estates, dear husband, our trees on the Darss peninsula bending in the wind, red deer trotting down to the sea early in the morning, bending their heads and drinking salt water, I see dunes where seagrass grows, reed beds rippling, and the white-flecked meadows by the brackish water where the singing swans raise their cygnets and graze, they bend their long necks and dig holes as they search for roots, further on, near the outskirts of the village of Ahrenshoop, the first buttercups are in bright yellow flower, and our kindly, fat cows walk among them, cheerfully crushing them. Cautiously, Ella opened her eyes and looked to see whether Thomas was listening, picturing the pretty cattle with their gentle eyes and tender tongues. Ella licked her lips. This is delicious!

Thomas ate a mouthful of bean casserole and looked at her. Your cheeks are glowing.

Here's to glowing cheeks! Ella raised her wine glass and drank to Thomas.

Here's to you. Thomas raised his own glass and emptied it. What makes you so cruel, Ella? Don't you ever think of any living creature but yourself?

Heavens, where would that get us? Who else would you like me to think of? Aren't I thinking of our cattle and our deer on the Darss peninsula? Are we nothing but creatures, then, do we do so little creating ourselves?

Thomas shrugged his shoulders. When Ella was getting on his nerves he could manage not to look at her for hours on end. One of those long periods could have begun just now.

Cheer up, little one, this is all about the fact that I like eating meat, right?

Thomas put down his wine glass, threw his head back, raised

it again and belched gently at Ella. It's an experiment, take it that way. No one has to kill and eat animals. My pacifist contribution to the world.

Ah, I see. Ella nodded in agreement, as if she were finally accepting what he said. A waltz was followed by slow music intended for couples in love and newly married, like them.

Shall we dance? Ella winked at Thomas and dabbed her mouth ceremoniously with her napkin. He put down his wine glass. Taking his sleeve, she led him through the double door to the dance floor.

There's only one man I can be happy with, Ella whispered in Thomas's ear, and that's you. All the others want to touch me, stick their tongues in my mouth, fuck me, hurt me. Ella shook herself. It's disgusting, they're as greedy for it as animals. You're different. She turned right, holding Thomas so close that he had to turn with her.

You think so? Thomas's eyelashes fluttered, and he did not step back but danced hesitantly on the spot, so that Ella trod on his toes.

I certainly am. Ella nodded vigorously. No doubt about it, you'd never want that, not with me, and perhaps – she hesitated – no, certainly not with any other girl.

Ella pushed his arm, pressed her knee against his so that he would keep moving his legs. She pushed him on, but he turned against her arm. What is it, don't you like dancing? Your shoulders are drooping as if you were a sack of potatoes. Thomas had blue eyes with a green glint to them on many sunny days, and when he was happy. Today they were a shade of grey in the dim lighting of the restaurant. Are you tipsy already? Ella giggled.

Thomas shuffled from foot to foot on the spot. I wish I were the one.

What one?

The one you look at, the one you want. Thomas's sad expression intrigued Ella. He went on: I'm not sure if I'm really any different from other boys. You hope so. But why would I be different?

You just are different, you're not an animal.

Yes, I am. Thomas was nodding now, I'm a mammal. Or if I may say so, a human being.

You're not your body's slave. Ella impatiently guided Thomas through the dancing couples, and he let her lead him, but that was not enough of a signal.

Not the slave, maybe, but the servant. Not just of my body, of other people's as well.

Then human beings are barbaric because they're born through sexual intercourse?

Well, aren't they? Thomas looked doubtfully at Ella. Barbaric, I mean? Maybe it's not just because of the two sexes, there are a few other details involved.

I don't know. Ella was laughing now, she held Thomas's arm up so high that it served as an arch and she could twirl in the dance under it. I can't imagine you doing it with Violetta or any other . . . you don't want to, do you?

Thomas did not reply; he didn't know what to say. I'll have to sit down. He was moving more slowly, and looked as if he might stop.

Not yet. Ella twirled again. There's nothing nicer than feeling dizzy as you dance.

Do you think, whispered Thomas, searching for words, affectionately, sternly, do you think you're the only one to feel helpless? What can I do about it? I'm a boy. I don't want to be a girl.

You're drunk.

Thomas shook his head. How would I be different when I'm going to be a man, when I'm a boy? He felt exhausted and wanted to lay his head on Ella's swaying shoulder. She was tireless when she began dancing, they could go on all night like this with him following her, holding up his arm for her to twirl under it, holding out a hand while she moved to one side as soon as he wanted to rest his head. Can I stop nature in its tracks?

Yes, stop it in its tracks. Stop all nature in its tracks. Come on, let's swear never to grow up. Ella raised her fingers in the air, her eyes were shining. I'm going to stay small and never be anyone's wife.

Is that what you want me to swear? Never to be anyone's wife?

Husband for you, of course, swear never to be anyone's husband . . .

They danced, and Thomas watched their shadows on the dance floor.

There's something I must tell you, he called out so that she could hear him; she had moved so far away that only their fingertips touched now and then.

Ella raised her eyebrows, but showed no sign of getting closer to him, so he would have to say it louder, shout it. He couldn't manage that.

Later, when they were back at their table, raising their full wine glasses, drinking to each other, he said: I can't do it.

Do what?

Stay a child. I can't.

Disappointed, she shrugged and assumed her haughty expression, that negative look from under her long lashes that laid all the Johnnys of this world low. She drank the wine in her glass straight down, waited for the waiter to arrive, gave him a half-smile and enjoyed his awkwardness. As soon as he had topped up the glass she took another sip. The wine was pleasantly astringent, her gums felt rough, her teeth felt rough when she ran her tongue over them, her palate felt rough. She had slight

63

nausea, in line with the intoxication of her thought. Of course, Thomas had begun loving girls some time ago, the looks he gave them had not escaped Ella, he couldn't see enough of them, when a certain girl crossed his path his deep gaze was embarrassing to Ella, and to Violetta if not also to Michael; Ella guessed it, but she didn't want to know about it. His desire was not of the flesh, it was a sacred, spiritual, crystalline desire, she felt absolutely sure of that. She nodded to herself, so as not to lose her certainty. Never mind all that talk of gazelles – Siegfried liked her legs in particular. Her knee was a bulging mound, a clumsy joint run wild, she thought as she crossed one leg over the other and jiggled it in time to the music.

You are different, she said, and smiled at her own earnest tone of voice. I didn't have time to want anything, Eduard was just there, and I hadn't even started bleeding, I mean before. I wasn't a woman yet. He thinks he made me one. But I'm not letting anyone make me anything. Do you understand?

Thomas nodded vaguely, took a large sip from his glass, and he might have been thinking of God from the way he gazed at the ruby red of the wine. He probably wasn't listening to Ella.

And now here's the lodger. Oh, what luck. Ella said it in a cold, contemptuous voice. Well, we're really in luck after that mess we were in, she said, imitating Käthe's tone of enthusiasm, he got us heating, genuine oil-fired central heating for the whole house, and we needed it so urgently.

You scratch my back, I'll scratch yours. Exhausted, Thomas shrugged his shoulders.

I don't want him scratching mine.

What do you mean? Thomas's mouth dropped open, as it so often did.

Close your mouth or you'll catch the flies. What I say. You know exactly what I mean. Didn't you say so yourself in the poem about the Red Way? The central heating demands tribute. Her eyes were sparkling with an unpleasant, angry, impotent light.

Would you like chocolate cream with vanilla sauce or red-fruit fool with sago and whipped cream for dessert? Soundlessly, the waiter had approached, and was looking from Thomas to Ella and back again.

Yes, very snug, aren't we? A lodger like that who doesn't bother anyone? Ella tightened her lips.

Stop it. His voice was not angry but pleading. Thomas was begging her to stop talking about Eduard and the lodger and other men. Tell Käthe, tell her about it and then you can get rid of him.

You think she'd believe me? She doesn't believe anything else I say, she'll only think I'm showing off. Her lodger is beyond reproach, haven't you noticed?

Excuse me, chocolate cream or red-fruit fool with sago and whipped cream? The waiter cleared his throat.

One of each, please. The chocolate cream for her, the fruit fool for me.

No, I don't want either. A cigarette, please, do you have a cigarette? Ella interrupted him, banging the table with her fist angrily, as if their air of distinction was getting her down. The waiter disappeared backwards as silently as he had come.

Shall we order another bottle of wine?

Thomas's eyes were fixed on Ella. She had been ignoring him for some time now, she wasn't looking at him but straight past him, cutting him out of her field of vision.

I'm so sorry. His lips were quivering almost imperceptibly. He moved his hand in Ella's direction over the white tablecloth, half clenched into a fist, an old signal between brother and sister; perhaps he thought she would push her own fist against his, a silent token of forgiveness. But she didn't know what she was supposed to be forgiving him for. The waiter had placed a small silver salver beside her. It held a piece of dark blue felt, with a single cigarette in the middle of it.

Go on, cry. Ella reached for the cigarette and placed it in her mouth. When the waiter struck a match and lit it for her, she drew on it strongly. Once again she smiled at the waiter. He stumbled, and she quickly snatched at his hand, turned it over and inspected it in its white glove. What a hard-working hand. A glance up at him. Have you been working here long?

Excuse me, he stammered, and red shot into his face; with his left glove he touched his gleaming nose, his right was caught in Ella's hands. Is everything all right?

Oh, very much so. Ella smiled and drew on the cigarette, holding it with one hand while she still held the waiter's hand in the other. Smoke came out of her nostrils, a lot of it. She practised that because she though it was funny to breathe smoke like a dragon. She batted her eyelashes. Would you take this out of here, please? She looked deep into the waiter's eyes.

Excuse me? His glance wandered over the table, on which only the refilled wine glasses now stood; he had cleared all the rest of the china and cutlery away.

My cheek, my face, me, I'm a girl, take me out of here with you.

Now the waiter looked at Thomas. Can I be of any assistance, sir? Would you like the bill now, shall I call a taxi?

That would be a good idea, yes. Thomas rolled his eyes. Chandeliers hung from the ceiling, their glass droplets reflecting the lights. My wife isn't feeling very –

Huh, my wife – I'm not his wife. That's my little brother. I'm paying the bill. And then I'm going away with whoever I want. Tell me, will you take me with you?

66

The waiter preferred not to answer this question, and hastily went away.

Ella reached for Thomas's glass, which was still full to the brim, put her lips to the rim of the glass and blew bubbles into it, sucked up wine, raised her head: Oh, my dear little brother. She put her forefinger in the glass, put it in her mouth, deep, deeper, she sucked her finger and put it back in the wine. If I could only love, you know – she tried whistling on the rim of the glass – everything might turn out well. Really well. I'd be happy with Johnny. Or Siegfried. If I could only love.

Without moving his head, Thomas looked surreptitiously to all sides. They were being watched; the older, distinguished-looking customers were entertained by the young couple. But Ella, with her tongue out, licked the rim of her wine glass. Couldn't you play a musical note on the rim of a glass? Which is worse, do you think, not being able to love or not being loved? She directed her question at the glass, putting out her tongue as far as it would go, perhaps getting it right to the bottom of the wine glass before the glass itself suddenly shattered between her hand and her mouth. Perhaps she had pressed it too hard, had bitten it?

The wine had spilled over her dress. Ella carefully removed a gossamer-thin splinter of glass from her tongue. She spat, several times, to get other shards out of her mouth, she spat on the tablecloth and on her dress, waving the stem of the glass, which she was still holding, back and forth like a conductor's baton. Thomas had jumped up and hurried round the table. He mopped at her with his napkin, carefully collecting the tiny shards of glass.

Don't swallow, show me your tongue again. Sure enough, he found another long, thin splinter on her tongue.

Your taxi is here. The waiter had brought the bill in a small silver booklet.

Where's the money?

There . . . there. Ella's mouth was making baby sounds as she spat, dribbling, so as not to swallow any broken glass, and she pointed to her school bag lying on the floor. Thomas crawled under the table to retrieve it, and had to empty the whole bag to find the money at last lying loose in it. He picked out all the coins and the note and placed the money on the little silver booklet that the waiter was holding open. As the waiter went on standing there motionless, Thomas put his hand in his own pocket and added something to it.

I'm sorry, sir, that's not enough.

Can you send us the bill at home?

What about your taxi?

We'll take the suburban train. I'm sorry about this. Thomas took a pencil out of Ella's bag and wrote the address on the bill for the waiter. Another waiter brought their jackets. But Ella couldn't stand up on her own, and had to be supported. Thomas hauled her up, got his arm under hers, supported her back while her sour breath blew in his face. His poem was still lying on the table. How could he ever have mentioned his doubts of the Red Way to her? She'd hardly listened to his poem, he had written it for nothing, given it to her for nothing.

Can I walk? Ella spoke like a small child now as she sank to the floor and fell to her knees, holding Thomas's hand.

You can, yes, you can. Thomas was sweating all over and wondering how he was going to get Ella home.

Daddy dear, I love you, said Ella, pressing her cheek to the back of Thomas's hand, kissing his hand, turning up her eyes soulfully, I love you and only you.

Standing

What's the matter? Don't stand around like that, get undressed. Käthe turned her back to her adolescent son, cigarette in one hand, holding her chisel against the rotating whetstone with the other. She called through the noise, in her powerful voice: If you're cold do some knee-bends. He could hardly hear her, and only guessed what she was saying. The screech of the chisel against the whetstone raised gooseflesh on Thomas's arms and legs. It was a noise that seemed to flay him. He stood motionless and watched her smoking, which she seldom did. Käthe's blue working jacket, the one she often wore when she was working on stone, particularly in winter because she wanted to keep the stone dust from settling in her sweater, was white on the back; perhaps she had draped it over the side of the vat of plaster when she was making a model, or had brushed against the freshly painted wall later. Thomas took off his shoes, his trousers, his socks. It was cold. He breathed deeply and imagined the warm sand under the pine trees beside the Müggelsee, sun warming his skin. Under the soles of his feet he felt cold concrete with small stones scattered over it. The screeching stopped. Käthe switched off the motor of her whetstone and tested the edge of the chisel with her fingertips. The silence could feel like warmth to Thomas. His gooseflesh went away. A cool, glittering November sun shone through the opaque upper window of the studio. He took off his sweater and vest, finally his underpants. Käthe scrutinised him.

His body hair was still sparse, his chest smooth, nothing but blond down growing in his armpits and on his upper lip, and you could easily see not only his armpits but his testicles as well. Thomas crossed his arms over his chest, rubbing his skin to warm it up until it showed red weals.

Käthe looked him up and down. Weedy for a model, aren't you? Don't quite make the grade. She stubbed her cigarette out. Don't make such a fuss about it, she said. A boy who lounges around his room all day writing poetry ought to go swimming now and then, run in the woods. It's all on your doorstep. A lad like you needs fresh air or you'll waste away. Käthe took several steps towards him. Put your arm up in the air. She showed him the angle she wanted. He knew it already, he'd been holding it at that angle for many days, hand behind his head; he had stamina, Käthe valued that in him. And he cost her nothing. Now, move your right leg slightly forward. There, that's it. Käthe took another step towards him. Thomas could smell the garlic on her breath.

He was good at standing still; for several years he had been sitting for Käthe as a model, not to mention standing and lying down for her. It made sense, it was only natural, since after all they were living under the same roof, and he had some years to go yet before his school-leaving exam. Weedy was a nasty description, Thomas squirmed when he heard it, nor did he like to be told he didn't make the grade, but he didn't want to show that she had hurt his feelings. In her mouth those didn't sound like mere insults. Käthe was describing the kind of person who, in her eyes, was an inadequate and lesser being. She would never say such things to one of the sculptors or writers she revered, nor to any woman friend of hers. They were reserved for inferior creatures, for Thomas, for children, for subservient models. She could speak to Ella in a way that demeaned her too. Käthe walked across the big room to her radio, which stood on a low bookshelf, covered with dust like everything else in the studio, and searched for a station broadcasting music. She loved Brahms and Vivaldi, Handel and Shostakovich, music for strings, powerful Romantic concertos full of universality and emotion, melancholy and cheerfulness. Up in the smoking room Käthe had had a record player for some time, but the records and needle were too sensitive to stone dust, so as she worked she had to listen to whatever was being played on the radio. If she couldn't find any classical music, she listened to the discussion programmes. She was lucky today; the familiar female voice announced the string quartet no. 2 in A minor, op. 51, by Brahms. A Romantic start to the day's work. She put on her protective goggles and took a few steps round the block of stone on which she had been working for three weeks, assessing it. Thomas thought he could sense her impatience. Käthe was breathing fast enough to make her big breasts heave. Her eye held the keen glance of an eagle about to discover and perceive the potential of every moment: she was already chipping away at the stone. Thomas sensed her hope, which to his mind had something childish about it. Käthe believed, defiantly and to some extent arbitrarily, that her creative work would succeed. He admired her for her lack of doubts; he himself had doubts at every moment of his life, and even deciding whether to buy potatoes and carrots or cabbage and meat when he went shopping cost him a great effort. Maybe he just didn't have much taste? Thomas thought of cherries and how much he liked the taste of those, so much so that they gave him a stomach ache every summer. But shopping called for more than taste; it meant weighing up the preferences of other people who would be sitting at the same table with you, eating the meal.

Käthe seemed as certain of her taste as she was of her ability.

71

You could already see, in broad outline, the head of the sculptured figure and the arms, which were bent level with each other. They had a pale, warm glow, their sandy yellow and earthy ochre made the human form appear inviolable. The body and legs were still hidden in the block of sandstone quarried from the Elbe area. The lower part of the stone was almost black; if sandstone was left out in the open for a long time it darkened. Greenish shadows made you think of lichen, moss or mould. Käthe's stone had drawings in oil pastel on its surface, where she wanted to show the stonemason the places to chip away superfluous material in line with her sketches and models. Thomas knew how much Käthe loved the stones; he knew the look in her eyes as she tested a stone's qualities, how she would strike one and make her assessment of its content of iron oxide and quartz. She liked sandstone from the Elbe. It had strangely dark veining, it was soft enough for her to work at it for hours on end, and so firm and resistant to damage that it stood a good chance of keeping the shape she gave it for centuries, even millennia. There was something monotonous about her tapping at the stone, something that radiated calm, and did not just demand patience but engendered it, at least for Thomas.

Not all decisions were difficult for him. He thought of the swallow that he had found last summer in the yard outside the door of the studio. Swallows nested under the roof; they had built their round nests below the gutter and fed their young there without a pause. At first he had thought the swallow was dead. He knelt down beside it and saw the blue-black sheen of its feathers, the brownish black of its forked tail, the crossed wing tips; its breast was bright white. It lay motionless on its back, its eyes looking as if they were blind. He carefully picked the little bird up. A slight movement of its plumage made him think of the wind; he blew on it, but it did not move. Its light body was faintly warm. Next moment he saw its ribcage rise – it was still breathing – and fall again. Thomas felt tears in his eyes. He stroked the little head with his forefinger. Did small birds like this fracture their skulls? His eyes went to the nests, and he clearly heard the young chirping. The sky and the tops of maple trees were reflected in the upper windows of the studio. It must have flown into one of the windows. How smooth the down of its head was. It neither moved its head nor spread its wings by a single millimetre; it must have severe internal injuries. Its soft feathers ruffled up. Thomas put the bird down on a piece of wood and wondered how he could lay it down to die in peace, how and where he could bury it later. He heard the sound of an engine outside the gate. He didn't want to be disturbed, he didn't want company, he wanted to be alone with the swallow. He was going to stay with it and protect it by his presence, so that the cat wouldn't come along and eat it before it was dead and he could bury it. Suddenly its feathers moved. It flew up. Thomas jumped; maybe he had cried out in alarm. The swallow must have come back to life faster than he could watch it; it had dived off his hand, flew low close to the ground and then soared into the air, up and over to the workshops on the property next door.

The swallows were in the south now, the puddles in the yard were frozen, for the last few days it had been possible to walk on the ice of the reservoir in the woods with slide shoes. Thomas didn't have any; his feet had grown much larger in the last two years. So over the past few days he had tried to make some out of the brass he normally used to make bracelets and rings. But it was too soft; after his first attempt yesterday deep notches had shown in the soles; the alloy was not stable, and thus not smooth enough for going on the ice. He had promised to give Ella a pair of slide shoes, he just needed a little more money, so it was not surprising that

Käthe's purse caught his eye, a small black-and-white object with a catch on top to open it. It was lying on the radio set. Käthe briefly interrupted her work to switch on the standard lamp in the corner; its three necks with the tulip-shaped lights on them could be turned to shine on the high ceiling, or on the floor that reflected the light – in that position they also lit up her model – or turned on the block of stone. In spite of all the studio windows the natural light was getting fainter and fainter; the sun had disappeared long ago. At this time of year it was bright enough to work without artificial light only for three or four hours a day. A daddy-long-legs was making its way down from the windowsill; it stalked over to a weary fly and set to work on it.

Thomas was chilly; the wood and coal he had put in the stove that morning had burnt down long ago, and he was standing much too far from the little stove anyway.

Thomas thought of Ella, and what she had told him about the lodger. Käthe was chiselling away at the elbow of the sculpture, she took a step back, looked at Thomas, looked at her stone, tapped on the chisel some more, bent down, picked up a large piece of stone, put it on the wooden table and went on working with her chisel. Since Eduard finally went away three years ago, Käthe had been letting the room to a lodger. Thomas and Ella had wanted separate rooms of their own, but Thomas had to sleep on the veranda. The twins seldom came to visit, and when they did they slept on the sofa in the living room. With the lodger, Käthe explained, they could afford heating, central heating with a radiator in every room of the house, running off a big oil-fired boiler in the cellar. The lodger's name was Heinz. Ella and Thomas referred to him only as the lodger. If they ever did call him Heinz it sounded sarcastic, or at least subversive, and finally ironic, because they knew he had thought up that name for them, on account of his secret activities, so that they could call him something. The skin of the lodger's face was yellow, and so was his right hand. He was almost always holding an unfiltered cigarette. Käthe's tapping speeded up, short sharp blows that were to create the tapering of the arm on which she was working and give the impression of muscles. Thomas imagined the lodger with his yellow fingers quietly opening the door of Ella's room at night; she had told him about it. In his mind's eye, Thomas saw the lodger pulling off Ella's quilt, looked at the sleeping Ella, pushing up her nightdress, pushing his yellow fingers between her legs. Ella was awake now, but looked paralysed; she pretended to be still asleep, her heart was in her mouth, she feverishly wondered whether she was dreaming – she had a headache that was spreading – and how she could end the dream, she felt as if her own heartbeats were stifling her, she knew she must resist but she didn't know how. She had been able to recognise Heinz at once in the darkness of the room. What other man was already in the house at night and could get into her room? He was not wearing his soft peaked cap, his bald head shone instead, the thin wreath of hair above his ears was picked out by the faint light coming through the curtains from the street outside. The tapping of hammer on chisel struck Thomas's eardrums, he was in the darkness of Ella's room, it was as if he felt the lodger's yellow hand creeping under Ella's nightdress, groping around for her breasts that had only grown in the last few years. Ella turned away, the movement gave her strength, instinctively she sat up. They had exchanged words, Thomas heard them, they were louder than the tapping on Käthe's stone, stronger than any oblivion, words that echoed inside him as if he had been there with them; it was all happening in his mind.

Hush, the lodger had said to Ella. You don't want to wake anyone up, do you? Ella shook her head in the dark. Out, she whispered, get out of here. No, the lodger was laughing now, his quiet, snarling laughter. You know very well I'm not going. You're a girl, Ella, you want it too. Ella clutched the quilt to her. Was he flinching back? Get out, she whispered, louder now. The lodger grabbed her wrist with one hand, and ran the fingers of the other through her hair. Your daddy told me how you like it. My what? You know who I mean. His hand was clutching one breast. Eddy's little wife. Your mother threw Eddy out. Was it that he didn't bring enough money home, didn't he bother about things? Did she neglect him? Did he always have to turn to you? We know that, we and you. Eddy and I know each other, did you know? We work together, Eddy and I, you must keep quiet about that. No one must know. His grip on Ella's breast was so painful that she wanted to scream. But she couldn't. Go away, please. Words gulped down, pleading. It wasn't a good idea for her to beg, he would notice her uncertainty, smell her fear. Ella's head was ringing. Not likely, said the lodger, bringing his face close to her. Ella could smell the cognac he had been drinking, the tobacco that oozed from all his pores. The lodger pressed his mouth on Ella's and tried to push his tongue into it. His stubble was prickly. Ella clenched her teeth to keep his tongue outside, she pressed her lips together so that they tingled, pressure, rough, felted, tongue, his hand under the quilt. Ella kicked out with her legs, teeth gritted. The light came on in the corridor, it shone under the door of the room. Now the lodger was whispering. Eddy told me you have a sweet mouth. You really do. Eddy would have taken you with him, you know that. His little wife, that's what he called you, didn't he? My little wife. The lodger's breath smelled horrible. But you were still too young, it wouldn't have done. Are you sad? No, I'm not. Cackling laughter. He was still clutching Ella's wrist and pushing it down on the mattress, it was a firm grasp, she couldn't wriggle out of it. Ella's fear receded as faintness took over. Not a dream, I'm just fainting, she told herself, thinking almost coolly of a way to make him let go. A door closed, the light in the corridor went out, a second door latched. Silence. You like that, don't you? The lodger had licked his finger and was searching, with the wet finger, for a way to get between Ella's legs.

Tell me, aren't you listening? Now Käthe was slapping Thomas's arm. Get it down lower. I want to see that shoulder looking relaxed.

You like that, don't you? Stop it, will you?! Hey, whispered the lodger even more quietly, can't you call me comrade? What with burrowing between the quilt and Ella's legs, his finger had dried, and the lodger put it back in his putrid-smelling mouth, not just one finger, almost his whole hand. The wet hand sought, groped, took hold. Hey, call me Heinz, little Ella, call me uncle, say ooh, you bad uncle . . . Now he let go of Ella's wrist, perhaps to reach for his trousers. But Ella took her chance, jumped off the bed at lightning speed and ran to the door. The lodger was laughing quietly. Get away, push off! Go back to Hamburg or wherever you came from, just go away, hissed Ella, the doorknob in her hand. You saucy little madam, he snarled back. Who said anything about Hamburg to you? You don't know anything. We're fighting for a free Germany, a socialist Germany, we're at work everywhere. Hamburg is only a name, like Heinz, you just remember that and don't make yourself look ridiculous. He left, disappeared into his room, the room that Thomas had secretly occupied in the weeks when the lodger wasn't there and before he had put a lock on the door. Ella had told Thomas about the lodger's visits, every word, everything she felt, every expression; perhaps she had left something out, perhaps she had added something. Thomas knew it all inside out, the dialogues, the incidents, he had only needed to hear it once and he knew every word. There was nothing he could do about that, he couldn't forget it. His memory for words spared him nothing.

The knocking stopped, Radio GDR1 was broadcasting the news, and Käthe took off her dusty goggles, cleaned them with the hem of her blue jacket, and poured herself tea in the green-and-yellow cup that her potter friend had made and given her for her forty-fifth birthday.

You mustn't tell her anything, Ella had insisted. She wanted Thomas to swear not to. He had sworn, for Ella's sake. And what would he have told Käthe anyway? She probably wouldn't have believed a word of it. She might have been furious: what did Ella think she was doing, going around in such provocative clothes? Käthe certainly had no idea of what went on in the house. It probably didn't interest her. How was she to guess at something that didn't interest her? She was gulping tea from her cup, breathing out heavily; Thomas could tell from the sound how good it tasted. She was a noisy drinker. She would never think of offering her model something to drink of her own accord. Thomas knew that, so he asked if he could have some tea as well, and his voice was hoarse because he had been standing naked for so long in the cold dust without saying a word.

What a silly question. Käthe ran her fingers through her short hair and shook her head in surprise. The peach stones of her necklace rode up to her throat. Her full lips smacked slightly as she spoke. Go upstairs and get yourself a cup. It sounded as if she didn't like the news; she went over to the set and turned the tuning button until she found an animated discussion on the admission of African states to the United Nations.

We're coming closer to peace, murmured Käthe, nodding with satisfaction. At least they're rid of their masters. It's about time the world recovered. She knocked on the stone, not waiting for any answer. Käthe very often made some pronouncement without wanting an answer, and if anyone did answer her she could be very annoyed.

Thomas looked around the studio; he didn't want to go up to the house naked and look for a cup in the kitchen. He saw a glass with a little water in it beside the radio on the bookcase at the back of the studio. Can I use that glass?

Käthe didn't answer; she obviously hadn't heard him, or didn't want to hear him. She was bending down looking for something in her box of tools.

Thomas went over to the radio, where his eye fell on Käthe's purse again. He picked up the glass; there was a thin film of stone dust floating on the surface of the water. He tipped the water out on the huge cacti growing in the window, and poured some tea from Käthe's big teapot.

Give me a hand, she said, pressing her hammer and chisel into the naked boy's hands. Knock that bit down there away, the whole corner, or I can't work when the stone here is still in the block. Get at least that corner off.

Thomas grasped the hammer higher up the handle and knocked the corner off the block. It was not the first time he had helped her. The stonemason had gone to the Baltic on holiday for two weeks. He had applied for a holiday two years earlier, a summer holiday. Now he had been given one in November, but his wife and children would have to stay behind in Berlin. Käthe shook her head: all this bureaucracy. The stonemason wouldn't be back to do the preliminary work on shaping the stone until next week. Out of sheer impatience, because the sketches and small model studies in wax, as well as a larger plaster model, had been done weeks ago and were only waiting to be transferred to the stone, Käthe had already begun at the top of the sculpture and was turning to the fine structures there. Now she wanted to work on the lower part. What was a young man here for, after all? She wanted Thomas to knock the other corner off the block as well, working along the line she had drawn in wax crayon. She nodded with satisfaction as she watched him working. He felt warm; that was good.

That's enough, said Käthe suddenly. You're taking too much off it there, I'll need that bit later to shape the knee. Leave it alone for now. She pushed Thomas aside with her shoulder and hip, like an animal nudging another with its flank, so that he stumbled over the wooden plank on which the stone stood. Mind what you're doing. Käthe examined the stone again with a critical eye, put the rubber-framed goggles that she had pushed up into her hair back on her nose, bent down and began knocking a piece off the lower part of the sandstone. Then, still bent over, she turned her head and looked attentively at Thomas. You're standing around like a bad penny, get back into your pose and we'll carry on.

Thomas raised his arm until he thought it was at the correct angle. He knew that Käthe seldom began a conversation with her models; she needed all her attention for what was to come out of the stone. Thomas thought of his chemistry work. The chemistry teacher was glad to have a student like Thomas in his class. Recently he had asked Thomas to stand in for him and teach the class when he had been summoned to a meeting with the headmaster. Thomas felt diffident; he began by explaining the part played by oxygen in organic combinations with hydrogen and carbon, while his fellow students listened with vacant expressions, and he couldn't be sure whether they knew what he was talking about. And there were indeed more exciting things in chemistry, Thomas thought so himself, so in mid-sentence he ventured on a change of subject and tried to explain electro-negativity according to Allred and Rochow, as his American Uncle Paul had described it last time he visited early in the year. The class preserved their vacant expressions; they obviously hadn't noticed that he was now talking about something different. Thomas wrote the formula on the board and said that you had to imagine electronegativity in proportion to the electrostatic power of attraction; he drew a diagram of the inner and outer electrons and was about to describe the power of attraction exerted by the nuclear charge on the bonding electrons, but he very soon realised that no one was imagining anything at all, indeed no one in the room could follow him, so he interrupted himself. Something stung his cheek. With one hand he searched his trouser pocket, found his elastic band and a green sweet wrapping with a strong smell of eucalyptus. He made a small missile and shot it at his best friend Michael's forehead. Hands reached into pockets and school bags. The boys got out their catapults and began shooting at each other.

When the chemistry teacher appeared in the doorway with a stack of books under his arm he saw that some of the students were not in their places, they were laughing, shouting and fooling around. He told Thomas, in a loud, stern voice, that he had abused his trust. No sooner had he said that, reaching for the cane he liked to use at such moments, than an expression of the utmost misery spread over his face.

Open your books at page one hundred and three. There was total silence around him, no one whispered a word, and even after the bell went they still sat there listening, but the teacher said nothing until, at the end of break, he said the boys could pack up their things. When there was a chemistry test in class a week later, he gave Thomas seven extra questions as well as the six that the whole class had to answer. The idea was not to keep Thomas sitting twice as long as the others over the test but to show that he was able to solve more difficult problems and do twice as much as everyone else. You want to study at university, don't you, Thomas? The teacher knew he could ensure that his best student failed the school-leaving exam. He didn't need an extra-difficult test for that, he could interrogate him about politics, test his knowledge and his conscience there, call his attitude into question. But he was giving him a chance to show what he could do. Thomas had not managed to answer the last of the additional questions within the hour allowed. He hadn't been quick enough. For the first time in five years he did not get a One. The teacher was wearing his miserable expression again as he gave back the tests and stopped beside Thomas's desk. It was hard for him to see Thomas fail, it obviously troubled the teacher, he ran the knuckles of his clenched fist over the desk, there was strength in it, the will for pain as if the boy's failure physically hurt him. Thomas lowered his eyes; it was awkward, indeed impossible, for him to meet that gaze. It would not be the only test in class this last winter before the school-leaving exam. But the teacher had made it clear that Thomas depended on his goodwill if he expected to get marks corresponding to his achievements. Then the final exams could take whatever turn they liked; nothing would come of Thomas's plans to study at university if the teacher didn't want him to. Nothing would presumably come of plans for university studies anyway, since they had decided at the Ministry of Education to give the children of the working classes preferential treatment, in the cause of a more just society. Disobedience was a quality that Thomas would do well to discard. The collectivisation of agriculture had been completed, there would be a pressing need for young men like Thomas to work on agricultural production, he could work with farm animals, for instance, then he and those like him would not be forming elite groups, and university studies would be left to the other sort. Thomas wondered why art didn't count as work. Wasn't he the son of a worker?

Oh, for God's sake, take your hand away from your mouth! Käthe's voice sounded brusque, she took a step towards him and grabbed his arm. Biting your nails the whole time, I'll tear them right out one of these days if you don't stop it.

Startled, Thomas looked at his hand; he didn't notice when he was biting his nails. Even if he was standing in the middle of the room stark naked, as he was now, one hand behind his head, his arm crooked at the correct angle, the fingers of the other hand could land in his mouth without his thinking about it or being able to prevent it. The leg he was standing on hurt, he felt a pulling behind his knees. That was growing pains, he had often been told so over the last few years, and he must hope that his left leg, which was only minimally shorter than his right leg, could still catch up. He wasn't fully grown yet at sixteen, all kinds of things might happen to him. Thomas was a year younger than Ella, but right at the start he had gone up a year at school, so that they were in the same class. His hair might grow, his leg, his attitude and his obedience. His feet were cold as ice just now, but he knew Käthe wouldn't let him wear socks – even when she wasn't working on the feet of her sculpture at all. She needed a clear view of human anatomy, she claimed.

Käthe looked at the boy critically. You must watch that arm, it keeps sinking. Hold it higher up. No, not as high as that – that's better. The tapping of hammer and chisel went on to its regular rhythm. Amplify, hushabye, quantify, saygoodbye. Thomas tried to think of words that would sound good to it. You could avoid misunderstandings if you trusted the sound. He was sure that something like humboolabye fong fong, properly pronounced, sounded more impressive than just cold feet.

He liked sounds. Mortify, justify, purify, rectify. That last word made him think of the border official who promised the bearded German and his heavily pregnant lover, who wasn't married to him, to get them papers, or at least to get the pregnant woman papers, because the bearded man already had them. After that the two of them spent a whole week in a cave, but they had no illusions about the unfortunate predicament they were in without papers, snow outside, a little fire burning day and night inside, because they thought the border official meant it seriously and would really help them. Thomas remembered the walk by night that he and Käthe had taken last year. She was fetching her twins from the grandparents in Pankow, it had been late in the evening, and she had let him sit behind her on the motorbike. But halfway there the motorbike had stalled at traffic lights and wouldn't start again. So Käthe and Thomas had walked over half the Berlin borough of Pankow by night. He had asked her what his father had been like. Oh, a great guy, Käthe had replied. Then she had begun telling Thomas the story. She called his father the bearded man, because at the time he hadn't shaved for weeks. She spoke of herself in the third person, as if it had not been her story. They waited in the cave, heavily pregnant Käthe and the bearded man. But after a week in the cave they had to accept that the kind border official was not himself a nice guy but more of a counterspy. Counterspy from Lombardy, they called him later. They could freeze just as well walking through the snow over the mountains on foot. On the watch for border patrols, they would neither of them remember their carefree life in exile in Sicily, the heat haze over the olive groves, the red soil, their happiness. On the second day they walked into a snowdrift and heard the calls of a man pulling his sledge on the other side of the valley. The man was looking for someone who had probably climbed up to go skiing a few days earlier but had not been seen since. It wasn't easy for him to interrupt his search, but he told the two of them to get on the sledge. He had several furs on the sledge, wood, and hot embers in a cauldron; he heated three stones in it, and put them among the furs to warm the woman. Where were they going? he asked.

Käthe's tapping died away. She stepped towards Thomas, looked at his throat, his collarbone and the hand he was holding behind his head.

Come over here. When I'm working by hand I can't see you behind the stone.

Thomas changed his place.

Now, raise that one. She took his other arm as if he were a puppet and raised it, pushed, pressed the ulna. No; she shook her head. Now let it drop. Just let it hang loosely. She took his dangling hand in hers and looked at the fingers. Back to the angle again. Thomas crooked his arm as he had been doing for weeks. Käthe walked round him, taking small steps, stared at his collarbone again, his armpit and finally his fingers. She chose a different chisel and put it to her stone. Thomas blinked; the hand she was working on looked gigantic, his hand, as big as a log.

The bearded man and Käthe had reached Tessin with frozen toes. Thomas saw the scene in his mind's eye, the two men taking it in turns to haul the sledge with the woman's heavy weight in it over the mountains. But didn't anyone help you? Your father who was my grandfather? Nothing doing, Käthe had told him abruptly, without a shred of self-pity. They had sent telegrams to friends and relations in Germany and France from the post office in Bellinzona. After a long time, they had heard the first news at the post office: heroic fighting in Stalingrad. Soldiers sheltering in foxholes. A German U-boat had torpedoed a British passenger steamer off the Azores. Nearly seven hundred people said to have lost their lives. The destruction not only of civilians but of civilisation, Käthe called it. Perhaps that was a quotation, perhaps Thomas's father had said it. How had he thought, how

85

had he spoken? Käthe and the bearded man stayed in Bellinzona for a good two weeks, going to the post office every day. But in such circumstances friends in the north did not respond, and help was in short supply, Käthe's father, that worthy professor, sent a telegram asking his dear Käthchen not to come to Berlin. Her condition would create a great sensation, her arrival could endanger her mother's life. Humboolabye fong fong. On that walk through the night, Thomas had looked for any kind of emotion in Käthe's face, but it was too dark for that. Her voice was steady: So fat Käthe was holding the telegram from the professor. The bearded man tried to take her in his arms, but she shook her head. My dear father, he couldn't do anything else. He has always been able to protect us, all of us. Thomas wondered whether Käthe hadn't been seething with indignation and despair, at least at the time. Of course, he thought now, the realisation that her father, to whom she owed everything and who meant everything to her, was now powerless and could only warn her in no uncertain terms not to go back to them, not to come to Berlin where she had naively been hoping for his help, must have sunk inexorably in and finally made its way into her mind. In addition, Käthe's dismissal four years earlier from the masterclass she was taking had presumably shaken her self-confidence. Finding out that a professor's daughter had no immunity had not only hurt her feelings but astonished her. And then her self-confidence was to be not simply shaken but destroyed, like her will. Back then in Berlin, being thrown out of the university had been a fleeting source of annoyance; the beauty of Italy had moved her more deeply and more enduringly. In the scent of orange blossom there she had entirely forgotten that in the opinion of some people in Germany she herself ought not to exist. The danger had been left behind in the north, thousands of kilometres away. Until Käthe, driven out of the orange grove at Castelvetrano, had no idea where to go and went to knock on the southern gateway to Germany. Thomas himself, at such a moment, would have felt no injury and betrayal as keenly as that of a father who a few years ago still did all he could for his children. It must have sickened Käthe to find that he of all people, the man who had opened up her fatherland and half the world to her, who had not only taught at the university and headed the nitrogen research programme, the man who only ten years ago had taken his wife and children travelling in the Engadin valley, to fashionable Paris and the Uffizi Gallery in Florence, had shown her the fractured beauty of the Alpine slate, the turquoise glow of Lake Constance and the Musée Rodin in Paris, that this man, her father, was now skulking in his gloomy house in the Westend district of Berlin with the curtains drawn, not allowed to teach, dismissed from his position as head of research into nitrogen, was whiling away his days in his laboratory and was in bondage to those who obliged him to keep his wife in the cellar of his house. Käthe guessed that he was hiding her there, if not in the bushes in the square in front of the building then in his own father's garden house on Wannsee. Her mother was in danger. Mortal danger? Would she be taken away, was that possible? Käthe knew that her father had been told, several times, that he ought to divorce his wife, mother of his four children. In fact it was a good sign, thought Käthe, that she was endangering her mother, his wife, as they reached Rahnsdorf after two hours of walking and crossed the bridge. It meant she was still alive. It meant that a certain amount of protection was still possible and was tolerated. Heavily pregnant Käthe had been glad to hear that her mother was well, was still alive, and was still under her husband's protection, even if in hiding and conditions where she could not be sure of toleration. Käthe would make it on her own. Perhaps the bearded man would stay with her.

They had trudged through the snow to their hotel room – hamboolabye fong fong. The bearded man had said he was going to the post office again to see if his parents had sent any money. He stood in the doorway and Käthe looked at him: Are you coming back? The bearded man could say whatever he wanted – was he to be trusted? The bearded man's father, not a professor but an upright pastor in Halle on the River Saale, replied to say God be with his son. He could give his regards to the pastor of Bergalingen near Bad Säckingen, when he passed that way in the Hotzenwald district of the Black Forest. His call-up papers for the front had arrived and were urgent, said his father. Not a word by way of invitation to them, no money transfer, nothing about the woman who was trying to palm her coming child off on his son. Perhaps pregnant Käthe didn't even exist in the mind of the pastor at Halle. God be with him, it sounded chilly. Yet the bearded man and his pregnant lover saw the message for the pastor of Bergalingen, the precise information conveyed by its geographical situation, and its proximity to Switzerland as a hidden sign that they might hope to find help there. Hip hip hooray!

Inside himself, Thomas stretched; his exterior maintained almost the attitude that Käthe wanted. He pressed his shoulder blades together, straightened his backbone. All that standing in front of Käthe's eyes hurt; when he thought of Bellinzona, Thomas felt like bursting into tears. She had told him about it only once, as a result of that motorbike breakdown and their nocturnal walk, and she had told him about it with her usual rock-hard cheerfulness. But there was a glitter in her eyes, something was tipping over and cracking deep inside her. He wanted to hug Käthe. He had tried several times, but to this day she always just stood there like a chunk of wood. She was strong. He admired the way she set her chisel to the stone, carved her stone, and never complained on her own account.

Käthe put her tools on the wooden table and stretched her arms, she was jubilant, she yawned and straightened her back. Working on stone might be strenuous, but it made her happy. Käthe's rosy cheeks were glowing like a girl's, her cry of glee was the shout of a child.

Thomas smiled at her, but Käthe didn't seem to notice his smile. She shook the stiffness out of her arms and hands and cleared her throat noisily, in a way that Thomas had only ever heard otherwise from men in company. He tried to imagine what she must have looked like back then, a young woman with a big belly. Käthe picked up her chisel, took the wooden smoothing tool and shaved tiny pieces of stone off the head.

Ella wanted to go away, leave home, have a place of her own, a room of her own. She had taken Thomas into her confidence. The lodger lay in wait for her as soon as he came to Berlin. He had pestered her in bed at night, he had taken her by surprise in the bathroom, he had followed her through the woods from the house towards the suburban railway station and tried molesting her there, until luckily some people out walking came along the path. If only to get away from the lodger, Ella had to move out. Thomas was going to help her find a place. He would be left alone with the lodger's avid desires. He might be able to cope with that, he hoped he could put up with it. The lodger had made advances to him as well; there had been just the two of them in the house that afternoon, the lodger and Thomas. They could have a nice time together, the lodger had said excitedly. First he had talked to Thomas, then he touched him.

The smoothing sound died away. Käthe was inspecting her stone. Johann Strauss's 'Persian March' was playing on the radio now. Thomas feared it; it was music that chased and tormented you. All the merriment it was supposed to contain, the daring, the triumph, attacked him, challenged him and made him feel weak. Undisturbed, Käthe went on pecking at the stone. In spite of the announcement that the violin concerto in D major in three movements by Brahms was to be heard over the next three-quarters of an hour, played by a certain Henryk Szeryng, there was a long silence after the woman announcer's voice stopped, with only crackling noises, then a swelling rushing sound, and just as Thomas thought he could make out musical intervals in it, the music abruptly stopped and gave way to soft crackling. Thomas froze. For a moment Käthe stopped what she was doing; she didn't like to miss the opening of a piece of music. The first deep notes on the strings sounded. Käthe put her tools down and drank some of her tea, took a couple of steps towards her stone and examined the rough shape of the elbow. Thomas felt as if he were seeing through her eyes and knew exactly what she was thinking. Something was wrong about it; the angle wasn't sharp enough yet. The violin was playing in the foreground. Käthe did not often put her head on one side while she closed her eyes. She swayed, she didn't dance but almost imperceptibly her body bent and stretched, she was melting. Dada, dadi, she murmured, singing along with the melody on the violin. Only her voice and the instrument existed, no stone, no Thomas, no one and nothing to whom she wanted to show her attitude and speak her mind. Thomas had never seen her like this before. Wonderful, Käthe purred and opened her eyes, her gleaming eyes. What music! She stood close to her stone and inspected it; she ran her short, strong hands over the rough curve and stepped back to pick up her chisel and peening anvil again. She worked on the elbow with short, fast taps. Thomas's glance went to the window looking out into the yard; he heard voices there, footsteps, then he saw two figures on the other side of the window. Someone opened the small door into the studio.

A stocky, short man with red hair and a moustache, and a

man with dark, curly hair marched into the studio. Thomas recognised the curly-haired man; he was a sculptor like Käthe, a sculptor from Leipzig.

Käthe beamed, she pushed up her goggles and put the peening tool down. Rüdiger, so you're still around! She put out her arm, and she and the curly-haired man shook hands.

And this is Wiegand, said Rüdiger. Käthe greeted the redhead too.

A comrade and a colleague, added Wiegand. Käthe's eyes were shining. There was a military sound to the clap of their hands as they met.

We thought we'd look in and talk about the competition. That bunch haven't a clue.

Käthe nodded, and her smile turned to fiery earnest. We must work out a good idea, nothing will come of nothing. We must get the announcement right first.

Thomas was looking at his gooseflesh, a thousand tiny hairs standing proud in the light.

Rüdiger looked around him. Are you working on much just now?

Oh, this and that. Emerging from her throat, Käthe's voice was a harsh rasp. I don't have much here at the moment. I finished the relief for the hospital in the summer. Her voice rasped again; it sounded as if there was something in her throat. After that, just messing about, plaster and clay models. I've been waiting four months for this block of stone. Now it's here and my stone-mason has been sent on holiday. In the middle of November. Käthe laid her hand on the stone she had been working on just now. Her face brightened, her voice softened. A lovely stone, look, no great inclusions, not much dark veining. I already have a title: *The Upright Man*.

Thomas realised that his fingernails were between his teeth

again; they made gratifying snapping sounds. He heard the three sculptors chattering as if they were birds twittering, again and again one voice would be raised, it was positively rhythmic, they were eager, sarcastic, rebellious. The voices grew louder and louder; they were deploring the ignorance of the ministers and leaders of the artistic associations. The yapping was like that of Thomas's fellow students at school recently, complaining of their parents and present conditions. A pointless undertaking in both cases, it seemed to Thomas. Talking themselves into dependency and compliance, not out of it. Soongalaroo, varon te mai. Inventing words seemed to him a suitable reaction, something new and unique, a game against blind faith, the individual could and must move something in our society, they were saying, every individual was responsible for our democracy. Zumplepumple rumple-didum. Yet all eyes were blindly closed. How pitifully powerless talk and wishes were. The state had decided against the individual long ago. No one was waiting to hear about Rüdiger's answer based on artistic principles, or Käthe's love of Michelangelo and her commitment to the workers; conversations like these were pure boastfulness, blowing bubbles. All one class! Thomas saw the glitter of their words, which were shimmering in all colours of the rainbow. They didn't need much light, the froth of what they were saying moved through the room in tiny flakes. A huge bubble, first the size of a breast, then as big as her head had come away from Käthe's mouth, it was rising in the air, ooh and aah, said the marvelling mouths. Käthe was hardly ever happy, but she was proud. Her words tumbled over each other. Her pride sparkled, making the bubble shine more and more fantasti-cally. Was she at one with her bubble? Did Rüdiger recognise its dazzling deception? Or was Thomas getting a distorted view of her through the curve of the bubble? Her nose was bending and growing, it looked enormous, the dark down on her upper lip vibrated under it, her full lips pouted, defiant and insinuating. Thomas laughed quietly to himself. The louder the froth and bubbles of the talk between Käthe and her friends, the more easily they thought they could recognise the signs of the times, identify the real news, and keep their eyes open for what had been going on over the last few years in this German Democratic Republic. Well, something was going to happen in the next few years, and they wanted to bring their influence to bear on the opportunity offered by this competition.

Wiegand had brought some cigarillos. They came from a tobacco dealer in Leipzig who sold only under the counter, and who had been obliged to close his shop down some time ago because the sales of tobacco had been centralised. The smoke of them rose from Wiegand's nose and mouth and went back into his body with the next breath he drew. He held his breath for a minute during which he couldn't say any more, thus allowing Käthe to take over from him in mid-sentence.

The workers in Leuna need something beautiful, mankind needs hope, needs an incentive. Bread and art.

The three of them nodded in a single synchronised movement, and they bowed their heads as one.

If we think that art is only for an educated bourgeois elite we are doing ourselves and the workers down, that would be a rejection of the working class, of a socialist society. We want to create art that is for everyone. Giotto painted for everyone, so did Dürer. Picasso didn't cut himself off from other people, *Guernica* doesn't stop short of the suffering of everyone. Suffering is universal, it affects us all. By now Käthe was in full swing, entirely enveloped in her magnificent froth. Thomas wondered whether, clad in that glittering garment, she could even see the others.

Why go on about suffering? Rüdiger looked at her in surprise.

We want peace, don't we? Käthe looked sharply back at him.

Yes.

Everyone wants peace. Käthe spoke firmly; she had no doubt about it. Her visitors were looking at her expectantly. The Africans have liberated themselves. Germany has been liberated. Now we have to found a society in which fascism will no longer be an option.

Yes.

Wiegand was nodding now, too.

Käthe carried on. Her manner made Thomas think of the word declamation. Of words making sounds like delectation, reclamation. Declamation. He was sorry he couldn't learn Latin. Subjects from the old humanist educational timetable, in which classical languages were taught, were thought undesirable these days; young people today were not to remain trapped in the elitist mindset of their past origins, they were to keep their feet on the ground, Russian was the language of choice. Not that anyone had any choice. Including Thomas. The three sculptors talked, smoked, argued and never gave a thought to the naked boy who stood there useless for some time, arm raised, then lowered, and finally, after a good half-hour, he moved from his pose in silence – he didn't want to interrupt the conversation – picked up his vest and shirt and was about to put them on and go away, thinking he wouldn't be needed any more.

As soon as Käthe noticed Thomas preparing to pull his vest on she took a couple of steps and snatched the shirt out of his hand. If you're cold move about a bit, Käthe snapped at him, we'll be going on again in a minute. She turned to her visitors and said: Years ago that governmental oaf over there began arming his soldiers again. In the administration and the courts, in government posts, everywhere you look you see the same old warriors, men who made their careers and their money and their reputation among the Nazis. Getting all the benefits. And now they reap a fitting harvest, their time has come.

The struggle of the working class against their rulers can succeed only if everyone joins in, agreed Rüdiger with a nod. His voice sounded muted; he recited the maxim as if reading it off a board.

Blood on their hands!

Blood?

I mean that lot over there in their fine posts, said Käthe, shaking her head, are you blind? Thomas was watching Käthe, marvelling at her manner, which seemed to him brave and sometimes naive, almost stupid. Käthe implicitly believed that all those in the creative arts who said they were socialists must be good people.

As Rüdiger and Wiegand did not know for a moment what they ought to say about the blood on the hands of people over there in the other Germany, Käthe cleared her throat and raised her voice again: No French Revolution without Joan of Arc. If we're to get anything done it can only be through commitment, and everyone can help there, you and you, and so can I. Käthe was beaming, her cheeks were flushed now with heat and enthusiasm.

Thomas turned away. He thought it was embarrassing to hear three grown adults talking in such childish clichés.

Another half an hour passed while Thomas walked up and down the studio, naked and useless, until in the middle of her animated discourse she told him to come over to them. Here, she said to the small and rather flat-faced redhead, this is what I mean. Käthe tapped Thomas's shoulders and the back of his neck as if he were made of stone. A grown man's shoulders aren't as narrow as that, you can guess at the imposing stature to come – stand up straight, Thomas, do! – but it's present only as

95

potential in a young man. And look, added Käthe, pointing to his loins like a teacher pointing to the blackboard, the genitals are hardly there yet. So saying, Käthe tapped Thomas on the hip and turned him like a jointed puppet so that he could be seen better from behind. Michelangelo exaggerated them as well, in his David they're fully formed, stylised, or no one would realise that he'd grow to be a man. A man who stands tall and fights!

Thomas lowered his eyes. He did not stand tall. He was not a fighter. It depressed him to hear Käthe, in the firm belief that she could dissociate herself from every manifestation of National Socialism, taking him of all people, his body, as the example of a man standing tall in the class struggle. He wasn't. He felt a hand moving down his backbone, presumably Käthe's, but it could belong to someone else.

One of the men said: He's not man enough for that yet. His shrill, cheerful laughter rang sharply in Thomas's ears. But the others interrupted, drowning it out.

So let's suggest a plaque for the chemicals plant, we'll show the workers at work, the miner, the welder, the nurse, the factory hand.

Thomas kept his back turned to the others. He longed for calm, and thought of Käthe's brother Paul, who like a great many other people had got out of Germany at the right moment. If Thomas had been around then he was sure he would have done the same. He was not a fighter, and the idea of triumph left him cold. Thomas wondered what his life would have been like if he had been born in America as the son of Käthe's brother. Perhaps Käthe had simply missed the right moment back then. That was not how she described it; she had never wanted to go to America, she said; she wrinkled her nose very slightly at the thought of her brother, who had seized the first opportunity with both hands and emigrated in 1936. There was no art in

America, said Käthe. No one was about to contradict her, neither Rüdiger nor Wiegand.

At that moment the door from the yard into the studio opened, and two long-haired, giggling women appeared in the doorway, each with a bottle of wine under her arm and another, already uncorked, in her hand. The door stayed open for a while; soft snowflakes were drifting down in the blue twilight outside. As if at a word of command, both women put their bottles to their mouths and took a large gulp, and then bent forward spluttering and laughing.

Wipe the snow off your shoes, Käthe told them, pointing to the scraper just inside the door. The Leipzig sculptors' girl-friends giggled at their wet shoes, but obediently wiped the soles over the scraper several times. The hydrogen blonde flung herself on the little red-headed sculptor's shoulder, belching; perhaps she was feeling sick. But then she raised her swan-like neck, and she towered over not only the little redhead but everyone else in the studio.

Oh, how sweet, cried the swan-necked girl as her glance fell on the naked Thomas and his genitals. She stared at his prick as if she had never seen a naked man before, or at least not such a young one. Thomas blushed.

What's all this about, my pretty? said the redhead, patting his girlfriend on her back in its winter coat. Käthe said how during her Italian year she had noticed how much Michelangelo reduced the size of many male genitals in relation to their real proportions, and that very thing bore witness to the high force of attraction, the revelatory view with which he had depicted the human figure. The power of its shoulders and loins compared to the tiny member. Käthe spoke of the member as if it were an arm or a leg.

So he had a *member*, reflected Thomas, a member that was

part of the body and needed no more precise description? Now he heard Käthe talking about the human race, the male sex, his head was ringing with all the words she used, while the swan-necked girl went on staring at his prick and he feared that, under her gaze, it might grow and grow. No strength in his narrow shoulders and such a sweet little sex, he felt, it was going to be only a little willy, his blood was throbbing, something was echoing, and Thomas feared that his blood might go down to his sex and then up to his cheeks, back to his sex and back to his head.

Only now, apparently, did Käthe realise that Thomas was still standing there naked and useless, unoccupied. She said sharply: Didn't you hear me? Pick up that broom. And then get dressed; why are you standing around here without anything on?

Thomas picked up the broom that stood in the corner; he used it every evening after they had finished work to sweep the floor. The visitors followed the naked boy and the broom with their eyes, saying nothing, perhaps daunted by Käthe's imperious tone of voice, perhaps waiting for Thomas to leave the studio at long last so that they could go on with their conversation undisturbed. Thomas had to bend to pick up the dustpan. Käthe and her guests were still silent. He tipped the pieces of stone into the waste bin standing by the door, placed the dustpan on it, stood the broom beside it and straightened up. Tantantaraa! Thomas bowed to his audience and spread his arms submissively. The Upright Man; mentally Thomas could only shake his head, Käthe's name for the sculpture made him laugh, an angry laughter. He took his clothes and went up the wooden staircase that had no banister rail two steps at a time, and so into the house where it adjoined the studio.

Unlike Ella, Thomas seldom felt hatred. He was not annoyed with Käthe, he was annoyed with himself. What did he expect?

Käthe had often told him and Ella not to make selfish claims. Moderation was all. No one had a right to love and protection. Käthe wouldn't help him to get a place to study. She disliked the elite to which, as a girl of good family, she had once belonged. All that mattered was for people to create art for their own society out of their own strength. Her children were to learn to work like anyone else, that was what she demanded, that was what she expected. Thomas liked her glowing cheeks, but he distrusted the reason for them.

Those who want to change society had better begin with their own children, said Käthe, putting one of her favourite Bulgarian wines down beside the bottles brought by her guests. The guests were sitting round the large table listening to Käthe. Ella put coal on the stove. Thomas laid the table; as directed by Käthe he had warmed up the bean casserole, and she wanted him and Ella to wash the dishes after the meal.

Sit down, Thomas, you two can eat with us, come on, sit down. Once upon a time children ate in the kitchen with the domestic staff, and only French was spoken at their distinguished parents' table.

The guests looked at Käthe. Why French? The swan-necked girl stretched, her high voice trying hard not to betray her Saxon accent.

That's how it used to be at our home in a professor's house. We children ate with the domestic staff in the kitchen, we sat at our parents' table only on special occasions. That's what we learned French for. Käthe looked around at her silent audience.

Really? The strange movements of Rüdiger's mouth made his moustache jump up and down. The two women also let out noises of surprise. Really?

. . . and so that we could read French as well, anyone who wants to read Balzac and Molière has to know French, added Käthe, as if that were a better explanation for her visitors. Away with social rank! We don't want the language we use to show the status of our professions any more, not under socialism. If the son of the chef who speaks in Berlin dialect studies chemistry, and the doctor's son who speaks High German learns to be a chef, our society will be mixed up in a new order, and then we'll have done it. Everyone must make a contribution. My father was a professor, I carve stone.

Wiegand nodded appreciatively. What Käthe was saying obviously met with his approval. While Thomas filled Wiegand's plate with the steaming casserole, he realised what Käthe was getting at. The dialect someone spoke showed only if he came from Berlin or Leipzig.

Käthe solemnly held her glass aloft: The cook toils all day in his large kitchen, the milling-machine operator in the factory, I carve my stones – and now let's drink to the People's Own Works, the Leuna and Buna chemicals works! Santé! She held her glass out in all directions, and there was a muted clinking.

Some time ago Thomas had found out that glass sounded best only if the bowl of the glass was free in the air. You had to hold the glass by the stem, but no one here was doing that. And it shouldn't be filled to the brim. Käthe began eating even before Rüdiger had wished everyone *bon appétit*. Maybe she thought it more modern not to give herself away by any more French table-talk. Käthe didn't notice that Ella wasn't sitting down with them yet, because she was taking the ash bucket out into the yard, and that Thomas was sitting at the other end of the table with an empty plate, because there were not enough beans for everyone. The raised arms of several wax models of the Upright Man in the middle of the long table obscured her view.

She tried a saying in Saxon dialect, and looked expectantly round the circle at the table. But although they came from Saxony, maybe they didn't know the saying, which depended on the Saxon pronunciation *Oogen, Fleesch, Beene* for *Augen, Fleisch, Beine*: eyes, flesh, legs. Thomas said them after her in High German, assuming that that was what she wanted to make her meaning clear.

No, no, said Käthe brusquely, waving his contribution away. It all depends on banishing fascism from the way we think. I meant to say that we're all human, no matter what dialect or accent we use.

Understood, said Rüdiger. Käthe seemed to like this obedient response, and she went on.

We must affect everyone wherever we can. Everyone has children, and they have friends, and the friends in turn have parents, so we can exert extraordinary influence through our children.

Thomas went into the kitchen to fetch the big bowl of salad. When he got back into the smoking room he thought he would suffocate.

The golden tassels of the velvet cushion on which Käthe was sitting swung about. Thomas looked at her Biedermeier chair and the Persian rug. In this bourgeois living room her idea of society sounded not just adventurous but fantastic. Her lecture had moved away from Michelangelo now, words like Gommern and People's Own Works were flying through the air. They were also talking about the extraction of mineral oil and various sites of production. The workers and their rights, a revolution from within, Buna and Leuna sounded like fairy-tale words, the honour of the worker and his right to art, zarroolafrutzi kuttodamnutz, thought Thomas, taking refuge again in imaginary words, fleck-ibutz schnuttikutz, he must not only enjoy the benefits of art but be depicted in art himself, workers must be shown engaged in heavy labour, at the conveyor belt, in the lab, with their hands on the pistons! The mere word *worker* obviously moved and excited Käthe. Her eyes shone when she talked about the workers. While Thomas listened to Käthe he saw her firing up, so to speak, and recognised the unconcealed joy with which she devoted herself to the assumed influence and heroic power of her own existence. She told no story in which she did not feature as the heroine: who had the ideas for the worker, who spoke up for them, whose mouth was opened? Open your mouths, she told Thomas and Ella, a precept that came out as if propelled from a mechanism as soon as one of them appeared at the table to take the guests' crockery into the kitchen. Then she brought the palm of her hand down on the table, uttering a high-pitched squeal, and she laughed, because she could see how easily she was succeeding in making her guests enthusiastic, impressing them, carrying them away with her. The guests nodded, yes, of course, everyone wanted to help the workers to get their due. Glasses were filled and clinked. The muted sound made Thomas uneasy. Young people, said Käthe reproachfully, well within earshot of Ella and Thomas, young people must take responsibility for themselves and learn to speak up for others, or nothing will come of our new society. Nothing at all. There are plenty of people around here already who are moral cowards and hangers-on. Not to mention a few wimps.

People around here. Thomas could tell how little Käthe felt she was one of them, how urgently, perhaps by means of her heroic deeds on behalf of the workers, she wanted to be a part of the whole, adapt, fit in, adjust to the place and belong to a Germany that had cast her out a good twenty years ago, when those like her were no longer wanted or needed, were banished, hunted, killed. A Germany that was now recovering only with difficulty.

Drying

It began with the air losing humidity, drying up, so that her throat was scratchy, her eyes stung and there was a tickle in her nose. Dry air made life impossible in the long run, or at least very difficult. Ella turned the heating off. If you were a scorpion you could survive in the arid desert, but it wasn't so easy for a young girl.

No one needed intense heat in winter, so Ella turned off the central heating not only in her room but also in the smoking room. Someone or other kept turning it on again. Ella seldom left her room except to go to the bathroom and fetch water – she wanted to keep her eye on the heating and the bowls of water she put out. She couldn't discover who kept turning the radiators on again. The heating dried out the air, dried out the carpets, pictures and walls. Cracks appeared in the fabric of the house; eyes wide open, Ella watched them proliferate daily from her bed. The plaster was crumbling above the curtain, just where the wallpaper met the ceiling. Right beside Ella's bed the wallpaper came away from the wall, buckling because it was so dry. At first it had been only a crack, but for some time Ella had been able to lift the wallpaper so that a length of it came off all the way down the wall, a dry strip of paper with remnants of paste behind it. Ella herself was drying out, scales flaked off her skin, not just out of her hair, the skin of her shins and her arms was getting scaly too, her lips were brittle. Ella did not often embark on a conversation. If she was asked a question, she nodded and saved her saliva for herself, like her tears. She would rather keep her mouth shut to minimise the tickle that made her cough and that she felt whenever she opened her lips and said something. Ella filled all the buckets and basins in the house with water and kept them in her room; she didn't want to dry up entirely. The basins and buckets stood close to each other on the floor, all the vases and bowls that Ella had gradually been able to find over the last few weeks were on her desk, Ella spread wet towels over the radiator to keep the air moist if someone went and turned the controls on again behind her back.

On the first of February Ella was going down the corridor to the bathroom; she had to take a pee. She did that as seldom as possible so as not to lose fluid, but she couldn't avoid going to the lavatory once or twice a day. For she also had to drink, and if she sweated she lost fluid only to the room that was so dry. As soon as she had the handle of the bathroom door in her hand, the door was opened, someone seized her wrist and dragged her in. Blue evening light outside the window. Touch me, said someone whose hoarse voice Ella knew, he took her hand and guided it to his trousers, pushed it inside the waistband from above, stuffed her hand down until her fingers felt the skin right there, smooth and slightly damp. She knew the vague sounds he made, Ella didn't want to see the lodger as well, she looked out of the window at the yard, the evening now drawing in, what you would expect in December, there was the motorbike in the light of the courtyard lamp, and then she saw Käthe and one of her assistants from the studio, perhaps she was telling him how to get the motorbike over the iceberg and into the garage. The lodger smelled yellow, smelled of cigarettes and schnapps. He pushed Ella down on the bench, her hand fell out of his trousers, he pressed her hand, stuffed it back against his thin body, inside his sweaty trousers, and moved it with his own so that it rubbed against his skin, good, yes, that's good, rub, damn it, rub me, you dirty little tart, you filth, and he rubbed until Ella felt the sliminess, the moisture, and the lodger let go of her hand.

He blew his broad, fleshy nose in a check handkerchief, the same handkerchief that he used to wipe his trousers down. There's little errands you can run for us, Ella; he opened and closed his zip, wiped the fabric one last time and stowed the handkerchief away in his trouser pocket. Information about that teacher Matzke, little reports on the salon in this place, your smoking room – he imitated Käthe's tone of voice – when Käthe has visitors, when her brother comes from America, her friends from Paris, her cousin from London, that's what we need. Everything about the bourgeoisie. What about your grandmother? Is she still alive, does she still keep her domestic staff, is she spending the money she raked in? Jewish decadence. Write a little report. What did Käthe and Eduard quarrel about? Go on, you can tell us everything. It will be to your advantage. If you work for us you'll get your school-leaving certificate. That's an offer. Ella's eyelid was trembling, some of the slimy stuff was caught on it. Fluid, anyway. With all the information he had, didn't the lodger know that she had hardly ever been to school in the time before Christmas, and since Christmas she hadn't been there at all? What was she to say about which teacher, and who to? The slimy stuff was dripping from her eyelid to her cheek. Ella didn't want to soil her sleeve with it. She stood up and tore off a piece of the newspaper that was stacked beside the lavatory instead of proper toilet paper. Carefully, she dabbed the slimy stuff off her eyelid. Who needed proper toilet paper? Did everyone in this house have a regal, velvety soft behind? What a waste to buy toilet paper if you had old newspapers in the house! Once read, those not used for lighting fires and cleaning windows would only be thrown away.

Do you hear me, Ella?

Maybe she ought to shake her head so that he'd know she didn't hear him, or more precisely didn't want to hear him? Ella turned on the tap and washed her hands. Soap wasn't much use. She drank from her cupped left hand, she couldn't drink from the right hand, the one he had used. She didn't need a towel, she could leave those few drops of water on her face, they did it good, her dry face, her burning skin.

Can I go now?

With his curiously slender, short-fingered paw the lodger groped between Ella's legs. We have a secret, you and I. It would be better for you to go along with me. Paw still between her legs, he pushed Ella over to the window. Do you see your mother out there? Do you think she'd like to hear that you're chasing her lodger? Now, get out. The lodger pushed Ella over to the door. She left.

In her room, Ella crouched on the floor and then lay down, her hand turned away from her body as if it wasn't hers any more.

The water that Ella had poured into old wine bottles didn't evaporate easily. Thomas had said that was because of the small surface area and the narrow necks of the bottles. So she had knocked the necks off the bottles, robbed them of their narrow necks. She had to be careful not to touch the sharp broken glass when she topped them up with water. Ella lay flat on the floor, a flounder in the desert. Drying up alive. A flannel on her mouth, under her nose, that was how she thought of the water that brought hardly any relief. Ella breathed in moist air. On the floor was better than above it; Ella preferred sleeping under her bed. She curled up on the floor, she forced her bones under the bed.

At first no one noticed that all the containers had disappeared.

Crusted residues formed on their sides and rims, yellowish scabs showing former water levels, like the annual growth rings on timber. Ella thought it was salt, encrusted salt tracing the course of her dehydration. No, said Thomas, it was calcium, the calcium in the water leaving a deposit. A strange idea. The wet flannel on her mouth was drying, she was breathing more calmly now, dry air paralysed her. Her eighteenth birthday was approaching. If anyone came into her room these days, said something, asked a question, she simply lay there flat on the floor under her bed in silence. Her eyes were sometimes closed, but she was not asleep. What she missed most, now that she had stopped sleeping, were dreams. Someone came into the room.

It's me, said Thomas. He lay down on the floor so that his face was level with her, and pushed a glass of water under the bed towards her.

Ella drank. It wasn't easy; she could hardly raise her head, only tilt the glass and put it near her lips.

Coming for a bike ride with me?

Ella shook her head. The blue elephants are out there, and I don't want anything to do with them.

I'll shoo them away.

If she'd had the strength for it, Ella would have laughed. As it was, she just said: If only you could.

Thomas thought. Tell me about the mountain when our father came up it, with his bike and his easel. He had a bike, didn't he? Wasn't our father glad to see you? Didn't he pick you up and hug you, you were his little doll, weren't you?

What?

Go on, tell the story again. Thomas turned on his side, one arm under his head, and looked expectantly at her.

When our father came back I was in the way.

Nonsense, you were his little doll, he picked you up.

Only when he left.

No, when he arrived.

Ella shook her head. She didn't remember much, but she did remember that she had lied. For herself and for Thomas. She had said their father tossed her up in the air. But that was nothing but her made-up picture; she saw a man tossing a little girl up in the air. So it couldn't be true. If it had been her, she wouldn't see the little girl in her memory, she would feel the dizziness of being whirled around, she would remember her father's arms. But there was no such memory. Only a physical memory of being in the way. Her body, what Ella was and would be, was in the way. I was in their way. There were little mauve flowers where I was sitting, the meadow was full of cranesbill. They wouldn't let me into the house. They locked the door on the inside. I can still hear myself screaming: I want to come in. And I'm shaking the door, and I know it will never open again. Like in the fairy tale. A door that will stay shut for ever. It will be overgrown by plants, one day it will be invisible. One day no one will ever find any trace of that door. So I scream as loud as I can: I want to come in too. Let me in. I want to be with you. I cried as loudly as I could.

What about me?

You were happily waving your legs in the air under the tree, that's where she put you to sleep in the daytime, in the handcart under the walnut tree. Later you screamed too. And I went over to the handcart and pinched your hand to make you stop.

Do it again. Thomas reached his hand out to her. Pinch me again.

I can't, I don't have any feeling in my hands. I don't think I can move them any more.

Stop making things up, Ella. Thomas withdrew his hand and lay on his front, propping his head in his hands. Stop it, please! You drank out of that glass just now. Maybe Thomas thought he could outwit her.

Just now, yes.

And not now, this minute? Thomas waited for a while, probably hoping for Ella to answer. But she didn't, and he got up and left the room.

She couldn't even think of sleeping. It was cold under the bed. It was dark when Ella stole down the corridor to the bathroom. There she turned on the geyser and waited until the water was hot. She lit a candle so as not to attract attention in the middle of the night; it might wake other people up. The candle stood firmly on the floor, fixed to the tiles with drops of hot wax. The taps crunched as she turned the cold one off, the hot one on. The white stream of water poured into the tub. Steam rose, the air was so cold, the water so hot. When Ella climbed in, the soles of her feet burned, her calves burned, all her skin burned. Gooseflesh without a feather coat to cover it.

Ella lay in the tub, the nape of her neck against the rim, which was still cool. She felt dizzy. There was a rattling at the door. It must be her imagination. No one went rattling at any old door in the middle of the night, it might wake other people up. Ella said nothing, and held her breath. But no one else woke up, and while the rattling of the door went on Ella saw, by the light of the candle, how the bolt was lifting bit by bit away from the door frame. Until the door sprang open. The lodger fell on his knees. Looking up, he saw Ella lying there naked in front of him. He kicked the door until it latched. Still on his knees, he approached the bathtub. Hey, look at that, a nymph. I knew it!

That made Ella giggle. *Numph*, he said, sounding as if he had a hot potato in his mouth as he turned his exotic word over on his tongue, which was already hanging out of his mouth. Ella hoped her dizziness wouldn't overpower her. You're insane, sick.

We still decide who's sick around here, he said, putting one hand in Ella's bathwater. Ella didn't move. Nausea paralysed her.

Have you made up your mind? The lodger put his hand on Ella's breast. They're putting pressure on me. You're going to cooperate, aren't you? You want peace, you love your country?

Ella didn't take in what she was hearing and didn't believe what she saw. It was as if the lodger were taking the candle in his hand, putting it into the water, extinguishing the flame against her body.

Ella turned in the bathtub, until she couldn't see anything. It was nice and quiet underwater. She felt something strange against her body, her hands, fingers, limbs. Was he pushing her into the water, extinguishing himself on her body? Darkness and cold. Something pushed into her and tore at her until silence came.

Then glaring light, only for a moment, she kept her eyes tight closed. Something was pulling at her, she was being raised and held tight and pushed underwater, but she knew nothing about it, and trusted the dizziness that made everything go dark.

A cold sheet. The yielding mattress made her backbone soft. Ella sat up; there was a light on the bedside table, there was twilight on the other side of the curtains, either morning or evening twilight, the door was ajar. Käthe appeared.

At last. She went up to the bed and put her hand to Ella's forehead. We thought you were never going to come round. How long ago was it since Käthe last stroked her hair? What were you thinking of, having a bath in the middle of the night? Ella had seldom heard love in this woman's voice.

Ella bowed her head.

Did you go to sleep?

Ella looked at Käthe in astonishment. Did I do that? She smiled, she'd been trying to sleep for weeks. Was she supposed to have fallen asleep in the tub? What about the lodger?

You can be grateful to him for finding you. But for him you'd have drowned.

And I didn't?

He revived you.

He . . . what?

He pulled you out of the tub, revived you and then called me. Käthe looked tired.

Ella didn't know what to say. Her body knew that she had not been dreaming, had not fallen asleep, it hurt and burned down where he had been.

You must get better now, sleep a bit. And then, before Monday, we must talk. You have to go back to school. This can't go on.

Ella nodded, the sheet was clammy with sweat, someone had put a hot-water bottle and several hot stones in the bed to warm her up and make her sweat. Sweat was clinging to her forehead, running down her temples.

Come on, I'll help you. You need a dry nightdress. Käthe went over to the wardrobe and took a nightdress out. She went over to Ella's bed and pulled at the clammy fabric. Raise your arms, it won't work unless you do. Ella tried to raise her arms, but they were too heavy.

Ella. How long was it since Käthe had spoken her name.

Your voice is as soft as whipped cream, Mami, I love your voice.

Now, raise your arms in the air. Impatiently, Käthe tugged at Ella's nightdress. You're not a baby. She said 'baby' in a stilted voice, contemptuously, as if she were quoting her American brother and his wife. Affection made her uneasy. Maybe she just didn't have the patience for love. Ella raised her arms in the air, lost her balance, and while Käthe was still pulling the nightdress off Ella tipped over backwards on the pillows.

Aren't you eating anything? You're nothing but skin and bones.

With some difficulty, Käthe got the dry nightdress over her head, turned and lifted her from the mattress, pulled it down over her torso. At last her head lay still again, no more dizziness, no cold, only the burning between her legs and the miserable dryness.

Mami, my dear, dear little Mami. Ella whispered it like a magic spell to make Käthe sit down again and stroke her hair, oh Mami-Mami-Mami dear. But Käthe didn't sit down and wasn't doing any more stroking. The first shock had given way to a sense of relief that probably struck Käthe as useless, and had been quick to go away again.

Stop calling me Mami. I'm Käthe. And you're not a baby. Baby and Mami sounded just like each other as she spoke them now; apparently both were words of horror. Yuk, thought Ella, the word was on the tip of her tongue, yucky, but she wouldn't say, couldn't say a thing like that. Käthe dear, oh my dear, dear little Käthe. Ella closed her eyes. She wouldn't be sleeping. She felt her heartbeat flutter in her eyelids. Ella heard Käthe switch off the bedside lamp and leave her room.

During the next few days Ella listened intently, she kept a keen eye on the bowls of water. She took up her position under the bed. Every hour she crawled out and inspected the bowls, reassuring herself, she went from container to container, topping them up with water from the big enamel jug where necessary, doing her rounds. Before going to the bathroom to fill the jug she listened intently, to make sure of not meeting anyone. Not the lodger, not anyone else either. She just wanted it all to be quiet.

At night she waited for morning twilight, which was late coming in February. In spite of all the containers of water she was drying up, her rough skin was scaly, the corners of her mouth burned, they were so brittle and sore, and so did her eyes.

One morning Ella couldn't stand the itching any longer, the nightdress felt scratchy and hurt her. She had to undress and lie down naked under her bed.

Small feet pattered past the bed, red and blue socks, two voices, or was it only one? The voices were just like each other. They were sliding over the floor on their knees, splashing the water in the bowls with their hands. Whee! They were kicking their feet and shouting with glee. Strange children, the twins whose names Ella had forgotten.

What are you doing there? One of the girls put her head under the bed and reached her finger out to Ella. Ella bit it. Ow!

The other girl looked under the bed. What are you doing there?

What are you two doing here?

We're visiting.

Visiting. It's carnival time, it's the holidays.

I'm an Egyptian, said one of the girls She didn't look like an Egyptian.

And I'm a duck, said the other, sitting down, fully clothed, in the biggest of the containers, an enamel washtub. She wiggled her arms and legs, water slopped out on the floor. One of the twins quacked, and the other, who was tired of being an Egyptian and wanted to be a swan, cackled. They were splashing in competition.

It would have been a relief to Ella if they had put the light out. Please switch the light off, said Ella, but no one heard her. Maybe she had just imagined saying it? Perhaps she was asleep and dreaming, talking, but no one would hear her because no sound came out of her throat? The twins' screeching was loud, the water was splashing close to her ear.

What a performance! The indignant voice would have suited hard hooves. The door was flung open. What's all this supposed to be? Someone pulled at one twin to get her out of the big tub. Who said you could play with water here?

It wasn't us, said the twins in chorus.

Ella!

Ella didn't answer. She heard whispering, the giggling twins gave her away, they got down on their knees and pointed under the bed. Even before Ella could bite, they shrieked: Ow! The woman with the hard hooves shooed them out of the room with the help of a broom. Get out, go on, out you go! At first the children thought it was a game, they sat on the broom, wanted to be swept away, squealing with delight. It took force and stern orders to stop them. Get out of here or you'll be sorry! Scratching, biting, kicking. The girls were forcibly dragged to the door and pushed out. Their howls were like puppies yapping. Agotto barked outside, the door was finally closed. A gloomy silence; the hard hooves were coming soundlessly closer.

A woman's hairy face appeared under the bed. Ella recognised it from the eyes.

Mami, whispered Ella through her brittle lips, my big strong Mami! She put out her arms to the face, but the face flinched back and disappeared, leaving only a pair of calves above Mongolian shoes in sight.

Come out from under there. Come on out, do you hear me?

Ella didn't move; when no one could hear her she couldn't hear anyone, and she didn't think of anyone. The light went out, darkness settled, the light of the street lamps fell in from outside, Ella recognised the outlines of the windows on the floor, and the containers. She couldn't sleep, she slept less and less, and for a shorter and shorter time. But she wasn't awake now either. Her thinking didn't obey her, she begged her memory please not to leave her. Time passed. She could watch herself from outside. Two faces appeared, four arms that took hold of her and put something on her. You're not going out into the street naked, said Käthe, helping the girl into her coat. She was so weak that it took Käthe some time and trouble to get the sleeves of the coat over her clothes. Come on, help me, Käthe told the girl.

Ooooh – it sounded like a fluttering breath. Ella's knees gave way, Käthe's arm held her up more firmly. Mami dear, my little Mami, I'm so sorry. Ella laid her cheek against Käthe's, but Käthe straightened her head, her face was firm and her eyes wide with worry. Mooo, groaned Ella, pushing her forehead against Käthe's throat, mooo.

Stop that, please, Ella. Käthe showed the man the bag she had packed for the girl, and he heaved it into the car. Then Käthe was going to hand the girl over to him, but she was clinging tenaciously to Käthe herself.

Mooo, and she let her soft throat bend, her head sink down on Käthe's large, soft bosom. Oh, look at your cow eyes, Mami dear, let me be your little calf.

We're taking you to a good place, said Käthe, a place where you can rest.

Deciding

I'd like to see you having to put in a travel application for every journey, having to ask permission – Käthe was kneading the wax in her hands, strong fingers pressing and working the yellow mass to make it soft and malleable. She was outlining the body, a long back, slender legs, the loins. The head was what mattered in the model she was making. The forehead was domed, the eyebrows should stand out better, the mouth struck her as too soft. He was handsome, her young man, as she called Thomas. Sometimes she talked about him as if he were a stranger, a Greek model without a name. Her star, her hope, her gift. No statue ever had silky eyelashes, but Thomas did, and there must be some way of showing them. This time she was concentrating only on the head, he hadn't had to undress, they were sitting close to each other at a diagonal. The slate covering her workbench shimmered in the yellowish-grey light. Spring rain pattered down on the veranda roof. Käthe didn't like him to prop his head on his hands, but it felt heavy.

Permission, applications, you sometimes talk like a functionary, Mother. It's easy for you to talk. You can travel wherever you like.

Pull yourself together! In a bad temper, Käthe flattened the wax forehead, made the dome a prominent back to the model's head instead. I have work to do here, we're building a new society.

And where would she have gone? He knew, only too well, that her supposed freedom was nothing but the truth of necessity.

After all, his mother did not lack driving forces, felt capable of sacrificing herself to higher duties. Wasn't he himself the incarnation of her necessity, even if the reasoning behind it could be questioned, never mind whether you went along with Hegel or Marx, depending on your society? Without financial means, without a reputation, still single at the time and with two bastard children, now divorced with four children, deep in the shit? She wanted to be a sculptor. There was no other society that offered someone like Käthe a place. He bit his lip to keep from saying what he was thinking: in this country, you have to have been persecuted by the Nazi regime. Thomas whistled through his teeth. Do you know what I dream of doing? Swimming round the Galapagos Islands. Quietly, he added: And writing.

Käthe laughed. She couldn't take such dreamy notions seriously. You'll grow up, study, work, show what you can do. He heard the mockery in her laugh. What, swim round an island on your own? Who? Who wants to read accounts of delightful travels? Her certainty struck home, surprising him. He supposed she wanted to remind him of what mattered in life. So that he wouldn't dream of worlds no one had ever promised him, worlds that didn't exist. He knew her warnings.

It's all about renewing our society, never mind the chameleon's tongue. Käthe put the wax model on the table and viewed it from all sides.

Your society, thought Thomas, not mine.

It's said that Michelangelo idealised his models. No one has to invent anything like that about you, the gods were keeping an eye on Michelangelo's fingers. She laughed. Käthe stroked the regularly formed back of the wax model with one finger. Thomas yawned so as to avoid hearing what she said. She wasn't speaking to him, anyway, she was speaking to the room, to herself, maybe even to her wax creation, he hoped.

Now, come and sit down properly.

Thomas straightened up and rubbed his face with both hands to get rid of his weariness. She was talking about beauty; he was talking about what was to become of him. He had often known her to fall abruptly silent and turn to other subjects when he was talking about his own wishes, when he read a poem aloud and said he wanted to work with words and make writing his career. Something about that must seem improper to her. He was not trying to make her proud of him, he was just afraid of feeling that she was ashamed.

Why shouldn't I be a journalist? Do you think my poems are embarrassing?

Embarrassing? Oh, good heavens, no. The poems themselves are – what can I say? You're seventeen. Käthe squashed the wax nose of her model with some force. You don't know what work means. Who trusts words today, and by what right? She was modelling the body in a perfunctory way, the legs, the chest, the arms. Thomas felt that she was impatient, he guessed that she would stand up in a moment.

Käthe wiped down her hands. I must go down and work on the stone now. Come with me – she went ahead – the heating's not on, but you can stay as you are, all I need today is your head.

Thomas followed her downstairs to the studio. She put her glasses on, took the wooden peening anvil, chose a fine chisel and began working on the stone.

What are you thinking of? Käthe's question came unexpectedly.

Thomas felt bad about his lack of sophistication; he would never enrich language or experience. The world seemed to him large and powerful, it didn't need him. Why scrabble around like an animal? Language was not political in itself. What you made of it could be political, what many people made of it had to be political. Thomas, however, wanted to snatch language away from the political field and win it back for the world of beauty. He owed her an answer, he ought to tell her what he was thinking of.

I could write about the primeval dragonflies in the Himalayas, he said, and hesitated when he heard her snort. I could write about modern architecture in London, he tentatively went on. Isn't an uncle of yours an architect there?

You mean the baby of the family?

Didn't your father send you the newspaper cuttings about those tower blocks he designed? Thomas thought briefly of the odd fact that to this day the youngest sibling, envied by his brothers, was known by everyone as the baby of the family, even if the family no longer existed, still less the bosom of the family, Thomas's great-grandparents were dead and all the brothers had families of their own. Thomas had never met the English great-uncle who was called the baby of the family. He was seldom discussed, obviously his relations were indifferent to his absence, and it did not bother anyone that since his emigration a great expanse of water lay between them at the very least, perhaps a whole culture.

What do you know about journalism? The sound she made clearing her throat was intolerable. He knew nothing about it, his ears were burning. Wasn't she the one who was always wanting people to think critically, put resistance to the test, show civil courage? Thomas thought of the pictures from London that he had seen, and said: Why is London extending its city centre today, a good fifteen years after the end of the war, with the help of an architect who fled from Germany? A man who built them air-raid shelters and finally, in the middle of the city, wants to develop beauty of form and buildings for the English metropolis in post-war Europe? Huge apartment blocks that looked almost socialist, providing so much dwelling space all of a sudden in an environment full of single-storey and two-storey houses? Don't you think that's interesting?

Do you? Käthe impatiently gave one of the curt answers designed to cut a conversation short, end it, or at least change the subject, getting away from the theme that might interest the other person concerned and moving on to what seemed significant to her.

And the Botanic Garden in West Berlin: did you know they have Guatemalan giant ants there, I think by mistake, but no anteaters? How does man create a balance between plants and animals? Does he succeed, anyway? I could write about that. If I were a journalist I could write –

Thomas stopped. Käthe's aversion and bad temper could be heard as her tapping grew louder; tiny fragments of stone hit his arms and legs. He had to raise his own voice to drown out the sound.

You could do this and that, huh, you must be joking! You want, you want, and your enthusiasm makes you blind. No one can do that. And I'll tell you something: it's obscene to tell people about the giant turtles on the Galapagos Islands while they're standing in factories here making your shoelaces for you.

Why? Thomas looked at her. Käthe wrinkled her brow. She believed she could transport Michelangelo from Florence to East Berlin, she believed in the idea of people, in people themselves – but not in her son. Her son was not to want anything independently of her, certainly never anything outside her system of coordinates. Her love was pitiless, but it was love, there was no doubt of that. She grimly distorted her beautiful face. What do you know of the world?

Woof woof, he felt like saying, and laughed to himself, because the way she barked like a dog was only too familiar to him as a

120

sign of her unrelenting love. He nodded his agreement. Exactly. But I want to find out about it.

If you want to know about the world stay here, do something with your hands, study chemistry or geology. You could do research into mineral oil, be a professor like your grandfather.

Her eyes were shining. Thomas wanted to turn away, but he couldn't. There it was again, the noose round his neck, the noose round his legs, the gleam in her eyes. He needed a pair of scissors to cut himself free. Thomas knew how Käthe idolised her father and wanted to please him. If her son would only emulate her father, become a research scientist, a professor at the least, he would make her happy or at least content, for a moment.

Over in the West there's a lot of loud shouting. Freedom, they call it, but they're exploiting people. Fascism flourishes over there, take a close look. She was working on the temples of her statue's face.

Over there I could study journalism without having to be a member of the Free German Youth, said Thomas, but his words were lost in the noise of her tapping. She tapped and tapped and his ears went on burning. He knew she despised people who made off to the West, went there for a comfortable life under capitalism, but he couldn't stop wondering how it might still be possible for him to get there, in spite of her scorn.

Käthe tested the edge of her chisel, went over to her workbench and picked up a narrower one. Study something sensible first, then we'll see.

It sounded easy, the way she said that, simple. She never guessed the stifling sensation he'd felt for weeks. He had hoped for a while that the world would expand once he had his school-leaving certificate, but the opposite was the case, it was closing in on him with every minute he spent standing in Käthe's studio discussing his future.

Sometimes I think I'm choking, he heard himself say, and saw her narrow chisel pound the sandstone. Maybe I'm just going crazy, the ground is firm but my feet sink in, inside me there's . . .

Her tapping resonated on his eardrums. It was pointless to say anything. He stood there in silence for a while.

Can someone open the door? asked Käthe as she paused for a moment to examine the stone. That could be meant for only one person present, so Thomas went over and opened the door into the yard. It had stopped raining; the air smelled of earth and leaves.

Over there it's Adenauer, here it's Ulbricht.

Yes? Thomas turned to Käthe. Why was she stating that fact, what deduction was he supposed to draw from it?

Yes, said Käthe.

You think all the old Nazis have banded together in the West, but good people are in charge here? retorted Thomas.

Käthe put the peening anvil down on her workbench, pushed up her protective goggles, and was now gesticulating with her arms. There's a chance here. At least there's a chance. That's what matters. She took a deep breath and closed her eyes. She hated to let someone else have the last word. Thomas didn't have to explain the world to her. She was working like a woman possessed on the rebirth of a society. Thomas did not believe any of that, and he was ashamed of himself when he felt her hand on his shoulder.

You came up against the border at school. Refusing to join the Free German Youth! Baffled, she shook her head; her bitterness hurt him. Perhaps Käthe was horrified to realise that she had raised her voice in anger. She whispered her warning now: There's no future if you won't join in. She was not expecting an answer; she raised her chisel and the peening tool and struck the temples of her statue.

Hesitantly, Thomas replied: Isn't there? He thought of those autumn weeks last year that he had spent in the ranks of the Free German Youth, helping to drain the former marshland of the Friedländer Grosse Wiese, he thought of the flocks of birds whose resting places had been disturbed, he had lain in wait for otters and water rats, but to no avail, they had made off long ago. Thomas remembered rolling off the plank bed in the youth camp one morning to go on duty, and the image he had of himself that morning as he dug his spade into the earth, one of the ranks of all the Free German young people who were fooling around, chattering, grousing, and how he had felt like a monstrous mammal appearing there in the pack of all the others. There was no turning back now. And there was no real decision, for he had felt unable to join the organisation, he could not hold the spade in his hand, he was no young hero, and he was anything but free. Käthe did not take her admonitory glance off him. It wouldn't be any good if he didn't join in. How was he to tell her that he couldn't, that there was something he lacked, he was mutating, he was becoming someone else, he was already someone else? Are you joining in, he wondered, when you go to France to see Henri and your other friends, when you go to England to see your sister? Have you ever signed a statement about someone? Maybe saying your children would join the Free German Youth? Is it all up to your Party, then? Do I have to join some damn association to be allowed to study journalism? Thomas was seething. Käthe's lowered forehead made him tremble, he couldn't rage, run wild, he felt only weakness.

At the very least. At least you should join the Free German Youth, even better to join the Party. She looked up, and turned a challenging gaze on Thomas. Even then journalism wouldn't be advisable. You're intelligent. I've taught you both that nothing in life comes for free. Go in for scientific research, Thomas. Or you could be a mechanic.

I don't want to be a mechanic . . . Thomas hated the desperate, pitiful tone he heard in his voice.

Even though you like metalwork? Make use of your talents.

He didn't want any encouragement. Her well-meaning severity was repugnant to him, her heartening words tormented him. He was supposed to make concessions, but he couldn't, his throat felt too tight, his legs too heavy. How could he counter her mockery, her severity and love, tell her that he thought she had it all wrong, and he wanted to find a life of his own? As a mechanic I'd be in some industrial works, welding tractors and axles and no one will ask about my talent. Talent is dangerous, you might want something, want to make something. Better ten tractors a day. I don't want to! Can't you understand? I don't write poems to please or annoy my family. My poems have nothing to do with any of you – I want to write, I want to get out. How arrogant of him that was, his words were intended to attack her. Thomas heard his voice cracking; he had been lying. There would be no poems but for her and his birth in a place that he wished he had never seen. Every poem he wrote was about getting away, escaping and the impossibility of escape.

With delicate little strokes, Käthe was tapping stone away from the back of the head, the nape of the neck. She stopped and turned to him: Then our ways obviously part here. And don't imagine you can come back, just like that. Anyone who leaves is a coward, a traitor. It's open to everyone to make off, he can live in comfort in the West. If that's what you really want, I can write to my brother. Maybe Paul will know of something for you in New York . . . Her tone was threatening, Thomas clearly saw how hard she was trying to drive him into a corner by holding out this prospect, and although he saw through her intentions he couldn't throw off the alarming effect they had on him.

And see the rest of you only every few years? Thomas hated his weakness, his capitulation.

No one has to visit anyone. Those who want to get out had better get out, and that's that. But let me tell you, 1961 isn't 1936. Paul went to America because he wanted to study and he was threatened with a camp under Hitler, he had no choice. I went to Italy for the sake of art. It's all about society, not your private life.

Why didn't he shout at Käthe? He ought at least to turn away. It sounded pitiful when he said: I can't do that. I don't want to leave you. Against his will, his voice sounded pleading. He didn't love society, nor did he have faith in what was good. He just felt love for the woman who had given birth to him. And he couldn't be sure even of her.

Käthe went to the open door, stretched, raised her arms in the air and let out a cry of delight in the direction of the beech tree. She was pleased with her work, with herself, with the scent of rain. But the tea in her cup had gone cold; she wrinkled her nose, threw the dregs at the elder bush, and then poured herself more from the Thermos flask.

Thomas felt nothing but shame for his love, which seemed to him terrible, and his failure to understand Käthe's better society. However, he wasn't going to be talked out of his own views so easily. It wasn't just that he wanted to travel; journalists, words, explanations, he thought were needed close to home as well as far away. And someone ought to write about the factories, someone from the stone quarries, the building sites, and about the new buildings, he said quietly. He didn't believe himself.

She nodded. As you say. From the stone quarries, the building sites. That's not what journalists do, it comes from inside.

Journalists write propaganda, but enlightenment comes from within. We want to do away with educated elitism. That sort of thing goes into the works newspaper. There are wall newspapers in all industrial works, and many other ways of expressing yourself. If you look beyond your own nose for once and you want to do something for society, there's always the Party and the associations with their journals. We need committed young people.

Your Party is a jail. Thomas scared himself.

What?

Your Party is a barrel, he emended his statement. A bottomless barrel. A band of enthusiasts who believe in salvation through socialism the way others believe in the son of God. I call that blind.

Käthe wasn't listening to him. With determination and conviction she said, seamlessly: It's about justice, a more just distribution of all goods, those of the mind as well as material goods. Only if we achieve that can we conquer the fascist spirit. If someone cries, I want more, then it's only a short step to crime. Why do you think the Nazis murdered communists and Jews?

Thomas, baffled, looked at Käthe. She was radiant when she dreamed of a better society.

He wasn't expected to respond, she added the answer herself: Out of pure avarice. They wanted everything for themselves. Communists wanted the same for everyone, that endangered the Nazis' raid on the nation and the many who supported it. She put the chisel to the nape of her statue's neck, chipped away, stepped back, looked at her stone, chipped and chipped.

What am I to do, then? Thomas asked that question out of deep exhaustion. Although he knew what he had to do anyway. Work. As long as he could remember, he had never worked enough, and work was the watchword of life. Only those who worked could share, and proved themselves equal among equals.

Käthe stepped back, inspected her stone, inspected her son, and bent to pick up a small fragment. Here. You like the stones, don't you? Her voice was gentle, she had misunderstood him, so she wanted to give him some concrete advice. What's the point of journalism? What does anyone want with some charlatan of a woman denouncing liberty? Stones last. They lie in the earth, they're always where mankind is. Käthe dropped the bit of stone on the floor again. First you ought do something manual, a practical year, in industry, in production, an apprenticeship, anything like that. Your training will be continued at the Buna works; they need strong young men like you. And later you can study geology.

Thomas said nothing, even when she paused in her remarks as she did now.

Those who are always clamouring for freedom will only be unhappy; they'll never get where you are now.

Perhaps she was right; he couldn't be sure. Thomas had no arguments to oppose her. His eyes fell on the red carnations in the bow window; they were still fresh. Why did Käthe let the lodger give her red carnations on her birthday? What did they stand for – secret signs? Thomas thought of Ella, who had been asleep for weeks. Briar Rose, Snow White, it was like those fairy tales. She wasn't allowed visitors in hospital. If she woke up everything would be all right. Or at least much better than before. But no one asked for a reason, no one wanted to know anything. They decided on her treatment, they induced sleep. She was to rest. No thinking, no talking.

Käthe tapped away at her stone. Behind the carnations, there was something moving in the yard. Thomas went closer to the window and looked out. A hawk with long thin legs, shining yellow in the scuffle, was plunging down on something black. It dug its talons in and pecked its prey, black feathers flew up, it hacked and gnawed until the black bird under it was still. Judging by its size, the prey must be a crow, not very much smaller than the hawk. The tapping on the stone stopped. On the flat roof of the shed opposite, Thomas saw another crow following the spectacle curiously.

Switch the radio on, I want to hear the news. Thomas couldn't take his eyes off the scene in the yard.

What's the matter – why don't you move? Her tapping began again.

The hawk skilfully gutted the bird with its claws. It crouched horizontally, like a predatory cat, back and neck in a straight line, above its victim and dug its beak in. It ate organ after organ. A second crow joined the interested bird on the roof, and a third came along. The hawk kept burying its beak in the tangle of feathers.

We rejoice, we celebrate, we wave to our friends. In Vostok 1 Cosmonaut Gagarin took only 108 minutes to orbit the earth, we are proud of our friends, we salute the Soviet Union. Käthe had obviously switched the radio on herself. For days the same remarks had been broadcast at this time of day; pride knew no bounds. Gagarin, a calm man, laughs as he steps out of the spacecraft; he has seen the earth from above, he is the first man in space, our hero.

Black feathers were sailing through the air, the crows on their higher perch had ventured to the edge of the roof, squinting greedily down over the gutter. They were getting restless, it was taking too long for their liking. The breast feathers with their black and white markings flickered before Thomas's eyes.

And in a few days' time you'll be taking your exams. Käthe proudly announced this fact as if it were a new discovery.

So?

The Soviet Union flies into space, you finish school and start in an industrial works – doesn't that mean something?

Thomas shrugged. He thought of Violetta, who had told him yesterday that she'd like to go to the cinema, smiling as she said so and hoping for him to invite her. The corners of her mouth had twitched, she was waiting in such suspense for his answer. But he had said he was busy all weekend. It had hurt him to see her disappointment. He had looked away from her. It wasn't so much that he didn't have the money, it was her hand that had felt for his last time they went to the cinema. She had taken his hand and placed it on her skirt. How was he to respond to a warm, sticky hand like that? He liked Violetta's dark eyes, her tender, delicate mouth, the snow-white skin of her cheeks. She was waiting for his mouth, for his kiss, he sensed it every time they met, every time they parted. Her longing frightened him. Instinctively, images of the lodger shot through his mind, images that pursued him, that tainted everything male in him with disgust. He didn't want to be him, not a man like that. But he couldn't think who else. The fear was left. He saw the binoculars on the workbench behind Käthe. Going over there with long strides, he looked through the binoculars at the scene in the yard. The orange eye of the hawk turned towards him showed no movement; the raptor had gutted its prey neatly, and now it was looking around, eyes fixed and piercing, watching every movement in the yard and the crows on the roof. Thomas admired the brief, fast movements of its head, no glance too much, no glance too little. The orange eye was cold, glowing, beautiful. The grey feathers of its plumage shimmered. The hawk pecked at the dead bird's head; perhaps the tongue was still left, or an eye, a cheek or part of the entrails that it wanted to eat. With a tiny scrap in its beak, it took off from its victim and soared up into the evening air with outspread wings. What did the world look like from up there, what did the hawk see, what did it recognise? What it saw clearly had significance, but did a warm, yellow evening simply hold out the prospect of more insects, was it more comfortable than rain and a stormy wind, and nothing else? Did the hawk see beauty? And if human beings believed they could tell the beautiful from the ugly, was that because their perception derived from their own imperfect nature? What had Gagarin seen from space when he hovered there and his eye had no other perspective? Blue light. Did Gagarin wonder what the purpose was, or had he been selected because he had no doubts of any kind? As soon as the hawk had gone, the crows flew off their roof and set about the remains of their brother. Two more crows came to join them, but the first two squawked angrily and defended their treasure.

There was cheerful jazz music on the radio. Käthe pushed her protective goggles up into her hair, placed the peening anvil on the workbench and laid the chisel beside it. She went to the sink to wash her hands. I'll make us something to eat, after that you can sit for me again for the wax model. An announcer's voice told listeners the time: it was 17.30 hours. Käthe turned the tap on only a little way so as not to drown out the news. The sound of running water mingled with the voice of the radio newsreader: We learn from Cuba that the invasion by North America has been repelled. Let us take the Bay of Pigs as a sign of resistance to American imperialism. Fidel Castro calls on his country to defend itself against the aggressor. The coming together of nations couldn't mean much to the crows; they had left the yard, leaving only black feathers lying on the ground. Had they taken their brother's head with them, had they hacked it to pieces, eaten it? Had some other creature slunk into the yard unnoticed to steal the head?

Just think of that. The towel she was using to dry her hands still moving, one ear bent close to the loudspeaker, Käthe positioned herself beside the radio. She would have liked to hear more about the Bay of Pigs, but now the radio was playing music, *two good friends, two good friends, they don't say goodbye when they part, because for two good friends, two good friends, there's . . .* She had turned the radio off, she had even less liking for Fred Frohberg than for Freddy Quinn. The world will fall victim to kitsch yet, she said disparagingly, hanging the towel on its hook.

Why does the lodger give you red carnations?

Käthe smiled. Well, he values me. He values my work – she batted her eyelids jokingly – maybe he admires me?

Why did you give Ella that mound of sugar?

Sugar?

Two years ago, don't you remember?

Why, why! What makes you think of that? What odd questions to ask!

That was how it had begun. Perhaps Käthe hadn't noticed, perhaps he ought to jog her memory? She got thinner and thinner, the mountain of sugar got hardly any smaller. Thomas thought of the expression on her face, it had entrenched itself there as the months passed, as if she had been paralysed. She had felt revulsion.

Well, so now she's asleep. The way Käthe said that it sounded sensible, practical. In Käthe's mind there was no connection between the mountain of sugar and the waning of Ella's body to a slender crescent. She disliked memories, she did not like to look back, everything ought to go forward. This year I'd have given her a few hours of extra coaching as a present, if she hadn't been in hospital. Her eighteenth birthday, and she thinks herself grown up.

When you talk like that I get the feeling you're making fun of her. Are you angry? She can't help being sick.

131

Nonsense. Go ahead, defend her. She skips school. When she comes home in a few weeks' time you'll have finished your exams. A year younger, and you're ahead of her. With these words Käthe marched up the stairs.

Thomas didn't like the way she was playing him off against Ella. He felt ashamed. Maybe, as she saw it, he ought to feel proud because at last he'd be starting real work in the summer. What could be a more suitable period of probation before he studied than experience working in production, industry, a combine? Anyone wanting to study geology had to work for one or two years coal mining, or at least in a quarry or on a drilling rig. It was called practical training. At last he was to show what he could do – manual labour, helping to build the research institutes of tomorrow. The idea was that that made studying possible ... perhaps. Thomas didn't want to disappoint Käthe. He heard her dictum clearly: If you thought you needn't bother about celebrating adult citizenship when you were fourteen, if you thought you needn't bother to join the Free German Youth, then at least show your attitude to the class struggle by working. Anyone who sits around doing nothing doesn't deserve to study.

He had registered; in September he was to go to Gommern near Magdeburg and begin working in the stone quarry there. In the pit, in the gravel works, crushing rock, never mind which. There'd be a job for a young man like him; oh yes, everyone was useful. He couldn't tell Violetta that he had to go away for several months. He wouldn't find out what her lips felt like under his. He already missed seeing the rhythm of her breathing under the skin around her collarbone. Did anyone have a prettier collarbone? When she was happy he could see her pulse beneath the thin skin of her throat. How often had he watched her breathing as her small breasts rose and fell? He sometimes put an arm round her. Once he had put both arms round her and hugged her. It might have been only a moment, a moment he liked to remember, even now. But then he had let go of her, had taken a step back, had said something unimportant so that Violetta wouldn't notice his arousal, so that the lodger would get out of his mind, and with him Ella's drought. No more of that.

In a few weeks' time, Ella was supposed to have slept enough. Siegfried and Johnny were asking Thomas almost every day when they could go and fetch their friend Ella from hospital. He didn't tell them.

Celebrating

Minga la bye, dingula tu, shnagulaia shnoo. Ella couldn't help giggling, her brother's breath on her throat tickled, he was playing the flute on her skin. Thomas puffed at the hair on the nape of her neck, raising it, and placed the velvet ribbon smoothly round her throat. He carefully put a safety pin through the ribbon to hold it in place while Ella examined herself in the mirror, ran the palms of her hands over her hair, and checked her Prince Valiant fringe for any hairs out of place. Even in the muted light of the reading lamp her dark hair shimmered. She had put on a dark red, rather well-worn felt cap, and now she pinned the red-and-blue parrot feather in place with the golden brooch she had once found under the table in the smoking room when she was sweeping up after a large party. A keeper in the Zoological Garden had given Ella the feather; he had probably liked her covetous expression, the thin, bare arm she had put through the bars and was swinging, and the hand dangling from the end of that arm as she tried to pick up the feather lying on the floor. Her fingertips had landed again and again in the bird shit that covered the floor of the aviary. Then the keeper had come to her aid with a long-handled pair of pincers that perhaps he used for collecting sandwich wrappings or animal droppings. The feather adorned her today, attractive rather than magnificent. Ella turned her head so that she could see herself in half-profile, and checked the back of her

134

neck in the mirror and the bottom of her hairline, which she had moistened and curled around her little finger until it no longer stood out like weeds shooting up in the wilderness, but fell smoothly into place like the fur of an animal. She felt her brother's warm hands on her shoulders, he fleetingly passed his forefinger down her backbone, warmed her neck and let his hand stay there; he knew how to soothe her. She would give him the first dance, certainly the second, and maybe the last dance too.

Guests had been arriving for the last two hours. Through the closed door of the room, Ella heard them knocking rain off their umbrellas and coats in the corridor, the walls of the house quivered to the noise of chattering, laughing, cries of surprise. In the long corridor Ella and Thomas heard the bell ringing and the guests knocking, the shrill tones of greeting. As guests passed, someone's elbow might hit the door of the room, something scraped by, perhaps an umbrella brushing against the door; Käthe's dog barked shrilly. Only guests coming here for the first time rang the bell – everyone else knew that Käthe's door was always open, you could walk in at any time. Whoever wanted to, whenever they wanted to, with flowers or empty-handed. It was a railway junction of parties, gatherings, meetings. Even secret and personal, intimate and riotous encounters took place behind unlocked doors. Those who came were responsible for deciding to come and for what they would see and hear.

Käthe's colt-like whinny penetrated the noise. She had invited the man who cast her models to join the guests. In his presence her laughter was particularly shrill.

Zabula budy kaparak vi llilli marushnick plavy, rickey pickedy. Ella straightened up and raised her eyebrows enquiringly: Zalunalafye? There was surprise on her face. Only now did she notice that Thomas was still in his pyjama trousers and carrying a garland of dried leaves and flowers. He had fixed the blooms of yellow roses to a willow shoot, along with the umbels of hydrangeas, once blue, now faded to grey-green, and silvery-white poplar leaves. He laid the garland neatly round Ella's shoulders. From his smile, Ella could tell that he saw how beautiful she was. She needed his eyes more than the mirror, she trusted only his eyes, she could believe only in them. Ella tied the goatskin lying over the chair at her desk round her hips like a skirt, securing it with string.

What about this? Thomas held out the goat's cloven hoof that Käthe's dog had once found on a walk in the outskirts of the wood. Since then the goat's hoof, dried and useless, had been lying on the mantelpiece over the stove. Ella strapped it to her stockinged foot.

That afternoon Thomas had worked away on a stick with his knife, first paring the grey bark off the white wood, then spending hours making holes with a corkscrew and patiently hollowing out the stick, making her a flute as the finishing touch to her Pan costume. Ella put the flute to her lips, her breath filled her stomach and her lungs entirely, and now she blew with all her might. The shrill note tugged at the roots of their hair, hurt both ears until they turned away.

Ahhksy, lizzizumma! Thomas turned round in a circle, pressing his hands to his head, his ears, eyes, mouth – a monkey who didn't have enough arms for three, whose apertures, holes and pores were exposed unprotected to the world of which it wasn't supposed to, didn't want to know anything. His feet sprang into the air as if the floor were too hot for him, the air burning with the sound of the flute.

Wasn't she a magician?

Ella laughed. She blew the flute again and doubled up with laughter, because Thomas had flung himself on the floor and was acting as if he were dying from the high sound of her flute.

Pizzei ... piri k'h ... z'ho ... f'hu ... L'iiiii. Thomas stretched out, contorting himself, on the linoleum, his limbs lay slack, his eyes stared fixedly in one direction, far away from a sister who only wanted to be the god Pan today.

Ella bent over him. Falu? She looked at him from all sides; no one else could die as artistically as Thomas. And hadn't she killed him? Hadn't he carved the flute that she would play, and then he could die beautifully at the sound? Kattampeu? Not an eyelash moved, not an eyelid twitched, nor did the corners of his mouth. Ella giggled. Vooo, she whispered, her lips tingling, vooo, vooo. She cautiously nudged his body with one toe, then nudged rather harder so that his hips moved forward and Thomas was lying face down on the floor.

Ella took the parrot feather off her cap and crouched at his feet. They were bare, and cold although it was summer. She tickled his soles, first gently and lightly, the feather scarcely touched him, then she ran it round his toes, the balls of his feet, brushed the deepest hollow in his soles with the tip of the feather until he jumped up, spluttering and dancing about like Rumpelstiltskin.

Aren't you going to get dressed? Ella laughed and tried to grab the leg of his pyjama trousers. Hey, are you going in your pyjamas today?

Naked, he cried, I'm going naked! And he shook the trousers off his legs and took the pyjama jacket off. I'm going like this. Are you ashamed of being seen with me, then?

Ella rolled her eyes and yawned.

The Emperor's new clothes, pu'foo, pu'foo? Singsaladye. Thomas the naked man.

There was no reason for her to be alarmed or overawed by her naked brother, half man, half boy – he had only a few soft blond hairs where others had wiry bushes. Thomas put a soft dog mask over his head; it covered his face, his hair, his throat – anyone who knew Thomas naked would recognise him. But who did, besides Ella? Käthe maybe, he had had to model for her all winter. However, that was months ago, and Thomas had grown taller and stronger now. Käthe had seldom been able to dispense with him as a model last winter, and when she did she sent for a young man from Friedrichshagen instead. The two young men would certainly know each other naked; they had met in Käthe's studio. Maybe the stonemason who sometimes carved the broad outline out of the Elbe sandstone might also know what Thomas looked like naked. Ella remembered how Thomas, red in the face, had once come storming into her room in desperation, indeed in shame and rage, just as he had run away from Käthe, humiliated.

But summer parties like this evening's were not dangerous, at least in their early hours. Käthe was so busy greeting guests and dancing that it would be ages before she got round to holding forth. There was a pleasant sweetish smell of pipe tobacco that someone might have brought back from the West. Or was it a perfume? It smelled of the West, of another world drifting into this house.

Thomas raised his nose and sniffed the air, he barked, he snapped at Ella's hand.

He got down and jumped around on all fours, he whined and howled.

Ella patted her big dog. She ran her fingertips over the soft skin on his back, a nakedness that wouldn't hurt anyone. The dog licked her hand, rubbed his head against Ella's leg, and she patted his muzzle and the fur on the nape of his neck where the dog mask covered it. Where did you get that fur? She stroked the ears sewn to the mask.

Thomas barked.

Stop barking, where did you get the fur? From the rabbit?

What rabbit?

Why did he ask? The whining could certainly be pretence. Ella was surprised by the sadness that suddenly came into Thomas's

138

voice. The one that was lying dead under the larch tree. You shot it, Thomas, admit it. You took the airgun and shot it.

Thomas shook his head vigorously. No, that's not true.

Ella thought it strange that Thomas often found not only empty snail-shells and dead insects that he displayed in small cigar boxes, flies, bumblebees, honey bees, a dragonfly, peacock butterflies, brimstone butterflies, moths, large blue dung beetles from the woods. He also simply came upon dead mammals, a mole, the prickly skin of a hedgehog whose killer had obviously been unable to eat it and left it lying in the woods, the bloated body of a dog that had been drifting in the Fliess, and Thomas had fished it out before it reached the open water of the Müggelsee. He brought all these things home; he collected the insects and buried the mammals. Had he caused the rabbit's death? He certainly fired the shotgun, and not just into the air, shooting down the clouds and the sun. The rabbit had shown no external injuries.

Heart failure on its way from a dandelion back to its burrow, I just found it. Thomas shook himself. Once again Ella stroked the soft rabbit fur over Thomas's head and down over his bare back.

You've got gooseflesh, you're freezing.

Not too badly. He knelt in front of the chair with his short coat thrown over the back, removed the felted lining button by button, and put it on. Let's see if I can pass unrecognised. Thomas whined. He held his muzzle in the air, sniffing. Can you smell them? I can pick up their scent.

And indeed, Ella thought she could smell not only the warm, almost sweet fragrance of the pipe, but the guests themselves. The air seemed to be pregnant with their sweat and their flowers, someone had delivered lilies that afternoon, a big bunch of heavy, large-flowered lilies with a scent that came into Ella's room. Thomas was still naked under his coat lining; if he stayed on all fours only his bare arms and legs would be visible, since the lining just covered his bottom.

Let's climb out of the window. If we come into the house from the garden and over the veranda, we could be strangers. Ella felt her feather to see if it was back in the right place.

Here I go.

It's raining, watch out, the grass is wet.

I don't mind. Thomas opened the window and climbed out on the sill. Getting wet is okay if you don't have any clothes on. Thomas was already bending his knees slightly, and he jumped out into the plantains and dead nettles. Once in the garden, he spread his arms: Come on, I'll catch you.

Ella didn't trust herself to jump. She sat on the sill and hesitated. When she looked down she could already feel the pain of her foot breaking, she didn't want to break anything, feel any pain. She put her tongue out; she liked the summer rain. She liked feeling the raindrops on her bare arms. She'd have to be careful of the garland, she didn't want it to be ruined when she jumped.

Come on!

Thomas had never disappointed her, he had always caught her, he had always found food when Käthe left them for weeks without money and nourishment in the dark house, it was Thomas who had carried Ella's school briefcase home when Ella had been furious or sulky and hadn't wanted to carry it herself.

Come on! My feet are getting wet and cold!

You're crazy! Summer rain is warm. Ella was laughing at him.

He had taken his school-leaving exam two weeks ago. He had caught up with Ella and passed her without meaning to. She couldn't do maths, and had missed many weeks of school when she was staying away and then having the sleeping cure. Or had it been months? It was said she'd had typhoid fever, had been asleep with typhoid fever as a cure for the weakness. Ella wasn't quite sure about that; she had been given tranquillisers, maybe Käthe had only taken her to the hospital so that she herself could get better. Ella was glad to have been out of Käthe's house in February and March, away from the lodger, far away from algebra and other little things that she couldn't remember. But coming back was difficult. All the rest of her class had taken their school-leaving exams in those weeks.

Thomas would help her, he would spend every day studying with her for the next few months, studying patiently until she knew everything, or at least the most important parts. He had promised.

Come on!

Ella leaned forward as far as possible until she could touch his hand, her eyes fell on the stones and broken shards beneath the window, limestone and green fragments, the dead-nettle flowers were white; she felt Thomas's hand, his warmth, he was strong, he could catch her.

Now, she called, pushing herself off from the windowsill, and he caught her in both arms. Their heads knocked together, that was all, but it didn't hurt.

It was drizzling, the raindrops were warm, sunlight fell through the trees, the sun was just setting. Maybe they could see a rainbow? Midges settled on Thomas's bare skin. Ella went ahead. The wet grass tickled and squeaked under the soles of her shoes.

Maybe she ought to pick some flowers for Käthe? But that would annoy her. The fuchsias glowed violet and pale pink, drops of summer rain glittered on their dark green leaves in the red sunset light. The lawn was wet, and Ella's stockings soaked up the lukewarm moisture. Maybe she ought to go barefoot like Thomas? Vines climbed over the wall of the studio and up to the roof. Ella's mouth watered at the mere thought of the tiny, sweet-sour bunches of grapes. She picked one and pulled off two or three green berries.

Come on, little doggy, come on, she said, bending down to Thomas, who was already kneeling on the ground and panting like a dog. Look, you'd like these, wouldn't you? She held out the grapes on the flat of her hand in front of the mask, giggling. His rough tongue came through the muzzle opening in the mask, but wasn't long enough to lick up the grapes. Two men were sitting at the back of the garden under the spreading willow tree, talking and smoking, and didn't notice Thomas and Ella. Shlabbidiwabb.

There was light in the veranda windows. The leash that Käthe put on her dog only when they went into the town hung at the bottom of the steps. Ella took it and put the collar fastened to it round Thomas's furry neck. There's a good boy, then. They climbed the steps and opened the veranda door. Someone was barring their way, a kneeling figure who had to move slightly sideways so that the door could open and Ella and Thomas could slip in. The kneeling figure wore a transparent veil with flowers on it, and a nightshirt under it, he wasn't made up, no mask, obviously he was half-hearted about fancy dress. The man seemed familiar to Ella, but she wasn't sure if she had ever seen him before. He was kneeling in front of the bookshelves leafing through mildewed pages reverently and carefully. He lowered his nose to the paper, smelled it. No doubt about it, he had found a treasure – and the shoving and laughter and celebrations around him didn't seem important to him, he didn't notice any of it, he turned pages and read.

An elderly gentleman was standing by the window, watching the guests. He stood out because he seemed to be the only one not wearing fancy dress. He had a suit on, jacket, waistcoat and trousers all in the same finely woven dark green material, a pair of gold-framed glasses, and his hair was going grey. Oh. His mouth dropped open when he saw Thomas. A scantily clad young man in a dog mask being led on a leash by a girl. His eyes went to Ella. Not the smallest trace of a smile appeared on his face.

Uncle Paul? Uncertainly, Ella took a step towards him. She smiled. Are you Uncle Paul?

The gentleman scrutinised the slender figure of Pan and shook his head.

Have we met? He instinctively reached for the handkerchief in the top pocket of his jacket and held it as if to blow his nose or clean his glasses, but he did neither.

I don't know. Ella was stammering, and felt that she was blushing red. It was several years since she had seen her uncle, and it was only an idea, obviously a wrong one. She wasn't sure whether she could even recognise him. Thomas and Ella revered their American uncle, although they saw him so seldom.

No, said the gentleman, shaking his head, fancy dress, costumes, there are limits to those as well. Young people these days could be ashamed of themselves, he said slowly, they should be ashamed of themselves, but they aren't. Don't you two know the meaning of shame? It was an honest question, not a reproof.

Dismayed, Ella looked at her dog, who was panting in a friendly way. He would certainly have wagged his tail if he could. It was only a joke, she didn't want to upset anyone, specially not this nice old gentleman whom she had taken, in her high spirits, for her American uncle.

The man turned away and did not look back again. Ella patted her dog's head. No one laughed.

Thomas howled quietly and whimpered.

A young lady bent down and offered the dog a glass. Thirsty? She laughed. Maybe a little water? The lady looked round, saw a flowered plate and tipped her white wine onto it. There you are.

Thomas panted, he got up on his knees and pawed the woman's stomach with his hands. She almost fell over, she took a step or two backwards, supported herself on several people and stood her ground.

That'll do, that'll do. It was getting too much for her.

Ella jerked her dog's leash and said: Bello, what did I tell you? You're not to jump up at people. Calm down, Bello, come on, calm down. Thomas snuffled his way along the floor with the muzzle of his mask; he obviously couldn't see enough of the plate through the openings for his eyes. He lapped up the wine with the tip of his tongue.

Ella, what an enchanting feather! Alfred offered Ella his hand in greeting. He was a fine figure of a man, a sculptor and not very keen to be friends with Käthe, but he always turned up at her parties. Next moment Alfred's eyes fell on the half-naked dog.

And that is?

Enchanting, yes. Ella nodded.

And that – who do you have there?

My dog Bello.

I see. Alfred suppressed outraged laughter only with difficulty, snorted hard, and looked at Ella. Your dog? And you walk around here with him on the leash like that?

If I didn't he'd bite. Ella tickled her dog's head. Sorry, but he has to be kept on the leash.

Alfred bent down and clapped the dog on his back. Well, well, my good fellow. The dog growled. As Alfred straightened up his hand touched the garland round Ella's shoulders. Then he tapped the skin of her flat bosom with his forefinger, clearly below the collarbone. Would you like some wine?

Thanks, but no, I must look after my dog. Ella tugged at Thomas's leash and ducked under Alfred's arm. The dog barked, he was barking at Alfred, the greedy finger had not escaped his notice.

And he's looking after you, right? The lovely Ella and her naked dog! You could hear that Alfred had been drinking, maybe drinking too heavily. At least, several guests turned to Ella and Alfred and their eyes fell on the naked figure of Thomas, still unrecognisable

144

in his mask. A big, fat woman with red ringlets and a peacock-feather dress cried out in delight. Could she sit on the dog? Her hand was already groping for the furry neck, her long fingernails dug into it, and before Ella realised what was happening she let her heavy buttocks down on Thomas's back. There was a cracking sound, a groan, and Thomas collapsed on the floor under the peacock feathers. The woman rolled over to one side, lay on her back, spluttered and roared with laughter. Thomas's prick was exposed as he lay sideways, one leg at an angle, the coat lining falling aside, the mask slipping up, his face distorted, his eyes closed in pain or shame.

Ella stood beside him, clapping. As long as she went on clapping, she hoped, more of the guests would look at her than at him. And a lot of them were looking. She nudged Thomas with her foot and hissed: What's the matter? Stand up. Thomas hauled himself a little way up. Ella grasped the furry nape of his neck in both her hands, held it firmly, the way you pick up a cat by the scruff of the neck, and dragged him through the crowd. Loud music was playing, the plucked strings of a guitar, One morning very early. A dark-haired woman, throwing herself into it, was singing the Partisan song. Ella propelled her dog through the dancing throng, sometimes he crawled on all fours, sometime she had to push him, and among the dancers who were singing along Ella could clearly make out Käthe's clear, high voice. She was the only one who could sing the Italian text, their struggle for freedom, every verse, every line of it, her voice drowned out the rest. *O partigiano, portami via, ché mi sento di morir, e se io muoio su la montagna, o bella ciao, bella ciao, bella ciao, ciao, ciao, e se io muoio da partigiano, tu mi devi seppellir.* Ella heard her own voice in Käthe's, and she knew every line: what her mother said, what her mother sang, when you sang it your arms and legs tingled, you wanted to burst apart and open up. She felt like dancing too, but first she had to get Thomas out of the crowd.

As soon as Ella had closed the door of her room behind her, Thomas tore off the coat lining, took the mask off his head, and threw himself naked on his bed.

Bastards.

It was your idea, Ella pointed out. She sat on the chair and smoothed out her parrot feather. You wanted . . . she had to giggle again . . . you wanted to go out there half naked.

Thomas rubbed his fist over his hip bones. Very funny, he groaned, so was that an invitation to crush me? Bastards.

Bastards, Ella repeated.

Not because of that clumsy idiot. What gloriously lousy blindness. How long do they think their freedom will last? What kind of stinking freedom is it if they lock us up?

Lock us up. You say that as if we were going straight to prison.

So we are. Straight to prison with the raving lunatics. They all look, and no one says anything, no one's surprised. What do you think they need their damn Wall for? He's lying, old Walter is, when he calls it a little fence.

Ella turned the quill of her parrot feather between her hands so fast that it looked as if it were a bluish goblet shape.

What use are the sky and the suburban railway and your friends to you if the world doesn't notice what's going on here? Communist decadence, that's what it is, dictatorship. Do you want to live behind a wall, surrounded by a wall? *Bella ciao*. Käthe will never see her beloved Italy again. What a joke, she says she'll take us to Italy some time, she'll take us to France some time. Maybe we'd even have been able to go to New York and visit Uncle Paul?

Was that him just now?

She's never once taken us anywhere. And now she'll just have to go round in circles herself, always following the Wall, maybe to the shores of the Baltic for all I care.

Thomas stood up, put on a pair of trousers and a shirt. Through

146

the open window, they heard the rain pouring down, the willow tree and the ruins of the mill on the other side of the road were suddenly brightly illuminated, a flash of lightning, the air smelled of damp soil, they heard thunder rolling quietly in the distance. Maybe, and he went to the window where he had hung herbs up to dry a few days ago, maybe that's the death wish of the people here, they torment themselves if not blindly then with pleasure. Thomas cut some of the herbs off with a pair of scissors and collected the rustling leaves and dried stems in his hand. He smelled the herbs, spread his hand out flat, and cut them up smaller and smaller. It's like being in kindergarten, the world is too large for them, they'd rather build a little fence round it and then no child can get away. Be good and stay in the guardianship of the collective, never put a finger outside it, not a foot, not a thought. Build a wall round it, keep people away, there'll be no time off from your servitude to the state, you brought it on yourselves. Thus spake Walter Ulbricht.

What do you mean, a wall? Where do you see a wall? Ella let her jaw drop; she wanted to show him that she couldn't follow his fantastic train of thought, and didn't want to.

That's what Ulbricht's been talking about recently, exit permits to the world outside or not. The scissors clicked as he snapped them fast, the leaves must be cut up smaller and smaller. He denies that it's being built but he already has a name for it. Don't make me laugh!

They could hear music in the corridor, obviously the guitar player and the woman whose singing he accompanied were going through the whole house. *Flying into space, past the stars to race.*

Hear that? They're composing a song for Yuri Gagarin. The world is getting larger, not smaller. Come on, let's go out and dance.

I wish I had your dreams, Ella. It's trickery, all of it. Gagarin flying into space doesn't make our world larger, it makes it smaller with the help of exit permits. They'll close the border. Don't be so blind.

Ella slowly shook her head. What made Thomas so sure, was he obsessed? A few days ago Ella had come into the garden when Thomas and Michael were lying in the grass making up poetry. They didn't feel as if they'd been caught out in something, they took no notice of Ella only a few metres away, pretending she had to see whether the washing on the line was dry. She listened to the words clattering back and forth between them. *The world is overcast and grey, / timid is the wind as well. / Leaden, the sea surges this way / breathing in a sluggish swell.* The typewriter on which Thomas clattered away stood between them; he stopped, sat up, took the sheet of paper out of the machine, put a new one in so that he could touch the keys again, noting down Michael's words. Those words sounded like an answer, a mingling of their ideas, a duet. *We sit sadly here and talk, / we do not hear each other's words.* Did he love Michael? *All we hear is words, and know / that in the morning light we'll see / a road that's bound to part again. / We know it well, and we could weep.* They had been talking about the metre of death, because as Michael saw it poetry was not the only thing to observe metre, so did the vanishing of life, they had been talking about death, farewell, prison, the blind alley in which they saw themselves trapped. Ella now lost her temper again. She had found it more and more difficult recently to fire Thomas's enthusiasm for the other world, the world in which they played at being animals, at being other people, danced at a party like a married couple.

Why are you so pig-headed? You doubt everything but yourself.

As for my doubts – for a moment Thomas stopped and smelled the herbs on his hand – maybe it's just that you don't know my doubts about myself? Thomas packed the herbs into his short-stemmed pipe, tamped them down and tried to light them with a match. The very week after the school-leaving exams Michael and Roland were called up for auxiliary service. Walling up the doors of buildings. Putting up fences, that's what they call it. So why are they guarded by soldiers and police officers while they work? Digging their own graves, guarded while they do it. Digging our grave. How stupid do they think people are anyway? To be or not to be, that's what it's all about.

Calm down, little brother. Ella felt boundless anger rising in her. The readiness is all, the rest is silence. So there. She laughed mockingly. She could have hit Thomas, or at least the floor.

Don't make fun of me.

Why not? Aren't you Hamlet, isn't everything rotten?

Ah, that's a state secret. Building a few fences taller in the middle of the city, where they've decided the frontier of the state will be. Is that coincidence? Barbed wire for rabbits? Thomas filled his pipe again and drew on it, struck a match, drew on his pipe until smoke rose in the air.

You're crazy. Ella let out a hissing sound.

Let's hope so, yes. Let's hope I'm crazy. Puffing at the pipe, Thomas made a face as he tried to smoke it without breathing in, choked and coughed.

Well, maybe they really are just fences?

Oh, sure, and you take a pledge of silence. Thomas held his breath. Smoke built up behind his lips, he pursed his mouth and blew smoke rings into the air. Masonry fences with barbed wire, and soldiers on guard during the building works. Do you know my poem 'Farewell'? With his free hand he reached under the bed and brought out his blue folder of poems.

Must I?

The great house of parting, / thronged by countless crowds, / rises, gleaming with light / in the night-dark city.// And once in the dome of farewell / the cruel, impatient urge / will carry you away, / on cold rails that never diverge

. . .// Past the warmth of human dwellings / as familiar voices fade / and
pictures fly backwards past you / blurred by tears / from the light to the shade
. . . // Rails glowing pale red in the sun / dull grey as they pass into mist, /
linked lost places left behind / that for us do not exist . . .

Ella leaned back until her head hung down over the back of the
chair, enjoying the silence that followed the poem. His lament did
not move her. She simply felt angry. Face turned to the ceiling, Ella
said, slowly: Do you know what I think? You're just envious that
Michael and Roland can start studying at once. School-leaving
certificates in their pockets, places to study waiting for them. Never
mind, I want to dance, let's go and dance.

Tell me, what am I supposed to do in Gommern?

My God, Gommern, Gommern, Gommern, that's all you talk
about these days. And it's not even clear yet whether or not you'll
be sent there.

Into the army or off to the stone quarry. What are they planning
for me? What am I supposed to do there?

Ella took a deep breath. She could not share his fears, she was
impatient and wanted to dance. Thomas wouldn't let it rest, he
obviously didn't want to dance, and the noisy party going on outside
the door meant nothing to him.

What am I supposed to do there?

Ella whistled softly through the gap in her teeth, sat up ramrod
straight and told him what she thought: You're supposed to show
that you don't feel you're too good for it. That you're not superior to
it. Not the know-all who always gets good marks. Your work at school
was too good, that's just your bad luck. Käthe is not one of the
workers or she'd have had to stay a stonemason instead of becoming
a sculptor. Bad luck again. And you don't have an electrician for a
father!

As his pipe refused to burn properly, Thomas tipped the herbs
back into his hand and crumbled and rolled them between his

palms. The hell with Hamlet. You think I'm the only one affected. Everyone's affected.

Well, well, well. You're not everyone. Not everyone attracts all that attention at school, not everyone always thinks he knows best. Ella raised an admonitory forefinger.

Thomas was in no mood for joking; he stayed serious. Once you have your own school-leaving certificate, do you think she'll let you go straight off to theatrical college?

Ella put her feet on the desk and drummed her fingers on her knees. She pressed her lips together; she had accustomed herself to not answering every question. Particularly not those asked by Thomas when he wanted to open her eyes and dash any false hopes. She heard the hiss of the match. Out of the corner of her eye, she saw him sucking at his pipe, sucking away as if for dear life. Who says I'm even going to take my school-leaving exams? At this moment it rather looks as if I won't.

Thomas puffed at his pipe. Because of special aptitude? Don't you see that it doesn't depend on that any more? That's the principle of subversion. You told me yourself how the lodger tried to blackmail you . . .

You're being horrible. Ella adjusted her position in her chair. Why did Thomas have to start on about the lodger? With his dirty fingers that he tries sticking into everything, his slobbery tongue, his stinking prick . . .

Didn't he ask if you'd like to work with them? With his stupid Security Service? To protect the state? Didn't he say the teachers would take a softer line with you then, you could pass the exam?

There was pressure at her temples, the roots of her hair were burning, Ella felt hot, the skin of her face was burning, her throat, her voice sounded rough. So? The lodger's not Almighty God – she shook her head – the lodger has no power at all, just don't think of him, do you suppose it's his fault I've been ill and I couldn't finish the year at school and I can't remember anything? Ella felt sick.

Who knows? Thomas leaned back against the door of the room. Now that I come to think of it – he wrinkled his nose – yes, he did have something to do with it.

Ella heard Thomas going on, but only from a distance; the hissing in her ears had swollen to a rushing sound and she could hardly understand him. What was he saying? That Käthe wasn't innocent of all blame either. But what's innocence, and what's the meaning of guilt when we're talking about responsibility, about decisions? Ella swallowed, the burning of her skin was barely tolerable, her nausea ebbed and flowed, her heartbeat fell and rose, she was breathing deeply, as Thomas had always advised her to do in such situations. But this time he didn't seem to notice, he was still talking, and she vaguely heard what he was saying: Käthe believes in communism, even if it's called socialism these days, otherwise she could never have afforded to rent a huge house like this with a garden, and turn the stable into a studio – penniless as she was in spite of her distinguished family. He said objectively, almost gently, without a note of reproof or sarcasm: Perhaps the lodger came along at just the right moment.

Ella didn't have to listen to what she couldn't hear, her ears closed, she shut her eyes and enjoyed the dizziness. Thomas loved Käthe, but they couldn't talk to each other. In Käthe's eyes, he was a talented young man, she let him make her brass bracelets, lovers' rings, a silvery belt that she wore proudly as if it were a chastity belt. He could write his poems, he was to study geology, he was to model for her as well because he was so good-looking. One of these days, as she saw it, he could study chemistry, physics, medicine, whatever he liked; maybe. But not journalism, when not a word was free, let alone the news. Skin could flare up, like the herbs in his pipe, it could burn brightly – but first Thomas was to do Käthe credit, save face for her, show everyone he didn't think himself superior, her son was not above working in the stone quarry like all the others working in factories and industry. Ella's itch was overpowering, she scratched.

Her hands scratched frantically, her arms, she scratched her arms, her legs, she scratched her crotch, under her stockings, her throat, she scratched her face hard.

What are you doing? Don't scratch like that, you'll bleed. Thomas stood up and tried to hold her hands tightly.

It's that acrid smoke makes me feel sick. Admit it, you're smoking henbane, some kind of poison! Put your silly pipe out, will you? Ella could scream shrilly, hysterically. She was beside herself. The burning wasn't the guests out there, not Käthe or some kind of wall, the burning was her brother with his silly pipe and always talking about prison. Ella screamed.

Thomas put his pipe down, knelt in front of her and held both her hands. Look, you're bleeding already!

Yes, because of you!

You're going red all over, you're coming out in spots. Her bare arms were covered with raised marks. Tears rose to Thomas's eyes. Ella – he tried to hold her firmly – stop scratching, stop it. With all his might he tried to grasp her wrists in his hands.

You're hurting me!

He let her go, wound his arms round her, wanting to put an end to her fury, but she knocked them away.

Ella? She heard anxiety in his voice. Well, let him be anxious. Ella, she heard gentle determination in it as well, just let him try it, he wanted to save her, however much he wanted to keep her safe he couldn't.

He put his arms round her again, stroked her back, and this time she let him, let her arms dangle, put up with his concern, he must be able to feel her sobbing under his hands.

I've come of age. In tears, Ella sniffed. I've been able to go anywhere I like since February.

Thomas held her even more firmly. Of course she could go anywhere she liked. On her eighteenth birthday she had been in hospital. He had visited her there, she had liked that, and she had liked the blackbirds singing outside her window early in the morning. But then she had been sent home two months later. Cured. So they said.

I don't want to stay here any more, I can't stand it here any more. She nestled close to his throat, dried her tears on him, rubbed at her wet eyelashes, no one but Thomas could comfort her. Her skin was still burning, but she could bear it as long as Thomas held her in his arms. The lodger . . .

Shh. Thomas laid a finger on her mouth. We'll find you a room, an apartment, we'll get you out of here.

The lodger . . . he . . . she sobbed.

That's a promise. Thomas held Ella close; he thought he knew what she wanted to tell him. But he didn't. Applications would have to be made, the housing management committee of the commune would have to be convinced.

. . . I think I'm pregnant.

Abruptly, Thomas held Ella away from him. He had taken her by the shoulders, he stared at her. He looked defeated. Ella could see him searching for sensible ideas, something sensible to say. Whose is it? He swallowed, looked down as he suddenly realised how foolish this question was; he knew the answer and whispered it quietly, without looking Ella in the face.

His arms dropped, slack, powerless. All his love, his unconditional concern for Ella, his watchfulness, his careful silence in spite of the boundless fury he felt, none of it had been able to help her or prevent this.

Ella nodded, gritted her teeth and looked straight at Thomas.

He had only to open his eyelids for her to see herself in his eyes; he opened them, his eyes were brimming over.

When? Thomas asked so quietly that she had to lip-read the word.

A few weeks ago, when you were camping with Roland and Michael. The weekend after your exams.

He lowered his eyes again wearily, a tear was running down his nose. Why didn't you tell me?

What could I have told you? The lodger came back? He lay in wait for me and he fucked me?

A woman's screech of laughter could be heard from the corridor, a man was talking non-stop to her, she laughed, something went off with a bang, presumably the cork from a bottle of sparkling wine.

Thomas leaned forward, reached under Ella's chair and picked up the parrot feather. She must have dropped it. He held the feather in his hand and said nothing.

What is it?

Perhaps he didn't know what to say. His silence made Ella despair.

Oh, say something, speak to me! Do you think I didn't resist? Do you think I just let it happen? I threatened him, he threatened me. He can do us all harm, Käthe won't get any more commissions, she's already lost her lectureship . . .

Thomas lay down on his bed and folded his arms behind his head. He stared at the ceiling, but only briefly; then he closed his eyes. He certainly wasn't asleep. No one could be asleep now, with the party merrily in progress outside. Was he thinking?

Ella crossed her legs. She mustn't cry.

It can be got rid of, she said quietly. But Thomas did not reply; his face showed no emotion.

Maybe it will just go away of its own accord.

Thomas said nothing.

Are you asleep?

No. He sat up and slowly picked up single sheets of paper with his poems on them, typed on the only typewriter in the house, which belonged to the lodger.

What are you reading?

Once again, Thomas did not answer. When it took him so long to find his answers it made her furious. Recently he had often resorted to going away.

Leave me alone. I can't talk any more, he said without looking at her.

Ella waited for a while. Maybe he would read one of them aloud to her, maybe he would close the blue folder of poems and come over to her, be with her. But then she saw the shame in his face. Helplessness tormenting him. He could neither protect nor save his sister, he couldn't do anything. She could hardly bear to see him, she was ashamed of herself; she shouldn't have told him about the pregnancy.

She wouldn't be able to bear it here much longer. Someone had put a record on outside. Dance music.

Am I in the way? Shall I go out? Ella was not expecting an answer. She positioned herself in front of the mirror and, with a brush, painted huge red marks on her cheeks, outlined her mouth and eyes with the same brush. Let him read poems if he liked, write new ones, regret the damn freedom he talked about, lie miserably on his bed – she was going to dance.

Hymn of gratitude
After the final end
(Autumn 1961)

The stones iron
The shadows have long lashes,
They beat in the wind . . .
Cries cooing, a sound like bone
On the slopes
Decomposition grins back
In the dark
Statistics are silenced
For ever.
The moon has a yard
With little crosses
The night weeps
Horror limps on crutches
To another star –
which is glad to see it!
God has
Drunk himself to death.
He stinks of schnapps.
Tears clink like glass
A pearl necklace –

Endless!
Death sleeps
For ever –
He has been overworking!
He can't rub his hands
Any more.
He's too tired!
The light has dried up
Ice does not drench –
If God were not drunk
I would thank him!

Bending

The lodger's room was taboo. Käthe sent Ella and Thomas into it in turn just to kneel and clean the floor. They drew back the curtains, aired the room and scrubbed the floor. All through the hot, stifling month of August he hadn't been there, dead flies lay on his windowsill, and in sultry September he still didn't come. It could hardly be a guilty conscience that kept him away, for it hadn't been the first time he had raped Ella, and apart from Thomas no one knew she was carrying a child. Presumably his superiors at the Ministry of State Security had other plans for such a glorious and versatile lodger as he was. The anti-fascist struggle certainly called for conspiratorial meetings along the border which was making such waves. Perhaps the conspiratorial meeting place, the room under Käthe's roof for entertaining officers and spies working under-cover, seemed rather risky to the Ministry of State Security after 13 August. Ardent and zealous as the communist attitude of someone like Käthe might be, she went on welcoming friends and relations from abroad, whose true intentions and convictions could not be guaranteed as harmless. Hadn't Thomas heard Käthe telling her American brother Paul at her summer party that her lodger was a State Security officer whose spying activities, as she saw it, were above all harmless, but also a lucrative source of income and necessary if she was to practise her profession? It was possible that this conversation had not only lingered in Thomas's mind but had made its way into higher circles. How secret and secure was the Rahnsdorf room now? The question of whether she talked to her brother about her lucrative sideline entirely inadvertently, or on purpose, knowing that bystanders would hear this confidential remark and she would be rid of her lodger, gave him no peace. After scrubbing the floor, Thomas sat in the lodger's armchair and would have liked to take a nap. Outside the window, the maple rustled in blood-red fire, its glow anticipating winter, and the wind bowed its branches. There had still been a lime tree beside it last year, with heart-shaped brimstone-yellow leaves and a black trunk. But it had been felled after Käthe managed to acquire a Wartburg. For the Wartburg – its acquisition being entirely due to that lucrative sideline of renting out a room, and maybe the lodger himself had something to do with it – Käthe needed a broader entrance to the yard, and had simply picked up a saw. She had been furious when Thomas refused to hold the other handle. In the end her hired model from Friedrichshagen had helped her.

Why was a dying leaf so beautiful? No mating took place in the maple's autumn, only death, yet it magnificently outshone the courting of other deaths.

Ella had given birth to the child in the lavatory, she claimed. For the first time Thomas didn't believe her. How? Thomas had asked cautiously, and regretted his question when she began to tell him. After all, there were such things as phantom pregnancies, couldn't she have had one of them? Hadn't the child maybe disappeared unnoticed, as people so nicely put it? But Ella would have no truck with such pious wishes. First she had drunk a litre of hot wine, she said, later a large glass of vodka, she had jumped off the bed to the floor, had drunk more vodka, had jumped again, it went on all night, hadn't he heard her? He had been asleep, he hadn't heard anything. Towards morning she had drunk castor oil, then she sat on the ice-cold lavatory seat waiting in pain as the cramps set in. Ella's nostrils quivered. Hadn't she moaned and groaned? she asked. Distressed, Thomas shook his head. He had been asleep. He hadn't heard anything. Her wild eyes troubled him. How could he not believe them? He was her close friend, devoted and obedient. He placed his hand on Ella's forearm, he placed his hand on her temples, he touched her forehead. He wanted to stop the noises she was making, stifle her twittering, and he held her close, to no avail. Ella went on, crackling, burning. First there had been pale scraps. Wouldn't he believe her? The flashing of her eyes almost caught him out. But then the hairy tangle had fallen into the pan.

Mouth sealed, eyes blindfolded as befitted a confidant's loyal silence. Not a word to a soul. Thomas had nodded, Ella had gone out dancing. In a few days' time Thomas was to board the train for Magdeburg. Gommern was the name of his future. One day, surely, he could study geology in Freiburg. Someone who scored top marks in all subjects in his school-leaving exam ought to show that he has two good hands and can work in a stone quarry. He was to stay in the hostel on the spot. Working for the class struggle. Thomas closed the window looking out on the maple tree and drew the curtains again. No wind at all, it was as if he had never aired the room, which smelled stuffy. Thomas watched a spider that had woven a close-meshed funnel of a web between the curtain pole and the wall, and was now weaving another that seemed to be loosely connected to the first; the spider made skilful use of the weight of its body and the consistency of the thread. A knock on the door. There was only one person who didn't ring the bell or simply walked into the house through the unlocked front door. Thomas went to open the door of the room to Michael.

Our lodger's gone missing, Thomas announced to his friend,

leading him into the stuffy room. He would never talk to Michael about the dubious aspects of the whole affair. He showed Michael the half-full bottle of wine he had found on the veranda. Laughing, Michael took a small package out of his net bag. The smell of grated lemon peel, warm egg yolk and love streamed into Thomas's nostrils; he accepted the package, which was still warm, his mouth watering.

Michael shrugged his shoulders apologetically. She couldn't get any vanilla, and she knows you don't like raisins. She's really worried, a young man can't grow without cake, she thinks.

She's right. Thomas nodded, he smelled the paper and soaked up the love of his friend's mother, he could already taste the butter. He wanted to share the cake, but Michael waved the offer away, smiling and saying he had plenty of it at home. Thomas ate alone, the little package on the windowsill in front of him; he broke a piece off the cake and then another, eating it straight from his hand, licked the palm of the hand that he had used as a plate, munched the sweet dough. The warmth of the radiator rose from the grille, he went on eating the cake with his back to Michael, who wished him *bon appétit* again as he ate the last of it.

One of the greatest mysteries of mankind is that Käthe doesn't do any baking. You know what my mother's like. She's afraid Käthe lets you two go hungry.

Thomas nodded, agreeing with him; he rolled up the paper and let the crumbs trickle into his mouth.

A narrow ray of light fell through the curtains onto the brass picture frame, making it look golden. His radiance comes, his radiance goes. Thomas pointed to the black-and-white photograph. An altar to His Majesty, explained Thomas, pointing solemnly up at Walter Ulbricht; he bowed reverently to it and offered Michael the armchair. We have a desk with its only drawer locked, we have a bed that isn't used, we have air that isn't moving. His stomach was grumbling; more and more often these days, Thomas felt hungry directly after eating. It might be better not to eat any cakes, and particularly not to eat the love of other people's mothers. Thomas filled his pipe with the herbs that Michael had grown in his greenhouse on the plot of land near the woods and dried in the loft of his parental home.

Let's paint the walls black. Thomas pointed to the two buckets of paint in the middle of the room. The colour wasn't dark enough yet; he tipped black powder into the viscous paint and stirred it in with the long handle of the scrubbing brush. As he puffed the pipe Thomas kept his gums closed and enjoyed the bitter taste cutting through the sweet flavour in his mouth. He handed Michael a broad brush. Under cover of the falling dark, they tarred the air and their mouths, they painted the walls black in the smoke. Thomas spread paint with the scrubbing brush; now the floor was clean and the wall was black. Michael made two newspaper hats and handed one up to Thomas. Thomas stood on the ladder and worked on the ceiling with the scrubbing brush.

The future's unthinkable in a self-contained system. Michael swung his arm well back and stretched so that he could pass the brush over the wallpaper. The Wall will turn us into animals in the zoo.

Thomas laughed at the idea of freedom and the doctrine of frugality. Ulbricht's monkey house.

No monkey has to go near the fence.

No lunatic has to climb a wall.

Keep quiet and be good. Michael bent and dipped his brush in the black paint.

No one's forced to take a jump into the water and venture into the muzzle of a cannon.

Their anger alternated between bitter grief and silliness. Their hair and shoulders were black now.

Death to the tyrant!

They would stay in this room for the rest of their lives. A bunker in prison, no one would dare to drag them out of the crypt where they were buried alive and into a class struggle, it wasn't their struggle and they didn't want to be the class. An airgun fired more than just gas into the world. You could use it to kill.

The first shot broke the protective glass; it shattered into umpteen pieces, splinters of glass lay on the desk, on the floor, and there were still a few inside the photo frame. The brass sparkled like gold; there was a hole in Ulbricht's cheek.

Let me have a go. Michael laughed and took the gun from Thomas. He doesn't need any eyes now. Michael hit Ulbricht's left eyebrow. They took turns to aim the gun.

Death to the tyrant, death to the Führer, death to the just man. They had been shooting for about half an hour when the door opened, and the figure of Ella showed in the bright light behind her. She looked at her brother, at his friend, at the picture on the wall that was now full of holes.

What are you two doing?

Our life is over! Michael was lying on his back on the floor aiming the airgun. He fired and said: Wall closed, monkey dead.

The swallows have gone this year, there was an epidemic, they abandoned their nests. Do you know the breeding pair of barn owls? Have you seen them soaring through the air? Pipe in the corner of his mouth, Thomas took the gun from his friend, aimed, shot, and handed the gun back.

What are you doing? Baffled, Ella looked from one to the other.

Shooting, explained Thomas. Ella was in the way, she had no

idea what it was all about. He drew on his pipe and blew smoke rings into the air. All that pointlessness has seduced us. We're devout believers now, we believe there's no point in life.

To emphasise his faith Thomas, grinning, put one hand round the other and raised them in the air as a double fist, holding the pipe.

Nonsense. Michael shook his head, he stood up, the gun held loosely in his hand, went over to Ella, raised an admonitory forefinger and said gravely: It has nothing to do with belief, we know it. Michael looked at Ella; you would have thought he was in full possession of worldly wisdom. All he needed was to predict the entry into the earth's atmosphere of a meteorite with absolute certainty. God doesn't think in terms of sense and nonsense, God thinks only beautiful thoughts, added Michael, things of this world were seldom enough for him, God's existence was evident to him in all thinking. Only man, unfortunately, has no talent for beauty, or not usually. He's trapped in functions, intentions, all that nonsense – Michael took a step to one side and threw the airgun to Thomas, who caught it and aimed, keeping his pipe in his mouth. Michael excused himself to Ella; he had to go out for a moment. Thomas shot and immediately aimed a second time. Shot. He took the six-chamber magazine out of the gun and reloaded it with diabolo pellets. Taking no more notice of Ella, he pushed the magazine back into the gun, looked through the sighting notch, drew a bead on Ulbricht's forehead.

You two are crazy! Ella cried. She stumbled against a bucket of paint; it fell over and left trails on the pale bouclé rug. She put her hands on her hips. You pair of stupid nihilists. Stupid, stupid, stupid! Her voice caught in her throat. Are you disappointed to find that we're not in Paradise?

Only pretended sympathy. Exhausted, Thomas grinned at her.

You can keep your daft grin to yourself, idiot!

Michael came back. Right, we were going to paint the rug black as well. He nodded his agreement. All that elegant white was bothering me. Smiling gently, he reached his hand out to Ella. Thanks, Ella, thank you very much.

Ella flinched away like an animal. The hand seemed to her as untrustworthy as his thanks. She stood in the doorway with her legs apart and her arms folded.

But Thomas wanted no female spectator; he closed the door of the room in her face.

Stupid nihilists, shouted Ella through the door.

Thomas thought her anger out of place; he put his ear to the door and heard the tip of Ella's nose still touching the door on the outside, he heard her exhausted breathing, her jealous whispering: stupid, stupid, stupid.

You tell me yours, I'll tell you mine. Thomas bent down to the floor, took a sip from the wine glass and drank to Michael. He took a folded piece of paper from his trouser pocket, holding the glass in one hand; it was difficult to unfold the poem with the other alone. He had written it in pencil and hadn't got round to typing it yet. 'A Call'. The wine was pleasantly rough on his palate. *I tell you, away so far – / I tell you, far away – / Far away on the star: / Here is what I say! / Noisy men stride by, / And much is broken – / The silent weep in silence, / No law is awoken! / Those who stab us, / Judge them now / Who break our eyesight / Judge them too. / Noisy men stride by / Broken freedom was bright – / Blood flows in the pool of water: / Give us light.*

He went to Gommern on his own. Käthe had given him a sketch-pad and charcoal to take with him, bedlinen, a spare pair of trousers, soap. Even from the train he saw the pillars of dark smoke, and soon after that the two chimneys from which they

166

were rising came into view. Going south through the woods, he passed the great wandering dune that lay on the Kulk, one of the oldest lakes filling the stone quarries at Gommern. The sandy soil threw up ripples. The hostel, three huts, stood on the road to the quarry. Behind it was the manager's house. They slept four to a small room, two bunk beds, a table and a locker in each. Thomas was sent to a room with the apprentices. There was an acrid smell of sweat, alcohol, urine, something going bad. You got up at five in the morning when it was still dark, work began at six, gloves were provided. At first sight the apprentices looked to Thomas rather younger than him, one might have been seventeen, like Thomas, the other two were more probably fifteen. Were they apprenticed to learn about stone quarrying? Was that a profession you trained for? The boys made fun of him when he said hello, asking what sort of posh guy he was. No one asked him anything else. Thomas took the free bottom bunk, his bedclothes were too small for the long, scratchy blanket above them, which could have been woven of coarse wool and remains of plant substances. Thomas thought of thistles, he turned to the wall and scribbled words on the sketch pad with his well-chewed pencil. *Instead of silence: lonely helpless pointless / Always beginning – / Always the same / Life, you are death / I am great in the shadows – / I am endless waiting / A small, dirty scrap of fear . . . / Your sphinx eyes are fixed / for millions of years!* Later he closed his eyes, although the neon tube on the ceiling was still lit, and the boys were playing cards. They were bawling. The prize on offer was a certain lady from the Wasserburg. The boys raised the stakes, the atmosphere was heated, in spite of the cold they sat there in their vests sweating. They reminded each other of intimate details of the woman. Her big boobs, her behind, but also how much she obviously enjoyed it. She was the prize for whoever had won at the end of the evening, and the others were going to watch.

In the morning Thomas opened his eyes and heard a splashing as if someone had turned on a tap. But no one was washing. The boy with an ear that stuck out and freckles who had been sleeping above him that night was standing beside the bunk bed peeing. Thomas blinked; perhaps he was wrong. The boys murmured, laughed at a joke that Thomas hadn't heard. He pretended to be asleep.

Someone held an alarm clock right against his ear. Thomas threw back the blanket and was going to slip his shoes on. They were wet with the boy's piss, it was running out over the tongues of the shoes, over the leather and so to the floor, it was trickling through the seams, the boy hadn't aimed straight and Thomas's shoes were standing in a puddle. Six eyes were resting on him. He looked up. Get dressed!

There was nothing to be done; Thomas had no other shoes. Got any ciggies? The youngest boy stretched out his hand to Thomas, patted him experimentally down, his jacket, his trouser pockets. With the bunk bed behind him, Thomas couldn't avoid his hands. What was the boy looking for? Thomas took the packet of cigarettes out of his trouser pocket; the boy snatched it from him.

It was still dark in the stone quarry; they had pickaxes. The water was high in most of the pits, shallow in the later ones, pits had been closed over the last few years as soon as groundwater emerged and rose. The new boy had to show his fins. He was surrounded by the laughter of the apprentices, who had been joined by four other young men. Thomas was the new boy. Show your fins!

Maybe he was a girl, someone suggested, not wanting to undress? Hey, the girlie's coy! They were crowding round him. Scaredy-cat! Their laughter echoed against Thomas's ribs. He was not cowardly, he undressed. His wet, stinking shoes, his shirt, his underpants.

The water was soft and cold. The bottom was stony, obviously the bottom of a former quarry. Thomas showed what his fins could do. The water glowed dark blue, he had never seen water like that before. Maybe it was quartzite that gave the water its colour. When he came out of the shallow lake after a few minutes, his shoes were where he had left them. Ten eyes rested on him, no one was laughing.

Where are my clothes?

Clothes, anyone seen any clothes? Seen her dress anywhere? The boy with the sticking-out ear whose name Thomas had not asked, and he was not going to ask it now, stood in front of him, legs planted apart, the pickaxe swinging in his hand. The boys were roaring. They looked around. A little way off, the group leader was patrolling the ridge between lake and quarry, he blew his whistle, they were not to stand idle. The group leader swung his arm: they were all to come over to the stone quarry. Good luck, he called, the miners' greeting, as if they were miners. Like a monster, the crushing plant towered up among the trees. The young men climbed over the terraced stones, along the rails, and down into the pit. Thomas, naked, clambered after them.

They were to break up the roughly hewn stone into smaller pieces. Thomas would have liked to know the size and shape to which they were to reduce the stones. He couldn't see whether the others knew. For the first few hours Thomas hacked away at the stones, still naked; he was freezing, but he wasn't going to beg. Day was near dawning. A small stone hit his back, a larger one hit his thigh. His knees almost gave way, but he managed to stay on his feet. Don't look, he told himself, just don't look at them. That's what they want you to do. He heard them cracking jokes behind him, the sweat was not pouring off his back but it tingled, making him restless. Without looking up he turned round as he hacked. If they wanted to hit him, he thought, let them hit his head. A gust of wind rose, blowing sand that stung his eyes. His hair was almost dry. When the group leader made his rounds he grinned happily at Thomas. It was as if he knew why Thomas was working naked. The wind puffed out the group leader's jacket. He was wearing boots. Thomas had his wet, urine-soaked shoes on and nothing else.

Around ten there was a new assignment. Along with two men, Thomas was to load the trucks. Both men had crosses tattooed on one forearm, with the words Faith – Love – Hope. One man's cross had rays like the sun, the other was on a hill like a tomb. As soon as a truck was full it was winched up the inclined hoist. Thomas stood on the heap of stones bending and bending until his back hurt. On this first day he was the one to do the bending; he picked up each stone and passed it on to the man with the cross like the sun, who passed it on to his friend with the cross like a tomb, who put it into the truck. After a while Thomas put a hand to his aching back, but the man in front just told him, with a mocking look in his eyes, to get a move on, he'd soon get used to this, work wasn't for the squeamish, and he held out his arms waiting for Thomas to pass him the next stone.

At twelve the group leader blew his whistle for the midday break. Mess-time. Thomas bent down and carried the next stone to the truck himself, since the two men in his chain were already climbing the steps.

What's the matter, the group leader asked Thomas, don't you want to get dressed? Thomas nodded. He was not cold any longer, but he certainly didn't want to climb out of the pit and go to the hut naked.

Go on, then.

Where are my things?

Ooh, lost your things? What a shame. The group leader bit his lip, rubbed one earlobe and grinned. Not hungry?

Thomas shook his head; in fact he was only thirsty.

Well, no slacking, you're not here to dawdle about. If you don't want anything to eat you'd better go on breaking up those stones over there, and he pointed to a heap of roughly quarried stones. As soon as the group leader had disappeared Thomas went looking for his clothes, but he couldn't find them. So he went on breaking stones; he didn't want to freeze.

After their midday break the stoneworkers came back smoking cigarettes and joking. They took no notice of Thomas. Sometimes they broke up stones, sometimes they sat on them, smoking. Around three the group leader whistled. Some of the men could knock off work now, the others were to do overtime. Because winter would be coming in a few weeks' time. The men leaving could go up to their huts. Thomas watched them go. At six the whistle went for the end of the second shift. The remaining men disappeared, leaving only Thomas and the group leader behind.

Cigarette?

Thomas nodded.

Comrade Günter. The group leader offered his hand.

I'm Thomas. He shook hands with Comrade Günter. When he stopped breaking stone the cold crept under his armpit and into every other crook and hollow in his body.

A packet was held out to him. Thomas was about to take a cigarette, but Comrade Günter took it back again. Oh, sorry, don't have many left. The comrade put one in his mouth and tucked the packet away in his breast pocket. It was windy. The group leader cupped his hands round the match, which didn't light. The wind was whistling now. Thomas felt a drop fall on his shoulder, then another. It was raining. The group leader took a step aside, turned his shoulder to Thomas, lit his cigarette and blew smoke out quickly. Aren't you cold?

No, claimed Thomas. The smoke narrowed his pores, he felt a greedy, boundless longing for the bitter-sweet taste, for a warming cigarette.

Comrade Günter drew deeply on his cigarette, blew the smoke in Thomas's face and stepped towards him; he inspected Thomas, his eyes passing over Thomas's smooth, bare chest, and he drew on his cigarette again. It was raining harder now. Thomas heard the lighted cigarette hiss softly. He felt Comrade Günter's breath against his bare collarbone, he heard him begin to say something, then hold his breath, and finally breathe in deeply again. I could help you, said the group leader, and now, with the cigarette in the corner of his mouth, he came even closer, so that Thomas couldn't bend down to hack at the stones. He felt the heat of the cigarette dangerously close. Come on, said the group leader, and he was going to take Thomas's hand, but Thomas flinched away. The group leader's hand landed on his hip, slipped down, dug bony fingers into his naked buttock.

No thanks, no. Thomas clutched the handle of the pickaxe in both hands now. From the distant road, another quiet whistle could be heard. Thomas saw a group of people, heard distant sounds mingled with the wind and rain, maybe another group of workers, young labourers and apprentices on their way back to the hostel after their day's work. The group leader held his cigarette between his thumb and forefinger, he blew the smoke straight into Thomas's face, then salivated noisily and licked Thomas's face slowly. Thomas hardly trembled, but he held his breath and closed his eyes in shame. The group leader's tongue passed over his lips, he clearly heard the man gathering saliva in his mouth again, to leave as thick a slimy trace on his face as possible. Taking small steps, Comrade Günter trod from one foot to the other, and thrust his tongue into Thomas's ear. Thomas heard him salivating, felt the slobbering, it sounded like spitting.

Maybe some other time. The group leader let out a brief, harsh sound, perhaps meant to be laughter. I'm off now, I'm hungry.

The wind blew more strongly, it roared through the tops of the pine trees above the stone quarry and the little poplars, the raindrops were larger now, the poplar leaves rustled and Thomas kept breathing deeply, he didn't want to shiver. The smell of Comrade Günter's spit lingered in his nose. Out of the corner of his eye he saw the group leader climbing out of the quarry up the stone steps beside the hoist. The street lights on the road above had come on. Thomas stopped and did not move. He wasn't going to let the cold get to him. His body was wet, the wind carried not only rain on it but also sand and tiny twigs and leaves that stuck to his skin and flew into his eyes. He was waiting for darkness. He broke stones now to keep from getting even colder. Rain washed the stone, and with the rain the dust disappeared, the air was clear, washed clean, satisfied. It was as if no one had been here breaking stones all day. And why should they? Thomas had stopped asking himself the point of all this. Stones were quarried from the rock of the pit so that up above they could be poured through a funnel into a breaking machine that would crush them with its steel jaws. Maybe they would end up only as ballast and gravel. They were simply broken up small. He could do that now, naked in the rain, he could break them up on his own as darkness fell. No one would see him.

When darkness had fallen over the fallow land here, Thomas climbed up the wet stone.

The boys were playing skat, anyone who won a trick got to drink spirits from a wooden mug painted in the Russian style. Rain beat against the window. And anyone who won a game could drink from the bottle as long as he could without putting

173

it down. Thomas found his clothes in the corner beside the bed; they were sandy, and so was the rubbish bucket they were lying on. The showers behind the manager's house could be reached only with a key after previous application. Thomas washed at the basin; there was a cold-water tap.

A newspaper cutting was pinned on the wall, Brigitte Bardot with her big breasts, the drawing pin went through her throat.

A second bottle of spirits was opened. Thomas put on his underclothes, trousers and sweater. Ella had found a place in the wardrobe department of the Deutsches Theater. She wanted to learn dressmaking. She had gone to the interview in her Pan costume. She had been asked to make a small bag with neat seams in front of the wardrobe mistress, sew on a button and make a buttonhole. To her own surprise, she had succeeded at the first attempt. There were huge rooms in the theatre, Ella had told him enthusiastically, breathing deeply through her nose with her eyes closed again and again, because she liked the smell there so much. She could prepare for her school-leaving exam at the adult education college, which held evening classes for people with jobs. Thomas would help her study when he was allowed to come home at Christmas. Now he lay down under the blanket with his clothes on and closed his eyes, although the noise the boys made kept him awake. He pulled the blanket over his head. Perhaps you could choke on your own breath? Or at least lose consciousness and go to sleep? The Fatherland calls you. Thomas heard that rallying cry, soldiers came marching up, and a band of wind instruments and drums was drilling him. He couldn't march, couldn't get the rhythm of it, he stood still. The soldiers fired their guns, formed a wall around him, came closer, threw their guns his way, he was supposed to take hold of a gun. He couldn't catch one, he didn't want to, the guns hit him, their butts struck his bare body. He wanted to escape, he ran but he couldn't move from the spot, again and again he saw the wall of soldiers in front of him, guns were thrown to him, banners. Fluttering. Drumming. Music blaring. Fanfares. Protect the Fatherland, protect the Socialist Republic! There it was again, loud and clear. What might have been a dream just now reminded Thomas of reality, the hostel, the hut, the room, the bottom bunk bed where he had been trying to sleep. Thomas thought his eyes were encrusted, gummed up. The boys were still talking noisily at the table, bottles clinking, Thomas pressed the blanket to his eyes. Anyone who joined up now could look forward to a place in the Socialist Republic, training, studies. Solidarity and the right role seemed within touching distance. The boys here were determined. They were talking about the women from the prison on the way into the village, high-spirited laughter, skirt-chasers! All the noise circled around the Wasserburg and its female inmates. When Thomas dreamed again, fast asleep, surrounded by silence, he saw Violetta naked as he had never really seen her. Her red hair shone under his hands, he tasted her skin, it was sourish, unpleasant. There was scarcely any encrustation left when Thomas opened his eyes, dim light was coming through the window from a street lamp, it was silent, and he lay sweating under the scratchy blanket. His trousers and sweater were damp with sweat, the hair stuck to the nape of his neck. Thomas heard the boys breathing, snoring. He didn't want to undress, he wanted to be rid of the blanket. Cautiously he felt the scratchy thing. The blanket too was damp on top, crumbly, it smelled of vomit. Thomas withdrew his hand, he sat up, the metal springs of the bed above him scratched his scalp, he ducked. Head down, he looked at his bed in the faint twilight. Someone had thrown up on his blanket while he was asleep. It smelled of spirits and vomit, it was what Violetta had tasted like in his dream.

You don't have to show your fins today, said the older boy in the top bunk as Thomas pulled his sweater over his head. You go diving today.

The other boys laughed. Today Thomas would go diving. Take a header. The pit was over twenty metres deep, but the day before the water had been low, Thomas remembered it, the rocky bottom had kept scratching his stomach when he went full length underwater.

Test of courage, said one of the boys, everyone has to take it. Thomas didn't reply. He heard the voices of the older stone-workers in the next room. Thomas opened the door. He would join the older men before the boys were out of bed.

The group leader decided who had to load trucks down in the quarry, and who stood on the edge of the pit by the funnel, or spread the stones over the load surface of the big truck with a spade. He positioned Thomas at the foot of the hoist today. Muscles, that was the idea. Anyone with poor muscle tone would build it up, crushing and loading the stones. Fitness training, the group leader said, was the name of the game in this position, and like all new trainees Thomas was assigned to fitness training. In the morning he broke and crushed stones. Only after a good hour did he decide to take a sip from his water bottle. When he opened it, the bottle had a suspect smell; someone had peed in it. Thomas asked all the men working with him, but none of them were prepared to give him a drink from their own bottles.

When Thomas, following the others, went back to the hut for the midday break for the first time, a horrible smell of blood sausage met him. Dead Granny – the boys were delighted. Thomas went to the toilets and drank cold water from the tap until his stomach was taut. Then he washed out his water bottle several times and filled it with fresh water. He couldn't eat blood sausage. Potatoes were heaped on his tin plate, and afterwards there was semolina with raspberry syrup. The sticky semolina clung to his mouth, he worked the sticky mass with his tongue and palate, it was like sweetened cement.

Days of rain had left the bottom of the stone quarry underwater in parts. One afternoon, when the first sleet was burning the men's faces and their gloves, shoes and work clothes were drenched, the group leader stationed himself in front of Thomas, his booted legs apart, put his hands on his hips and said: Your turn today. It's dry in the explosives storeroom. The gallery's only eight metres deep. You'll get your kit from the demolition expert up in front. The lads will show you what to do. Thomas obeyed, he propped his pickaxe against the rock and followed the group leader over the terrain. From the demolition expert he got his equipment, a helmet, a box with the explosive in it, a belt to strap the tools on. The demolition expert explained something to him, something about switching on the lamp and the importance of the water. Thomas found it difficult to listen; he was in the clutch of his fear of darkness. Thomas turned at the entrance to the storeroom. The group leader clapped him so hard on the shoulder that it hurt. Just so as you know, not everyone gets to go down, but you do. Whether that was a threat or praise, Thomas couldn't make out. At the moment he felt he no longer knew anything about people, what they said and the meaning of their words. Good luck, he heard the group leader call out his watchword. Thomas put the helmet on. His hand was trembling so violently that he couldn't find the eyelet in the strap. No one here could know how much Thomas feared the dark. There was no Ella for miles, an Ella to scrabble about in the low-roofed gallery for him in return for his doing her maths homework, to put on the helmet instead of him. He was shaking, the rigid fingers of his trembling hands sought the eyelet on the strap of the helmet and couldn't find it.

Want me to help? The group leader laughed, he didn't mean it, he certainly hadn't noticed any knocking of Thomas's knees, however slight; he brought his heavy hand down on Thomas's shoulder for the second time and gave the demolition expert a sign. Thomas went downhill in cramped darkness, groping his way forward on all fours. What had the group leader said about the lamp, how did you switch it on? Thomas couldn't remember if he even had the lamp with him, and if so where. Cold darkness surrounded him. He strained all his muscles, fear forced him on, he worked his way forward, legs at an angle and hurting, feet numb, as if the tension in his limbs had sent them to sleep, he could hardly move them. The deeper down he went, the colder it was. How could he know when the gallery came to an end? Eight metres, said a voice in his ear, it couldn't be long. But he saw no end to it. Nor did it seem to him certain whether eight metres was really the right measurement. The galleries were short, the others had said, they were just below the bottom of the quarry.

He wasn't getting enough air, he felt that clearly, the weakness, the mist in his head, he could be about to faint. He must pull himself together, how often had he heard that, pull yourself together, no weakness, no fainting, no moment of thoughtlessness. Keep thinking, resist the darkness, the Should and Must of the school of socialism, think of your last German essay before the final exams, the flexibility that he should, could, must show. *I was lucky!* He had written that because he had to show that he was worthy to live and study in this society. *I was able to go to school, and my teachers were people who made real efforts to form the personality of the generation now growing up. With their help I realised that this was the time when I too could give something to our human society, could support it in its struggle for the freedom of mankind.* He was hardly struggling himself, his legs like pillars of stone, no more feeling except that his hands hurt when he had to grope his way over the stone with them, he wasn't free, he knew very well what a look at West Germany would reveal. *And I also know only too well the cry of freedom that comes to us from across the border. Over there it means the right of the stronger over the weaker, the right to go hungry, and the right to die a hero's death in pursuit of foreign goods* ... The ins and outs of it were strange, the cold walls of the stone into which he was burrowing as if into the shaft of a tomb, surrounded. What did freedom and goods say, familiar or strange, what could they be to him? *But true freedom is insight into necessity – their struggle is the unconquerable will to liberation of the entire nation, to unlimited rights to all the good things of life for everyone who has earned them.* What had he earned? Darkness, labouring at the stone. *I have come to know life in our Republic, and I have enjoyed all the advantages that can be granted to a young man in this state – I have become what I am now. How often has the term fatherland been misused in the past! The fatherland of a people is where the great mass of it is in the right and is free to choose its fate. Born in this Republic, we owe great obligations to the pioneers of socialism, obligations in the present.* But what was it that he should, could and would do? *The battle for socialism that will be for the good of all mankind. Although contradictions and doubts sometimes emerge in me, and not in me alone, out of the sad situation of our divided country, yet I hope for the victory of our cause, for which I with all my might will fight and which I will defend! I hope I am not alone in knowing it!* He knew how it went, turn away from your own soul, go into silence, endure darkness. No stars shone down here, no icy light from above, deep down in the distance there was a warm glow now, it was no illusion, a light was approaching, taking him into it, he could see his hand, something dazzled him, he closed his eyes, but his own soul was strange to him. Today he knew more about stone and his own being. Perhaps he was dreaming; he was amazed to find that in a dream he could remember his essay, word by word, understand and feel contempt for it.

When he opened his eyes there was no light, no glow. It must have been an optical delusion. He had to lay the explosive, reach the end of the gallery, but symptoms of paralysis were preventing him. Hadn't the explosives man given him gloves? Where were the gloves, why had he crawled into the gallery bare-handed? He waited where he was. Suddenly he remembered where the lamp that the explosives expert had mentioned was: on his helmet. Thomas cautiously felt for it. Sure enough, his fingers found something round. The tip of his forefinger found and pushed the switch until it clicked. But no light came on. The battery must be finished. How long had he been in the gallery? Was anyone calling to him? He heard words in the distance, a call quite close to him. Someone tugged at his shoes, seized his calves and pulled. Out of here! That was the man calling. But Thomas hadn't laid the explosive charge yet, hadn't reached the end of the gallery yet.

His knees creaked, his legs wouldn't obey him, he was scraping over the rock, the man pulled him backwards up and out of the gallery. Warm light made its way past his eyelashes. Confused voices at the entrance to the chamber. The light was dazzling here. What was wrong with him? the men asked, one of them bent over him in concern. Another was raising his legs and took Thomas's feet on his shoulders. The beam of a flashlight dazzled his eyes.

Hello? Hello, can you hear me? I'm Kurt, what's your name?

Thomas moved his lips, which had turned cold and dark; no one could talk with cold lips. The palm of someone's hand slapped his face. A thousand cells burst, his skin swelled up. He ought to say something, show that he was conscious, that he was all right. Another man took his legs, someone grasped his shoulders, he was

180

carried and put down again, they leaned him up against the steep wall of the stone quarry and shouted at him. He opened his eyes.

Someone took his water bottle off his belt and sprayed his face with water. He had ten minutes to recover, they told him. He smelled blood in his nostrils and kept his sleeve in front of his face, so that no one would see when it began to flow. Putting his head back, he leaned against the rock and felt a fine trickle of blood running down his throat. Be brave, he heard Käthe say, he saw her before him and the glow of hope that she inspired in him.

Eyes closed, he crawled on far into the darkness. Water splashed in his face again. He couldn't open his eyes, didn't want to. Had he failed? Was he nothing but a coward to her? Without gloves – there was no missing the indignation in the group leader's voice. A beginner, said other people. No guts, that's for sure, some of the others said. Thomas kept his eyes closed, he didn't want to see their faces. He crawled into the gallery, he tried to turn round but the gallery was narrow, he came up against stone everywhere. As long as he could hear the man behind him, it went on. He saw nothing ahead of him now, not even his own hands, he himself had become the last to cast a shadow. His own shadow pointed into the darkness, no outlines were visible. Thomas was filled with fear. He thought of Ella, who would surely be sitting in a huge workshop flooded with light, in the middle of brightly coloured fabrics, sewing tiny little bags, each prettier than the last. In spite of the gathering cold in the rock, Thomas was sweating, his sweat, wet and cold, ran down under his armpits into the fabric. He crawled on, his eyes were streaming, perhaps only because, even wide open, they couldn't see any more light.

Someone hit the soles of his shoes, telling Thomas to take his helmet off.

In the distance, Thomas heard an explosion, and jumped.

And don't take fright, there are explosions all the time, small, harmless detonations. Nothing to worry about, we're all right here.

Thomas nodded again. He took off his helmet. Someone must have taken the box with the explosive away from him. Presumably another man had been sent into the gallery now, someone who knew his way around. Thomas tried to stand up. He reached for the pickaxe leaning against the rock next to him, which he thought must be his. He tried to take a deep breath of air, but there wasn't any, or so it seemed to him. He mustn't turn round, that wouldn't be any help now, he was staggering. He searched his mind for lines of verse that would let him walk forward, go upright. He wanted to cross the bottom of the quarry. *The blaze will die down.* Perhaps his fear forced him, wouldn't let his lungs unfold properly, he breathed and breathed, *it tumbles and falls.* His ribcage was moving up and down, but that wasn't air, or not the sort he knew from the world above. He saw the other workers climbing out of the quarry. Come on out! Last call, everyone out of the pit! Only the group leader and the explosives expert were busy at the entrance to the chamber. Thomas turned his back to them. He dragged himself towards the pile of stones at the southern end of the quarry. They were lying loose all over the ground there. Debris. Maybe you could breathe without air. Ella had told him that was how she dived. While he kept his head above water swimming in the lake, breaststroke, crawl, never diving down, she would suddenly come up, and she sometimes disappeared for minutes on end in the cloudy water. She claimed that she breathed without air down there, she moved her ribcage so that it rose and fell – it was wonderful down there, she told him how dark it was and how safe she felt, not like an amphibian, like an embryo, a small child rocking in the bosom of the lake as if inside the Great Mother, weightless, aimless, without any responsibility for a word or a direction in which to go. Thomas felt gooseflesh. What Ella had described to him as beautiful, like a dream, made him feel uneasy, oppressed him, made him afraid. He thought as little of the cold as of the darkness falling, he couldn't get any air. Detonated rock. Reaching the southern slope of the quarry, he crawled behind the heap of stone, he would find peace here, more peace than up with the workers, in the gallery, or above all in the hut among the rowdy boys, his knees and thighs met stone, sharp points bored into his chest, his hands were rough, paws must feel like that, clumsy, with a blunted sense of touch.

Would he have completed his mission with gloves on? He would rather feel the stones than the dulled, sweaty, leathery inside of gloves that left his hands with an animal smell. He didn't mind if the stone roughened his skin, he picked up fragments large and small, he collected every stone that came to hand. Did quartzite like this have inclusions? If so, what were they? The fine rain was falling harder. The ground shook. Stone thundered, explosive force discharged the tension of stone in his ear. Thomas lay still on his stomach on the floor of the quarry, his view of the explosives chamber was blocked by the heap of stones, he was safe here. He felt the quivering, the breathing of the stone against his diaphragm. The explosives expert and the group leader had set off the charge. Rain pattered down on Thomas.

More rumbling, the earth around him was shaking, small explosions, nothing dangerous, of course, far, near, the stone preserved him, sand filled the air, gummed up his eyes, his nostrils, he had to cough, he would suffocate on the sand, on the darkness, turn to stone.

Dragonflies glittered under the willow tree, glowing red ones;

where the branches bowed down, the sunlight from the Fliess shone up on the slender leaves; a swarm of red and blue, gleaming blue dragonflies; Michael lay beside him, his hair tickled, Michael's delight laughed in his ear, his hand touched Thomas's, the sun flashed in their bodies and eyes. I'd like to know, said Michael, his voice becoming one with Thomas's. His own thought in Michael's words and mouth, his own curiosity on his friend's lips.

His chest was burning. His mouth felt rough with sand, he heard his own rare heartbeat in his ear as it lay on the stone, his head motionless; he rolled a small stone fragment out of his mouth with his tongue. *From somewhere, desired by all, / A spark kindles the shadow. / The light rises, reaches out.* Thirst tormented him. So much that the darkness sank away. He tried to move his toes, and didn't stop until the tingling in his calves and legs showed him that he was alive; he took slow, shallow breaths. Hadn't that man been right? All harmless little explosions, nothing would happen here. If he stayed lying where he was weeks could pass before anyone thought of looking for him. How long had he been lying there? Boundless thirst. Beneath him, on his stomach and near the burning pain, he felt something wet in his navel, on his ribs. He knew he hadn't pissed his trousers, not that. When he could move his arm, he pushed it under his body, felt the moisture and the water bottle. For some reason unknown to him, its contents had poured out between him and the rock. Be brave, hadn't his mother said that when she noticed his hesitation, fearing failure even before he could fail? The only way to defy the cold and darkness was to move. Now he wiggled his toes and stretched his legs, pushed them forward and back until the tingling died down. The working clothes rubbed his skin, the burning pains were coming from the side of his chest, under his arm, no way of moving forward without pain, pain even in silence. Thomas stopped and waited, motionless, he listened to sounds, distant noises. He heard no voices. The men must have knocked off work by now. Friday evening, many apprentices had gone home. And if home was too far away, they went to the Wasserburg and the secret meeting place among the dunes. Thomas did not want to go for walks, nothing attracted him to the Wasserburg, indeed he was frightened of its female inmates. And on no account did he want to come upon men and girls among the rainy, wet dunes. He spent the weekend in the hut, hoping that when the other lads came back they would have forgotten about the test of courage and the header that he hadn't yet taken into the shallow lake.

Writing

Ella leaned back against the stove. She was wearing two pairs of trousers, one on top of the other, a pair of long johns, two pairs of woollen socks and a cardigan over her sweater. The time when she was afraid of drying up was over. The thermometer showed that the temperature in the room was fifteen degrees, and it would probably rise higher. Before Käthe went away she had turned off the heating in the cellar and locked the door. She must have taken the key with her; at least, Ella hadn't found it anywhere. Käthe suspected Ella of wasting heating oil behind her back. Suitcase in hand, pilot's cap on her head, Käthe had said that if Ella really felt too cold she had better heat one of the stoves. It was indeed too cold, and had been for some days. But obviously Käthe had also hidden the key to the coal cellar, which proved impossible to find. A week after Käthe left, Ella had written a letter to the Walter Ulbricht Leuna Works, asking Käthe to write to her or phone her and tell her where the key was. But there was no reply yet; the post could take a week. Maybe all mail was opened by the manager of the works before being passed on to its recipients? Maybe Käthe simply didn't want to answer the letter. She hated requests and begging letters. She thought Ella was not just a parasite but a thief as well. Ella's request for the key to the coal cellar might seem presumptuous to her. It wasn't easy to make it sound respectful enough and yet as casual as possible.

It had been a few more days before Ella ventured to go over to Michael's place. Ella was freezing, and hadn't got out of bed all day. She had put on a cap and a scarf, she had drunk hot tea and broth, and after supplies of both were finished she had drunk nothing but hot water all day. In the end it was too much. She put on several pairs of trousers, looked at the thermometer, which showed minus nine degrees, and found a thick woollen coat in Käthe's wardrobe. Snow was falling as if in slow motion, fine flakes sailing through the twilight. She stood outside the house. Under the apartment where Michael and his family lived there was a butcher's shop. The shutters were rolled down. Steam came from a small air vent, carrying a salty smell of smoked meat. Ella looked up. The lace curtains at the top windows were illuminated from inside, warm light, there must be candles burning there, the family believed in God and Sunday was the first Sunday in Advent. Ella had never been here on her own before. Whenever they had needed something in the past, she had sent Thomas over to his friend's family. Thomas could get anything there. But Thomas was in Gommern and wouldn't come home until Christmas.

Ella, how nice! Michael's mother was glad to see her and asked her in. How was Thomas, she asked, had Ella heard anything? Ella shook her head, no, nothing, there had only been a brief postcard since he left in September. Arrived safely, will write again. However, Thomas had written two long letters to his friend Michael, but Michael, while giving her a friendly smile, kept quiet about their contents. Ella didn't like to ask.

Michael's mother sent her son down to the cellar to fill a rucksack full of coal for Ella.

Would she like to sit down for a minute? Ella nodded unde-cidedly, it was warm in the living room here. Michael's mother was sure she would like tea, or would she rather have some cocoa?

Ella drank, gulping greedily. Michael's mother wrapped up some cake for her too, walnut stollen and dried apple rings. A jar of plum compote so that Ella wouldn't go hungry while Käthe was away. Ella nodded, and took the rucksack from Michael. Michael would help her to carry the things, said his mother as Ella was wrapping her scarf around her hair and her cap, and going to the door. No, Ella assured her, no, it's only two streets, I can manage that. The kind glances of mother and son touched her; the love was for her brother, thought Ella, and was glad to feel some of it rubbing off on her. Did she have enough money? Michael's mother asked as Ella was standing in the doorway, legs apart, stooping forward slightly with the weight of the heavy rucksack. Ella had shaken her head. In fact Käthe had left five marks on the table for her, but she had spent that on a kilo of smoked sprats and a bottle of wine in the dance-hall cafe on the first day. Johnny had carried the tipsy Ella, half asleep, home on his back, put her down outside the door and thanked her for the lovely evening. Ella had slammed the door in his face: she had wanted to sleep and nothing else.

Michael's mother now disappeared into her nice-smelling apartment and came back to the door with the purse containing her housekeeping money. She wanted to give Ella ten marks. Ella said she felt embarrassed to take it, and as she made that claim she imagined herself really feeling ashamed, and sensed that she was succeeding, she was blushing and awkward, indeed, she was looking meekly at Michael's mother's brightly coloured apron. But she took the ten-mark note, folded it and put it in her coat pocket.

Michael's mother touched her cheek as she might have touched the cheek of a poor child. All alone, she whispered. Her soft hand was alarmingly warm. Ella felt herself deliberately making the shame she had conjured up into misery, a yawning abyss of what seemed to her untold depths, she felt tears come to her eyes as she took a faltering step backwards.

Look after yourself, my dear, said Michael's mother. Ella felt dizzy. The cold reinforced the rushing in her ears. Even when she was at home, heating the stove and getting a spoon from the kitchen, she felt dizzy. She stabbed a hole in the screw-top lid of the jar of compote with a knife to let the air out, and opened it. She ate the plums spoonful by spoonful, swallowing two plum stones, drank the sweet liquid until the jar was empty, and leaned back against the stove.

Her stomach ached, the thermometer rose, it was dark outside now. Ella lit a candle and proudly examined the ten-mark note that she had placed on the carpet in front of her. She put her head back until her hair felt hot against the stove; her shoulder blades tingled with heat through all the layers of shirts and sweaters she was wearing.

She heard a sound outside the front door. A rattling, the door was opened. Ella sat there rigid. She wasn't expecting anyone, it was dark outside. Käthe wouldn't be back for another ten days, and she had taken her dog Agotto with her as usual. Also, Käthe wouldn't be likely to come through the front door; she usually parked in the yard, where she unloaded her baggage and then came in by way of the studio or the other flight of back stairs. Ella would have heard the Wartburg. Now the door was being closed. Ella listened, keeping quiet. No one knocked, no one rang the bell, no barking, no one calling out who's there? Should she call out herself, stand up, find out who it was? She didn't dare. The light in the corridor was switched on. She heard footsteps, bumping and banging. The bathroom door was opened, and Ella heard the splashing of a long jet into the lavatory bowl. Someone was taking a long pee. The intruder must think he was alone in the house, because apart from the faint candlelight that no one

189

could have seen from the outside there wasn't a single light on. The stove was hot against Ella's back, she didn't want to move. The lavatory was flushed, more water flowed in, Ella heard it gurgling as if she were right beside it. The lodger. Yes, it seemed he was busy in Hamburg, and the Wall might make it more difficult for him to travel, but he still had a key. He could have passed it on to someone else who worked with him. Steps came closer. But the intruder passed Ella's dark room, probably hardly noticed the candlelight in the bright light of the corridor, went on and opened the door to the smoking room. Now Ella heard a voice talking to itself: *Your mirror is time – / Endless! / Like mine / You are not flesh, life – / you are fear*, and she recognised the voice, *I live on fear – death is boring – / and so are you!* Ella pushed herself away from the stove, stood up and hurried out of her room, running the last few metres down the long corridor. She pushed the door open with both hands and fell into Thomas's arms.

What are you doing here? In her relief, she snuggled close to him.

Ouch, watch out, you're hurting me. Thomas tried to free himself from her embrace, but Ella didn't want to let go.

Oh, I've missed you, dear little brother. You never wrote. I thought you weren't coming home until Christmas.

What about Käthe? Thomas was still trying to get out of Ella's arms.

Käthe, Käthe, oh, away on business as usual. The combine in Leuna wants to give her a bigger, more important commission. Ella rolled her eyes. So off she goes for discussions and preliminary sketches. She won't be back for another ten days.

Please, Ella, let go of me. Thomas grimaced as if he were in great pain, drew in air between his teeth and gripped Ella's arms so that she couldn't keep them round him.

What's the matter with you? Thomas had never before pushed her away so harshly when they were reunited. He was pale, with red rings under his eyes. Have you been crying?

Don't talk nonsense, he said, but Ella didn't entirely believe him. Ah, now his grin was back, a forced grin this time, but it was back. When had it first appeared, when had it wormed its way into her company? That cynical grin, how distant he wanted to show himself. Ella breathed deeply; she didn't want to see that grin.

How about the trolls?

They won't be here until Christmas, they're in that home in Werder. Did he really want to know how they were? No one else asked after the twins, only Thomas. Going backwards and forwards couldn't be good for them, if it hadn't been for Thomas they'd have been forgotten long ago. They probably wouldn't even come back from their home for Christmas. They're fine, they really are. At least, we can suppose so as long as there's no letter.

I've got something. I don't know ... Hesitantly, Thomas pulled at the sleeves of his sweater. The grin had gone.

Got what?

What . . . He looked around in search of something. Ella sensed his eyes looking for Käthe, chasing Käthe and failing to find her.

Don't be like that, tell me what's the matter.

They've sent me home.

Sent you home? Ella couldn't take it in. Wow, that's great!

Why was her little brother acting so strangely? He'd never got up to anything bad, surely they wouldn't have turned him down for labour service? Why wasn't he grinning?

I'm not well.

Not well? Incredulously, Ella looked at her brother. How did he really seem? Did an invalid look like that? Were the rings round his eyes real, pain expressed in those short sentences? People didn't fall ill in this family, at least not physically ill. The body proved itself flawless by enjoying unbroken good health. Moments of weakness were for shirkers. Such weaker vessels attracted pitilessly derogatory nicknames, a kind of advance warning. Those who were capable of coping with life and enjoyed their work were people like Käthe who took a cold shower in the morning all the year round, jumped into the icy waters of the Baltic in February, and stood chiselling away at stone or doing other work in a bikini in summer. For some time Ella had suspected that Thomas was Käthe's favourite child because, apart from his fear of the dark, he had no little aches and pains, there was his radiantly sunny childhood, romantic poetry in his teens, there were the rings, circlets and belts made from brass by Käthe's golden boy, and of course he always got top marks at school. Above all, however, he was never ill. Nothing about Thomas dried out, no need for him to rest and sleep in a sanatorium. And now he said he was ill? Ella felt resentment, heretical derision. What do you mean, you're not well?

Don't laugh. Thomas wrinkled up his nose, looking as if he were about to bare his teeth. The works doctor says it's shingles.

Shingles? Ella rolled the word around on her tongue. Show me. She was going to pull up his sweater, but he held it down in place. You can die of it if the blisters form a circle all round your body! Ella's nostrils flared as her fear rose.

Nonsense. Don't shout like that.

Thomas was suffering, no doubt of it. Ella could hear it in his voice, he was in pain, real physical pain. He sat down in the low leather armchair, Ella knelt on the floor and put a hand on his shoulder. There are old women, you know, witches who can treat that with an incantation, cast a spell and the shingles will go away.

It just has to get better of its own accord. Otherwise I'll be in pain all my life. It mustn't spread any more.

Show me, please.

Only if you promise not to show you're disgusted.

I promise. Ella lifted two fingers as she swore.

And do me a favour, Ella, stop looking at me like a dog. It makes me furious.

I won't look at you like a dog any more. Ella raised her two fingers again and swore.

When Thomas raised his sweater, carefully, holding it up and away from his body, luckily he had the fabric in front of his eyes and didn't see Ella's face. Her silent scream, the open mouth, the look that said she couldn't believe what she saw. She tried to keep quiet, looked at the raised skin covered with blisters, fiery red, yellow in places with pus both wet and encrusted, mauve like clotted blood at some of the edges of the rash. A devastating, horrible burn spreading everywhere, said Ella, clearing her throat. Looks as if you've burnt yourself.

Thomas lowered the pullover.

Where did you catch it?

You're disgusted after all. Thomas was already smiling his forgiveness. He knew Ella too well, she couldn't pretend with him.

Not at all. She waved the idea away, and Ella believed what she said, she already felt objectively cool superiority. I'm not disgusted by anything. But where did you catch it?

Don't worry, it's not infectious.

As he leaned back in the chair and asked if there was anything to eat in the house – and Ella did not mention the plum compote any more than the stollen, which she had not yet eaten, but she

193

planned to keep for herself – all she could think of was what he was bearing, suffering, enduring.

Don't look at me like a dog. Thomas spoke sharply, the beginning of the sentence very quiet, the end of it in a voice not very much raised, but she sensed his anger at her helpless pity.

All right. On tiptoe, arms spread wide like a tightrope walker to make a show of her extreme caution, mocking her poor sick brother, Ella left the smoking room and went back to her own room, where the wax of the candle had run down over the holder and onto the rug. Here she crouched in front of the stove and ate her stollen; smacking her lips with relish she licked the burnt sugar off the walnuts. Let Thomas sit there in his armchair, grinning, let him see who could bear it if she couldn't. He could wait a few more days for Käthe. Would he venture to go and see Michael with his shingles? Or Violetta?

In the morning, when Ella opened the door of the lodger's room, where Thomas had been sleeping more and more often during the prolonged absence of the lodger himself, he was lying on his bed with his forehead wet with sweat and his face distorted. The skin of his face was reddened by strain, with only a white triangle around his nose left free. A sure sign that he was seriously ill. He was biting his pillow to help him bear the pain.

Help me, please, Thomas groaned, turning on his side. The top buttons of his shirt were undone, and Ella could see the rash under it.

What am I supposed to do?

Ella thought about it; she didn't know any doctors. She went into the smoking room and looked in the telephone book, but apart from a vet and a dentist she found only a paediatrician and a GP who didn't have any consulting hours that day.

Get me some painkillers, Thomas called from his room, anything, and maybe the pharmacist can call a doctor. Please!

Ella put Käthe's woollen coat on. She wondered whether to write to Käthe. Maybe a phone number for the Leuna chemical works could be found?

A doctor came in the evening and examined Thomas. He confirmed the diagnosis: yes, it was shingles, and he couldn't say what had caused it or suggest anything much in the way of treatment. Apart from painkillers and powdering the rash, there was nothing to be done for shingles.

As soon as the doctor had left, Thomas was whimpering with pain. Ella stuffed cotton wool in her ears to keep the sound out. But in the middle of the night his screaming woke her. She couldn't bear it, it was sending her out of her mind. She went into his room and shouted at him. Yes, she said, of course it was bad that he was in pain, but if she herself couldn't get a wink of sleep all night either, it wasn't going to help anyone. He'd better bite his pillow, she told him, going back to her room, and she took her quilt and lay down on the sofa on the veranda to be out of earshot. Thomas tried to keep quiet.

Five days later Käthe came back. Although she had gone in the Wartburg, she was wearing her pilot's cap, probably because it was so cold. Agotto was already barking in the yard. He raced in through the doorway ahead of her, wagging his tail. He had jumped up at the door handle and opened it before Käthe came up the stairs with her baggage. There was no greeting, no hello, no how are you? Käthe was indignant. Are you still at nursery school? This is a state commission I have, an important piece of work! Don't you two have any respect for me? Just because one of my children, almost grown up, is ill, I can't drop everything back there! What on earth were you thinking of, sending the manager a telegram? She snorted. Am I a professional mother?

Don't shout at me, Käthe. I thought you ought to know. The works doctor at Gommern sent him home. He's been here for a week now, screaming with pain day and night. Ella ran both hands through her hair, scratching her scalp nervously and energetically. Honestly, I've been sleeping on the veranda the last few nights because I can't stand it.

So where is he now?

Where do you think? In bed, of course.

Of course, of course. People don't go to bed in broad daylight. Käthe took her pilot's cap off and stalked through the smoking room, opened the door to the corridor and called to the rooms off it: Käthe's back, everyone rise and shine!

But no one rose; no one appeared at all.

Ella had seldom seen Käthe so annoyed with her favourite child. Didn't he always do everything right, didn't he say the cleverest things, wasn't he the most handsome boy in the world?

From a distance, Ella heard Käthe finally walking down the corridor. She stayed in Thomas's room for quite a long time. When she reappeared she had changed. Her annoyance had given way to deep concern.

If we don't find someone who can cure this thing he could die, Ella, do you realise that?

For a moment Ella hesitated; then she nodded. I heard of a woman in Erkner. Ella quietly tried explaining her idea. They say she can work magic – with her hands and with spells.

A witch? Käthe laughed heartily and put her blue working jacket on. First you can give me a hand getting the statue out of the car.

Ella looked enquiringly at Käthe. Käthe turned and led the way downstairs and into the yard, where her Wartburg was standing with its tailgate open. A monster wrapped in cloths and a blanket, all tied up with coarse rope, lay on the folded-down rear seat of the estate car. A smell of wet dog came from the car. Presumably Agotto had had to lie beside the statue on the way.

The plaster wasn't even dry when I had to set out. But it was wonderful, the Brigade there had never seen anything like it. The director's eyes popped out of his head. Along comes Käthe to show them what art is! Käthe spread her arms wide. Careful, take it by the plinth. No, wait, turn round. Käthe harassed Ella, making her go this way and that, she was to hold on more firmly, bend her knees sooner, more to the left, and be careful where she was treading when she walked backwards. It was the same as usual, as if Ella were helping her for the first time. Every order struck home. No sooner had Ella put the plinth carefully down on the wooden turntable, pulled away the blanket from under the stand and undone the packaging from below, to help Käthe get the statue erect, than Käthe said impatiently: Go a little way to the side, and pushed the statue towards Ella. Ella caught the package in both arms. Two heads came into sight, the bodies scarcely separated yet. A dancer with two heads. Maybe two dancers who were still merged together. Ella could already guess whose leg would belong to a man or a woman later, one of the woman's legs was coming away from the bulk of the rock at the back, one of the man's legs was wound round her. They shared a body, their heads were separate.

Do you like it? Käthe was watching Ella's expression. This woman in Erkner – well, why not? Erkner, that's some way to go. I have things to do here. You'd better take your bike and cycle there. We want the woman to cure Thomas.

Ella nodded. She rode her bicycle to Erkner to fetch the woman who could work magic.

The woman couldn't come until the following day, because she worked on Saturday and had to fill the shelves after the shop closed. She was a sales assistant in a grocer's shop in Erkner.

You don't think I can work magic, you don't think that, do you? said the woman, reassuring herself as she came through the doorway and shook hands with Käthe. She looked anxious. Ella was curious; she had never seen a real witch at close quarters before.

We think only the best of you. Käthe led the woman to Thomas's bedside. Ella draw back the curtains. In full daylight the sales assistant looked even slimmer. Shyly, without any grand gestures, she took off her patterned green headscarf and her fine white gloves. She had delicate, slender fingers, she wore thin tights under her pleated skirt, and she had slightly bandy legs with graceful ankles. Her feet were in flat patent leather shoes. Hesitantly, she unbuttoned her coat, which so far no one had taken from her. Ella saw no warts, no hairy chin, no evidence, however small, that this was the genuine enchantress she had hoped for.

I'm not a witch. The sales assistant looked at Käthe and then back at her patient. Thomas was blinking in the bright light.

You've helped other people. Go ahead. Käthe was not just expressing confidence; it sounded more like an order. Without a word of goodbye Käthe left the room; she probably had to go down to the studio where her dancing couple was waiting. She had worked on the thing with wax half the night, the plaster had been mixed, the carving was as good as done, she'd even been promised a place at the foundry next month. Two naked models would be sitting downstairs in the studio, waiting for her. Time was pressing.

The sales assistant looked around for something.

Do you need anything? Ella wondered whether the sales assistant would want a cauldron or some herbs for her magic.

Well . . . The sales assistant looked down, not at Ella.

Take her coat for her, please, groaned Thomas from his bed. His voice came hissing through his teeth so that anyone could guess at his pain. He braced both fists against the mattress to help himself sit up.

May I? Ella took the sales assistant's coat, and the slender little woman stowed her headscarf and gloves away in her handbag.

Would you, the sales assistant's voice was getting quieter and quieter, so that Ella had to stand still to make out what she was saying, would you leave us alone, please?

Why . . . and Ella wanted to ask, why should I? But she bit the words back and said: Why not? Ella left the door wide open; she didn't want to miss anything. As she hung the sales assistant's coat up on a hanger, she heard the door to Thomas's room being closed behind her. Wasn't she a witch herself? Didn't she know as much about herbs as this sales assistant? Maybe more. What was the woman supposed to know that she didn't know? She could hardly hear her voice through the door. After a few remarks had been exchanged, there was silence. Ella pressed her ear to the door, she couldn't hear any rustling, any voices. Once she heard a footstep. After a long time that seemed to Ella like an eternity, Thomas said something that she couldn't hear properly. She moved away from her listening post on tiptoe, and waited at the end of the long corridor for the door to open.

There you are. The woman stepped out into the corridor and looked around her.

Do you need to go to the lavatory?

What? Oh no, I was looking for my coat.

Here it is. Ella went to the coat stand and handed the sales assistant her coat. Well?

What did you say? The sales assistant put her coat on.

Well, has it gone away? Have you cured him?

I'm sorry, the next few days will show. The slender woman took her headscarf out of her handbag and put it on.

We can't wait. Ella opened the front door for the woman with a deep bow. The sales assistant did not take much notice of the bow, but stepped over the threshold. Outside the door, she turned to Ella.

It would be a good thing if he didn't have to go back to that stone quarry, you know where I mean, to Gommern, she said quietly, and with a slight smile she shook hands with Ella.

This was not the way Ella had imagined a witch. She took the big silk scarf that no one must touch or wear but Käthe herself – it had been given to her a few years ago by the French boyfriend of her youth – off the coat stand. She draped the scarf over her head and went into Thomas's room. Whooooooo! Hocus-pocus, abracadabra, when shall we three meet again?

Oh, leave me alone. Thomas was sitting on the edge of his bed, as weak as ever. Ella asked what the woman had done, how she had worked magic. She had only put her hands on his shoulders, said Thomas, she hadn't even touched his rash, no spells and incantations, or not aloud anyway. Ella couldn't believe it.

Maybe I can do better. Can I have a go? Ella raised her hands as if conjuring up spirits. But to Thomas it was serious; she had better go away.

While Käthe was finishing the *Dancing Couple*, and Ella was in her room trying to burn small lumps of resin – she had scraped them off the bark of trees in the summer and kept them in a box – to try out her own powers of witchcraft, Thomas's rash turned darker and formed scabs. The resin didn't burn, it only sweltered and turned black where the flames had licked it. Ella invented magic words: Guttlenuts and Shatzlebrutz.

After tomorrow we can all go back to our work, stated Käthe, relieved, at the end of the second week. They were sitting at the supper table, together with a certain Susanne and a certain Kalle, models for the *Dancing Couple*. What did I tell you? Käthe proudly looked round the table. Thomas's rash had dried up and the scabs were already coming off many places on his skin. The magic powers of the sales assistant from Erkner had proved their worth. There was no doubt that Thomas's cure was all due to Käthe, it was her success. Ella wondered how she could let it be known that she, too, had powers of witchcraft.

I know a fairy who works magic, I gave her a quick call, and guess what, Thomas is better now! You just have to know what will help. Pass the butter.

Susanne passed Käthe the butter. A real enchantress?

Well, it helped, anyway. You'll be taking the early train to Gommern tomorrow, won't you, Thomas?

Thomas sat hunched at the end of the table. He was chewing his coarse wholemeal bread very thoroughly, and had taken no part in the conversation yet.

Thomas?

Thomas nodded obediently; he wanted to have chewed the bread well before he opened his mouth. Since he ate so slowly, the conversation had usually got away from him before he could contribute to it.

What they do there is just fabulous, Käthe now told her guests happily. They're bringing stones from all different eras to the light of day, the famous quartzite and slate of the Lower Carboniferous period, fine sandstone from the Pleistocene. Truly unique. Well, of course Ulbricht hopes we can be independent and find our own oil – for Ulbricht, there has to be that bit of hope. But for scientific research it's all gain. Do say something, Thomas.

What do you expect me to say?

Since you've been home you haven't told us anything about Gommern. A piece of cauliflower fell out of Käthe's mouth; she wiped her greasy lips with the back of her hand.

What do you expect me to tell you? We're just breaking up stones, hauling them to the truck or taking them to the next station. Thomas was smiling like an angel.

Don't play it down. You're acting as if you were a building worker.

Not at all, I don't build anything. Quite the opposite, I'm hacking away to destroy the earth. A miner, maybe, no, not even that. I just help, I just lug stones about. Bored, Thomas yawned. He put his hand in front of his mouth and looked gloomily across the table with his sick eyes.

Children! Without deigning to give him so much as a glance, Käthe made a brief and clearly dismissive gesture in Thomas's direction; she turned cheerfully to their two guests, not much older than Thomas and Ella, who had spent the day modelling for her. Didn't you say you're studying economics in Karshorst now? That's amazing! Käthe drew the cauliflower salad towards her and ate what was left of the stem straight from the bowl.

Since Susi's been a Free German Youth leader we're on the move round the clock. And we're doing handicrafts too, making things for the Christmas market, and going into the schools in January.

Making things for the Christmas market? Käthe articulated the words Christmas market as if they evoked Popocatepetl. Her mouth had dropped open. But why?

We do our bit everywhere, you know that. The Free German

Youth goes into the factories, into the schools, among the people, everywhere. Susi sipped her wine, smiling.

Terrific. Fabulous. That's what I call fabulous. Käthe seemed relieved at first. Then she stopped and thought. But how do you manage to study as well?

Oh, working with the Free German Youth is fun, said Susi, putting her glass down.

And but for the Free German Youth it wouldn't have been so easy to get a place to study. Kalle spoke with a heavy Berlin accent; Käthe liked that, and was tempted to emulate him. But it was clear that she had had difficulty in understanding exactly what he said. How was she to react? She knew that Thomas was obstinate enough to decline to join the youth organisation. And even with the prospect of taking her final exam as an inducement, Ella had made the mistake of leaving it again.

If we got places to study at all, Susi pointed out.

I believe you! Käthe looked past Thomas and Ella, an expression of reproof in her eyes. Two clever young people sat there before her who supported the Republic and did not, like her children, refuse to lend a hand.

In mid-December Thomas came back to Berlin from Gommern for the second time, only a week earlier than expected. But he had been sent back because of a recurrence of his rash. Once again the sales assistant from Erkner who worked magic had to be called in, and the doctor came to see Thomas as well. On the same day the phone rang. After a long illness he had passed away, were the words with which Käthe's mother gave the news of her husband's death. Perhaps it should be described as a blessed release, he didn't have to suffer any more. He had been Käthe's father the professor, the Vati she revered, she didn't believe in blessed releases. She sat at the table in silence, staring at the tablecloth.

Her brother Paul and his family were coming from America for the funeral, and her sister Erna and Erna's husband were coming from England, so the professor's son and younger daughter would both be here. However, the German Democratic Republic wasn't going to let them into the country on flimsy grounds. The family did battle with all means at its disposal against formalities, documents were certified, sent off, file numbers were communicated, and two days before the funeral the entry permits were granted. For the funeral, and between Christmas and New Year, Uncle Paul's family and Erna with her husband stayed with Käthe. Käthe warned her children not to tell their relations about Thomas's illness in case they feared infection. She was obviously embarrassed by the fact that Thomas was ill. As their beds were needed for the visitors, Thomas and Ella had to share a bed with Käthe. In the daytime Ella lay on the sofa on the veranda, dozing; the door of the smoking room was open, and she couldn't help overhearing a conversation between Käthe and her sister Erna.

Who keeps house for me when I'm earning money?

Surely Ella and Thomas don't get up to any mischief? Erna whispered.

Thomas is eating me out of house and home, hissed Käthe softly, and Ella lies and steals whenever she can. How am I supposed to pay for it all? The rent, the stones, a studio, it all costs money. Haven't I been bereaved?

Not in the eyes of the law.

I mean as a widow, from back in the past.

You weren't married to him.

But we loved each other.

Erna said nothing in reply to that, and Ella didn't see what she could have said.

After a moment when they were both silent, Käthe whispered: Aren't I entitled to anything?

Perhaps Erna pressed Käthe's hand. You're strong, you can work.

Of course I can work, no question about that. Käthe was getting heated. She could easily get annoyed with Erna, with her immaculate respectability as a married woman and her part-time job as a teacher. To Käthe, her sister's life was the quintessence of a secure existence. But I need money to work as well, I don't have a wife to look after my children. By way of reply Erna started crying. Was she shedding tears of sympathy or of shame for her own better situation? Käthe came marching firmly out on to the veranda, and saw Ella there with her eyes closed. Don't just lie around idling like that, you'll sleep half your life away. There are dishes to be washed in the kitchen. Get up, Pimpernel, off you go.

Käthe had bought an enormous carp for New Year's Eve; Ella and Thomas feared that carp every year. While Käthe was gutting the carp in the kitchen, and her sister Erna was supposed to be helping her to clean the vegetables and peel the potatoes, Uncle Paul and Thomas were playing badminton in the smoking room. Uncle Paul had suggested moving the big table into the next room so that they could run back and forth more freely. He showed Thomas the way he served. Ella sat in front of the radiator, with no one taking any notice of her, rolling a ball of wax with the palms of her hands. Her eyes kept closing, and then she heard the whoosh of the shuttlecock in the air, heard its springy ping and then the firmer plop as it fell.

Thomas was not to put himself under any strain, the doctor had said only just before Christmas, to speed his recovery from shingles, but no one forbade playing games, so Thomas was leaping into the air, bright red in the face. Uncle Paul spoke with a strong American accent, as if he hadn't been born and gone to school in Germany. You have to jump higher!

Thomas jumped higher.

Faster!

Thomas jumped faster. Ping. Plop. Plop. Plop.

Once Thomas stumbled, gasped for breath and collapsed. Uncle Paul crouched down beside him. In concern, he put his hand on Thomas's shirt, which was wet with sweat. He patted his nephew like an animal. Oh boy, you're not on good form.

Thomas shook his head.

Oh boy, repeated Uncle Paul, nodding sadly. Sport is so important. How are you going to study if you don't keep fit?

I want to get out, whispered Thomas.

What did you say?

Out, Uncle Paul. Out of here. O.U.T.

You mean? Uncle Paul looked around as if he feared someone might be listening to them. Only now did he see Ella, but he just smiled at her briefly, bent over Thomas and said: You know perfectly well you can't do that to your mother. She loves you.

Thomas sat up, supporting himself on the floor with one arm, blew back his fringe and wiped the sweat from his brow with the back of his hand. In the middle of his overheated face, a white triangle stood out around his nose. Something was running down his cheek, Ella couldn't be sure whether it was sweat or tears.

You can help me, Uncle Paul.

But Uncle Paul shook his head. Your mother will get you a place to study, you wait and see.

Please! Now Thomas gripped his uncle's arm and held it tight. He was gasping. Please.

At this point Ella threw her ball of wax in Thomas's direction, but although she hit him on the leg with it neither of them took any notice of her.

Thomas, that won't do. His uncle pinched Thomas's cheek as

if he were an impudent little boy. I'm sorry, Thomas. He stood up and gave Thomas his hand to help him to his feet.

Can't someone set the table? Käthe opened the door. Do get a move on! Isn't anyone going to bring the table back in? We'll be ready to eat in ten minutes!

On New Year's Day all the visitors left after breakfast. It was not Käthe's style to go to the door with her guests. Whether or not they were family members, whether they had stayed the night or only an hour, they all had to open and close the door for themselves. Käthe was testing the dampness of her Rosa, a clay figure on which she was working in these winter weeks and which stood on the veranda, wrapped in pieces of cloth. The brim of Rosa's hat kept breaking off. Käthe was annoyed by her inability to force the clay to do what she wanted.

As soon as she heard the door latch behind her departing family, Käthe heaved a deep sigh, said: *L'ospite è come il pesce, dopo tre giorni puzza,* and without another word set to work.

In spite of a second visit by the shop assistant from Erkner, this time Thomas's recovery was slow.

He had become familiar with the pain of his skin over those weeks. Thomas wondered if there was a condition beyond loneliness and pain, beyond cold and the stars, a place where he wouldn't be seen by anyone, wouldn't taste piss in his mouth, wouldn't hear anyone bawling in his exhausted ears, and wouldn't have to be anyone's poor boy.

On New Year's Day he woke up without pain for the first time. Thomas wondered what they had paid the woman. He looked at his ruined skin and fanned it with his sweater. His nerves felt exposed, sometimes the wind cooled him, sometimes it burnt him.

Paid her? Ella shrugged her shoulders. No idea. Anyway, I didn't give her anything. Perhaps she was asked to choose one of Käthe's little reliefs?

No, seriously: what did Käthe give her?

The first time, Käthe said hello to her when she arrived and I said goodbye. And the second time Käthe wasn't there at all. Don't you remember, she was with her painter friends beside the lock that day? I spoke to the sales assistant, I let her in. So if that's what you're asking me, no, she didn't get anything.

What sort of people are you? You can't just ask the woman to come here and not give her anything.

You might have thought of that yourself. Ella wasn't accepting a reproof. Anyway, she had doubts of the efficacy of the sales assistant. Guttlenuts Shatzlebrutz, she could work much better magic herself. How do you know she was the one who cured you? I did it: Guttlenuts Shatzlebrutz.

That's pathetic. Downcast, Thomas shook his head. Whether the rash goes away entirely again this time or not, she started the improvement, twice. She has to be thanked. Thomas ran his hands through his hair. I'll go there.

Look out of the window. It's snowing, it won't get properly light at all today. Maybe a real witch doesn't accept payment, hmm? She can make you better by magic if she wants to. Maybe taking money is against her honour?

Then I'll send her a thank-you present. Thomas brought out the cardboard box in which he kept the bracelets and rings he had made himself from under his bed.

Are you crazy? You're not going to give her that bracelet, are you? Don't you remember, that was the one you promised to me?

Dismayed, Thomas turned the bracelet in his fingers. Did I? He seemed to have something on his mind. Sometimes I feel afraid I'm forgetting things.

You mean you hope you are. Ella laughed. You hope you're forgetting me. You're not giving that woman any of those things. Or not unless you want to forget me.

But we must give the woman something. Are you sure Käthe didn't give her anything?

I'll just go and ask her, said Ella, walking out of the room. Käthe had been down in the studio all day, and hadn't even come upstairs to eat.

Agotto was lying on the back stairs, wagging his tail. Käthe didn't like to let him into the studio, because he disturbed her work.

Ella opened the door and went downstairs. *What to some are happy dreams* . . . it wasn't often that Käthe listened to pop songs; perhaps she hadn't been in hearing distance or had changed the radio station by accident . . . *what to others* . . . Before Ella reached the bottom step she could see Käthe's bare breasts hanging down to the floor, heavy as melons, almost as if she were mopping up dust with them . . . *hard cash means* . . . Freddy Quinn, 'La Guitarra Brasiliana', Käthe on all fours, head down, backbone slightly bent, naked and grunting. Behind her knelt a man whom Ella didn't immediately recognise. Shocked, she went up the stairs again backwards, step by step, without turning round, quietly, making as little noise as possible, she opened the door and closed it behind her. Agotto jumped up at her, licked her hands and whimpered.

Well, what does she say? Thomas came into the kitchen, went past Ella and over to the larder.

Nothing, she's grunting.

What?

Ella followed Thomas into the larder. She's grunting. Go and see for yourself. She's crouching on all fours and grunting, along with a naked man. Ella laughed, and made a graphic gesture with her hands.

Thomas raised his eyebrows; he didn't look at Ella's hands, he looked into Ella's eyes. He felt uncomfortable. Aren't there any apples left?

All sold out. There may be some more in spring. But there's dried apricots, sweet and juicy. Ella climbed on the narrow stool and reached purposefully for a tin on the shelf. Käthe keeps them hidden from us up here. Before she climbed off the stool she opened the tin and handed it down. Thomas took it. You don't mind maggots, do you? There are a few little maggots in there, but they have to live on something too. She ought not to have said that, she knew as soon as the words were out of her mouth. After all, maggots were living creatures.

In revulsion, Thomas gave her the tin back.

Do you want to save the maggots? No? Ella took an apricot out and put it in her mouth. Delicious.

Thomas turned away. I'm hungry.

They had spread newspaper on the big table in the smoking room and peeled the wrinkled, softened potatoes as well as they could. Where they were sprouting, Ella broke the sprouts off.

Potato soup for the New Year.

Go over to Michael's, I'm sure they'll give you a cut off the joint there. Ella threw a piece of potato peel at Thomas's head.

Thomas threw one back at her. Not today, the whole family is visiting.

Well, aren't you part of the family? Ella pouted, making her mouth look like a beak, and pretended to be sympathetic.

Not entirely.

Ella picked up each peeled potato separately, examined it, and cut out the dark eyes with a knife. Nightshade, she said, and repeated the word, nightshade. Potatoes belong to the nightshade family. You know everything, why are they called that?

Good evening. Käthe's fluting tones were accompanied by the barking and whining of Agotto as he stormed in. The way he licked their hands reminded Ella of the naked man down in the studio.

Ella craned her neck to see whether anyone was following Käthe. But there was no one else, the door latched, Käthe sat down.

Why are you two in such a dismal mood?

We're not in a dismal mood, just wondering what there is to eat today. We found some potatoes and that was all. They cut the potatoes in pieces.

Oh well, then one of you must go shopping. And do some work, right? Käthe was rubbing her hands, but there's time for that.

Ella rolled her eyes.

I have some good news. Listen to this.

What?

Roguishly, Käthe looked from Thomas to Ella and back again. Thomas can't possibly go back to Gommern again. He'll just fall ill, and that won't do.

Ella and Thomas looked at Käthe in surprise. She took her time, the pause lasted too long.

Then what? Thomas uttered a nervous laugh.

I'm not really allowed to talk about it. You must promise me that this will stay between us. Promise?

They were to be Käthe's accomplices. Promise, said Ella and Thomas in unison.

Well, Thomas, there are certain prospects of your getting a place to study medicine.

Medicine? Thomas forgot to blink, and suddenly his eyelids were fluttering. Had he understood Käthe correctly? Medicine was for those who toed the Party line, the children of officers, those who proved their worth in other ways than just getting brilliant results in their school-leaving exam. Thomas couldn't believe his ears.

In Berlin. Käthe nodded proudly. What did I tell you? Your Käthe will find ways and means. She was singing the words out, carried away by her own joyful news.

And you think of something like this . . . Ella hesitated, wondering if it was fair for her to doubt . . . something like this in the middle of the holiday season? I mean, the phone hasn't rung once today. This is New Year's Day. So how do you know this now?

Hush, don't ask silly questions. Käthe cut Ella short. You're pleased, Thomas, aren't you?

Thomas nodded, yes indeed, he managed to smile. He had learned to do that. The way he looked at her, his silky lashes cast down, his eyes hidden behind them. He felt there was something uncanny about her now, the woman he loved so much. The astonished Ella looked Käthe straight in the face. But how do you know?

Don't be so inquisitive all the time. Käthe put her head on one side, looking mysterious. As with the naked man who had been kneeling behind Käthe in the studio, Ella felt laughter rising in her, but she suppressed it. She could be serious, pretend to be serious if necessary, she could pretend anything. She poured water into the pan of potatoes and put it on the stove. Ella wondered whether the naked man in the studio had been the lodger. But then wouldn't she have recognised him? It had been only for a fraction of a second that she saw him, how familiar can a face seem to you in a fraction of a second? Had she recognised someone? Him? Her head was in turmoil. So Käthe's golden boy was getting what his heart desired, had desired? But he wasn't jumping for joy, his muscles had wasted during his illness, especially, so it seemed, the muscle of his heart. Ella felt uneasy. The dry air of winter sent her crazy, when she let her hair hang over the table dandruff fell out, like snow, she picked it up with a fingertip and put it on her tongue. The Host, wasn't that what you called it? Give me this day thy holy bread? Why should she, Ella, be jealous? Jealous of the golden boy.

But you must do a period of practical training, of course. You must work in a hospital for a few months, you know that?

Thomas obediently nodded. His smile had long ago vanished.

You are pleased, aren't you? A shadow of cautious doubt appeared in Käthe's eyes. Had she misjudged her darling? Wasn't she bringing him joy?

Yes, he said firmly, yes, I'm pleased. Just tell me, would you, who's behind it?

It's thanks to your grandfather, said Käthe, a mysterious gleam in her eyes. She pointed to the ceiling, probably meaning heaven.

Of course, why had no one thought of him before? The soul gone to heaven. What use was a professor as a grandfather, a great and illustrious mind? Maybe Käthe had spoken to someone of importance at the time of the funeral, made a contact, been able to fix something for her golden boy? Thomas's strained face showed no joy. Ella felt sure that he had never thought of studying medicine before. The human body interested him less than any plant, any animal. Maybe he had once mentioned that he would be interested in studying botany, that was the name of the course of study he would have dreamed of if he had dreamed at all. But presumably Käthe hadn't noticed. A place to study medicine must seem to her like a big win on the lottery, a win achieved with the help of the lodger's friends.

Later, Ella lay on the bed in the room that the lodger hadn't used for months. Thomas, like a hermit crab, had taken the room over, since he had no other room of his own in the house. Ella listened to the clacking of the typewriter. She had almost finished the wine in her glass, and put it down beside the bed. The clack of the typing sounded like heels going clickety-clack on paving stones, sending messages in Morse code, enticing you. Only the muted light of the desk lamp shining on his hair lit the room. Ella could think of no one she would sooner be close to than

Thomas. Lying on the bed, listening to him writing, being with him in his light. How could he help it if Käthe loved him so unconditionally?

Read to me.

Thomas turned round. Holding the sheet of paper in his hands, he began: *To Morning: I have lines on my face.* His voice faltered, he crossed something out with a pencil and wrote in something new. *The rest is great, immensely deep, / with lines on the outside. / Inside there are torn places, and a letter / to my dream of yesterday. // The dream was my word, my song and my life / Filled until then by a draught of hope; / Now I have woken – to a day with no scope / for dreams, that hope wasted on the eternal day. // The loud voices around me / are tinny, scornful in my ears. / No one asked me, I was born / guiltless, of night-time fears. / What's the use of echoing / others' loud and cheerful singing? / Inside, in the end, I am at . . .* How often had she lain like this, letting his words cradle her? The wine made her arms, her forehead and her lips tingle pleasantly.

Are you asleep? Thomas was leaning his hands on his knees, his voice was loud now. She must have nodded off without noticing. You're not interested. Thomas put the sheet of paper back on the desk.

Yes, I am, of course I'm interested, go on reading, I wasn't asleep.

Don't tell lies, you were snoring, loud strong snores.

Ella couldn't help giggling. Wearily, she turned her head from side to side. Her eyelids felt so heavy that she couldn't even shake her head.

Can you actually listen without falling asleep? Thomas rubbed his eyes.

Of course I can. Ella sat up with a vigorous movement, and her head fell forward. I saw a smile on your face, she pointed to him, there, I knew it, I spotted it. In between the lines. A smile you didn't want to show. I know, Ella closed her eyes, I mean, who wants to smile? You were fond of Grandfather, weren't you?

Thomas breathed in deeply and audibly. Did he have to be patient with her? Ella made her own sense out of his poems; it had as little to do with understanding them as simply listening to them. She just couldn't listen, she knew that herself, and she couldn't help it.

We're all saddled with our own guilt, innocent only when we're born. Was that a preachy note in his voice? Was he going to deliver a sermon now?

Oh yes? Ella smiled a tipsy smile; sometimes Thomas thought in a very simple, almost plain way.

I did love him, yes. The childish side of him, his bib, the way he dribbled, his hearty laughter when we went to have a meal with the grandparents. Words like bockletop, suddlefoot, snickety-snack, he invented them in the first place, do you remember? He talked to us like that for days when we were little. *Covered with the scabs of wounds / In the grip of frozen snow.*

Ella shook her head. She had not loved anything about Grandfather, not the professor or his childish side. With the best will in the world she couldn't see what her brother saw in him. Perhaps her will just wasn't strong enough. How often was it? Ella found it hard to hide her amazement at the love he suddenly said he had felt, or at least had unexpectedly expressed. If they saw their grandparents two or three times a year, that was often enough.

What does often mean? Love doesn't observe the frequency of opportunities. *And very rarely, sometimes, I forget myself, / as I dare to remember. / As it came, so it goes, / under the pressure of petty things. / I cannot hold it fast, that lovely, lost / ruined dream in the past. / Only the letter I wrote him in his grave / I remember painfully*

well. // The words are burnt on my mind / they are my only faith — /
Now you must forget — it says there, in the blood — / Forget, be silent,
wait!

So that's the end of your poem. Ella leaned over until her hair
was dropping on the floor and tried to drink from her wine glass,
which was standing beside the bed. Always blood, death and
forgetting — you're mad about them. Well, that figures! The wine
glass tipped over, and Ella tried to catch it with her lips.

Thomas gritted his teeth. He was annoyed with himself for
reading his poem aloud to Ella. Couldn't he be happy that she
followed his voice into sweet dreams? And what did he want to
know about her? What did she know about death? Obviously
not half as much as he did. At least she didn't hope for anything
from him. Her troubles were different: the heavy tongue that kept
her from speaking well. And Johnny's unhappy letters were embarrassing, now she came to think of it. She reached for her glass.
Better drink a little more. Forget, be silent, wait! Ella was powerless
against it, she had nothing to say in answer and nothing to say
against it. Glass in hand, she stood up, bobbed a little curtsy and
said goodnight: Zumbledum. Sleep well. Would be nice if you're
really better now.

Beginning

Thomas got off the tram and walked along beside an old wall made of rounded, natural stones. Ivy clambered around it, clinging to the stone. Thomas had checked on the street map that the hospital grounds must be in the next block. He was to report to the Personnel Office at 8 a.m. A glance back at the tram stop, but the clock had obviously stopped. His hands sweated if he found himself on the way to a new place on his own, a place that was to mean something to him, a place where he had to prove himself. They had sweated last autumn in the train to Gommern, they were sweating again today. He clenched his hands into fists inside the pockets of his jacket, spread his fingers, then clenched them again. Before he shook hands with anyone he would have to wipe his hand on the lining of the pocket. He had his school reports with him. There was nothing wrong with them, and nothing he could do about it now – good marks hadn't helped him in Gommern either. Didn't he need a letter from the Ministry? he had asked Käthe yesterday. He felt naked. No, no letter had come, and she was sure he wouldn't need one, not this time. Thomas pressed his briefcase more firmly under his arm and put both hands to his mouth, breathing warm air into the loosely clenched fists. Even though his hands were sweating, they were cold as ice. When he reached the gate and passed the porter, it struck him that he hadn't combed his hair. There were boys who always had a comb with them, even if they didn't need it. They had been brought up to have it ready. Thomas was not like that; he was uncombed, badly brought up. Anyone could see that at once. Anyone who wanted could simply see it. Thomas ran one sweating hand through his hair. However, he could smile. He smiled.

He would probably be accommodated in the brick building to the right of the entrance – the crematorium. Why else did it have the big chimney? The laundry, the kitchen, the boiler room – he was sure none of them needed chimneys of this size.

Ahead of him there was a broad path with flower beds down the middle. To the right and left of the beds you could walk on small, light-coloured paving stones, and the flower beds were surrounded by cast concrete stones with pebbles in them. A glasshouse on the left might once have been the hospital's own nursery garden, they must have grown vegetables there during the years after the war; at least, the glasshouse was mended with cardboard and other materials in places, although it was certainly no longer in use. Thomas thought of the Botanical Garden, which since last August seemed to him like the garden of Paradise. It was over a year now since he had last been there, he had gone over to the west of the city on the suburban train with Michael. They had looked at the carnivorous plants and the collection of poisonous plants. For the last time, although they didn't know it. They would never go there again. By way of compensation there was the Natural History Museum here in the eastern part of the city. Dusty animal specimens, embryos of mammals preserved in formaldehyde. Ammonites and fossils. Never again would he be able to admire a *Drosera omissa*, however unpretentious. Or an alpine butterwort. When would he ever see *Aldrovanda vesiculosa* again? True, it was said that the magical waterwheel plant, hanging in the water as lovely as a green bride, also grew in Europe. But he and Michael had searched the reeds beside the Müggelsee in vain last summer, they had waded along the bank, they had also parted the rushes beside the river, but they had not discovered the beautiful plant anywhere. She was a sensitive bride who liked only clear, clean warm water. You could draw a lesson from the plant; it grew at one end while it died at the other. Life as a waterwheel plant must be good.

I can show that I laugh / if you want me to / and that is often. / The rest is my business.

A robin sat in the black foliage of the borders, pecking. The snowdrops were over. The young green leaves of crocuses and grape hyacinths were coming up. How they shone against the black of the winter leaves. A man on crutches was standing on the path, and Thomas almost ran into him, his eyes were so captivated by the robin. Thomas swerved to one side and apologised. A clock hung from the first low building; it was ten to eight. His hands were sweating. Thomas practised walking with a steady step. This slightly uphill path was a long one. Two gardeners were kneeling on the paving stones, putting plants in the soil. Another gardener was removing blackened leaves from the beds with short, sharp movements, using a fan-shaped rake. Why hadn't Thomas thought of it before? It would be good to be a gardener. He wouldn't find his hands sweating if he were a gardener, he could kneel on the ground and sow the seeds of flowers, he would prune rose bushes and take snails to places where they would be safe from the birds.

In the Personnel Office he was received by a woman in a white sleeveless overall. She took his reports into the next room to be examined, and told him to wait out in the corridor meanwhile. A good hour later she called him in again, stamped a small card and told him which ward to report to: 3 A. First he was to collect his work clothes from Building C, Room 132. It would be a good idea to get to the ward by ten o'clock when the doctors would have done their rounds, and the ward sister would have time to show him the ropes. When he left he was not to go the way he had come, but go down the corridor on the left down to the little staircase, and out of the back door of the building. Over the yard, diagonally right, then through the open gate. Thomas nodded. His stamped card and the docket for the work clothes in his hand, the folder with his school reports under his arm, he went out of the door, turned left, and looked for the way to go.

In the ward they showed him where to change his clothes. After that he had to sit down on a bench and wait again. The doctors had not finished their rounds at ten. There was a penetratingly sweet and rotting smell, as if of bacteria, and then a sharp smell of vinegar. Thomas could also pick up the scent of floor polish.

Marie, said a soft voice, and a slender hand was offered to Thomas. I'm the ward sister, I'll show you round.

Thomas felt that the handshake was encouraging. She must notice his cold, damp skin, and he felt that he was blushing. But her own hand was not as warm as he had feared. It was light and firm.

Don't worry, I won't bite. Her voice was not only soft but also husky, with a slight scratchiness in it. Thomas got to his feet and followed her. She stopped outside a narrow door with the letters Staff WC on it, turned on the flat heel of her shoe, folded her arms, and smiled at him. First you must wash your hands. That's always the first thing to do when you come on duty. Do you understand? Washing your hands is essential.

Thomas nodded. He had to smile. He hadn't thought of that. He opened the door and washed his hands. Never in his life before, he felt, had he washed them with so much soap and such hot water and at such length as he did now. They were red when he dried them.

When he came out again, she was leaning on the windowsill opposite and gave him a mischievous smile. Let me see.

Unsure of himself, Thomas held out his red hands.

Turn them over. Now she unfolded her arms and touched his fingers as if to help him.

Thomas turned his hands in all directions. Okay?

Almost. It's important for you to cut your nails as short as possible. And you must brush the nails. Get them nice and clean. In a hospital everything has to be clean, at least everything about us. You want to study?

Thomas tentatively nodded; obviously she had read his personal file.

You see, even if you don't become a nurse but you're maybe operating later, your hands have to be clean. Sterile. No germs. Just like they are now. Come on, she said, turning on her flat heels. Come along, she waved enticingly to him to follow her, I'll find you a pair of scissors.

A slight aroma rose to Thomas's nostrils. Was it egg yolk, sweet yeast, warm butter? It reminded Thomas of the cakes that Michael's mother made. The young woman was already turning the next corner, and Thomas had to stride out to keep up with her. He had seldom noticed a woman's neck before. The pattern where her hairline began touched him, its symmetry was breath-takingly beautiful and made him think of metal filings in a magnetic field. Her hair was pinned up under her cap with thin hairpins, and the finest of little hairs curled at the nape of her neck, shining chestnut brown in the late-winter sunlight. Her shoulders were as narrow as a young girl's, although she must be several years older than Thomas. She had finished her training, she was in charge of the ward, at least today, when Matron was off duty.

She introduced Thomas to her colleagues in the nurses' room. Thomas is our new auxiliary. He'll be staying until October, she said, looking at him for confirmation and winking as she did so, as if they were accomplices. And then maybe he'll get a place to study. The other nurses said hello, looked up from their tables of figures and their cups and nodded to him.

Marie turned round, opened a drawer, took something out and went up to Thomas. She gave him a small pair of nail scissors that she was holding in the hollow of her hand. Take them into the toilet with you, and I'll wait for you here.

Thomas did as he was told. He cut his nails so short that the skin of two fingers was left sore, and one thumb was bleeding.

Now I'll take you round the ward, said Marie, and Thomas followed her. Maybe he could follow this woman a good deal of the time? She seemed to know exactly where to go. First she showed him a storeroom where brooms, cleaning cloths, bowls, containers, bedpans and hot-water bottles were kept, as well as vases for flowers.

For if there's an accident, she said, and her delicate lips sketched a smile.

An accident?

Don't look so anxious – quick as a cat, she licked her upper lip – we don't have a patient dying every day. I mean if something goes wrong, if a patient vomits or doesn't make it to the toilet in time, or a bowl of soup gets spilt. Things like that. You'll find buckets, scrubbing brushes, all you need in here.

Thomas nodded vaguely. He hadn't thought of having to wipe up sick and other fluids. There was something glazed about the smile on Marie's delicate lips. The way she avoided his eyes told him that she had practised smiling, just like him. She could do it on request at any time. There might not be anything more than politeness behind it.

There were nicer things in the next room, where all the cupboards were full of bedclothes. Little notices were fitted above the handles of the cupboard doors. Sheets. Hand towels. Duvet covers. Pillowcases. Draw sheets. Foot sheets. Shrouds. Molton cloths, large, medium, small. Large terry towels. Hand towels. Tea cloths. Bibs. Nappies. Large nappies. Nightshirts. The early shift makes the beds, and the used bedlinen goes in that cart, said Marie, pointing to the large cart standing in the corridor outside the laundry room. Sometimes we'll be asking you to wheel the cart over to the main laundry.

Thomas nodded. He'd have liked to tell her that she didn't have to smile for his benefit.

And you won't be going into this room. Marie pointed to the next door. It's locked. Apart from the doctors only Matron and I, that's to say the ward sister on duty instead of Matron, have keys. There are cupboards for medicaments in here, and supplies of cellulose wadding, gauze, cotton wool, muslin bandages, plasters and so on. When the packs of those run out in the nurses' room you must tell Matron or me.

Wasn't she cold, with her bare arms under her white nurse's coat? Her arms were immaculately white, but two long, thin scars aroused Thomas's curiosity. Where did she get those scars on her arm? Had a patient scratched her, or maybe a cat?

Thomas's stomach was grumbling. The sound was so loud that even Marie couldn't miss hearing it. She smiled briefly and looked down. Now for the kitchen. She went ahead of him, taking small steps. Halfway there she turned to Thomas. Of course I'm just going to show you the kitchen. It's occurred to me that you may be hungry, but there's nothing for us to eat there. Meals for the patients are brought from the main kitchen in the cart in the morning, at midday, in the evening. They had reached the kitchen. There are two small immersion heaters here. Cans down there. And camomile, peppermint and fruit teas up there in those bags. She stretched to reach a high cupboard door. Thomas wanted to help her, but at the last moment he held back, for fear of touching her. She turned to him and looked startled, because she hadn't noticed how close to her he was standing. Her perfume stirred an electrical impulse in him. Thomas took a step back. This time her smile was natural, and she looked at the door as if assuring herself that no one was watching them through the open doorway. She folded her arms and placed her right hand in a curiously upright position on the inside of her upper arms. Her fingertips touched the fabric of her coat under her armpits.

Sometimes the tea is served black, usually not. We don't have any coffee for the patients. If a patient brings coffee we brew it when we have time, but that doesn't often happen. She reached up to the top cupboard, and then closed the cupboard door again with a practised movement. He could see the outline of her panties under her white coat. Sometimes we'll be sending you to fetch the cart with the meals, or to take it back to the kitchen later. Depending on what we have delivered, there are also fruit juices, sauerkraut and apples. But only with the doctor's permission, not all the patients can or should drink fruit juice.

As she recited all this, she licked her upper lip now and then. It happened so quickly that Thomas had to stare at her mouth if he wasn't to miss it.

Is something the matter? She had a very wide, large mouth, and her delicate lips were almost violet. She was probably cold. You're staring so. Is something wrong?

Thomas heard her ask, and had to tell himself to stop staring, blink, tear his gaze away from her mouth and look back at her eyes.

No, nothing.

Tell me what I just told you.

He liked her slightly husky voice, and repeated: And up there in the bags there's camomile, peppermint and fruit teas. Sometimes it's served black, usually not. We don't have any coffee for the patients. If a patient brings coffee we brew it when we have time, but that doesn't often –

– Happen, she said, laughing with satisfaction now. That's good. You notice everything. Her laugh disappeared as suddenly as it had come.

She had faint blue shadows under her eyes. A tiny vein shimmered on her left eyelid. He seemed to be familiar with those eyes, they looked so close and deep, it was as if he had always known them. Maybe she wasn't a native of the night, only when she was on the late shift? People of the night, and he was one of them himself, seldom dropped off to sleep before dawn. You watch over the darkness the way a Neanderthal man watched over fire in the cradle of mankind, Michael had told him in their tent, because Thomas had been sitting outside it half the night, smoking.

Marie looked at him attentively. She wore hardly any make-up, just a delicate black line on her eyelids, emphasising the almond shape of her large eyes.

Come along, she said again, gently, and when he followed her the delicately sweet aroma of her perfume streamed into his nostrils.

In the nurses' room Marie loaded up her trolley for the ward with thermometers, a pair of scissors, small knives, pipettes and syringes for blood samples, cellulose wadding, cotton wool, plasters, and one large and one small container for used instruments. We'll need these as well, she said, placing several bulb syringes for enemas and a manicure set in the middle compartment. She asked Thomas to wait outside the medicaments room. Then she took a long list from the clipboard, written by someone in meticulous, small handwriting, and Thomas watched her in profile through the door, which stood ajar, as she stood in front of the large cupboard, opened doors and stood on tiptoe to reach an upper compartment. She collected tablets, small bottles of tinctures and ointments.

In the next room she loaded up a second trolley with bedlinen, washcloths and towels that Thomas took down from the upper cupboards for her.

At Marie's request, Thomas pushed the trolley of bedlinen while she wheeled the trolley of medicaments. Before they reached the first door, Marie briefly explained what to expect. There were six men in the first room on the ward, two of them dying, it could take hours or days but probably not weeks, while it was to be hoped that the others would be discharged once the scars of their operations had healed or they had recovered from pneumonia. The old man by the window had to be attended to first. As he had not passed any stools for too long, according to a chart attached to his bed, he was to be given an enema, and then he must be washed. He's in pain, said Marie quietly, better not make too much of it if he screams. He'll scream terribly, he calls us names too. His piles must hurt like hell. She opened the door, and the dazzling winter sunlight fell on their faces. Thomas followed her. Without even thinking about it, he stood next to her beside the bed. She greeted the man, who was dozing, and had to speak to him twice and touch his thin shoulder through the nightshirt to wake him up properly. She pulled the covers back with one hand, with the other she held the man's hand, and with a skilful grip she laid the thin little man on his side and undid his nightshirt. She pushed it up and undid the nappy he was wearing. Could he sit up today? she asked. The man shook his head, he groaned, why couldn't they leave him in peace? he asked. He wanted to be left alone, that was all. There was no emotion at all in her voice, no impatience, no regret, only her quiet firmness allowed Thomas to guess at her sympathy as she said that now, unfortunately, she would have to give him an enema. Marie asked Thomas to hold the old man firmly, and showed him exactly how. It was a matter of holding his wrists, his hips, his rickety legs. Thomas held him as she turned round, did something or other, and filled a rubber bulb syringe with water. She bent down and took a bedpan off her trolley. Thomas had to hold the man's wrists tight. Marie put the bedpan in position on the sheet and skilfully inserted the point of the syringe past the raw flesh. The man's screams were deafening. Thomas turned his eyes to the window and concentrated on the muscular power of his arms and legs to hold the thin but very strong little man firmly, pushing him down on the mattress with all his might.

Behind him, two of the other patients were arguing, but Thomas couldn't understand what they were saying.

Thomas held out like that for about ten minutes, until his back hurt and the stink was taking his breath away. He would have liked to ask Marie how much longer he must hold the man. He couldn't open his mouth, because the stench nauseated him so much, and he could hardly breathe through his nose when the little old man suddenly fell silent in his hands and stopped resisting; his body lay limp, as if broken, and Thomas's own hands now looked to him like an animal's paws. Cautiously, he raised them and let go of the man, but he was not defending himself any more. Thomas saw his shallow breathing under skin as thin as paper, as his ribcage rose and fell. The man had half closed his yellowish, rather clouded eyes. He had discolorations all over his body, blue, nearly black, and brighter red marks.

Marie had disappeared with the bedpan. It seemed to Thomas that he stood there for an eternity, staring at the door and waiting for her to come back. Soon after that she brought a bowl of steaming hot water to the bedside. She handed Thomas a warm washcloth. You wash his face, throat, arms and armpits. I'll do the rest.

Thomas nodded, held the washcloth, and watched Marie washing the man's genitals and bottom with short, quick movements.

What is it? She stopped and looked up at Thomas.

I think, I'm afraid I . . . Thomas passed his forefinger over the old man's arm. I'm afraid I hurt him.

The blue bruises? That's normal. There's nothing else to be done. He's been here for a few weeks now, we're just glad he hasn't developed bedsores on his back.

Thomas nodded. If Marie said so, maybe it was true. Was old people's skin too thin, their flesh too soft, did they simply bruise more easily? Thomas took the washcloth and cautiously dabbed the old man's forehead. He turned the washcloth over and, with the other side of it, wiped his cheeks, chin and mouth. The stubble of his beard looked like little plants, dark little stems growing out of small pits.

Thomas. She stepped to one side and bent over to him from the other side of the bed. In her mouth his name sounded intimate, distinguished, tenderly beautiful. You must get a move on. We have five rooms and almost thirty patients to deal with. Their lunch will be brought at eleven thirty.

Thomas apologised. In her eyes, his attempts must look clumsy, hesitant, awkward. He had never washed another human being before.

With the diabetic patients, the laboratory values entered on the charts had to be consulted, the dose of insulin was calculated to match them, and Marie injected it.

228

The second room also contained six men, one of whom had not been properly conscious for two weeks; three others would be dead by summer, although two of them would presumably be discharged and sent home before that. Three men lay in the third room; the fourth bed was empty because the patient was in surgery, having an incipient ulcer removed.

Thomas saw two nurses going along the corridor with a trolley. They were making their way to the ward. Marie and he had begun in the first room, the two nurses in the last room, and later they would meet and finish their round in the middle. Or almost finish it. Only the strong or particularly expensive medicinal drugs would be administered by Marie in the other rooms. The fourth room contained five men, and a sixth bed had been vacant since yesterday, because the patient had died.

What of?

Cancer, replied Marie. Most of the patients on our ward have cancer. Diseases seldom come alone. Diabetes goes along with kidney damage and kidney failure, kidney stones and strokes. The older the patients are, the tougher their bodies, the more diseases they accumulate.

When they reached the last room Marie said, in her soft, husky voice, that Thomas had already made good progress. She licked her lips. Only her eyes were smiling now, not a grimace, a sign that she felt close to him, Thomas believed. She had sensed that he didn't want any pretence. Could he please, she asked, see to the last two patients on his own, because she had to hand out the medicinal drugs and write up entries in the card index and her poisons book. Marie explained what to do for the two men. One could walk, wash and shave himself, and he was to be discharged tomorrow. For the sake of routine, however, his temperature must be taken and he must be weighed without shoes on. The other man was still young, but as well as an ulcer he had a weak heart. Thomas was to help him wash, because he was too weak and careless to cleanse certain parts of his body properly. Thomas was to check his ears. Change his nightshirt. Make up the bed with clean linen, a job done much faster by two people synchronising their movements, and Marie promised to send him a nurse to help with it.

When you've finished, come to the front of the ward. You'll be taking the meals round. It's easy, the other nurses will show you how. At lunchtime I must write up the reports, but you can have a smoke with the other nurses, or eat your sandwiches if you brought any. After that we'll see each other again. Marie pushed a loose strand of hair back under her cap and left the room. He felt that he was all alone. Did the patients know how new and inexperienced he was?

It was a moment before Thomas noticed the ribald remarks of the patients, and realised who was the butt of them. Hearing their conversation made him embarrassed; he didn't feel that he belonged with these people.

At five, Marie went to sign off at the end of her shift. See you tomorrow, she said, shaking his hand. The other nurses giggled and cast him surreptitious glances. One showed him the door of the room where he could change. The nurses whispered, waved goodbye, and wished him a nice evening.

A little later, Thomas was sitting on the bench that stood on the broad path between the flower beds, smoking a cigarette. The tobacco gave him a pleasant sense of mild nausea; it occurred to him that he hadn't eaten all day. The first blackbirds were singing in the clear February twilight. Thomas didn't know how many ways out of the hospital there were, certainly there would be back doors and side doors, gates to let delivery vans in, access for ambulances and hearses. But he was sure that sooner or later Marie would have to come along this path. Signing off at the end of a shift couldn't take hours. Maybe he would smoke two or three cigarettes. He had plenty of time.

Although it was nowhere near dark yet, the lights in the grounds flickered and came on.

Just before the end of her shift, Marie had been called into a room where a man was having breathing problems. Thomas had been expected to follow her. At her request he had opened the window, while the man struggled for air and breathed stertorously. Marie had bent over him, put an oxygen mask on him, and finally sent Thomas for the doctor. When he came back into the room with the doctor, the man had died. He had not been one of those expected to die in the coming days or weeks. A patient with a small cancerous tumour on his liver, it had been successfully operated on, with no sign that any vital organ was about to fail. Where had they taken the body? Thomas wondered.

Thomas lit another cigarette and blew smoke rings into the air. The light nearby dazzled him. He heard a scream from somewhere. Perhaps one of the patients was angry, perhaps he was afraid. *A howling ray of light flowers in the cry, / when the ash flakes, / the last black egg breaks / shattered against the sky.*

As long as someone could scream he wasn't marked yet, wasn't black yet. How many marks had he left on the thin man this morning? It seemed unreal to think that he had known Marie for only a few hours.

He put his head back, and closed his eyes. The smoke tickled his nose pleasantly.

Horror stifled us now / And the proud trees seem / in the great dream / under the blood-storm to bow. Barely moving his lips, he began again at the beginning, *When the ash flakes*, reciting and beating time with his foot on the paving stones. He stubbed his toe on the stones, and began adding another line. *A second guessed at for a thousand years – .* She must come now, he could feel that

231

she was close. He sat upright and looked down the broad path towards the hospital in search of her.

He recognised her figure in the distance. She was on her own.

What are you doing, still here? She hardly smiled at all, she stopped not two metres away from him, her coat almost touching his knee. He was a boy, she was a woman.

He rubbed his eye with the back of his hand; the smoke stung. Throwing the cigarette on the ground, he trod it out.

I was waiting.

Yes? Her husky voice, the tenderness and certainty in it excited him. He didn't have to answer the question in it. I could take you home, it's getting dark.

She put her head on one side. Come along. She reached her hand out to him. No one had ever put a hand out to him like that before, just so that he could take it and walk part of the way with her. Now he was walking beside her, their hands clasped.

You can't take me home, she said as they went along. They were both silent. She almost floated as she walked, as if she were gliding, in spite of the delicate heels clicking on the paving stones. A few metres before they reached the porter, she said even more softly than before: My husband is waiting for me. I must do some shopping now, collect my child from the crèche, and then I'll go alone.

Go where?

To Friedrichshain. Home. To my husband. As they passed the porter, she took her hand out of his.

Thomas waited with her just outside the beam of the street light where it fell on the tramline. He could go with her as far as the Frankfurt Gate, where they would both change to different lines. He stood back for her to get in first, and put coins for their fares into the ticket machine. Then he turned the handle, which itself turned the compartments for the money, visible

through the glass pane, as it fed out the tickets. The tops of the
tickets fell out of the device with a slight rattle. Two tickets, one
for her, one for him. The light in the tram made the shadows
under her eyes look deeper. Her expression was weary and sad.
They sat down on a vacant seat.

I could go shopping with you, he offered.

Another time. She smiled and put her head to one side, resting
it on the window. She was wearing a woollen cap that covered
her hair, as the nurse's cap covered it in the daytime. How long
was her hair, he wondered, and where did it fall to when it wasn't
covered up? If they had known each other longer, he could tell,
she would have laid her head on his shoulder. Her slender hands
clutched the bag on her lap. Only now did he notice her bright
ring. The nursing staff weren't allowed to wear jewellery on duty,
she had told him so herself that morning, no bracelets or rings
because of the danger of injury.

How old is your child?

She'll be two in April.

A little girl?

She nodded. The corners of her mouth moved, almost imperceptibly, as she looked out of the window into the darkness of
the streets passing by. She would disappear into that darkness,
Thomas already missed her. His arm touched her shoulder, the
slight jolting of the tram brought the fabric of their coats sometimes closer together, sometimes further away. He wondered
what to say in goodbye when they left the tram at the Frankfurt
Gate and went their separate ways.

In Rahnsdorf, Ella was sitting in the smoking room, with a
brocade cloak over her shoulders and a cactus leaf on her head,
drawing. There was no one else at home. The twins had been
with a foster-family since the beginning of the year.

233

No one around? Thomas closed the door behind him. Ella carefully turned her head. Her neck was going to be stiff if she balanced the cactus on her head any longer.

Aren't I anyone?

There was something suspect about her expression. Had they quarrelled? Had something happened?

Käthe's gone to the theatre. Ella put her pencil down and looked at the fired clay head standing before her. Käthe had made it a few years ago, and its nose was rather too small. She bent carefully, keeping her head erect so that the cactus leaf wouldn't fall to the floor, and then straightened her back.

Why have you put that cactus on your head?

So that I'll sit up straight at last. Her injured tone of voice told Thomas that there must have been a quarrel.

I really wanted to go too, but Käthe wouldn't take me. She says I have to learn to draw properly first, and then maybe she'll get me a place at the fashion college. On her stool, Ella turned in Thomas's direction so that she could look at him. But on three conditions. If I'll take a serious interest in art, if I'll study drawing properly, and if I go to adult education classes.

So what? I thought you'd been going to those for quite a while.

Tears shot into Ella's eyes. Of course I've been going. For months. But not any more, she sobbed. I can't even say my multiplication tables from one to ten. I don't know what's the matter with me.

Thomas went over to her. He was about to take the cactus leaf off her head with his fingertips, but as soon as he touched the fine prickles Ella snapped: Don't do that! You must help me! She held on to the cactus with one hand, shrieked, and tried to put her hand in her mouth, which was much too small for it.

Wait. Thomas went into the bathroom, opened the drawer of the little cupboard, found the tweezers and hurried back to the smoking room. Wait, I'll help you, he cried, when he saw Ella leaning forward to bury her face in her hands.

What can I do? I can't do anything. What do I want? I don't want anything. What am I? I'm nothing. Ella was crying.

Stop it, Ella, you'll rub the prickles into your face. He removed one of her hands from her face, and began pulling the prickles out of her skin with the tweezers. As the fine ones kept eluding him, Ella let her tears fall on her hands, and Thomas had to pull himself together to keep from laughing furiously.

I'm stupid. Little-Ella is really stupid.

Please stop that Little-Ella stuff. You're not stupid. I'll help you. Thomas had found the easiest way to take hold of the prickles, and now he was pulling them out at increasing speed, until the first hand was clear. Ella had only a very few prickles in her other hand.

They sat down at the big table in the smoking room, and Thomas sharpened a pencil. A large book of pictures of Italian Renaissance paintings served them as a base on which to place a sheet of graph paper. Thomas drew a horizontal line on it, and a vertical line over the horizontal one. That's the x-axis and this is the y-axis. Imagine the y-axis as a thermometer. Here, this corresponds to one, this to two, this to three. Thomas drew tiny lines along the vertical. And in the minus area you have minus one, two, three, four, and so on. He quickly sketched the units. It's important to be systematic, always stick to the same sequence, or it won't work. I'll show you a simple example first. Assuming that f of x equals . . . Thomas noted down the little letters and brackets.

Why x and y? Couldn't the upright line be there too? Ella raised her eyebrows, with some effort, and fluttered her eyelids. Her shaky voice showed that up to this point she had hardly been able to listen. Already she didn't understand what he was trying to explain to her.

Of course. Anything could be. But this is about the area of definition, and if I decide that I want to look more closely at a curve, or represent its calculation graphically, then –

The what? Area of de-fit-ion?

Definition. Never mind, just look at this. This f of x corresponds to the parabola that I'll show you, $f(x) = (x - 4)^2 + 3$. Now we're looking at its situation in the system of coordinates, look where its apex is, see in what direction it opens, and how it is curved. You get the idea?

You act as if I ought to know all this! Ella struck the table with her fist. But I don't. Apex, f of x, what does it all mean?

The more agitated Ella became, the calmer Thomas was. He knew her moments of despair and impatience, her assumption that she was stupid, her suspicion that no one would ever manage to explain something to her if she simply didn't understand it already. Here, take this. Thomas handed her the pencil.

So what am I supposed to do with it now? She furiously scribbled on the top corner of the graph paper until the lead broke.

Sharpen it. Thomas held the pencil sharpener out to her. It's really very simple, he said calmly, smiling confidently at her. Listen.

Ha ha! Very simple.

Every quadratic function is a parabola. Draw the shape down here in the corner. Do you know what a parabola looks like?

No. Ella had cast her eyes down as if ashamed of herself. She sharpened and sharpened an ever longer coil of wood from the point of her pencil.

It's sharp now. Thomas took the pencil out of her hand and swiftly sketched a parabola. That's what it looks like. He gave the pencil back to Ella. The last number here, plus three, will show you at a glance where your zero point has shifted along the y coordinate. So if you assume that f of x is the point of intersection of the two coordinates, zero, then look for the level where the apex could be situated.

Here? Ella pushed the pencil to a place on the paper. With verve, she drew a line in the upper right-hand corner of the sheet, put the pencil to the paper again below it and drew a similar line to the left. There's your parabola!

Yes. Thomas wondered how to ensure that she didn't get even more worked up. That's a parabola. And he added, almost inaudibly: more or less.

What?

But not the one that belongs to the equation here. Your parabola needs another equation. It ought to be more like $f(x) = x^2 + 3$. He didn't tell her that in addition her parabola did not show the requisite symmetry, but bulged far too much, and was asymmetrical to the axis of reflection.

Well, there you are! Ella got to her feet and threw the pencil down on the table. I told you I couldn't do it. Anyway, what does f of x mean, why is it all supposed to have a function? I don't have a function myself, do I? She was shouting so violently that tiny drops sprayed out of her mouth.

Ella, it's not about you at all, it's not about your function. He spoke slowly and almost as softly as Marie when she calmly wished him good morning today. Was it really today? It seemed to him an eternity ago, another world, another life. Thomas rubbed his temples, he tried to catch hold of Ella's hand as she kicked out, pushed the chair back, tore the brocade cloak off her shoulders, flung it to the floor and ran towards the door. Quietly, he said: There is no such thing as a graph without a function. I mean, well, there is, but we can represent it precisely if we know the equation.

Now Ella was opening the door, and she slammed it behind

her as loudly as she could. He would go after her, not at once, perhaps in ten minutes' time when she had calmed down. He would try to begin again from the beginning.

But when Thomas passed the closed door of Ella's room later, he heard her laughter and the laughter of Siegfried, who had obviously dropped in for a late visit.

After changing, Thomas had arrived in the nurses' room while it was still dark, half an hour before he came on duty and the shifts changed. He used the time to study the duty roster pinned up in a small frame beside the door. His own name was entered in the bottom column, in pencil rather than the ink normally used. Marie had tomorrow and the day after tomorrow off, and she was on night duty at the weekend. In his own column, Thomas had crosses on all the weekdays, all of them for the early daytime shift, none at the weekend. Disappointed, he turned to a chubby nurse whose eyes were red-rimmed after her night shift. Who draws up the rosters?

Matron. You don't get any choice, specially not when you're new here. She yawned in mid-sentence and politely put her hand in front of her mouth.

Thomas thanked her, and left the nurses' room. It struck him that he had forgotten to wash his hands. As he rubbed them under the white stream of water, he wondered whether to bring an eraser, rub out the pencilled crosses in some unobserved moment, and then enter them in the column for night shifts at the weekend. When he returned to the nurses' room, a woman with bobbed white hair was standing there, giving instructions in a staccato voice. Thomas shook hands with the matron and told her his name. He confirmed that Nurse Marie had shown him around the day before. The matron issued her orders briefly to the other nurses as they arrived before the shift changed.

When they were all sitting at the long table, and just as the hands of the big clock on the wall moved to 6 a.m. exactly, the door opened and Marie joined the others on the bench. Her hair was immaculately pinned up, the narrow line above her eyes delicately traced. The pale rings round those eyes moved Thomas; she still hadn't given him even a fleeting glance. News of incidents and new developments was exchanged. Marie wrote down details in the ring-bound notepad on the table in front of her. Thomas was sent out to fetch a teapot. When he came back he put the teapot down within Marie's reach, went round the table and sat down in his own place. The nurses were discussing the new occupant of a bed; the man who died yesterday had obviously been removed. Taken away. The night shift had laid out the corpse and then taken it to pathology. Thomas thought about the pronoun. If there was no living person inside it, the dead husk became an it, not he or she any more.

Did you hear what I said, Thomas? The matron gave him a stern look.

I'm sorry. He hadn't been listening, or if he had the last sentences had escaped him.

The matron made a note in her book, and was now clearly summing up what had just been discussed. Because of the staff shortage, Nurse Doris is on short-term loan to Ward C for the entire weekend. Thomas, you will stand in for her here. It's a night shift, but Nurse Marie will be on duty with you. Not much usually happens at weekends, no doctors doing their rounds, no new procedures.

The morning passed in a buzz of activity. The doctor had begun his rounds, the formalities for two new admissions were concluded, preparations were made to discharge three other patients. While the matron accompanied the doctor round the ward, Marie was constantly issuing instructions, letting the nurses know who was to do what in which room. Thomas was sent over the grounds with the laundry cart, then he was told to clean a whole trolley of kidney dishes and instruments, another nurse was to help and show him how to wash the instruments, and then how to put them in a basket for sterilisation later. As she gave these instructions Marie did not look at him, but talked to her colleague who was to show Thomas what to do. Why didn't she look at him? Thomas stood at the sink for half the morning. Many of the instruments seemed to have been lying in a disinfectant solution with a strong smell for hours, but still they were not easy to clean.

At the midday break Marie disappeared with Matron for a discussion. Only when the food trolleys were taken away and Thomas has been told to take the temperatures of a small number of selected patients for the second time did he see her again. He was just shaking the thermometer down, and smoothing out the pillow at the request of the patient, who raised his head and looked past him curiously. The door behind him had opened, and Marie was there in the room, carrying a tray of gauze, clips and a bottle. She held the tray on the palm of one hand, like a waitress, while she put a strand of hair back behind her ear with the other hand.

Can you help me with the compresses? At last she looked at him, her cheeks were flushed, her eyes shining.

She put the tray down on the bedside table of a patient whose skin had a yellow tinge; he must have a liver problem of some kind.

Thomas was to hold the patient's arm up in the air while she tied the compresses in place. As if by chance, their bare arms touched. The scent of her intoxicated him. Motes of dust danced in the sunlight in front of her face, the light from the window fell on her shoulders, lay on her back as she leaned forward to close the compress, and briefly brushed past her face as she turned and gently touched Thomas. She held the clip of the compress in place with one hand, stretching the other out towards the tray on the bedside table. She didn't reach for it, she would have had to grasp him more firmly and push him aside to do that.

Will you give me another clip, please?

Thomas reached behind him and handed her the clip. They stood close to each other, side by side, in silence as Thomas held the man's arm. Marie leaned forward and clipped the compress in place, their hips touched. Thomas held the arm only a little way up in the air, so that hers could touch his when she straightened up. She picked up the tray, and he followed her out of the room. They were alone for a few seconds in the corridor.

Please don't wait for me this evening. My husband is coming to collect me. Marie turned round, as if to make sure that no one was listening to them. He's very jealous. If he sees me with a young man he'll ask questions. She put the tray down on the trolley and held the brown bottle of disinfectant tincture out to Thomas. Without further explanation, she pulled the trolley of kidney dishes and instruments along behind her. Thomas followed her over to the bed. The man in it was feverish, his reddened eyes gleaming.

Spare me, he said. Marie responded with her exhausted smile. She pulled off a piece of cotton wool and handed it to Thomas, then a piece of gauze, she pushed the covers back, raised the man's nightshirt and told him that Thomas would be seeing to him today. Thomas had to put down the tincture. Then he wrapped the gauze round the cotton wool and pressed the wad to the mouth of the bottle, waited until it was soaked, and dabbed the patient's skin with it. The tincture had a mineral smell. The long suture on the stomach of the man, who had a childlike look, was fresh. To keep from crying out, the man drew air in through his teeth with a hissing sound, spraying saliva in pain. A second wad of cotton wool, then a third. Thomas took the kidney dish with the used wads of cotton wool and went to the door. He waited for Marie, and they tidied up the trolley of instruments together in the corridor. What had been taken out of the man, he asked, what was his operation for? Marie told him it had been for fatty liver. The affected part had been cut out and taken away. Where to, he asked, where does the bit of liver that's been cut out go?

It's thrown away, burnt. Thomas felt a leaden sensation in the pit of his stomach, his limbs were heavy, he needed a break.

When he was down in the yard on his own, smoking a cigarette, he watched two men carrying rubbish buckets out of the surgical department. This way of dealing with human bodies seemed to him barbaric. The unworthiness of it disgusted him. The idea would have seemed ridiculous had there been a level from which he could have smiled down on it. Called to higher things, who could that be? The emptiness of it clung to him like a certainty. A doctor with a stethoscope round his neck came along the path, a surgeon, Thomas suspected, his gait was so proud and self-important, he was smiling so triumphantly to himself, and as Thomas watched him go the doctor shrank to a tiny figure with a certain helplessness in the way he moved, his hands not knowing what to do, clutching a thin file folder, looking without conscious intent through a pair of horn-rimmed glasses for which a bull had probably had to lose part of its body. *See the chin, once so defiant / helpless falling on his chest / And the striking Roman nose / pointing sharply nowhere much.* Soon, Thomas heard Marie's voice again, she was sure he'd be allowed to watch an operation. Thomas trod out his cigarette with the sole of his shoe, throwing livers away, cutting out cancerous tumours, taking corpses to the mortuary.

Back in the ward, Thomas found Marie in the corridor carrying the tray in one hand, pulling the trolley along with the other. Unasked, he followed her, caught up with her, walked along beside her. When she stopped outside the room where medicaments were kept and was looking for her key, he leaned against the door frame. He waited, and took the tray from her. She unlocked the door, took her tray back, disappeared into the room. He heard sounds, and closed his eyes. Heard her sliding something open, heard something clinking softly, a snapping sound, probably a cupboard door opening and closing, he heard her putting items down, placing and laying them in position. When she reappeared, she was holding a box of plasters and a small glass bottle of tablets. She closed the door of the room, slipped the key into the pocket of her coat, and went ahead of him.

How old are you?

Marie stopped and tilted her head slightly to one side. Twenty-six. Her eyes gave nothing away.

I'm almost eighteen, he said, and added quietly, I'll be eighteen in a few days' time.

A visiting relation came through the big double door in search of her father. Marie told her where to find him, saying she still had medicaments to give out and could go part of the way with her. Thomas waited indecisively, and then went into the nurses' room. He asked if he could have a short break to go to the lavatory and smoke a cigarette.

Since the turn of the year, since they had buried Grandfather, and Uncle Paul had gone back to faraway America, he had been trying to write him a letter. Maybe there was a solution that an uncle could see from America, whereas here, from inside the Wall, high as it was, you could hardly even see the stars these days. The drafts of Thomas's letters always began with questions.

Not about Uncle Paul's health. Questions verging on complaints: Why is the world watching us? That was one of them. How can you people out there pass by and see us pacing up and down behind the bars of our socialist dream? Maybe his uncle didn't care for irony, cynicism or doubt. After all, he himself claimed to have been in the Red Squad during his schooldays in Berlin. So obviously, even if you had origins in communism, you could live in America? Instead of a sender's name and address, Thomas drew a face on the envelope with the pupils of its eyes consisting of barbed wire in large, spiky tangles. Perhaps his letters were intercepted at the border, because the authorities were curious and would want to know what such remarks meant. Thomas waited weeks for an answer, and waited in vain. None of the nurses approached him as he stood out in the yard, smoking and scribbling something down with a pencil. They kept their distance, giggling, and waved to him now and then. Forgive my questions, but who should I turn to? Where could I go? Please tell me. He erased the salutation, and over the pale ghost of Dear Uncle Paul he wrote Dear Aunt Erni. Aunt Erna, as he realised when he had written the last letters of her name, was an even less suitable recipient than Uncle Paul. And Thomas didn't want to get anyone whom he had seen so seldom in his life as his aunt into trouble. Maybe he should write to the family's French friends, Henri, the friend of Käthe's youth, and his Natascha? Hadn't they cut and run when Germany threatened to stifle them, facing them with the prospect of imprisonment and a living death? Once again Thomas rubbed it out and began again.

At the weekend, the late day shift began at 1 p.m. and ended at ten in the evening. During that time, said the rules, members of the nursing staff could take an hour's break, but in reality that hour's break almost never materialised. Now and then they went for a smoke, or to go to the lavatory.

Marie had already seen him at midday; she was sitting in the nurses' room writing figures in a book when he opened the door, glad that he could work with her. Presumably the tiny figures denoted the weight and number of powdered medicaments, drops or tablets. She had to keep the records of all the medicaments administered on the ward.

Hello, she said, and he thought he saw a strange sadness in her eyes. Maybe it was the slight stoop of her shoulders, as if she was bending over, Marie who usually sat as upright as she stood, almost skipping. Perhaps she was just tired, perhaps her little girl had slept badly last night. Her face was strikingly brown; she had rubbed brown foundation into her face, no doubt about it. Thomas took a deep breath. He thought about it. Did she believe she looked prettier with that brown paste? The effect was like an actress at the theatre, the make-up coarse and almost crumbly on her delicate face. She lowered her eyes, and Thomas wasn't sure whether he had heard a sigh.

He was holding a greaseproof paper bag. Here, I brought this for us.

What is it? Curiously, she craned her neck.

Toasted oat flakes with sugar and cinnamon, smell them.

She obliged him by doing so. The things you can do, she said wearily. Was she forcing herself to smile? Maybe he was being a nuisance?

Thomas put the bag on the table and asked what he could do. Marie opened the window and looked at him. First he was to help collecting the rest of the plates left from lunch. Then he could take over from the nurse in Room 8 who was feeding the severely weakened man with the cancerous growth on his forehead. Later she would tell him what to do this afternoon.

Thomas did as she had asked. He had cleared away the plates, but feeding the man with cancer was difficult. The nurse had managed to get only three spoonfuls inside him. Thomas took over the spoon and the bowl of mush. The nurse closed the window, said goodbye and left the room.

Thomas tried to get the man drinking from a cup with a spout. It smelled of camomile tea with a slight touch of urine. But the sick man was obviously too weak to suck. He only put out his tongue, which had a furry, yellowish-white coating.

My whole mouth hurts, he said, slobbering.

One eye was badly swollen, closed and purple. Pus stuck to the eyelid. Thomas forced himself to see only the surface details, no emotion, he told himself, no disgust, no horror. Only the body is his. My brain is mine. I'm making a fuss because I have to get over a little obstacle, but this man will die. In fact he must. Thomas let his arm holding the spoon drop. You don't have to eat it, he said, staring at the grey mush. It had an unpleasant smell, no one, however hungry, would want to eat mush like that.

No, whispered the man, I don't have to. He sounded grateful, as if Thomas had let him off lightly. Cautiously, he felt the largest of the swellings on the back of his head. Then he dropped back, and his bib upset the cup with a spout that Thomas had not been holding firmly enough.

Thomas fetched a bucket and cloths, and cleaned the bedside table and the floor. The bed had to be made up again; he needed Marie's help.

They didn't have time until an hour later, when they put a clean sheet on the bed, turning and moving the man with the growths on his head. Marie fetched cotton wool and some tincture, and carefully dabbed the man's eye. Thomas watched. He could have watched her for hours curving her fingers, holding the wad of cotton wool, standing there and smiling, fresh, no courage or grief in her attitude, he admired her.

Please go and check the nappies of the patients in Room 1

and Room 6. Thomas went. It seemed that Marie found nothing difficult.

Her gliding gait meant that she could approach you silently, whatever shoes and height of heels she was wearing. Suddenly she was standing beside Thomas, and her delicately sweet perfume rose to his nostrils.

When we come off the shift this evening, then . . . She looked at him with her large, velvety eyes.

Your husband will be waiting for you? he asked, finishing her sentence.

No. She lowered her eyes, and once again she looked as sad as she had at midday. He won't be waiting at the gate, not today. She seemed to be wondering what to say to him, and how. Maybe I could go home to your place?

To my place? Thomas looked at her in surprise.

To your family. You still live at home, don't you?

Of course you can, said Thomas, nodding vigorously. Thoughts crowded in on him. What made her express that wish?

I can't go home today. I'll explain later. She turned and hurried down the corridor, where a patient could be heard calling out through an open door.

Thomas threw the soiled nappies on the laundry cart. His pulse was racing for the rest of the day; wherever he stood, wherever he sat, he was wondering how he came to have this unhoped-for stroke of luck. He also wondered whether Käthe would be at home, or Ella.

As she had on the first day, Marie reached her hand out to him as they went down the broad path between the flower beds towards the porter's lodge, in the darkness that had fallen some time ago. He held her hand, and felt the warmth that radiated from her.

Walking in the dark, with the light of a street lamp falling on their faces only now and then, they did not look at one another as they talked.

When I'm on late shift or the night shift, at weekends like these, my little girl stays with my parents. I take her to Bergholz on the Sputnik express shuttle, and I collect her again on Sunday or on Monday morning, depending which shift I'm working.

Thomas said nothing. Perhaps her husband worked shifts as well, so he couldn't look after the child when she was at work or at weekends like this. Thomas felt her hand in his and was glad that she didn't withdraw it as they passed the porter.

The tram was standing at the stop with all its lights on. They ran to catch it, hand in hand.

Thomas was still holding her hand as they sat side by side. Her ring shone, pale and narrow. He put his other hand under hers, so that he could clasp it entirely, covering it protectively from above, supporting it from below. He wondered if she would let him stroke it. Won't your husband be surprised if you don't go home?

Now she bent her gaze so low that he had the impression she felt ashamed.

What will he be thinking?

He thinks I have to work overtime on the shift. Sometimes the night shift is late. Her lips moved as she began, several times, to say more, and with her lips her nostrils moved almost imperceptibly. Fine crumbs of her make-up quivered there, ready to fall off at any minute.

We don't have a telephone, she said with an anxious smile. I told the nurse on night duty to tell him, if he calls from the telephone kiosk, that I was kept late, and then I went home to Sabine. Sometimes I sleep at Sabine's.

Now Thomas did press her hand. She freed it from his, opened the large patterned bag on her lap, and searched it until she produced a powder compact.

Excuse me, she said, turning to the dark panes of the tram windows and powdering her nose, forehead, cheeks and chin. Her skin had a grey tinge, and fine cracks showed everywhere in her make-up. Thomas wanted to tell her that she didn't need to make herself up, any more than she had to smile. But he said nothing and waited until she had put the compact away and had a hand free that he could take and hold in his again. At Alexanderplatz they got off, went up the steps together and waited for the suburban train going in the direction of Erkner.

All the windows in the house were dark when Thomas, still holding Marie's hand, had walked through the wood from the suburban railway station, and had then gone along the sandy path to reach the wide road paved with cobblestones.

The front door was locked, a clear sign that Käthe and Ella were not at home this evening. He switched on the light in the corridor and led the way to the smoking room. There was a smell of wax. Käthe had forgotten to turn off the flame under the little hotplate on the tea trolley. A tiny remnant of wax was bubbling in the pot, which was steaming. Thomas turned out the flame and stepped on the switch of the standard lamp. Marie held on to her big bag with both hands. Shyly, she looked around, her eyes wandering over the tall cacti by the window, the small clay models standing on the table ready for firing, the large chunk of stone on the windowsill, the shining bowl on the chest of drawers, varnished green. She marvelled at all the pictures on the walls. That bright yellow furze is by Kesting, Thomas said, pointing over to the charcoal drawings. And that one is by Kollwitz, like the etching beside it.

But Marie did not know those names. She nodded politely and said fancy that three times running, until Thomas mentioned no more names after Kollwitz, because he didn't want to make her feel awkward. What did it mean to her if a picture was by Schmidt or Beckmann? He did not mention the clay Rosa Luxemburg standing under its damp cloth on the veranda. Enumerating all those names would seem conceited to her.

Would you like some wine or some tea?

She couldn't decide, and then wanted both.

He offered her the armchair in his room and sat on the bed opposite her. She sat on the very edge of the chair, her slender legs crossed at the knees, swinging her heels in their delicate shoes.

May I use your bathroom? I'd like to have a wash.

Your hands?

No, my face. It's been itching all day. When the foundation dries I can hardly stand it. Now she laughed awkwardly and got to her feet.

He showed her the bathroom. Before he could explain anything she had closed the door. The bolt stuck. Thomas heard her struggling with it in vain. Since Ella's accident with the lodger, the bolt was bent so badly that no one could shift it.

Thomas opened the bottle of wine and filled both glasses. In the Johannishof, he had noticed that the glasses were only half filled at first. Only later, as the evening wore on, did they seem to be fuller.

Marie didn't take long. Her skin was reddened; perhaps rubbing off the make-up or the cold water had irritated it. But Thomas saw something else. It took him a moment to realise what he was looking at. The skin over one of her cheekbones was discoloured blue.

Marie must have noticed him staring at her. She put one hand to her cheek and said: I walked into an open cupboard door this morning.

An open cupboard door? Thomas knew he had better keep his mouth closed if he wasn't going to embarrass her even more.

Yes, I wanted to get the sugar out of the cupboard, and crash! Now she put both hands side by side on her lap, flat, as if she were praying.

Thomas tried to imagine Marie walking into an open cupboard door. Something like that might happen to him, but not Marie. Her eyes saw everything, they were everywhere, penetrating everything, they saw from a distance and close too, everywhere, he was sure of that. Why was she lying to him?

You don't believe me, she said quietly. Thomas did not reply. Holding his wine glass, he tipped it slightly, held it straight, and wondered whether he had to take hers off the table and press it into her hand so that she could drink. He leaned forward, took her glass and held it out to her.

Here's to you!

And you!

He had closed the door of his room, and when he heard footsteps and Agotto's barking in the corridor he knew that no one would open it, any more than anyone expected him to go out, say hello, or even introduce his guest formally. Käthe wouldn't even know that he had a guest, they were keeping so quiet.

They sat opposite each other until three in the morning, telling one another what they thought about life, in few sentences with long minutes of silence in between.

For instance, seeing her eye fall on the picture of Walter Ulbricht that had been shot at, Thomas said: He made monkeys of us all. He scratched under his armpits, grasped two invisible bars in the air in front of his face, and pressed his pursed mouth between them. Looks good out there.

Marie cautiously laughed, and moved a little further back into the armchair, placing the arm holding her glass on the arm of the chair while she stroked the smooth fabric of her trousers with her other hand. What sort of dog was it she had heard just now? she asked. Thomas told her about Käthe and her dog, who always got something from her plate at mealtimes, the dog she caressed and tickled under the chin. He had never seen Käthe caress a human being. He poured Marie more wine. *With alcohol, wishful dreams, oblivion and tobacco, / And we will hate ourselves with all our might. / Oh child, you need not weep, / We take nothing with us when we go. / We will only walk by night. – / You do not see in the dark when an eye breaks.* Marie raised one eyebrow. She liked the black walls of his room: It's like a cave, you can feel safe in here.

The universe, Thomas drank from his glass, but kept the wine in his mouth and did not swallow it, turned it over gently against his palate. His tongue in the wine. That afternoon Marie had said that the man with the eye oozing pus was going blind in it, and they would have to operate next week. By now he knew what it meant for something to be taken away. The eye would disappear. Now he swallowed the wine. Is there a place where no light comes in any more, a place no one thinks about any more?

The shadow of the moon? She looked attentively at the rug between her and Thomas. The loops of its bouclé fabric looked like moss in the faint light. He had the impression that she was thinking of something else.

Everyone thinks of that. Lunik 2 has even been there. Everyone wants to go to the moon. The silence inside the Wall since it was built round us. Over on the other side, where the order to shoot isn't in force, do people stand on the Wall shaking our barbed wire? Do you want to get shot?

He soon saw, from the way that Marie was suppressing her yawns, that she was tired and shivering.

He offered her his bed, and when she hesitantly agreed, his quilt too. She took the hairpins out of her piled hair and put them on the chest of drawers one by one, until her hair was falling down over her shoulders. Should he offer her a nightshirt? She sat on his bed and took her shoes off. Thomas plumped up the pillow and put it down for her so that she could sleep comfortably. Tentatively, she laid her head on the pillow, her hands under her cheek, her legs drawn up. Only just audibly her teeth were chattering; she pressed her lips together. Thomas put his quilt firmly round the beautiful, shivering woman. He took the sheepskin off the chest of drawers to cover himself.

He put out the small lamp. It was some time before he could make out her shape, the hollows of her eyes and her delicate mouth. Dark hair framed that pale face, and she was looking at him with tired eyes. He would look at her for a long time, for as long as he could.

When a blackbird struck up its trilling in the faint twilight of dawn, it made him blink. How different Marie looked in the dark, how good it was to be with her. We have to go to work tomorrow – his voice croaked, it was so long since he had spoken.

Afterwards, she whispered back.

Close your eyes, he said, putting out a finger to touch one of her eyelids. The skin there was smooth, warm. He would have liked to touch her cheek, but he didn't dare. Her slight smile under the closed eyelids infected him. In the midst of the darkness he saw her image and felt, even if he did not hear it, the light touch of her breath on his chin.

My husband likes to drink. And he has friends, colleagues at work. He gets together with them at weekends. He invites them to come and see us. And before my little girl was born, now too when she's away at weekends I have to dance.

Thomas did not like darkness, he wanted to see her, he wanted to see what she was saying, understand just what she meant. Thomas opened his eyes, but she had spoken with her own eyes closed. Dance?

Take my clothes off and dance.

You have to take your clothes off and dance?

Only at weekends, and when the child isn't there. She spoke so softly that he could hardly make out the words. He wanted to get closer to her, but the idea that he was lying in front of her, like a reflection, suggested caution.

Just dance?

Sometimes other things too.

Other things?

They give him money for it. It's amusing.

Amusing? He didn't understand what Marie was telling him. He says.

Thomas stared at her, his eyes burning, the dim light hurt, and he wanted to say: Look at me. He wanted to know how she would look at him now. But he couldn't do it. If she didn't open her eyes of her own accord he wouldn't tell her to, wouldn't try to put an arm round her.

His arms lay stiff beside him, his hands clenched into cold fists, nails digging into the sheepskin. *So warm and close, / So warm and close, within reach, / your being lay by mine, / but the great gulf yawns, / Where reason parts us* – Was her breath steadier, was she asleep now? He couldn't ask her, he could only whisper something, the beginning of the poem: *Where did love begin, / to stir in the heart again? / Who gave the signal / to reveal the pain?* Her breathing was so peaceful that he had to make sure she was asleep.

254

In the dark, she took his head in her hands, held it, and he wondered, as he pretended to be asleep, whether she also held his thoughts. Perhaps they were both asleep and dreaming.

You're a handsome boy, she said, putting the fingers that had touched his forehead to her mouth and kissing them, then running them over his cheek.

He felt hot under the sheepskin. The heating was on, he had forgotten to turn it off in the evening and open the window. His eyes felt swollen. Her lips, her fingers, his skin. He felt the blood draining from his hands as they went cold in the turmoil of his mind.

No one can make you dance. The defiance in his words alarmed him. As if he were her husband, as if he could make such decisions.

Perhaps to punish him, perhaps out of shame, she closed her beautiful eyes and kept her hands close to her sides now.

He turned over, lay on his back, helpless as a beetle. Beautiful Marie beside him, untouchably close.

She must have heard his arm on the sheet, smelt the cinnamon and burnt sugar, she opened her eyes. In daylight the blue bruise was yellowish green at the edges. She raised her head, sniffed, and brought her lips close to his hands. With her slender fingers she took a few toasted oat flakes and let them drop into her mouth. She licked her lips.

Do you have a mirror in here? She didn't want to have to cross the corridor to the bathroom without make-up on her face.

He said no, but went out and brought her the big mirror from the corridor wall. She crouched in front of it and put her make-up on. He asked if she would like some tea. They heard footsteps in the corridor. Thomas didn't know if they belonged to Käthe, Ella, a visitor or a model. Anyone could be walking about the house at this time, in the middle of a Sunday.

Marie said she would rather go down to the lake, which must be quite close.

A wind was blowing, already a mild, spring wind; bare trees towered to the sky, broken branches lay in the mire as they walked hand in hand along the Fliess and over the marshy land. Among the puddles and small pools, you could see the first little green leaves, scillas and anemones peeping through the blackened winter foliage. They had to pick their way around large puddles, and mud clung to their shoes. On the narrow landing stage made of piled boulders, a fallen alder lay in the brown reeds, its root pointing up at the sky, as if the earth were yawning, and Thomas scrambled up on it and gave Marie a hand to help her up. He led her along the trunk by his hand, out over the water, which grew deeper and deeper, to where the little breaking ripples had buried the crown of the tree. They could go no farther. Swaying in the wind, they kept their balance, held hands and looked out over the restless grey water. It was fresh here, cooler than in the wood. They did not talk, but sometimes their eyes briefly met, and their hands did not let go of each other. The wind blew over the lake towards them, raising little waves so that water sprayed in their faces.

Lurching

The caster, his journeyman and a potter from Weissensee were sitting with Käthe at the table on the veranda, munching the sorrel that Käthe, not expecting visitors, had sent Ella to pick in the meadow beside the Fliess, and that she was now serving as a salad with lemon, oil and finely chopped parsley. Ella brought glasses, a bottle of the Bulgarian wine of which, to Käthe's annoyance, there had been only mellow varieties in the shops for months now, and a jug of tap water. The windows to the garden, where tulips and daffodils were in flower, were wide open.

As soon as Ella had handed round the glasses, Käthe told her for goodness' sake to take the potatoes out of the oven or they would burn. Ella took the hot baking tray out with an oven glove and put it down in the middle of the table, on the tile with the painted picture of a naked woman. The halved potatoes, cut side down on the tray, were still audibly sizzling in the oil, and the aroma of the thyme that Ella had sprinkled over them rose in the air. The guests praised the sorrel salad, and Käthe beamed: What did I tell you? Käthe knows how to cook, no one leaves my table unsatisfied.

Ella filled the glasses with the ruby wine. The chair beside the caster's journeyman, opposite Käthe and the potter, was still vacant. Ella sat down and put some salad on her plate. The caster's journeyman had restless legs, and kept fidgeting about with them under the table. He had to sit with his legs wide apart. Ella wondered whether he was nudging her thigh with his knee by accident or on purpose. She concentrated on the sorrel. Across the table from her, she was aware of the potter's eyes lingering on her hands, her fork, her mouth. She didn't have to look up to know how his long, pale beard fell to his chest, how his curly, ash-grey hair came down to his shoulders. Nothing at all about the potter seemed to her attractive. How could she stop him looking at her? He had fallen into decline long ago. Nausea came over her. But Ella did like the caster's strong shoulders, his deep voice, his large, firm hands. As usual the caster had eyes only for Käthe, and today there was something persistent in his voice.

Pour the water, Ella, Käthe said, interrupting the caster. She held her nearly empty wine glass out to Ella across the table. Ella picked up the water carafe and filled Käthe's glass to the brim. The potter quickly finished his wine, put both hands round his glass, and waited meekly until Ella finally poured some for him as well, last of all. Water trickled into his pale beard.

The caster stuck to his theme, and was not to be distracted from it: If all the young men born between 1940 and 1943 are now being called up for military service, I suppose your Thomas is among them?

No, snapped Käthe. The caster's choice of subject was unwelcome. She drank half her glass of water. He's going to be a doctor now, he's studying.

Studying medicine, is he? There was a silly note of awe in the potter's question, and he asked it so quietly that Käthe didn't hear him.

Käthe cleared her throat. Thomas is a few weeks too young, born in '44, he's only just had his eighteenth birthday. Käthe drained her glass in a single draught, relieved to have thought of such a simple explanation. She helped herself to potatoes before anyone else. Even before the others had plucked up courage to take themselves, she speared a crisp piece of potato on her fork and blew on it loudly. Luckily. It would have been silly of them to take the young men out of the industries now. Snorting, she bit into the hot potato. They're needed, after all, those young men. Thomas has been on duty round the clock for the last week. Haven't you heard? They can't control the dysentery.

They have dysentery?

The whole city has dysentery. Käthe put another large piece of potato into her mouth all at once, and went on, chewing: In any case, they're using all the emergency beds they can find. Thomas is working two or three shifts running all the time. I can't think when they get any sleep. She stuffed a forkful of sorrel into her mouth, and a leaf soaked in oil fell on her blouse.

Doesn't he want to do his national service? The caster wasn't letting the subject drop; the armed forces were very important to him.

What are you talking about – what do you mean, national service? Käthe laughed out loud, and the oily little leaf on her mighty bosom heaved up and down. It won't come to that. The Germans have done enough killing already. Käthe asked if anyone wanted more salad. Without waiting for an answer, she pulled the bowl towards her and picked out the last leaves with her fork.

The caster did not seem to like Käthe's decided attitude. He turned to the potter. You say something, why don't you?

Listen, said Käthe, before the potter could take his eyes off Ella and answer, just because they've thought up national service over there we don't have to make the same stupid mistake.

The caster pushed his fork round his plate, and the potter

tentatively shrugged his shoulders, looking at Ella as if she might help him out.

Oh, silly me! I've forgotten my napkin again. Shaking her head, Käthe removed the little leaf from her bosom and put it in her mouth. She rubbed her blouse with her finger, but the oily mark wouldn't go away. Ella tried to get her legs into safety. The nudging of the assistant's knee was making her nervous.

We have a little society in Weissensee, a drawing circle, sighed the potter. His squawking voice disgusted her. We're looking for a young model to sit for nude studies, Ella. Do you have any spare time? Maybe we could even pay you something.

Go on, do it, Ella, said Käthe, before Ella could answer for herself.

Ella nodded. How often did anyone need her these days? Since she had left school, was only attending evening classes, and brought hardly any money home from the wardrobe mistress for whom she worked at the theatre, Ella had to do all she could to show Käthe how willing she was to work.

Suddenly Käthe looked back and forth in surprise at the potter and Ella, as if discovering something. Have you been painting your lips?

Two flies buzzed over the salad bowl, flew in a circle, settled and then flew up again. Ella did not answer; she felt the eyes of all three men on her.

And what have you done to your hair, Ella?

Ella wished she had a cap of invisibility. She pressed her leg firmly against the caster's journeyman's nudging knee to make him stop it. She had backcombed her hair a little before tying it into a ponytail. Was she supposed to explain that?

Comb your hair out, that just looks silly. Käthe gulped down the last of her wine, clicked her tongue, and turned to the caster. Wasting her time in front of the mirror instead of doing a good day's work. And calls herself a modern girl! Her scornful snort sprayed saliva in Ella's ear. Chair and all, Ella moved back from the table, and the chair legs scraped on the floor. She wanted to get up and walk out.

And the blouse. What's that blouse you're wearing? Käthe raised her eyebrows and jutted her chin, as if she couldn't believe what she saw.

Ella had gone bright red by now. The wine was throbbing under her temples, she looked down at herself. She was stupid. Stupid Ella.

I don't believe it, cried Käthe, indignantly letting her hands drop to her lap. I've been looking for that blouse everywhere! And I actually suspected that, oh what's her name, Thomas's colleague who's always flitting in and out of the house!

It's – Ella would have liked to explain how she had come by the blouse. It was true that she could find no explanation, but she was ready to think one up, anything.

Käthe interrupted her: I told you to keep away from my wardrobe!

Couldn't she have found the blouse under the fuchsias, blown off the washing-line? It wasn't me, Käthe, I found it in the garden –

Don't pretend. You'll take that blouse off this minute, said Käthe. Is this what it's come to? I'm not having my own child steal from me.

Ella flung her fork across the table and jumped up. The blue of the plate annoyed her, she smashed it on the floor and stamped on the pieces. Here, she shouted, here's your stupid blouse! How easily the fabric tore. Ella already had the thin silk blouse with its fine embroidery in her hand, she threw the scraps on the baking tray in the middle of the table. Before the potter could feast his eyes on her bare breasts, she ran through the door leading from the veranda to the dark house and slammed it behind her.

Silence in the smoking room, cool air in the corridor, peace in the day. Ella pressed down the handle of the bathroom door, but it was locked. None of the guests could have got past her – they were still sitting on the veranda. One of Käthe's cardigans was hanging on the coat stand, and Ella put it on, so as not to stand there bare-breasted in the cold corridor. She was trying the handle of the door a second time when the floor behind her creaked. Alarmed, Ella turned round. Thomas was standing in the open doorway of his room. He looked tired and pale. Don't, he whispered, Marie's in there.

Marie?

The ward sister from the hospital.

Ella let go of the door handle and went a step towards Thomas. Only now did she reply to his whisper: You keep bringing her home these days. Is she your . . .?

My . . .?

Your girlfriend?

Thomas put his forefinger on Ella's mouth. She's married, he whispered. At that moment the door opened and the slender figure of Marie appeared.

We'll get two or three hours of sleep, then we have to go back to the hospital.

In the middle of the day? Ella didn't believe Thomas. The woman's wavy hair lay on her shoulders, she wore a plain skirt, and greeted Ella with a little bob. Was she drunk or was she swaying with exhaustion?

Because of the epidemic. Thomas must mean the dysentery. Ella pretended not to know what he was talking about. It's been a long night, we worked until midday. Don't tell anyone we're here. Thomas took Marie's hand, put his other arm round her

262

shoulders and guided her into his room. We have to be off again at six. He closed the door.

Ella stood in the dark corridor, wondering, poffletoffle, whether simply to go in after them, open the door to Thomas's room, snipsnap, be there if he wanted to get some rest with this Marie. Would Ella be in the way?

In the bathroom, she put her mouth down to the tap and drank water from it. With an air of decision she went down the corridor, opened the door to Thomas's room without knocking, and asked: Have you seen my maths book anywhere?

Sorry, no, said Thomas, who was kneeling on the rug in the middle of the room. Marie was sitting fully clothed on the bed, dabbing her eyes with a handkerchief. They were reddened, her black mascara was so smeared that Ella wondered if she was crying.

Please. Thomas stood up and went over to the door, put his hand on Ella's arm. Please, he whispered quietly, leave us in peace.

Just as you say, replied Ella, annoyed, anything you like. If I can't find my maths book I can't study. And if I can't study, I'll never pass the exams, and it will be your fault, and –

Please. Thomas took a firmer grip of her arm to make her let go of the handle and leave the room. He gestured urgently to Ella. Just for today, I'll look for your maths book tomorrow.

Let go of me! Ella screamed, swung her arm back and then up in the air. She left it there for a second, two seconds, she could hit Thomas with his tired, angelic face if he went on waiting like that for her to leave him alone with this Marie. Then her arm dropped; Ella felt embarrassed in front of the weeping woman sitting on the edge of Thomas's bed. She went away.

Down by the Fliess Ella took off her sandals, turned up the legs of her trousers, and slipped down the sand on the little slope.

The water was still cold, she waded along by the low bank. Myriads of tadpoles moved apart and swam away.

She tried to catch some with her hands, but the tadpoles were quick. A bicycle bell rang over the meadow. Someone was waving. He swung his arm in a circle like a windmill and pushed the bike over the soggy ground of the paddock with his other hand. Ella made out that she hadn't seen him. She turned her back on Siegfried, bent down and held her hands in the cold water. When she bent down she was hidden, the slope to the riverbed protected her. The cardigan slipped over her wrists and its sleeves got wet. Ella waded faster, maybe she could reach the other bank and run away. But the river was deeper in the middle, and her trouser legs were already wet.

There you are at last! Siegfried had reached the sandy path that ran along the top of the slope. He let the bike fall in the grass and slid down the shallow slope to Ella.

You'd vanished off the face of the earth. He took his shoes off, took his old cap off his head, and waded through the water to Ella. Maybe he wanted to kiss her, but Ella turned away.

Where've you been these last weeks? There was a greasy shine to his leather jacket.

Working. Ella bent down and tried catching tadpoles again.

Why didn't you even answer me? I came to your place lots of times and left notes for you. Didn't Käthe pass them on?

Ella went after a little shoal of tadpoles, the water splashed up, she nearly slipped. The loosely knitted cardigan was wet all over now, and pulling heavily down. But Ella didn't mind cold water. What notes?

Letters and messages. I thought it would be nice for us to meet, I suggested times. Siegfried's eyes lingered for a moment on the place where Ella supposed he saw her breasts, small, pointed breasts, they could be standing out under the dripping wet cardigan.

I thought we could go dancing together at the May Club. Siegfried tried to hold Ella's arm, but she quickly swerved aside.

She had caught a tadpole, lifted it out of the water and examined it. You could already see tiny stumps on its sides that would grow into legs. It's over. Ella looked brightly into Siegfried's pleading eyes.

That can't be what you want. Siegfried touched her hair, looked with admiration at her ponytail, the slightly backcombed lift of the hair above her forehead.

Ella threw her handful of water with the tadpole up in the air, as if setting a bird free to fly, and the water splashed, making Siegfried step back. She wasn't smiling. What I want is my own business.

Horror showed on Siegfried's face. Dominique! He reached his hand out to her, clumsily. Ella thought of a jumping jack, but her expression was serious, with an iron gravity.

Have I done something wrong? Getting no pity, he gave himself some. He stooped his shoulders, his head fell forward, his hands crushed the crown of the Marlon Brando peaked cap into a small ball. There was a tearful note in his question: Tell me, what did I do wrong?

Nothing. I don't love you, that's all.

You . . .? His pitiful grimace showed that he didn't doubt what she said. He was going to shed tears any moment now. Is there . . . someone else?

Ella didn't want to see it, she wanted to turn round and catch tadpoles. What was this boy thinking of? How did he come to be asking her such questions? Were they married, engaged, promised to each other? Just because they'd sometimes played at husband and wife? Because she had made up her eyes like Brigitte Bardot, and he wore a leather jacket like Brando's? Had he thought those signs were real? Real jackets, real make-up, real love?

Dominique, he managed to say, putting out his hand to her hair, as if the memory of the film *The Truth* that they had seen at the cinema together last year, just before the Wall was closed, could persuade Ella to be his Brigitte Bardot again, his lover for ever. Even at the time she had wondered where love like that came from, where it was supposed to come from. Where did you get love if not by stealing it, if not by playing at it? Ella could play at it, that was all. His greasy hair shone in the sun, the bridge of his slightly reddened nose gleamed, he had a pimple on his forehead. She would never love him. Yet Siegfried couldn't help that. She just wondered why this new Siegfried was suddenly so strange to her, seemed so ridiculous. A wild character in a leather jacket. Whereas Johnny, over the last few years, used to stand at the side of the dance floor, looking soulful, Siegfried would wink at the company, sure of victory. He had always known how to conquer Ella, at least for a dance, for an evening, for that kiss. Now he was stammering clumsily, the afternoon sun dazzled him, he had to narrow his eyes, and what he came up with, stuttering and swallowing, seemed to Ella shallow and paltry: Ella, I love you!

Even her real name, Ella, sounded empty, worth nothing, like an insubstantial screen behind which she disappeared. Had she given him false hopes, ought she to feel guilty? His reddened nose was shiny.

Ella did not pretend to feel sorry for him. She folded her arms and said nothing. On the bridge, not a hundred metres away, she saw two figures holding hands and leaning intimately close. They stopped for a moment by the handrail, then went on and disappeared behind the hazel bushes. Presumably Thomas was taking his Marie to the tram, perhaps they were on their way back to the hospital together.

Wait, begged Siegfried, as Ella moved to walk past him and wade to the bank. What can I do? Tell me. I'll do anything.

Ella did not like obsequious people. She had often wondered what it was that Käthe liked about admirers and flatterers. How did the sculptor who portrayed the ideal of the Upright Man bear the way her friends and comrades bowed and scraped? Sometimes it was as if Käthe simply did not know when someone was pretending, she reacted so happily and openly to all attempts to win her favour.

There's nothing to be done, Siegfried. So long! She clambered out of the water, the sand was warmed by the sun. She picked a leaf from a flowering yarrow plant and stuck it in her mouth. The hard leaf crunched pleasantly between her teeth. She climbed the slope, holding onto bushes and enjoying the warm ground, the scratchy sensation of the old blades of grass and the soft, fresh growth under her bare feet. On the bridge Ella looked around, but there was no sign of Thomas and Marie, no waiting tram, not a single car came along the street. Ella swung herself up on the handrail of the bridge and walked along it, above the Fliess. She guessed that Siegfried was watching her. If he'd asked whether she wanted to go to the cinema, who knew, maybe she'd have let him take her. She'd have slept with him too if he hadn't wanted any romantic stuff and talk about the future.

When Ella entered the house she thought the corridor seemed gloomy. How long did it take for the cold of winter to leave the house every year? The sound of voices and laughter echoed across the yard, Käthe liked to take her guests to the studio. Smoke was still rising from the ashtrays in the smoking room. Ella knew she had to study. The exams would be in the summer. On Sundays like this, when she wasn't working for the wardrobe mistress at the theatre, she really ought to be studying. Yes, if she could, but she couldn't. She didn't feel any desire to study.

Someone had left his wine glass on the table half full. Ella drained it in a single draught. The door to Thomas's room was open, just a crack. Want to play badminton? That was what Ella would ask Thomas if he was there. She opened the door, but as she had expected, the room was empty. She hadn't won a single game against Thomas for months; last time she had thrown the racket at his head because his delight in winning annoyed her so much.

Ella almost closed the door; she didn't want everyone to see what she was doing in Thomas's room.

There was a full glass of water beside his bed, and an empty glass that had probably contained wine; the purple mark at the bottom had dried up. Ella looked around; maybe she'd find some trace of that girl Marie. The curtains were still drawn. Ella went over to the window on the right and moved the green fabric aside to look out into the street. A moth fluttered towards her, landed on the windowsill, flew up into the dark curtain with a faint whirr of its dusty wings.

Thomas's bed was neatly made. It was probably this Marie's habit to leave everything neat and tidy. Did her husband know where she spent her midday break resting between two shifts? What was it Thomas had said, she had a small child? Where was the child? With a foster-family, like the twins, in a hostel that took children during the week, or at home with the husband?

Ella knelt down and looked into the narrow space under the bed, checking what was there. Her fingers groped around until she felt paper. She pushed the water glass aside and pulled out the blue folder. Did Thomas read poems to his Marie? A sketch of a sleeping woman lay at the top of the folder. Ella recognised Thomas's style at once; he liked red chalk, and he seldom needed more than five or six lines for a face. She recognised Marie's eyes. A line here for her shape, the curve of a narrow hip, only a hint. A thin arm lying at her side, an almost tentative line. The drawing wasn't finished yet, he still had to draw her breasts, her stomach, her mount of Venus. There was only one leg so far, drawn up at an angle, a leg with a slender foot. Ella couldn't see any indication of the nakedness of her body. She turned the sheet of paper over, but he had only noted down a poem on the other side, also in red chalk. *It is especially / good to couple / in red light / The image strangely blurred / strange the face . . . // Endless the loneliness / smoke rises covering like a veil / In the shadow of the other / both unite!* Was this Marie just a colleague or a girlfriend, a secret one? Did they undress in front of each other? The disabling of the body, the desecration of the eyes, there it was again, the sanctity of loneliness. Hadn't he said, only a few days ago, that Marie had shown him a dying man? It was impossible to operate on that patient; he would be dissected only after death, in the cause of scientific research. Organs were removed from a dead body and thrown away, Thomas said, so next day the man would have to lie on his stretcher not only dead and naked but empty as well, before he disappeared into Hades. Zeshmendava. It was difficult for Ella to imagine Thomas touching that girl Marie, seeing her naked, undressing himself. The body was probably sacred to him, Violetta had once said, confiding in Ella, unburdening herself of her complaints. She had offered him her mouth, but he had kissed her only hesitantly, as if he were endangering gold dust. *Here and there heads rise / heavy, smoky vapour / mingles with flailing / arms and legs – The quiet / cooing of birds with full crops.* The next lines were crossed out with a thick pencil. Ella narrowed her eyes: *Stamped underfoot on rotting ground – / cries of pleasure crunch in the / orchestra's ecstatic raging . . .* Who was that poem for? *Apart, on the rim of the fleshly struggle / With secret silent expectation / washing around it / Covered by metallic trumpet cries / Forced by the drums to wild stamping.* Whose trumpets and drums were being brought up here? *He holds his breath and sees his face / blurred by endless helplessness . . . / . . . And grief mingles with disgust . . .* What part was Thomas trying out? A strong and desperate one? When something felt strange to him he would resort to disguise, to dissembling. Madness never took him in its grasp. The madness was hers alone. Picklydipuck shnucklesuck. Magic words, spoken only to herself, with no echo, bringing no happiness. What was he afraid of, what did grief and disgust mean to him?

There were footsteps in the corridor. Ella closed the folder and pushed it under the bed as quietly as she could. The footsteps stopped outside the unlocked door, no other sound met Ella's ears. Käthe might ask what she was doing there if she saw Ella kneeling beside Thomas's bed. As quietly as possible, Ella raised her right leg. Something creaked in the corridor. She heard a match striking. No breathing, no rattling of a cigarette case or rustling of a packet. The smoke of a cigarette came through the narrow gap where the door stood ajar. Even before Ella was on her feet, the door was pushed open.

The lodger stood there in his hat and coat, holding a briefcase.

Who said you could use this room? His glance fell on the black walls, the shattered glass of the shot-up picture which made Ulbricht unrecognisable, the desk, his typewriter.

Ella stood up, clutching her cardigan together at the neck.

They said last year you wouldn't be back.

Suspected of undermining our efforts – the lodger puffed out smoke – that's what we call it when someone talks too much.

Could be. Anyway, there was no one here for a long time, so my brother thought he could use the room.

Your brother – thought?

Käthe said so. No one comes here any more, so we might as well use it. She wants to rent it out to students as soon as I've found my own place. Then Thomas can have my room.

What kind of place are you hoping to find, a room on your own?

An apartment.

I see, a whole apartment for the high-class daughter of the intelligentsia.

The lodger was looking at the door. So you two simply changed the lock, did you? Took it off? The lodger took a step towards Ella.

Intelligentsia? Ella knew that on a Sunday, in full daylight, someone could come into the house at any time to use the toilet.

Barefoot, eh? The lodger ventured a grin. Ella looked down at herself. Only now did she realise that she had left her sandals on the bank of the river. Her toenails had black rims, and there was sand between her toes. The lodger put his briefcase down on the desk, opened it, and took out a loose-leaf file. He opened the file, studied a note with two official stamps at the top, and said, as a length of ash fell off his cigarette to the floor: But you know, don't you, that these items of furnishing are state property? This desk, the typewriter, the bed, the lamp, a picture – fleetingly, the lodger raised his head and glanced at the frame with the picture that had been used as a target – and a rug. Three metres by three metres. If I may ask, what have you done with the bouclé rug? Ella looked at the rug where paint had been spilt last summer. The place had dried up, no one had gone to the trouble of washing the rug. What rug? She could hear footsteps and voices in the corridor.

We brought a pale green rug in.

I don't know anything about that.

Doors opened and closed in the corridor. Well, this is a surprise, Heinz, what are you doing here? Käthe came into the room, closely followed by the potter; perhaps she had been going

271

to show him the bathroom. The potter stayed standing in the doorway.

Good day. What am I doing here? Checking the inventory. As you know, comrade, these things were to have been taken away tomorrow in a van.

A van? I don't know anything about that. Käthe put her hands on her hips.

Were to have been. But we're staying.

You're staying?

Can we talk privately?

Käthe turned to the potter, and then her eyes fell on Ella. Of course, yes.

We shall go on paying the rent. A friend of mine will be arriving at the end of May. Hartmut.

Hartmut?

Can we speak alone, please? The lodger pointed to the desk. And incidentally, there are personal possessions in this desk. I'll take those away today.

Ella squinted at the desk. Had Thomas never opened the desk drawer? Its lock seemed to be intact.

This is Heinz, my lodger. We have to discuss something in private, Käthe told the potter, who seemed to be rooted to the spot in the doorway. And you get out of here, said Käthe firmly, turning to Ella. How about this? Käthe took hold of Ella's cardigan. What a nerve! First my blouse, then my cardigan. She gave Ella a ringing slap in the face. Get out, and fast. How long since she had last had her face slapped? Was there an age when you were too old for it? Ella had never minded a slap in the face as little as she did today. Ella nodded, and she pushed past the potter.

Have you thought about the proposition? His voice squawked slightly.

Not yet. Without turning to him, Ella unbuttoned the

272

cardigan and hung it up on the hook. Her long hair tickled her back pleasantly. She thought only fleetingly of the discussion of parabolas and curves that she ought to have been studying. Modelling for a Weissensee drawing circle, thought Ella. The words Weissensee drawing circle made her think of circular French knitting with a spool and four nails. Is anyone hungry? The hell with this passion for working, this reverence for labour, all that wretched striving for assiduous performance. You could live without ambition. She wanted to paint, she wanted to draw with Indian ink, maybe a watercolour of a fading magnolia. Paper and paints were available in Käthe's studio. After that slap in the face she could leave the potter and the lodger alone with Käthe, her mind at rest. With her trouser legs rolled up to the knee, Ella went barefoot and topless along the corridor as if that were the most natural thing in the world, and opened the door to the smoking room. Was her cheek glowing from Käthe's hand, from the wine, from her wish to paint? Fongfong. There was a green bottle on the long table in the smoking room, still one-third full of the dark wine. Ella broke the cork, which was crumbling and soft, and the sourish smell of wine rose to her nostrils. She pushed the remains of the cork down into the bottle with her finger and drank, the wine gurgling down her throat, without putting the bottle down, without breathing or tasting it, until the bottle was empty. Ella could already hear the voices of the caster and his journeyman from the stairs. Käthe had probably left them to wait in the studio while she showed the potter the whereabouts of the bathroom up in the house.

The journeyman fell silent when he saw Ella, half naked, coming down the stairs. Ella ignored him, went over to the chest of portfolios, and pulled out the top drawer. Behind her back, the caster was now silent too. At her leisure, Ella tested the quality of the paper. Most of the sheets seemed to her too large and too thin. Paper for drawing was not suitable for Indian ink. She closed the drawer and opened the one under it. Here, Käthe kept pencils, charcoal, chalks, pens for Indian ink and erasers all in wild confusion; separated from them by a wooden partition in the middle of the drawer were brushes of various sizes, rough bristle brushes, silky mink and badger brushes, and also wooden sticks, flat ones and round ones, with dried paint on them. To the right of the drawer, again separated from the rest of the contents by an old water-level, lay the tubes, little bowls and bottles of gouache, tempera and oil paint, coloured ink, a small, round container of black Indian ink, and several tubes and small screw-top bottles of watercolours. It all smelled of turpentine. Her hands wriggled like eels among the tubes, pushed some aside, took others out of the depths of the cupboard. She found a half-empty little bowl of white Indian ink, a tube of pale yellowish-green watercolour and a blue one, now all she needed was purple. The silence behind her excited her. There was not a word from the caster and his journeyman. Ella thought of the caster's deep, full voice, and the powerful shoulders with which he had lifted the bronzes out of his car and carried them into the studio as if they were light wooden carvings. The wine was singing behind Ella's forehead, it sang in a ruby-red, a purple voice, it rushed along like a stream to which she would entrust herself and all the paints. Panther Rei, Thomas had once said to her, or something like that, and Ella had been glad to understand one of his cryptic magical words for once, because wasn't the *rey* the king, the king of the panthers? Thomas had laughed, not mocking her, but he had told her gently: *Panta, panta rhei.* Ella had to pull the drawer farther out to look in the depths of the chest for purple paint. She placed herself sideways on to it, her long hair fell forward over her shoulders, she ran her hands through the paints and swept and pushed them together with her forearm. Cobalt, aquamarine, indigo. Most of the tubes were rolled far up, the tops were missing from a few of them. Fiery red clung to the fingers of her right hand, and something dark as well, probably charcoal. Ella was now almost lying with her torso over the drawer so that she could reach right inside the cupboard with her outstretched arm. Ouch – she took her hand out and put her thumb into her mouth. Something had cut her, probably the sharp folded edge of a tube. Ella tasted oil paint, there was nothing for it, if she had cut her thumb saliva was the best treatment.

Can we help? There it was, the caster's deep and by no means agitated voice. Ella turned to him. He was trying hard to look into her eyes, but his glance kept slipping down to her breasts, at which his journeyman was also openly staring.

It's okay. Not too bad. Ella sucked her thumb with a smacking noise.

A plaster? The man was still standing there rooted to the spot, but was now looking around him.

Nonsense, I don't need a plaster. Ella took her thumb out of her mouth and held it proudly up. All there, I haven't cut anything off. Sure enough, the thumb shone as rosy as a baby's, except that there was still a crescent of red paint, not blood, under the nail. The cut was fine and only superficial; the skin was closing and looked almost white. Ella leaned forward again, her hair was hanging down into the drawer, and she fished in the dark depths with her fingers to where all she could feel was wood. She drew the huge, shallow drawer out almost to the point where it would go no further, stood close to the opening and stretched, swaying slightly and finally lying right over it, to get at the two tubes she had spotted at the very back. There was a glow of purple from the depths of the cupboard; her magnolia would have a blue tinge. Suddenly something cracked, the drawer sagged beneath her breasts. Quick as lightning, Ella took her arm out of the deep cupboard and braced it under the drawer, trying to hold the heavy thing in place, but next moment it crashed to the floor. Ella, bending over it, was swaying with the drawer against her knees, so that she slipped, she tried to regain her balance with her hands, the drawer dropped on her feet, and Ella propped herself up on it with her fingertips. The thin wooden bottom of the drawer had broken away from the frame opposite her, pencils, pens, brushes, paints, everything had been slipping about in it. Some of the contents had jumped and rolled out of the drawer. Only now did Ella feel her toes and the instep of her right foot hurting. The drawer had fallen half on the floor, half on her feet.

All right? The caster placed one hand on Ella's back. Her voice was shaking slightly, but she said: Yes, fine, it's okay. The warmth of his hand aroused her. Ella let out a cockerel screech: Cock-a-doodle-do, cackle cackle ackle, pant ha rh'ai, herbai, herbai.

Help me, will you? said the caster to his assistant, taking his hand off Ella's back, and together they lifted the drawer slightly to one side so that Ella could move her feet freely. She wriggled the toes of her left foot, all of them, except for the second, her longest toe, which had swelled up dramatically within a few seconds. Little spots of clear red blood were seeping through the grazed skin of her instep. The foot hurt so much that Ella could hardly lift her toes.

Can you put any weight on it? The caster held his arm out to Ella to help her to support herself. But Ella tried to do it without support. A step, another one. Like a dancer, she spread her hands out, away from her body. She could walk, but the pain came in waves; if it seemed never to have been there at one moment it overwhelmed her the next, making her grit her teeth at the same time as she cried out. Her cries were shrill but not piercing. She didn't want to bring Käthe down on them. Käthe would surely still be deep in an important discussion with the lodger of his possessions, the property of State Security, and as it was State Security and the people were the state, strictly speaking it was all about not just state-owned furniture but the rightful property of the people. Ella took a third step, the caster walked beside her, holding his arm at an angle in the air, so that she could catch hold of it at any time. Ella was lurching, but she was sure the caster didn't notice. She imagined a silk thread holding her up like a puppet, no pain in her toe could affect her, as a puppet it was easy to walk with your head held high. Right – Ella hesitated – right, left. Something pricked the bare sole of her foot. Now she did lean her left elbow on the caster's handsome shoulder, holding the back of his neck with her hand. She raised her left leg and looked at the sole of her foot. There was a drawing pin in the ball of it. May I? The caster wanted to help her pull the drawing pin out. He smelled of masculinity, of copper and of weight. Ella tried to think what the smell reminded her of. It was not a question of being able to take the drawing pin out, she could have done that for herself, it was only a harmless drawing pin pricking her, it didn't hurt. But Ella liked the way he had asked permission. Liked it that he was finally paying her attention, without falling for her straight away when her bare breast lay against his shirt, against his shoulder, and when he bent down, her hair falling around his head, when he bent down and she saw the pulse in his throat, when he bent down to pull out the drawing pin. The man who never tried to talk to anyone but Käthe, who hung only on Käthe's lips, well, she would open his blind eyes today.

The caster was red, red all over his face as he straightened up, and showed her the sharp little pin.

Pretty, said Ella. She was waiting for him to look at her, first at her breasts, then at her eyes, then at her breasts again. With slight pressure, she moved her hand from the back of his neck to his throat. It seemed to Ella that his pupils widened, his eyes shone. Was that lust in his eyes? His firm shoulders did not shake, that caster could hardly *fall* for anyone, at most maybe he might sink for someone a little.

Ella turned her head. The journeyman was standing in front of them, keeping watch, his arms hanging down, his hands, probably unknown to himself, clenched into fists.

Coffee time, master, said the journeyman. But Ella kept her hand on the caster's neck.

Coffee time. There's always cake on Sundays, master.

The master craftsman did not even nod, but turned his head, with Ella's hand on his neck, and looked at Ella's mouth as he spoke to her.

Want to come with us? My wife has baked a cake. She bakes a cake every Sunday.

Come where, to Schöneiche? Ella was amazed by this idea, and laughed out loud. What would she do in Schöneiche?

Wait a minute. The caster knelt down on the floor in front of Ella. He took hold of her ankle and told her to lean on him so that she could lift the foot. Ella did as she was told. She propped herself on the caster's shoulder with both hands, and obediently raised her foot in the air. The caster held her ankle, bent the foot forward and back, forward and back. That one's all right, now the other foot. Ella changed to stand on her other leg. The caster moved the swollen foot up and down, the sprinkling of blood was already drying up, no blood was flowing, a scab would form, that was all. The caster put his other hand round her ankle and placed her foot back on the floor. Involuntarily he touched her muscular calf, the back of her knee, and looked up, raised his face with his head tilted back. His mouth was level with her crotch, tiny dark stubbly hairs showed on his chin. There was a tingling in the pit of Ella's stomach.

The journeyman noticed, he was watching. Ella was sure that there couldn't be any noticeable contact between them. The journeyman believed in his master's honour, he was standing guard over it.

Thanks, but I'll just clear up here. Ella moved her feet. She saw her footprints in the white stone dust on the floor.

We'll help you. The journeyman sounded relieved; at last his fists unclenched, and he moved to help Ella. He handed her a small tube with purple paint sticking to it. Ella read the label: egg tempera. She wasn't going to mix watercolours and tempera, the tempera would absorb all the paints into it, there would be nothing light and watery and hardly any glow to her magnolia. While the caster tied his shoelaces with great ceremony, Ella and the journeyman turned to the drawer. With a small hammer that had been lying on the workbench along with larger ones, the journeyman knocked nails into the drawer so that the bottom of it fitted firmly into the frame again. Together, they lifted and slid the drawer into place; it took several attempts. As Ella was not looking at the journeyman, he probably thought she didn't notice him glancing at her breasts.

I can do the rest by myself, said Ella. She stood in front of the open drawer and put the old water-level that it contained on one side, the wooden partition on the other. How large had the separate compartments been? She bent down and picked up tubes of paint, pens, brushes, chalks. Most of the chalks had split, like the charcoal. However, they had probably been split already, Ella told herself as she picked up the pencils and the pencil leads lying about broken into many pieces. The caster was still tying his shoelaces. What was the matter with him, couldn't he tie a bow? Was Ella expected to help him? The journeyman bent down to collect the crayons that had rolled under the workbench and over to the door into the yard, and handed them to Ella, who put them in one or the other compartment of the drawer, depending on what kind and what colour they were. There wasn't a purple one. Ella put a magenta one that would have been better for fuchsias on the cupboard, along with the watercolours she had chosen, and added a bright violet. Why no aquilegia? A magnolia the colour of fuchsias and aquilegias. Out of the corner of her eyes, she saw the caster standing up.

The journeyman had noticed it too. Let's go, master, he said, coffee time will soon be over.

Dream?
(May 1962)

A grisly sound cries out in the night
A tooth grates on deep sand;
I climb from my grave –
And the vapours it gave –
With bloodstained rags on foot and hand,
And laughed as a madman might.

The stench rises to the tall tree,
Green leaves rot and fall.
Waxen hair blows in the wind wild,
With crunching teeth I eat a child,
Closing my lips, consuming it all,
I see pus and foam dripping down.

A cry for help sounds in the sun –
What I am there is not me!
Eating a child
Pissing on the undefiled,
What I see there is not me.
It's the death of all, and has just begun.

Collecting

Oppressive heat, the air flickering above the tramlines. Thomas was leaning against a lamp post, waiting for Marie. They had been working the early shift, and the afternoon was free. Thomas knew where Marie and her husband lived. But she had not let him take her home. In no circumstances was Thomas to be seen in Samariterstrasse, not by the neighbours or anyone else. No one was to tell her husband that she had been seen with the young man. Marie had told him to wait while she went home, packed bathing towels and fetched her little girl from the crèche at the end of the road, and then she and the child would come to the Frankfurter Tor underground station. The bathing beach by the Müggelsee would be overcrowded. Thomas wanted to show her the marshland, the little bay. No one would come upon them there, not Marie's mother-in-law or her husband's colleagues, and the husband himself was at work until six. Tuesday was the evening when he went drinking with his friends, and he wouldn't be home before ten. Thomas felt uneasy; he still couldn't think of Marie as a mother, his hands were sweating. A July day lay before them. Thomas watched the traffic; every few minutes a small column of cars came eastward here from Alexanderplatz, stopped at the traffic lights on the roundabout and clattered on. There was a smell of petrol. Thomas felt hungry. He went into the little greengrocer's shop and bought a bunch of radishes and a bag of dried plums. There were no apples yet. He licked the stone of a sweet plum and looked at the time. Shouldn't Marie have been back by now? He leaned against the lamp post again.

That morning, a young man in Room 1 had died; he hadn't come round from an operation on his pancreas. He died while Thomas was tending his wound, without warning and without holding the hand of the wife he had married only a few months earlier, who had been visiting him at the hospital morning and evening. Thomas felt his life ebbing as he put fresh gauze on the wound. It was as if he felt the shadow of death even before he heard the breath drawn that was, although he didn't know it, the patient's last. He looked up and saw the man's yellowish face, the eyes that had been looking at him just now had rolled aside, as if by chance. Thomas dropped the gauze, he had seized the man's arm, crying out: Breathe!

The plum stone stuck to his gums. How much longer would Marie need? A brand-new Trabant stopped beside him, its engine chugging, pale vapour enveloping the vehicle like a cloud, and also enveloping Thomas and cutting off his view.

The men in the neighbouring beds had sat up, curious. They wanted to know what had happened. Thomas felt hot and cold by turns. Tears poured from his eyes. One of the patients made his way, with difficulty, out of bed and rang the bell for help. The bright white of the sheet hit Thomas in the eye, his retina hurt, his ears, everything about him felt sore. Never before had he felt such a strong sensation of misery. *Lips now dry and cracked / once were fierce with lust / The mouth, a black sultry cavern / can't even say Mother now.* A nurse appeared and looked at him enquiringly. Should he smile, explain something that he couldn't explain? Even his own helplessness, and this was not the first time he had felt it, seemed to him small and ridiculous in the face of the general helplessness and immense misery of the world.

Let go of him, the nurse had told him with unusual emphasis; apparently she had had to repeat the remark several times, since Thomas had not done as she said. He had tried to open his hands, but they were stiff, it had been difficult for him to let go of the dead man. He felt humbled by nature, dismayed by mankind. Would the man have died if the operation had not been carried out? What was a body worth to scientific knowledge, what was experimental medicine worth, what was it worth to the man? Was he not, in the guise of curiosity, of bringing aid, of a better world, both discoverer and researcher, both a hypocrite and a destroyer? Never mind whether the name was Rutherford, Hahn, Meitner, Strassmann, or then again Mengele, Truman, Thomas. Who could tell a good intention from a bad one? Thomas felt queasy.

The engine of the Trabant flooded. Two men got out to remove something from the boot. Thomas must have been waiting for half an hour. The sun was hot, the black plums smelled almost alcoholic. In the distance Thomas saw two women in button-through dresses wheeling a large handcart full of children along. Thomas spat the plum stone out as far as he could; it landed in the tramline rails.

Man, in his hubris, thought that he could defy nature, domesticate it, that he was not just the slave of his curiosity, of his intentions, the moral value of which Thomas found it impossible to estimate. He bore the responsibility, whether he acted or was silent, whether he killed or died. Playing God, Michael had once said, meant ignoring all that. Thomas couldn't do it, he was repelled by the jaunty gait of the surgeon with his stethoscope dangling on his chest like an order. Subduing the elements, splitting the atom, removing a thyroid here, part of a liver there, listening to hearts, and that was that, and what could you really ever expect to control? *All that lives must die – passing through nature to eternity* – from Shakespeare's standpoint that might have been true. But recently mankind had set about eradicating things. Nature, eternity, perhaps life itself. It seemed to Thomas uncertain whether you could still think in harmony with nature and mean what Shakespeare made Queen Gertrude say. Wasn't suicide, to Shakespeare, the opportunity to speed up a life played out in every spectrum?

The sun sparkled on the shining paint of the Trabant, dazzling Thomas. He was thirsty; the plums were sticking to each other in their bag. He hoped Marie would bring something to drink when she finally arrived. Thomas looked in all directions; perhaps the children at the crèche were on an outing, so Marie had to wait. He felt in his trouser pocket, but he had no cigarettes left. He had smoked them all that morning after the man died.

The white of the sheet had hurt his eyes so much that Thomas could see only a blurred image of the dead man, the yellow of his skin, the glittering of the fresh wound. He felt weak at the knees, his pulse was driving him out of himself. If he didn't hold on to the bed he would collapse, fall over, now and next moment too. Marguerite daisies danced on the dead man's bedside table, little brides of the sun. Hadn't the surgeon spoken of making progress to the young wife? Told her what progress medicine had made, and surgery. His hands had relieved the man of part of his liver, and now the cure could proceed. Hypocrite. Thomas reached for the sheet and sat down on the young man's bed. He felt a roll of something, the covers turned back under him, he heard Marie's voice saying something to him, and he wanted to stand up, but he tipped over backwards and felt the dead man's knees under his spine. Someone took his hand and touched his cheek. Thomas had not fainted although he felt faint. The marguerite daisies on the dead man's locker bowed, fading in their dance. Thomas felt a sense of surfeit, felt that it was all too much. Who was going to tell the young man's wife the news? He would never be able to work as a doctor himself. Go outside the door, get a breath of fresh air, Marie told him. He shook his head. He didn't want to leave her alone, not with the nurse hurrying in, the woman doctor entering the room, and the dead man. He didn't mind death, it was the living he minded. Thomas took a deep breath, wiped his face with his sleeve, wiped it dry. Marie tried reviving the dead man, but because of the gaping wound over his liver the procedure was difficult. The doctor gave instructions, Thomas was told to lower the raised bed by winding the handle. But when he let go of the handle and was standing upright by the bed again, the doctor too saw that the man was dead. He was to be laid out and taken away. Thomas helped Marie. She had put back the sheet and wheeled the bed out into the corridor. From there, the dead man would be taken to pathology as soon as the doctor had made out his file and the necessary forms. Marie sent Thomas back into the room to fetch the bedside table. The dead man's wife had brought the marguerite daisies that morning, when Thomas was collecting breakfast crockery from the other beds. He had seen her taking the newspaper wrapping off the flowers and sitting down beside her husband's bed, when she had looked at her watch. She probably had to keep an eye on the time, visit her husband only briefly before she went to work, and she couldn't come back until evening. She had taken his hand and pressed it to her stomach. Her husband had said something quietly, whereupon she had kissed his forehead and his temples and said goodbye.

If you were standing on a large street on a July day, thirsty and waiting for Marie and a child you didn't yet know, you could get dizzy with the heat and the exhaust fumes and the thought of the first person to die under your hand. Thomas rolled the bag up. He rubbed a radish on his trousers and put it in his mouth. To some extent, radishes could quench thirst.

What do we do with this? Thomas had held up the little beaker with the medicaments. For the first few days after a patient had had an operation, a higher dose of morphine was prescribed, mixed with a barbiturate meant to allow that patient to sleep in spite of the pain. Day by day the medicaments were weighed, measured and given out by the matron or Marie, on the doctor's orders. Marie had taken the little beaker from Thomas, opened its screw top, looked inside as if to assure herself of something, and screwed it up again. She had put the beaker in the pocket of her white coat. He won't have any more use for this now, she had whispered, what do you think?

Thomas had wiped down the bedside table, sorting out gauze, muslin bandages and tinctures on Marie's trolley the way he had watched it being done for weeks now. He knew what order she arranged things in very well. As well as he knew her figure.

Now, even from a distance, he knew the way she walked, holding the hand of a little girl in a blue dress who must be her daughter. She was carrying a basket in her other hand. Thomas spat out the plum stone and went towards them.

He crouched down in front of the child and held the bag of dried plums out to her. But the little girl turned her face into Marie's skirt, clutched her mother's hand and rubbed her face hard against the back of it. She took a quick look at Thomas only for a tiny moment, and then immediately hid behind Marie's hand again. Later, maybe, said Thomas, standing up, and he offered Marie the plums.

The tram made its way through the thickets of the city. It had an acrid smell of sweating skin clad in nylon. Later, in the suburban train, the windows were open and summer had taken up residence in the carriages. The little girl sat next to Marie, snuggling into the crook of her mother's arm, and let Marie put a plum in her mouth. Marie had taken the stone out of the fruit with her finger. Suck it first, she told her child, don't swallow the whole plum down, suck it first and then chew. With her fingertips, she searched her raffia basket for a handkerchief, but couldn't find one. Thomas guessed what she was going to ask him, and had already tried his pockets. Sorry, he said.

She licked her fingers. Don't look at me like that, she said, shifting back and forth in her seat, as if Thomas were embarrassing her.

She leaned her bare leg against his, while longing glances passed between them.

With a loud smacking noise, the child put her fingers in her mouth, took out the plum, and examined it until it slipped out of her hand. She tried to catch the plum as it fell on her dress, but it dropped on the dirty floor of the train. The child climbed down from the seat, crouched on the floor, pressed a finger into the plum and turned it over, rolled it back and forth until its black gleam was gone. You could pick up a plum like that even with one finger. The child put the fruit in her mouth and climbed back on the seat.

Under the tall elms in the shady marshland, the irises were still in flower, and countless midges settled on their skin. Marie carried the child in her arms over the marshy ground, once sinking in almost up to her knees. Thomas held her hand so that she could support herself. She had wrapped her little girl in a bathing towel to protect her from the midges.

Only by the lake, after the child had crouched on the bank for a long time kneading the wet sand, and had gone to sleep playing with Marie's hair, did she ask whether he had brought the poems he had promised her. After they had bathed he could see her breasts. Now he was lying on his stomach to hide his arousal. The little girl was sucking her thumb in her sleep and clutching her mother's hair tightly in her fist, as if afraid that she might go away.

They were alone beside the marshy bay. Thomas had been coming here for years. No one who bathed in the bay put a swimsuit or trunks on, but this was the first time that Thomas had been surprised by anyone's nakedness. Often as Marie and he had been together over the last few weeks after work, sometimes lying side by side, touching and kissing each other, he had never seen her naked from a distance and in the open air; she was lying not an arm's length away from him with her child, her skin dazzling in the sun. If he closed his eyes he had a black negative image of her. He preferred to close his eyes to hide the expression in them. Her skin was an almost translucent white, her nakedness seemed to him so new and unique that it was hard to imagine a husband. Thomas could not picture the man who saw her naked morning and evening whenever he wanted to, the man who would offer her to his colleagues for a quick fuck.

Don't you want to? She removed the strand of hair from her child's fist and began lovingly tickling the little girl's nose with it. It was only when she raised her arm that he could see blue bruising on the inside of it where the husband or one of his friends must have grabbed hold of her.

Yes. He reached under the pile of clothes beside him, and a wasp rose in the air and flew a short way, only to come down again. The wasp bent its head, other wasps came in a curving flight to suck the dried plums. Thomas had forgotten to close the bag. He put his shirt to one side, felt around for his trousers and the pockets in them. He brought out several folded sheets of paper. Right, then; Thomas reassured himself that the little girl was still asleep between them. *Forgive me, swerve away, flee /*

ecstatic death, from me. / Leave me, leave me here, / My life is sweet, is dear. // Do not force me from the light, / out and into the void of night, / I still have life in mind, / to death I am not inclined. / No, no, keep back but stay, / We will walk together for a way, / since a fight for life and breath / Can only end in death.

Marie had stopped tickling her child with her hair. The little girl was drawing short, quick breaths, her eyes moving under their lids. The oblivion of dreams. Thomas dared not raise his head higher to where he would see Marie's breasts, and then her face.

What's holding you back?

What was holding him back? Thomas was thinking of his mother; Marie could obviously read thoughts.

Will she cry?

No. Thomas flapped his hand to drive away a wasp that was now hovering in small circles above the little girl. Of course not. My mother says I would make her cry if I didn't go along with her.

Go along with her? A smile flew briefly over Marie's lips.

In general, in principle. Go along with her claims, her ideas for my future, for what will become of me. She only says that. I've never seen her in tears. Thomas stared at the blade of grass in front of his nose. She's found me a place to study medicine now, and I tell her I can't do it. She thinks I'm just a shirker, a freeloader.

Did she really say that?

Now Thomas did look at Marie's face. Did she think I would invent such words, out of nothing? He, Thomas, the inventor of the word *freeloader*? Maybe he picked up words, used them, but he had certainly never invented a single word. *Mother. I bear you like a wound / on my brow that will not close.* Gottfried Benn. Did Marie know that poem by Benn? Was it the wound or the brow that wouldn't close? Ultimately they were one and the same, and held neither pain nor thought intact within them, if in that way one is united with the mark of maternal pain. He was an empty husk, a husk carrying pain. Maybe Marie thought it wrong for him to repeat what his mother had said, for him to remember what had slipped out of her mouth, his mother's words in Marie's ear. Has your husband been hitting you? Thomas bit his tongue.

Marie did not seem startled by his answer, a question on a subject that she had never broached. Nor did she mind it. Her eyes were as clear as the lake. A wasp circled in the air between them and came down.

His elbow hurt where he had been propping himself on it for so long, holding the glance of Marie's eyes.

Marie frantically waved her hand about to raise a little wind as the wasp came down on the child's little head. Marie blew at it, but the wasp had settled on her little girl's mouth. Perhaps its feet tickled, for the child's head twitched, turned back and forth, she opened her eyes and, at the same moment, opened her mouth too in a shrill scream, a scream that turned to crying before the child ran out of breath. Now Marie touched the wasp with her fingers, but it had fastened firmly on the little girl's lips. Thomas flicked his fingernail against the insect to make it fly up, a small scrap of skin in its jaws, leaving a tiny bleeding wound on the screaming child's lips. Marie picked up her daughter and held her tight, comforting her, until tears were running down her own face. She kissed the child, sang to her, rocked her. The little girl gradually calmed down and soon fell asleep as if she had only been woken by a bad dream.

No one ought to say a thing like that to you – Marie put her hair back behind her ear – a mother doesn't make fun of her child. The way she said that it sounded like an iron law. Teasing, yes. Oh, how my own mother teased me. But she never made fun of me.

What did I have in my head, I knew nothing at all about the world. You can't do anything, you don't know anything, in Käthe's eyes and in her words he became nothing. He could hear her resolute voice.

Marie was still cradling her little girl.

And it's true. I really can't do anything. Thomas smelled Marie's sweetish sweat, he saw the rocking movement that made her one with her child, a single body. He had never yet been one with someone else's body, or not at least since his birth. Marie would not be able to release him like that, he was sure. Carefully, he folded up the sheet of paper with the poem and laid it among the other folded sheets. He had meant to read her some other poems.

I'll be with you, said Marie suddenly.

You will?

Always.

Thomas had to smile. She leaned forward and came close to his face, the child that she was rocking between them, above the little girl her firm breasts, and her mouth approached his. But before their lips touched she drew back. The morphine that the man didn't need today – Marie sat upright, holding her child close. It wasn't the first time I've taken something away. Before you came, early in the year, I did that too. Only a small quantity, there can be inaccuracies in weighing the drugs out, so it didn't appear in my poisons book. Marie wiped her little girl's forehead, which was wet with sweat. My husband found it in my handbag and questioned me about it. I said it was something for a headache.

You can give it to me. I'll keep it safe. No one searches my things, no one questions me like that.

Marie carefully put her little girl back on the towel and drew the wicker basket close to her. Reaching into it, she held the little screw-top beaker out and handed it to Thomas. You'll look after it?

He nodded.

How much was there in the container? Marie had to keep meticulous notes every day of how much of what substance she took out of the poisons cupboard, how much she gave to which patient. If any was left over, that was supposed to be taken back and a note made of the amount too. But who was going to check up on whether the patient had taken the morphine to alleviate his pain before death so suddenly took him away? Who was going to check whether the prescribed, weighed-out amount had actually been given to a patient?

As if guessing his thoughts Marie said, sitting naked in front of him: It's only a small amount, it won't be enough yet, not by a long way.

Enough for what?

For disappearing. She wasn't whispering. Her child was breathing steadily. She picked up her panties, put them on, and put her blouse on as well. She crouched beside the little girl and stroked her forehead, ran the tip of her forefinger over her eyelids, tracing the line of the pupils, caressing her eyebrows, her nose.

Thomas was able to sit up at last; he no longer had to conceal anything from Marie. The alders cast long shadows in the evening sunlight, and a wind rose; Marie had gooseflesh on her arms and legs. She had bruises on her legs as well. Why hadn't he noticed those before?

Dreaming, that's all, sleeping unaware of anything. Marie got to her feet. She brushed the soil off the sole of one foot with her hand, and slipped into her narrow lace-up shoes, one of which was still black where she had sunk into the marshy ground earlier.

Thomas watched Marie get into her skirt and do up the short

zip. Something was fluttering inside him. He was overcome by fear that she would walk away now; he had to take her to the suburban train station and lose sight of her there. Her little girl was still asleep.

Would you like my pullover? He did indeed have in his bag the pullover that he had put on to go to the hospital early that morning, before the warmth of the day had set in. He gave it to Marie and watched as she raised her slender arms in the air, and the blouse over her flat stomach slipped up a little way: he had now known, for several hours, what that body looked like naked.

Hadn't she said she would always be with him?

Could he hold her tightly, was it presumptuous to want to touch your lover's body? Be one with it? He wanted to unite with her, be one with her, one and the same body. But he guessed what her physical experience had been. Marie must be afraid of him. He didn't want to hurt her, he didn't want to make her dance, or hit her and threaten her. The thought of her husband offering her body to others maddened him.

Her head emerged from the neckline. It smells nice in your pullover, it smells safe, it smells of you, she said, smiling.

Thomas picked up his trousers, which were rather damp on one side; his underpants were still inside them, and he put on both at once. He put the folded sheets of paper with his poems on them in the right-hand pocket of his trousers, and inside the left pocket he felt the hard little beaker with the amount of morphine that was not enough yet. If only we were a couple, Thomas began, without knowing where the rest of the sentence might lead him.

We are a couple, Marie interrupted him. There's no one in the world I feel good with and want to be with except you.

I mean, Thomas said, hesitantly, for he was glad to hear what she said, but he didn't mean the secret meetings, he didn't mean the almost incorporeal ardour that inflamed all desire and yet was meant to suppress it at the same time, a real couple, he meant, and went on thinking out loud, in real life, because he wanted to explain it to her and yet he couldn't. It doesn't have to be marriage. But I mean, if we could live together as man and wife, I'd study hard, I'd go to work, never mind at what, for the little girl, for you and me. Even as he said it he felt ashamed; the word *foolish* occurred to him, he felt how silly such remarks were, how impossible his hope was.

Marie shook her head. Her smile was weary and perhaps a little sympathetic. You know it will never be like that.

Thomas did know.

He won't let me have the little one. He's always carried out his threats.

Thomas knew what she was going to say to him now; he wanted to put his hands over his ears, but he mustn't and couldn't. He was telling himself he must make an effort to understand as he heard Marie finishing what she was saying: If he catches me having a relationship he'll get a divorce, and I'll never see my little girl again.

By what right?

Never again.

By what right?

Marie bent down, picked up the little girl's bottle, took the rubber teat off and washed it. She filled the bottle with water, poured the water out, filled it again. The last rays of the red sun lit up her chestnut hair. Her long, narrow back was lying in the shadows. When she stood up and turned to Thomas, he could hardy see her eyes against the shining wreath of her hair.

I can't live without my child. I can't live with my husband, and I can't live without you. She put the bottle in her wicker basket with the dark green tin from which they had been eating nuts and bread rolls in the course of the afternoon.

There's no duty about it. No duty to love or to live. Thomas put his hand out to her, as she had done to him so often in the last few weeks. He knew that he couldn't change her life for her. Only put out his hand and go beside her.

They stood close together, his nose in the shadow of her damp hair. The air smelled of the lake and twilight. His arms trembled when he couldn't put them round her. She pressed close to him, so that he felt her breasts. Closely entwined, they stood there in silence, and he was glad that she returned his embrace, in spite of the body that could not give the lie to his desire.

I can't do anything about love, she said.

Nor can almost everyone, he replied, no one can do that, and his dry lips moved over her hairline, her delicate brows, her lips. He put his hand in his trouser pocket and brought out the little beaker.

Take good care of it, she said. I'll give you everything I can take in the immediate future.

I'll look after our poison. Thomas put the beaker back out of sight in his pocket. *We did not make our own beginning / But we can make ourselves an end, / Longing says, forget the voices. / Every passing day is our friend.*

We'll go on collecting until we have enough for both of us; her warm breath in his ear was intoxicating. He wanted to kiss her, but the child was there and could wake up and see them at any moment. Thomas nodded, and as he nodded he felt her lips against his cheek, against his ear.

It will take a few weeks, they don't keep large stocks in the cupboard and Matron checks everything. It has to be done when we get an opportunity like today.

Marie's little daughter moved under the towel. She sat up,

rubbing her eyes. Thomas let go of Marie, although the little girl wasn't looking at them but poking her finger into her ear. Look there, she said, what's that?

Marie crouched down beside the little girl. A glow-worm, darling. She put the child's blue dress on her again and noticed the dampness of her back. Let's go, it's getting cool.

The little girl couldn't walk very well or very far yet, and she wearily stretched out her arms and clung to Marie's skirt. She bit Marie's leg to make her stand still and pick her up. Marie's back hurt – not from carrying the child, from work, she had told Thomas once long ago. She showed her daughter the glow-worms all over the ground, glowing green, like the fireworks known as Bengal lights. It was like star-gazing; if you looked for long enough you saw more and more stars in the sky. They had to keep stopping, and made slow progress. Thomas picked up a small twig with a glow-worm on it from the ground. Its light was dimmer when he held it, as if the movement had alarmed it, and its stumpy little wings reminded Thomas of how he and Michael had once examined a dead glow-worm through a magnifying glass. Thomas showed the little girl the glow-worm. It was black and ordinary-looking as soon as its light went out. It's a female, he said, she crouches on the ground, glowing, and waiting for a male to come along. She can't fly.

Not fly? The little girl took a step toward Thomas to take a closer look at the insect.

Otherwise they'd never meet. The female glows and waits on the ground, the male can fly and finds her. Thomas put the twig with the little glow-worm back on the ground. Come along, you can ride on my shoulders. He picked the child up, and was surprised to find how little she weighed.

Marie went ahead over the marshy ground between the tree, hardly able to see the path in the gathering darkness. When the woodland floor became firmer and drier, they reached the Fliess. There the path was wide enough for them to walk side by side.

Marie turned to Thomas. And when they find each other?

Then the male drops to the ground in mid-flight, they mate, and a few days after the female lays her eggs they both die.

Think of that, other creatures die for no reason.

They were walking through the tall plants on the meadow now, with grasses and St John's wort tickling their calves. Looking through the trees, Thomas saw the tram with its lights on waiting for late passengers at the terminus.

You can both come home to us, said Thomas, holding onto the child's soft calves; she seemed to be asleep on his shoulders, he felt her chin weighing down strongly and heavily on his head. My mother is in Leuna, working, my sister won't mind, even if she's there. She's had an apartment allotted to her, she's hoping to get the key any day now.

Marie stopped. She put one hand against Thomas's cheek, and gave her other hand to her daughter, who was now putting out a little arm to her mother. She opened her mouth and took a deep breath, but said nothing. Now the child was holding both arms out to Marie, so Thomas lifted her down from his shoulders and put her into Marie's arms. The little girl looked curiously back, as if seeing Thomas only now and wondering what this young man looked like, the young man with whom she had spent the afternoon and who had carried her through the wood on his shoulders.

There, said the little girl, pointing to Thomas.

Instead of answering, Marie turned away with tears in her eyes. With the raffia basket over her arm and the child on her hip, she went on in the direction of the tram stop. The child kept her arms outstretched, looking past Marie's shoulder and back at Thomas, who didn't know what she wanted him to do.

I'll go with you part of the way, said Thomas, following them. Wait, Marie, I can go part of the way into the city with you.

Marie hurried on, crossed the road, and Thomas followed her. *You tell me, don't go away, / but what would I have if we parted?* He spoke softly to himself, reciting the lines he had written a few weeks ago, when he still thought that only time would show what became of them. Time on its own showed nothing, only the living had to part. *I must go now, / you said, / and so it was indeed. / I could not hold you, there / was nothing I could do. / Those are laws not written by our love, / but laws that part us.* He caught up with her at the tram. Let me come with you. He touched her arm. She was still wearing his pullover.

In the electric light of the tram a few people sat on their own, reading the newspaper and waiting for the tramcar to leave. Marie put her child down on the step up into the tram, with the raffia basket beside her, and took Thomas's pullover off over her head. I love you, she whispered as she gave it to him, and got into the tram with her child and the basket. *For the answer / is the end / of searching, of the question.*

The buzz of the signal burned in Thomas's ears, the doors closed, and the tram, squealing, began to move. He could just see Marie sitting down with her little girl before the tram went round the curve and disappeared past the trees. He had two days off ahead of him before he could see Marie again at the hospital on Friday.

By night Thomas found himself on the street. He was not wandering aimlessly; it was a compelling attraction against which he was powerless. He could sleep less and less often these days, and when he did sleep it was for only a few hours. He would board the last tram or walk through the wood to the suburban railway. *You wept without a reason. / Do you believe in summer days,*

/ or like me, see cold coming – / your face is far away. As if passing
through a system of veins he went, never resting, on rails inside
the brightly lit carriage into the city, capillaries all going the same
way, Frankfurter Allee, Samariterstrasse, the stone of its pavement,
Marie. *Footsteps by night wear down stone outside the house* – and if
he did not look down at the pavement, he looked up at the two
windows behind one of which he sometimes saw a faint light
still on. *I fear the mist around us, / do not keep looking round – / the
planet on its axis / takes your face far from me.*

In spite of the dusty warmth of the summer nights, by three
or four in the morning at the latest Thomas was freezing, his
hands trembling, and he would sit down beside the gutter
diagonally opposite the building, making notes for his poems.
His mingled fear and longing to see Marie, or perhaps not to
see her, wore him out. The lights upstairs had gone off long ago,
the windows were dark. He never heard Marie, which troubled
him. Even when one of the windows up there was open, he did
not hear her singing a lullaby to the little girl, however quietly,
he did not hear her cry out when her husband hit her, he did
not hear her speaking or weeping, and he had never heard her
laughing. Was she asleep? Was he watching over her sleep there
in the gutter? *To light the dusty paving, / the way your steps have
gone. / To bring warmth to it, / when you return, / I stand here smiling
/ still, and waiting / still, and I know / that there's some sense / in it,
in waiting, even where / no one has ever been, / even there. / And I
am happy.* In his trouser pocket, like a pledge, he felt the little
beaker in which the white powder was collecting, milligram by
milligram. *The end is waiting there, / I do not know but do not fear
it, / and there is sense in knowing, in believing. / So I go on and feel
no weariness.* As day began to dawn he would set off, worn out,
on the way to Alexanderplatz, from where he sometimes took
the first train back to Rahnsdorf, but he usually went straight

to his shift at the hospital. *I do not look around, for I know well, / deep silence follows, happiness, / and I know you, beloved, loneliness is strange, / and the sin of fear – that I have never known.* So in the morning he would get out of the suburban train, the birds in the wood twittered, and coffee cups clattered on springtime tables when he reached the first cobblestones. He did not walk in fear now, but in great peace and certainty; how easily the handle of Käthe's door opened, how the cold of the dark corridor surrounded him, and here he could rest, and if not sleep then rest without dreams. *Days and nights I do not count, / you are with me, and a mighty sun / has risen, I do not doubt it, / and I can feel the freedom that is in me.*

Oh, to break free of her, lose sight of her windows, rest his senses, walk away from her! He hardly knew where he could go. Was there a place without Marie? Where did he belong, if not with her? *And I go on again / to the railway, to the cold. / I search every night for you, / every night I pass, awake, undreaming.*

Once he reached Samariterstrasse in the middle of the night, and all the upstairs windows were brightly lit, voices and music spilled out into the street, seeped into his ears, clung to the dust. Thomas could not be sure whether it was Marie and her husband entertaining guests. He imagined them drinking, saw Marie being made to dance, her husband collecting money from his colleagues as they came out of the bedroom one by one, *Often at times / I am afraid. / And when I stand like this, / my legs being made of stone / and so not tiring, / while the city holds me, / dusty as it is, / holds and embraces me / as if jealous of you, / then I'm afraid. / How, tell me how / I can be rid of the dust.* When the voices were quieter, the music had been turned down, and the light went off upstairs, he saw a shadow that might be her husband's at the window. A little later Thomas saw three drunks coming out of the house. He wanted to shout, to leap out, but he only ran up the street, and having reached the end of it, breathless, he slowed down, trotted, walked, then stood still and realised that he would not get away. *Someone's stuck up my mouth, / to keep me from crying out, / to keep me from crying out, with / sticking plaster, / sticking plaster, / on purpose, / on purpose . . .* His hand went into his trouser pocket and closed round the little beaker, her beaker, their beaker. He walked down the street again, calmly this time, and saw before he got there that her windows were dark and silent now. *My legs are restless, my mouth is dry, / we walked the endless streets.* Thomas went past and to the far end of the street, from where he would only have had to go along Frankfurter Allee to reach Alexanderplatz, but he went back and climbed the street the other way. *We cry out questions / that torment us, / and stony silence echoes back; / who, oh child, has burdened you with guilt, / who will now show us the way?* He was standing in the shadow of the entrance to the building opposite. Here he was invisible, no one saw his fear, only the glowing of his cigarette shining harmlessly in the dark. If he had been wearing heels, iron heels such as the whores at the entrance of a brothel in a harbour town had worn for decades and centuries, iron nails in high heels, waiting night and day – then the stone of the entrance would have given way, he would have bored holes in it on these nights. Eduard had told him about it once, about the deep holes in the marble threshold of a brothel. It was a long time since he had thought of Eduard, the old adventurer, the fallen warrior. Ella had felt sorry for him, she said, he had been stranded in the cold harbour, in Käthe's surfeit, she had felt so sorry for him.

It was true, survival at any price wasn't worth it. Thomas never wanted to be like that. *Footsteps die away, we have reached the house, / the house with windows always blind / She will not stay for ever / but she will stay for now, will stay for now / wearing the heavy yoke for years. / Life groans only slowly by . . .*

There was a kitchen window looking out on the yard, and he sometimes took the entrance gate into the yard. He stood in the back entrance and looked up to the second floor, where the light in the kitchen was still burning. Perhaps it would burn until morning. Weren't there people who left lights on at night? The moans of lovemaking echoed down, from whose window, where from? Once he had seen her at the window, closing it. Did Marie want him stealing around her apartment? She would certainly be afraid he would be seen, would be sleepless and freezing. *I know the leaves rustle in the wind, / it is cold, they fall from the trees. / I have walked long enough, long enough. / I will go home now to my grave. / Like me, lost armies / grope, searching, through the void / I see their desires but / there is nothing I can do.*

While Käthe was away working in Leuna for weeks, only sometimes coming to Berlin on a Sunday, the twins were brought back from their foster-family. All anyone could say about them was that they told lies, stole things, and fought. It was the summer holidays, so they didn't have to go to school. Thomas had no idea what they did when he and Ella were at work. On his free days, and whenever he and Ella had time, he sat on the veranda with her preparing her to take the final school exams. Her evening classes were over now, and the exams were at the end of the month. Ella didn't know very much. Thomas kept patiently explaining mathematics to her from the beginning, over and over again. For chemistry, he built a model from balls of clay and matchsticks. The clearer something seemed to Ella, the less she could remember it. Historical dates had been difficult; she simply couldn't keep them in her head. Not even the date of the founding of the German Democratic Republic. Thomas told her to write little notes for herself. After each of his questions, Ella rummaged among the pile of notes on the table in front of her. Now he asked: The founding of the Republic?

But instead of the date, Ella said: I heard just now on Radio Free Berlin that they shot someone at the border yesterday. He was just eighteen, the same age as you.

What else?

They left him bleeding to death. Our border soldiers watched, the Americans watched. No one helped him.

Maybe he was lucky. Thomas yawned. He had no time for digressions; in an hour he must set off to work the late shift. Ella had better spend her time studying, he thought, not indulging in pointless thoughts.

Lucky?

Free for ever.

And I've been thinking recently, the odd way you've sometimes been behaving, said Ella, chewing her pencil and stripping the paint off it with her teeth, I've been thinking that you may have the same thing in mind.

What, getting out of here? Thomas shook his head. He couldn't suppress a grin. Why would I make other people into murderers? He took the little beaker out of his trouser pocket, held it firmly and unscrewed the lid, then screwed it up again. And I couldn't lie around somewhere on the beach of the Wannsee, knowing I'd never see any of you again. Thomas tried to make the beaker disappear inside his fist, but it was a little too large, or anyway he couldn't close his fist round it entirely. Perhaps his left hand was larger than the right? When he looked up he saw that Ella had put her pencil down on the table and was picking her nose with relish. Hey, stop that, he said, trying to grip Ella's wrist with one hand. Thomas hesitated. He felt some excitement at the idea of letting Ella into the secret. The way she rolled her eyes showed how little she thought of any of his existential questions. Here – he held the open beaker in front of her nose – freedom can be for ever.

Ella narrowed her eyes. She firmly turned away. What is that? Poison, am I right?

Poison, yes. The two of them spoke at almost the same time. Thomas screwed the lid on again, and put the beaker back in his trouser pocket.

Keeping it for yourself? Her lips were narrowed, she had closed her eyes as if she had just fallen asleep sitting where she was. She said nothing for quite some time. She had seen nothing and heard nothing. As if the tension between them had to relax, she let her lips tremble. Thomas remembered the horses that used to pass through the garden, whinnying and snorting, their muzzles distending when they galloped. Ella bared her teeth, pursed her lips, rolled them and then squeezed them tight, and finally said, very distinctly: 7 October 1949.

Good girl, good student. It was a part that she played especially for him, as Thomas knew. She wouldn't hold him back; her own happiness was no more important to her than his. When did Ulbricht become head of state?

1960.

More precisely. What happened first, how did he do it?

Ella's eyes were still closed. She spoke like someone conjuring up spirits – first Wilhelm Pieck died – and as if some higher being were whispering the answers to her. Two new committees were set up, she tentatively suggested, as if the higher being was giving only cryptic answers to those questions, and she couldn't really understand what it was telling her. The Council of State and the Council of National Defence. And hey presto, Ulbricht was the first President of the Council of State.

Hey presto? That made Thomas laugh. Maybe you ought to

mention one or two of the aims of the construction of the Socialist state?

I could, she claimed, having briefly opened her eyes and squinted at him to make sure he was laughing, after which she closed her eyes again and gave him a lopsided grin. But I'm not going to. I'm not going to take those exams. She folded her arms and pouted, like a defiant child.

You will take them, we'll see about that.

I have to go and bathe now. Coming with me? And I've finally got hold of a bucket of paint. I'm going to start painting this evening. Don't you want to see my apartment? Now she was gathering up the notes on the table and stuffing them into a large envelope.

Sorry, I have to get to the suburban train. I'm on the late shift all weekend.

Ella took note after note out of the envelope again, studied them as if looking for a particular question or answer. She had written on both sides of many of the notes, the question on one side, the answer on the other. 13 August 1961? Baffled, Ella held the note. Did she really not know what the question about that date could be? Cautiously, she turned the note over, then she folded it, tore it in half, and wrote something on the blank half.

Thomas stood up. He wanted to find out where the twins were before he had to go to work, since he would not be home until tomorrow morning.

Wait a minute. Ella held the note she had written out to him. He didn't read it, but put it in his trouser pocket and went down the steps into the garden, where he had heard low voices. The twins were sitting on the bottom step, playing at kissing.

Loving

Müggel Schnüggel Flüggel, the rising sun had set the lake on fire. Ella was swaying, and in her dizziness she put one foot carefully in front of the other to reach the water. The sand was soft, and still cool with morning. The long pine needles of the Brandenburg Mark gave way under her bare feet. Ella was thirsty, she wanted to wash the acidity off her face. Was it only the wine, or had she thrown up while half asleep?

She put her right foot in the water first. Thomas would have stepped in with his left; as a left-hander, he favoured his left foot. The lake was still warm from summer. Her legs didn't want to walk, didn't want to stand. Ella lay down in the lake.

Swimming was out of the question; her arms failed her. She lay in the shallow water where it was not easy to drown. She could still feel the sand on her stomach, the air tickled her skin above the water. Her small breasts rubbed over the bottom of the lake. Sometimes people thought she was a grown woman already – but she would always be a girl. She let her arms drift, took her feet off the bottom, opened her eyes in the water. The finely rippled sand reminded her that the world didn't need her.

A limp body could lie comfortably in warm water as long as there was an above and a below – but Ella lost her sense of direction, felt dizzy, and crawled up on land on her stomach, over the pale sand to the shallow hollow where she had spent the last hours of the night.

She lay down in the hollow on her back. She could feel the ground beneath her, the sand on her bare back, her behind, her legs, her heels, and she linked her arms behind her head and looked up at a huge, fleecy, white tower of cloud, pink at the edges. An airy structure that, sublime in shape and sharply outlined, was making its way swiftly eastward over the Müggel Schnüggel. A bird of some kind flew up. If Thomas had been lying there beside her, he would have guessed, even without seeing it, what bird it was. She had already closed her eyes several times that morning, wanting to go to sleep.

She rolled over on her side, on her stomach, rolled on, working up impetus, rolled down the slope again until she was close to the water, a girl coated in sand like fish or meat coated in breadcrumbs. When she closed her eyes there was a bolt over a door, the images were strong, they reached for her, and she felt queasy. She had to open her eyes. It was Monday; in this country of workers no one but Ella had time to lie by the lake, so she was on her own. Today the wardrobe mistress would wait in vain for Ella to arrive at the workshop. September the third, whispered Ella. Did numbers have their own magic, as Thomas had once claimed? How could she simply say the date, how could she think; her pulse hammered, and there was a rushing sound of wind and blood in her ears. Whoo hoo, a date of no importance, only today's date, a date that certainly wouldn't signify anything else. Nothing else. Ella hated premonitions, especially her own. She was afraid of herself, wanted to reassure herself, and would need strength; she ought to get up, wanted to get up and walk through the wood to the tram stop, she must get up. Ella, get up, she told herself. You lazy beast, she told herself. Lazy was how Käthe put it, the beast was her own idea, but it didn't fit. She wasn't lazy, she wanted to do things, but she couldn't, couldn't manage to fold her legs up, stand on her feet.

Ella rolled over in the water, it lapped around her ears, splashed on her skin, gurgled in her mouth. She crawled up the slope on all fours to the hollow where she had left her clothes. First get dry, then get dressed. She must go to Rahnsdorf, back to Thomas. Kneeling over the hollow, she watched the water dripping out of her hair, digging tiny pits in the sand.

The best way to get dry was to lie on your back in the warm sand. The trunks and branches of the pines of the Brandenburg Mark shimmered with a reddish tinge above her, there was a smell of resin and late summer and barely stagnant water. Once again she rolled over on her stomach, her face in the sand, sand in her nose, on her lips, on her tongue. It wasn't easy to suffocate, she took shallow breaths and put her arms together above her head in the sand, as she and Thomas used to do when they were children, a bird that couldn't drown and couldn't stifle. She turned on her back again and brushed the sand off her breasts, where it was clinging like a second skin.

She heard the squealing of a tram in the distance. She didn't have to catch a tram, she could walk instead, back to Käthe's house. Ella imagined herself waiting and the tram ahead, coming towards her. She straightened one leg, but the knee gave way; it took her an effort to stand up and walk back to Rahnsdorf, where she had come from only a few hours ago. Before spending a wakeful night in the hollow. She had missed the last tram in Rahnsdorf yesterday evening, and she hadn't felt like walking through the wood to the suburban train station and back to her new, empty apartment where there was a smell of fresh paint. She had preferred to walk through the wood to the lake. Not over the marshy ground, not to the landing stage, she had gone to the pine trees, where the sand would still be warm from the day before.

The clouds were moving in the direction of Rahnsdorf, and

she must set off that way herself, but she couldn't. She didn't mind that her skin was encrusted with sand. She went on all fours, there was a trunk, the trunk of a blue elephant, a trunk that looked like her arm, and a waving hand that tugged at a trouser leg. Don't be afraid of it, she heard Thomas say, first seriously and then amused. She heard him laughing, and giggled too, her hand waved to the trouser leg, picked it up and waved it in the air.

Ella pulled on her corduroy trousers, put on her blouse, the sand clung to her long, thick hair. As she went up the slope and over the pine needles on the ground to the tram stop, she felt her hair making her blouse damp, her back was cold, she had gooseflesh. Had she left her shoes on the bank or in Rahnsdorf yesterday evening? She didn't look round, she didn't go back, even without a watch she knew it was time to go to Rahnsdorf, she must go there, she walked barefoot along the paved road, she could already hear the scorching squeal of the tram in the distance.

But the tram went past as if no one was waiting for it. Perhaps the driver thought he saw a blue elephant there at the tram stop.

She had been in Käthe's house only yesterday evening. She had gone to Rahnsdorf, wanting to see Thomas. She laughed briefly. You bastard, she had hissed softly, you lousy bastard. Why hadn't anyone come? Hadn't she issued invitations to her house-warming party, hadn't she given him a note two weeks earlier: Coming to my house-warming? Please do! And bring Marie with you. He hadn't answered. He had put the note in his trouser pocket, but had he ever read it?

Ella balanced her way along the rail. If she could make it to a hundred planks along the tramline, everything would be all right. What, everything?

One, two, three, four, no Siegfried and no Johnny, no one had turned up at Ella's new apartment in Köpenick on Saturday, no Michael and no Violetta. Eight, nine, perhaps she had only imagined the invitations and never asked anyone out loud, ten? Ella wobbled, regained her balance and went on. Eleven, twelve, around midnight, tired of waiting, she had gone to sleep. Only next day, on Sunday, had she gone to Rahnsdorf to see Thomas. Why didn't you come? She knew he had the note, he couldn't talk his way out of that, she had invited him, she'd even put it in writing. Fifteen, sixteen, or had she counted plank number fifteen twice? Eighteen, nineteen. Why hadn't he come to celebrate and dance with her? Twenty, twenty-one, he usually liked to be with her. Twenty-three. He had tried over the last two months, tried hard with her when she couldn't remember a figure or a name, let alone a date. Twenty-five. A fire salamander was lying on the rails in front of her, basking in the sun, Ella wobbled again, she didn't want to alarm the salamander, she got down into the grass and crouched beside the rail, stretched her hand out and waited. The salamander would come. Bubbles in her head, and blue elephants, they didn't need any formulas or correct spelling.

When she lost her temper with Thomas while she was studying, because she thought he spoke too fast, when she had cried because she thought she would never get any algebra into her head, where blue elephants still lurked round every corner, stealing as much space as they could, and even when she had been angry, calling him an ape, pulling his hair and throwing her compasses at him because she didn't understand something – he had just sat there, at the most ducking out of the way. If she had run off he would be waiting for her, handing her her pencil when she came back hours later. The salamander moved its head, it turned, went several steps towards Ella, stopped and waited with its head in the sun. Something had warned it, maybe it could sense Ella's uneasiness, she had no time to wait here for a sala-mander while the door of the room in Rahnsdorf had been closed all yesterday evening, and perhaps it still was.

Thomas had sat with her for weeks on end. Her clever little brother, who had simply overtaken and passed her at school, who had sat his final exams the year before. The stars, botany, poetry? Rubbish, good only for the back of beyond. Käthe was pleased, proud of her golden boy's many interests. Gifted, said Ella to herself, gifted, that was how it sounded when Käthe said it. Ella was certainly not jealous, as Käthe liked to claim. But gifts didn't do those in need any good, those who were to suffer were gifted. However, the German Democratic Republic had other plans for the sons of what it supposed was its intelligentsia. Ella got up, the salamander startled by her movement, scuttled away. It wasn't much farther to Rahnsdorf, she could be there in ten minutes' time if she wanted.

Why hadn't Thomas come to Ella's house-warming party? How could he fail to celebrate the most important day of her nineteen years of life with her? Her escape from that dark house, her first apartment of her own, the life of freedom that was just beginning.

Perhaps he hadn't wanted to leave the twins on their own. Käthe had been in Leuna for weeks, and wouldn't be back until Monday. Monday was today. It would take her several hours to get here from Leuna, she wouldn't arrive until late in the morning or around midday. Ella walked along between the tramlines where the grass grew high. She bent down and picked a stem of shepherd's purse. You could chew the seeds if you felt restless. The heart-shaped little pod lay on the tongue like a tiny sweet. She pushed it between her front teeth and bit it.

When Ella had arrived at Käthe's house yesterday afternoon, she found his door closed. She heard his voice on the other side of it, and Marie's voice too. Music was playing softly on the radio. At first Ella didn't want to disturb them; she thought she would wait for them to leave the room and then tell them off. Why didn't you come to my party? But when they still hadn't come out of the room an hour later, she had knocked. There had been no reply from Thomas. The twins ran along the corridor, one chasing the other, they pulled out tufts of each other's hair and waved these trophies in the air, shouting. Ella had gone into the garden, enjoying Käthe's absence. Was she a guest in the house now? Did having her own apartment make her a guest here, a secret, uninvited guest? Ella had lain down in the meadow beside the fuchsias to enjoy the last of the sun. Without Käthe there were no orders to do housework, no weeding, no cooking meals. When Ella came into the house later, the twins had bitten each other, and cheerfully showed Ella the bite marks. The door of Thomas's room was still closed. Ella had listened. Quiet murmuring, she hadn't been able to make out a word. Or perhaps she had only imagined the murmuring? She had knocked, but no one had answered. She had knocked a second time. All was quiet on the other side of the door. Later she had gone out at twilight to throw little stones up at Thomas's window. Are you ever going to open that door?

If today was September the third, then yesterday had been the second. Or was she wrong, hadn't she spent a sleepless night beside the Müggelsee, had she been there not just for a few hours overnight but for a whole day and a night? How long was Thomas going to hide away in his room with his girlfriend Marie?

Ella could see the ruins of the mill behind the trees already; in less than five minutes she would be in Rahnsdorf. Yellow St John's wort was fading everywhere, the tall grass had scorched during the summer, and the rusty red spikes of sorrel were drying to brown.

The twins had moaned and grumbled; wasn't Ella going to have something to eat with them? But Ella had not been hungry, and was restless, she kept going up and down the corridor, past Thomas's locked door, she listened, she went into the bathroom and back to the smoking room, always past that door. When she came into the smoking room the twins were sitting on the sofa, swinging their legs and whining. Ella closed her ears to them and went back to the corridor, the dark corridor, past Thomas's room, past Käthe's bedroom, she looked into her own room, the room she had occupied until a few days ago. Her former room, now taken over by the twins. They had tidied up and made their beds. Perhaps they had learned to do that in the children's home or from their foster-family. Back in the corridor Ella had to pass Thomas's door again. The silence astonished her. She stopped. Had someone turned off the radio? She knocked. Still no answer. Bastard, thought Ella, just you wait, when you come out I'll give you a piece of my mind. Where were you, why didn't you come to my party? Ella could hear her own breathing against the door. She bent down and tried to look through the keyhole. But now that Thomas had changed the lock you couldn't see through it any more. He might possibly have stopped it up, sticking something over it on the inside. She knocked a second time. Thomas? Ella heard herself asking, and this time she pressed the door handle down. Someone must have locked it. Ella held the handle down and leaned against the door. The new catch didn't have a key, but hadn't he fitted a bolt on the inside only a few weeks ago? So the door could be locked only from inside the room. Ella had gone back into the smoking room. The twins had come out of the kitchen with their hands full of raisins, which they placed on the table, dividing them, raisin by raisin, into two equal piles. Couldn't they cook something themselves? She knew very little about the twins.

Ella didn't want to pick a perilous way along the tramlines now, she walked between the rails, getting slower and slower, as if she could overcome her inner uneasiness by moving lethargically. At the tram stop she changed direction, hesitantly put one foot before the other, trudged through the tall grass to the street, where there was not a car in sight, although it was Monday morning. When she crossed the cobblestones and saw Käthe's house, she looked up at the windows first. The left-hand window of Thomas's room was not quite closed; the curtains were still drawn, hardly moving in the draught.

During the past week, Thomas had helped Ella to paint her apartment. It had been a hot August day, and they had opened all the windows. And Thomas had turned to her, looked up at her as she stood on the ladder, and asked her why she was so happy. Because I'm free now, she had told him, laughing. You're welcome to sleep here with Marie when I go to the Baltic in autumn, you and she can stay here for a week or two then. From his face, she had realised that he didn't understand her delight, and her suggestion seemed anything but tempting to him. He had said: You call that being free? Ella wasn't interested in the Wall, it was a few hundred metres away, not even in sight from here. She was interested only in what was close, very close.

Taking two steps at a time, she pressed down the handle of the front door to the house. The door opened easily, as it always did, as easily as if there were a spirit standing inside to open it just as you pressed the handle down on the outside.

The chill in the corridor reminded her of winter nights. Ella looked through the open doorway of her own old room. The beds there were still made, but there was no sign of the twins. The bathroom door was open, no one was in there, but the tap was dripping. In passing, Ella opened the front of the grandfather clock and gave the pendulum a little push to set it moving. She set the hands of the clock with one finger. How late might it be? Eight, nine, or much earlier than she thought? After a few minutes she decided on eight in the morning, which seemed right for a Monday.

Passing the door of Thomas's room, Ella opened the smoking room door. One of the twins was sleeping with her mouth open on the sofa, the other was lying on the carpet in front of the sofa, curled up like a small animal. Hadn't anyone told them to go to bed? Ella went back into the corridor. She stopped outside Thomas's door. Apart from the ticking pendulum of the grand-father clock, a sound that now filled the corridor, Ella could hear nothing. She didn't ask him, she cautiously tried the handle, but the door was as firmly locked as it had been yesterday evening.

Ella went into the kitchen, where she found plates with remains of food on them and a pan, in which the twins had obviously cooked something up for themselves the evening before. She washed the plates and ran water into the pan to soften the residue. She plugged in the little kitchen immersion heater, but when the water boiled she just pulled out the plug and didn't make tea. Back in the smoking room the twin on the sofa stretched, made a lip-smacking noise, yawned and opened her eyes. Why are you back again? asked the twin, seeing Ella sitting at the table in one of the deep armchairs.

I just am. Ella was cleaning her fingernails with one of the plastic sticks out of the Mikado game.

The twin stood up, nudged her sister with her foot, and disappeared into the kitchen. I'm hungry too, called the other twin from the floor, wait for me. She got up and ran after her sister. A bumblebee was buzzing against the windowpane between the smoking room and the veranda. Ella got out of her chair and opened the French door so that the bee could fly out. Ants had formed a little procession on the veranda table; maybe it hadn't been wiped down. Once on the veranda, Ella saw that the door to the garden staircase was open. When Käthe was at home she always made sure that all the doors were closed at night. She did not lock them with their keys; she was not afraid of anyone breaking in, but the wind disturbed her, and she didn't want birds and mice coming in from the garden. Now that the night was over that door might as well stay open.

Give it to me, shouted one twin to the other. It's not fair, you're taking a second bite! But the first twin held onto the bread crust and wouldn't hand it over. The crust was so hard that Ella could hear the girl's teeth crunching on it. Ow! Stop scratching me, shouted one of the girls, and Ella heard the thud of a blow. She stood in the doorway between the smoking room and the veranda. A squabble broke out, one girl hitting, the other maybe pinching, calling each other names that Ella didn't understand. They were animals communicating only through sounds and noises. As soon as you intervened in their fighting and bickering they would gang up together against you as the supposed aggressor. Ella's eyes fell on the long wooden ladder leaning on its side against the wall under the windows. They used it for gathering walnuts from the tree in autumn, and for apples. Ella picked up the ladder, which was not particularly heavy, but long; it must be twice as long as Ella was tall. It might be long enough. With the ladder over her shoulder, and walking carefully so as not to knock it against the bookcase or the pictures on the veranda, Ella went to the garden steps.

What are you doing? Are you picking apples already?

The twins came running up and watched Ella manoeuvring the ladder down the steps.

Can we pick apples too?

They're not ripe yet, said Ella, when she had the ladder down the steps.

Then what are you doing?

Ella did not reply; she put the ladder over her other shoulder and went round the house through the garden. She carried the ladder to just under Thomas's window and put it up against the wall there.

Are you going up the ladder? What are you doing?

The second rung was broken. Ella stepped over it and onto the third, climbed the ladder, and held herself in position with one hand on the frame of the open window so that she could pull herself up on the sill. Down below the twins were calling that they wanted to come up as well, but one of the sisters didn't dare to because of the broken rung, and the other was trying to persuade her to climb it all the same. Ella was now wedged into the narrow space where the window was open. She got hold of the inside catch, opened the window fully, and jumped down into the room.

It was a moment before she could make out the scene before her inside the black walls. She saw a long, narrow back, a woman's bare buttocks, her legs, one of them bent at an angle. One of her arms was hanging down from the bed, the other lay on the sheet. She was lying face down on something that also had arms and legs, and whose head was half hidden by her long hair. Ella knelt down beside Thomas's bed, took hold of the long hair and pushed it aside. His open lips are hardly recognisable; something white is coming out of them, something soft that makes Ella think of a cloud or of mould. When Ella lets go of Marie's hair she touches her arm, which is not really so much hanging off the bed as sticking out stiffly, it is cold, colder than the temperature in the room, colder than a stone would be if these two people had been carved out of stone, and the end of it, where the curled hand almost touches the floor, is a dark colour. Ella thinks of Käthe, who will come home from Leuna this morning.

Ella-a-a-a! Ella-a-a-a! Outside, the twins are calling her in unison, the same voice, the same word, the same impatience.

Sunlit motes of dust dance in the air.

No, says Ella, or maybe she just thinks No. She holds her left hand open and puts Marie's hair over it, strand by strand, holds it firmly, and looks at what is coming out of Thomas's mouth. His eyes are not quite closed.

She touches his forehead with her fingers. His forehead is cool. She touches the arm lying beside him; it may have slipped out just a few minutes ago from under the body lying on top of him. His arm is not cool, it seems to Ella almost warm, warm enough to move. But nothing is moving.

Is that a sound?

Ella's eyes fall on the bottle of wine, which is almost empty, a single glass stands beside the bed, they were probably both drinking from it. She lets go of Marie's hair.

Here I am, says a twin from the window – the curtain is still billowing between them. Ella gets up, goes over to the window and stands in front of it. The girl is standing at the top of the ladder, but she doesn't know how to haul herself over the sill, her arms are too short. She is smiling mischievously.

Climb down, Ella tells her sister. Go on, get down that ladder.

The other girl is waiting at the bottom, holding the ladder firmly with both hands. Come on down.

The twin nimbly climbs backwards down the ladder. Ella looks at the bed with the two bodies on it. Stark naked. Why does that term occur to her? Is there a difference between naked and stark naked?

Thomas's trousers are hanging over the arm of the chair. Ella picks them up, put her hand into one of the pockets, where she finds some folded sheets of paper, and reads. *And who will sit / in judgement on us? / You who see us, / do not forget, / we love each other.* She stuffs them back and tries the other pocket. She knows what she will read on the small, torn-off note: Coming to my house-warming on 1 September? Please do! And bring Marie with you. She puts the note in her own trouser pocket and arranges Thomas's trousers as neatly as possible on the chair again. Her glance falls on Marie's dress hanging over the other chair-arm, a special dress, dark blue with a black velour pattern that Ella would like to touch, a tiny pair of panties on top of it, like a child's, a little vest with thin shoulder straps. She has arranged her sandals as a pair so that the toes are touching. They are probably closer together than people's feet could ever stand wearing shoes.

Are you coming, Ella? The twins down in the garden are getting impatient. Ella goes to the window and pushes the curtain aside. Since when were colours so pale? Ella sees the dry grass with spots before her eyes. She climbs out on the windowsill and from there to the ladder.

The twins wait until Ella has reached the bottom.

Well? asks one twin, and then they both ask together: Are they dead?

Ella takes the ladder away; uncertain whether or not to carry it back to the veranda, she lets it fall in the grass. She walks off.

You're crying, says one of the twins, going along beside Ella and observing her with unconcealed curiosity. Why are you crying? asks the other twin, trotting along behind them.

A car clatters over the cobblestones. Ella walks along beside the wall of the house as far as the corner, but she doesn't want to go into the garden now. She goes back, past the twins, who are sitting in the grass beside the ladder. What are we going to do now? asks the first twin. Wait for Käthe, says the second twin.

Without a word, Ella leaves the twins sitting in the grass and goes round to the other side of the house and the entrance to the yard. Didn't Käthe take her car to the garage before going to Leuna? Has she had her motorbike repaired? It's been standing in the shed without a back wheel for the past year or so, going rusty. Ella hears the distant squealing of the tram. They can go to meet it. It's true that Ella does not know exactly when and by what means Käthe will arrive, but she must be here some time in the next few hours. Ella and the twins walk up and down outside the house. When a car passes once, the twins wave to it wildly, as if a steamer were sailing past on the bank. Ella sits down on the sandy path. She leans against the fence, folds her arms over her knees and puts her head down on them. She will look up only when one of the twins calls: Käthe! Until then she can count elephants to her heart's content. One of them has an almost purple skin, but that could be because of the sun burning down on it. The air above the asphalt flickers. Aren't the elephants thirsty? They are sinking into fluid tar with their heavy legs. Even making a great effort, they can't move from the spot, the tar around their legs is sticking them to the ground.

Here comes Käthe! Ella hears the twins calling. She's coming, she's coming! And they add: Come on, let's go and meet her.

Ella's arm is wet. She stands up, wipes her tears from it with the other arm, and with small steps, swinging her arms, waving her trunk, she follows the twins, who are running towards a woman coming from the tram stop, loaded down with a rucksack and a heavy bag, tottering as she passes the mill on the way towards them.

Thomas is dead, whispers Ella, but Käthe doesn't see her, looks past her, it is not clear whether she heard what Ella said. Or did Ella only think she said it?

Can't someone take this bag? says Käthe to the twins, putting the heavy bag down in the middle of the front doorway. Go into the studio, you can make something with the clay in there.

The twins do not obey. They are running back and forth between Käthe and Ella, until Käthe gives one of them a shove because apparently she trod on Käthe's toes. Didn't I tell you to go down? Out of here! Käthe grabs the twins by the scruffs of their necks, like kittens; holding them like that she takes them through the smoking room to the back door and right through the kitchen. She opens the nearest door, takes the twins by their wrists, hauls them over to the staircase leading down to the studio. You two stay here until I call you. And she shuts the door behind them, even turning the key, as if the twins couldn't get back into the house any time by going out of the studio door and across the yard.

Käthe telephones, she goes to the toilet, she leafs through her post stacked on the table in the smoking room. She brushes the badminton racket off her chair so that it falls to the floor, and sits down. Soon after that she goes into the kitchen and runs water from the tap. When the bell rings she opens the front door. She points to the door they want and goes back into the kitchen, where she finishes her glass of water.

And what are you doing, running about after me all the time? Ask the men if they'd like some coffee. Take them the sheet they asked for.

Ella opens the dark linen cupboard that stands in one corner of the smoking room. The telephone rings. Käthe goes to answer and says, into the receiver, of course I haven't forgotten the meeting . . . yes . . . no. With the sheet over her arm, Ella opens the door into the corridor. The men have broken down the door of Thomas's room. First there were only two policemen, now a doctor has joined them. Ella looks through the open doorway into the room. The doctor gives instructions. Can she spread out the sheet on the floor beside the bed? Ella nods vaguely; of course she can do that. She shakes out the sheet until it is lying flat and smooth on the bouclé rug. The doctor has asked one of the policemen to lend a hand. It isn't easy; they try it from different angles, but the bodies are stiffly entwined. Maybe here? Ella hears the policeman ask, and sees him about to take hold of the hip of Marie's body. The doctor advises the shoulders. Will it take long, will it take minutes, will it take for ever? They are clasping each other tightly. When they lift Marie's body off Thomas, it turns out that her radiant white skin, still dazzling on her back, is discoloured on her front; there are dark, purple, almost black marks on her stomach and her breasts. Carefully, the two men lay Marie's body on the flat sheet.

The doorbell is ringing again. Ella goes to the front door, opens it and lets the new men in. Carrying huge zinc tubs, they knock into things all over the place, there is much clattering and clanking.

The first policemen tell their colleagues they can put the coffins down and wait out in the yard; they haven't finished in here yet. Can they leave the coffins down in the bathroom, or where? Ella nods uncertainly. She approaches the bed and sits down at the far end, beside Thomas's feet. On the floor, the doctor is examining Marie's body, pressing his thumbs down on various parts of her stomach. He examines her eyes, and tries to look inside her mouth with a small flashlight. He has put down his stethoscope; it is hanging over Thomas's trousers on the arm of the chair.

Käthe stands in the doorway for a moment, hands on her hips. Come out of there, Ella, she says, come here, you're getting in the way. Ella stands up. One of the policemen is sitting at Thomas's desk, noting something down on a form. Do you have a goodbye letter? Now he looks at Käthe and Ella, who stand motionless in the doorway watching what is going on.

A goodbye letter? Suddenly Käthe is weeping. She shakes her head. Has Ella ever seen Käthe shed tears before?

A note, a letter, anything. Did the dead couple give any advance notice of their intentions?

Advance notice? Now Käthe is weeping uncontrollably. My boy.

Ella puts her arm round little Käthe, but Käthe is still shivering, her tears are shaking her where she stands in the doorway, my boy, my boy. She does not return Ella's embrace in any way. It is as if she were standing there alone, as if she neither notices Ella's arm nor understands the policeman's question, nor can she answer it. Ella tries to hold on to Käthe, but it is impossible, Käthe is trembling so much that Ella slips down past her, past the strong shoulders, past the huge, heaving bosom, there is nothing for Ella to hold on to, her legs feel weak, they give way, and Ella is sitting on the floor, she crawls out into the darkness of the corridor, where people come and go, come to parties, go away, come on visits, she lies on the floor under the coat stand.

Now the doctor would like to have one of the zinc coffins brought in, and asks the policeman to go into another room to question the relations. Would you please follow me? says the policeman, as he passes Käthe. But Käthe still stands in the doorway, my boy, she weeps and weeps, my boy.

Only when the policeman takes her arm and she tears herself away does she precede him into the smoking room. Ella watches their feet touching the ground, being raised off it again, coming back down, the policeman's large feet in gleaming black shoes, Käthe's tiny sandals.

The twins' small feet trip past. Ella stays lying under the coat stand, she can easily be seen from here, the feet come and go, but she also has a clear view of Thomas's room, where with the help of the other policeman the doctor is placing Marie's body in one of the coffins. The coffin stands on the right, beside the bouclé rug; on the left is the bed with Thomas on it. The coffin stays open while the doctor turns to the male body and examines it. Only occasionally does he try to manipulate Marie's fingers, seeing whether and how they are getting stiffer, moves the arm to the edge of the coffin. One of the twins squeals. The doctor asks the policeman to take these children to his colleague and their mother.

Ella sees the feet passing her. The twins do not want to go to Käthe; they hardly know the woman described by the policeman as their mother. The second zinc coffin is carried out of the bathroom and past Ella. It is placed on the bouclé rug beside the bed, where Marie's body was lying on the sheet earlier.

The doctor asks the policeman to help him. They lift Thomas and put him in the zinc coffin.

You mustn't do that, says Ella, standing up. She goes over to the doctor and the policeman. They both look up at her, they want to stretch out the legs and place the arms on the dead body so that it will all fit into the coffin.

You mustn't part them. Ella looks from Marie's coffin to Thomas's coffin. They want to be together for ever.

The doctor takes no notice of Ella, he adjusts Thomas's head. Here – Ella picks up the doctor's stethoscope to get at Thomas's trouser pocket. The doctor must have misunderstood; he takes the stethoscope out of her hand and tells her not to touch it.

It's not about your stethoscope, says Ella, perfectly calm now, it's about love, and she take Thomas's poem out of his trouser pocket. She doesn't have to reread it to know what it says. She holds the folded sheets out to the doctor: *And who will sit / in judgement on us? / You who see us, / do not forget, / we love each other*, she says, and she whispers: They must not forget me. But by now the doctor has bent all Thomas's limbs and fitted them into the coffin in the way he wants. The policeman puts the lid on Thomas's coffin. And here – Ella opens the blue folder lying beside the typewriter that is the property of the lodger or whoever is to follow him soon. She takes out the top sheet of paper. Last request. They wrote it on the typewriter, with the curving signatures of their names in pencil underneath. They want to be buried side by side. But loud as Ella speaks, even shouting, as she does now, no one listens to her. Marie's coffin is closed as well, someone must have done it when Ella turned to the desk.

Ella knows that no one will carry out their wish. In her mind's eye, she sees Marie's husband, whom she has never met, wanting the body of his wife, arranging to have Marie's body buried alone in a grave in some other cemetery in the city. But that, Ella knows, won't prevent anything now, and she smiles. The living people can sometimes do as they like, but sometimes they can't. She thinks: The two of you have the last word. They can bury your bodies separately, but you will love each other for ever.

Ella picks up the blue folder, climbs over the coffins, goes past the doctor and the policeman and out of Thomas's room. She thinks: You are dead. At your funeral, someone will say they would have killed you with their ideas. They don't know you well, they don't know that you are here and we are talking to each other.

*T*he author has taken the poems used in this novel, and the school essay of 3 January 1961, from the literary estate of Gottlieb Friedrich Franck.

ENGLISH PEN FREEDOM TO **WRITE** FREEDOM TO **READ**

This book has been selected to receive financial assistance from English PEN's Writers in Translation programme supported by Bloomberg and Arts Council England. English PEN exists to promote literature and its understanding, uphold writers' freedoms around the world, campaign against the persecution and imprisonment of writers for stating their views, and promote the friendly co-operation of writers and free exchange of ideas.

Each year, a dedicated committee of professionals selects books that are translated into English from a wide variety of foreign languages. We award grants to UK publishers to help translate, promote, market and champion these titles. Our aim is to celebrate books of outstanding literary quality, which have a clear link to the PEN charter and promote free speech and intercultural understanding.

In 2011, Writers in Translation's outstanding work and contribution to diversity in the UK literary scene was recognised by Arts Council England. English PEN was awarded a threefold increase in funding to develop its support for world writing in translation.

www.englishpen.org